NOTHING GOOD HAPPENS AFTER MIDNIGHT

A SUSPENSE MAGAZINE ANTHOLOGY

NOTHING GOOD HAPPENS AFTER MIDNIGHT

A *SUSPENSE MAGAZINE* ANTHOLOGY

EDITED BY JEFFERY DEAVER

JOSEPH BADAL
LINWOOD BARCLAY
RHYS BOWEN
HEATHER GRAHAM
ALAN JACOBSON
PAUL KEMPRECOS
SHANNON KIRK
JON LAND
JOHN LESCROART
D. P. LYLE
KEVIN O'BRIEN
HANK PHILLIPPI RYAN

SUSPENSE PUBLISHING

DEDICATION

To our girls:
Abigail, Ryan & Kensington Grace—may your dreams come true.

And to John Raab, Sr., for all the stories he told, over and over
again. We miss you, Dad.

PRAISE

"Something very good happens after midnight...just pick up this brilliant book and be transported—and very afraid!"
—Peter James, UK #1 Bestselling Author of the *Detective Superintendent Roy Grace* Series

"***NOTHING GOOD HAPPENS AFTER MIDNIGHT*** is a treat—dark, chilling, and delicious. Grab it."
—Meg Gardiner, Edgar Award-Winning Author of *The Dark Corners of the Night*

"***NOTHING GOOD HAPPENS AFTER MIDNIGHT*** proves that the witching hour still has the power to haunt in this suspenseful collection of stories by luminaries in the literary world. Inventive, twisted, and downright chilling, here is an anthology to be savored—well past midnight and into the dead of night."
—James Rollins, #1 *New York Times* Bestseller of *The Last Odyssey*

"This anthology showcases some of the best talent in the thriller genre—or in any genre. Whether quirky or creepy, each story displays the talent and uniqueness of its author. And since all are so good, this collection is a delightful read."
—Sandra Brown, #1 *New York Times* Bestseller of *Thick as Thieves*

"*NOTHING GOOD HAPPENS AFTER MIDNIGHT* is loads of fun. The stories from this lineup of all-star authors are a blast to read, with plenty of neck-snapping twists and heart-stopping thrills that will keep you turning pages way past the title's witching hour."
—Boyd Morrison, #1 *New York Times* Bestselling Author

"If you like intrigue and suspense, you'll love this salmagundi of tense tales from some of today's short story masters. This book is guaranteed to keep you awake until midnight and beyond."
—Steven James, Bestselling Author of *The Bowers Files*

"Readers rarely get a gift such as this—a superb collection from the giants of mystery and suspense."
—Robert Dugoni, Bestselling Author of the *Tracy Crosswhite* Series

"Midnight is the magic switch. Safe becomes dangerous, good becomes evil, quiet turns raucous. When the clock strikes twelve in *NOTHING GOOD HAPPENS AFTER MIDNIGHT*, a talented crew of writers unleashes a maelstrom of thrills so intense, you will never sleep again. Unputdownable!"
—K.J. Howe, International Bestselling Author of *SKYJACK*

"*NOTHING GOOD HAPPENS AFTER MIDNIGHT* is a treasure chest of novelties, curiosities and gems. From Kevin O'Brien's 'Cell Phone Intolerant' to Shannon Kirk's 'Tonight is the Night' and Jon Land's surprisingly heartfelt 'ATM,' you'll never step outside at night in quite the same way."
—Joseph Finder, *New York Times* Bestselling Author of the *Nick Heller* Series

CONTENTS

INTRODUCTION

I've had a soft spot in my heart for the hour of midnight ever since, at a young age, I knew that by then my parents would be asleep and I could pull the blanket off my head and continue to read Ian Fleming or Tolkien or Edgar Allan Poe without the risk of detection…or suffocation (though I *did* keep the bedside table light off and continued to plow through pages by the less-obvious beam of my Boy Scout flashlight—I wasn't stupid).

It also didn't hurt my affection for that transitional time that one of the films steering me toward crime writing was the gritty 1957 noir *The Midnight Story*, set in San Francisco and starring Tony Curtis and Gilbert Roland.

So it was with unbound eagerness that I leapt at the chance to edit this volume of suspense stories describing incidents of the curious, the eerie, the disturbed, the violent that occur in that netherworld after the witching hour (yes, yes, I know that purists claim that title belongs to three a.m. but *I'm* the editor and I'm bestowing it upon 00:00).

Another soft spot? For short form fiction.

We readers are long-distance travelers when we enter the world of novels, taking our time as we get to know characters and bask in their journey, their perils, their wins and losses. Sometimes, though not necessarily, we're treated to a big wallop of a twist at the end. A short story doesn't have the luxury of seducing us during the course of such leisurely transit; it has to grab us immediately with a high-speed plot and, in the end, deliver a gut punch of the

11

unexpected.

And the more spine-tingling the atmosphere the author has created, the better.

All of the tales in this anthology deliver that punch, and tingle that spine, and do so in a fascinating variety of ways, reflecting the wide-ranging talents, themes and styles of our contributors. You'll be reminded of Conan Doyle, Edgar Allan Poe, O. Henry, Agatha Christie and Stephen King, as well as episodes from *The Twilight Zone*, *Outer Limits* and *Alfred Hitchcock Presents*.

Let's meet our crew.

Rarely has a ticking clock been put to such keen effect—before, at and after midnight—as in Alan Jacobson's "12:01 AM." As the moments count down to the execution of a particularly nasty serial killer, we learn that there's much more to the crimes and the man's history than meets the eye. Jacobson's sharp, compelling series character Karen Vail, ace FBI profiler, joins forces with some familiar faces in the Commonwealth of Virginia in a break-neck race to save an innocent life before time runs out. The back and forth between Vail and the soon-to-die killer will also keep you on the edge of your seat.

You'd think it would be tough to write about the start of an entire social movement in a short story but Kevin O'Brien has done just that in the witty "Cell Phone Intolerant." The story hits all the right buttons—forgive that—and makes us smile with satisfaction at the exploits of Ed, a dyspeptic divorcé, who, to borrow from pop culture of a few years back, comes up with his own variation of "We're not going to take it anymore!" I, for one, recognized a bit of Ed in myself, and I suspect you'll feel the same when you finish the story.

Nothing is more exotic—and potentially eerier—than an overnight train ride. Think of *From Russia With Love* or *Strangers on a Train*, not to mention Agatha Christie's classic. Hank Phillippi Ryan's "All Aboard" perfectly recreates the claustrophobia and suspense of such nighttime travel on the rails. The setup is indeed Hitchcockian: a savvy public relations expert overhears something not intended for her ears, which sets the plot in motion. In addition to being a page-turning thriller, Ryan's contribution asks this telling question: is not information as powerful a weapon as a gun or knife?

In "Gone Forever" Joseph Badal takes us front and center to an event that is all too common in the news, a mass killing, this one in a church. We relive the event through the eyes of a stalwart police officer and the man she's interviewing, the shaken priest whose congregation was the target of the assault. I always like to see a storywright's skill at work in coming up with a title that does double duty. That can be a surprise in itself. In Badal's tale the phrase "gone forever" comes hauntingly home to roost on the last few pages.

Imagine this: you're on the phone with a crazy man, you don't know his identity and you're the only one who can stop him from a killing spree. How would you play that scenario out? This is the edge-of-the-seat premise of Linwood Barclay's twisty "Night Shift." As a former journalist, I know how accurately the author has recreated the atmosphere of a late-night newsroom, a place that is invariably placid and sleepy and dull...until it absolutely isn't.

What would a midnight-themed anthology be without a visit to a graveyard? Heather Graham's "Midnight in the Garden of Death" has us flipping pages in rapid order to see what happens next in her tale of teens whose on-a-lark sleepover in a cemetery doesn't go exactly as planned. Graham's fine depiction of the characters takes us straight back to those days when our world could be divided into the inside kids and the geeks—and the portrayal of that fraught time is as spot-on as the action is heart-racing.

Every suspense anthology needs a classic private eye story and Paul Kemprecos has contributed a great one with "The Sixth Decoy," which stars his immensely likable series character, Aristotle Socarides, ex-marine, old salt, and part-time P.I. In this tale Soc is hired by a wealthy recluse to track down a missing sculpture, carved by an artist who can only be described as the Michelangelo of wooden birds. This story will remind you of John D. MacDonald, the creator of Travis McGee, at his best.

My first novel was not in crime, but horror, and occasionally I'll pen a story in that genre, as I've done here. In "A Creative Defense" I aim for supernatural gothic in telling a tale of a horrific murder in a small New England town. The inspiration was this: trying to imagine the expression on the jurors' faces when the defendant's attorney pitches a particular argument as to why his client should not be found guilty for the slaughter. And just to try something a little different, the "midnight," after which something bad happens doesn't refer to the time, but to something else entirely. And, no, it isn't a cat's name.

It would simply be wrong to publish an anthology based on the theme of midnight without a Cinderella story and I'm pleased to report that we have not one, but two—and both written by the same author. In "After Midnight" Rhys Bowen has given us a clever retelling of the classic fairy tale of old, though we meet a protagonist who's a bit different from the one we're familiar with. Her second Cinderella tale is set in the modern time. Suffice it to say no mice, pumpkins or slippers figure in *this* story.

I've made up a variation on the old saw, "No good deed goes unpunished." It reads like this: "No bad deed goes unpunished… or does it?" In John Lescroart's whipsawing suspense offering, "Easy Peasey," plots aplenty unfold, as we watch the shenanigans of school kids—both innocent and otherwise—spiraling out of control. As always, the author takes us deep inside the motives of each character as he shifts masterfully from one point of view to another.

In D. P. Lyle's "Tonic" a couple of good old boys in rural America are cruising the back roads in an ancient pickup and simply pursuing the American dream of trying to make a living. Who could blame them? And, a more cogent question, what could go wrong? Oh, a thing or two, especially when they decide to explore a new business model and attract a little more attention than is wise. The cast includes a great small-town sheriff and a medicine man you won't soon forget, try though you might.

It was a dark and snowy night… In "Tonight is the Night," by Shannon Kirk, we meet George, an outsized ski resort trail groomer, known for his expertise on local-versus-tourist etiquette and his tall tales, which may not be as fantastical as his joshing fellow workers believe. With his mind on romance, and on the fierce blizzard, George learns that a dark past that has dogged him for years still has more on the agenda during the course of this one harrowing night. After reading this switchback-filled story, you may think twice about waxing up those skis and heading for the slopes.

Jon Land takes us to the mean streets of New York City in "ATM," where we meet Venn, a young man who's bottomed out and is desperately seeking to parley his last few bucks into something resembling a break. When reality and fantasy appear to blur, Venn's life takes a dramatic turn and he sets out on a mission at the behest of... well, I'll leave that for you to find out. Land evokes the after-midnight atmosphere of the boroughs of the city so well, you'll feel you're walking along the streets in person.

All right. Enough of the appetizers, now it's time for the main course.

Just let me offer some advice before you dig in: For your own comfort, I'd make sure your doors are barred and windows locked, and maybe you might want to have a flashlight ready, Boy Scout or otherwise, in case the power mysteriously goes out at an inopportune moment.

That is, at least if you're going to be reading our collection after midnight.

—Jeffery Deaver

12:01 AM

A *Karen Vail* Short Story

ALAN JACOBSON

PHELPS CORRECTIONAL CENTER
CULPEPER COUNTY, VIRGINIA

Stephen Raye Vaughn—no relation to the famed musician—sat on the edge of his death row cot. His "music" was a tune of a different sort, his cauldron of creativity emanating from death and mayhem—and finding new ways to wreak havoc on a city.

With his time remaining on this Earth melting away like a glacier in the throes of climate change, he was now reduced to digging out the dirt from under his fingernails. Why? He had no goddamn idea. He was due to die in 120 minutes and nothing really mattered anymore, did it?

Did it ever really matter?

Yeah, it did. Back when he was hunting for his prey, he had to present himself as an upstanding, clean cut individual. He had to play the part. Otherwise he wouldn't have been able to sit undisturbed in his van in parking lots while selecting the 16 women he would eventually murder.

His van. He missed that thing. He didn't know exactly where it was at this moment, but he knew who had it. Fortunately, he had disposed of it before the police caught him, so it could not be used as evidence against him. And man, was there a lot of evidence in it that could be used against him.

As it turned out, the one victim who got away went to the police and turned him in. It was very difficult to commit the perfect crime, although it did happen on occasion. People did get away with murder sometimes, but there was usually at least one major mistake a guy made that proved to be his undoing.

Stephen Raye Vaughn was no exception. For him it would be the mistake of a lifetime, one he could not take back.

But so be it. He was like a star in the nighttime sky, burning very brightly before going supernova. He had made peace with that. Not that he didn't want to continue living, but sometimes you just had to accept your fortune. It took him a dozen years, but he had finally reached that point.

Time was short, and his lifespan was now shorter, but at least he had lived a helluva ride. And unlike 99% of the individuals populating this planet, he had made plans to ensure his legacy continued on, at least for the near future. If all played out the way he figured it would, he would be forever immortalized in movies, television, books, Internet memes, and American history.

Stevie Ray Vaughn may be famous, but Stephen Raye Vaughn… he was infamous.

Vaughn glanced over at the sterile black and white clock across the way and wondered: Was that enough?

With so little time left to live, it would have to be.

THREE HOURS EARLIER

Debra Mead gathered her reusable grocery sack against her chest and trudged toward her Subaru. Taylor, her twelve-year-old son, sat waiting in the car playing a game on his iPad, not wanting to be seen with his mother shopping for groceries.

As she walked through an aisle of vehicles in the parking lot, a van door slowly opened. She heard it, rather than saw it, the sliding scrape of metal rolling on its track. As she turned her head in the direction of her car, something grabbed her shoulders and yanked her backwards. She felt her body falling through space, but before she knew what was happening, her head struck something hard and everything went black.

Debra awoke slowly, at first only vaguely aware that something was wrong. She was lying on her side, rocking to and fro as the vehicle she was in moved down the bumpy road.

With her vision and foggy thoughts clearing, she realized that her arms were drawn back behind her and her wrists were bound tightly with tape.

She tried to speak but a dry wad of cloth was shoved into the back of her jaw and a muffler was wrapped around her lips.

Debra forced some words from the deeper reaches of her throat. She meant to say, "Why are you doing this to me?"

It probably came out sounding more like a groan or even a poor attempt to hum a tune.

But the man turned around and glanced over his right shoulder. His right eye sat at half-mast and the brow was missing its hair, replaced by a thick pink scar. It gave his face an evil, tortured look.

"Everything's gonna be fine."

"Fine?" she tried to say, the disbelief no doubt registering in her furrowed expression.

"I just need your help with a few things. Then I'll drive you back home. You'll be on your way and I'll be on mine."

Debra looked in his expressionless eyes and knew she was in trouble. She did not think she was going to make it out alive.

Her thoughts turned to Taylor. His father had passed two years ago from a freak brain aneurysm. Now the boy was on the verge of losing his mother, too.

No, she told herself. *I can't let that happen. Somehow, I have to find a way out of this.*

FAIRFAX COUNTY POLICE DEPARTMENT
FAIRFAX, VIRGINIA

Stalwart homicide detective Paul Bledsoe had just finished a call with the medical examiner when he noticed a shadow engulf his desk. He looked up to see James Kearney, about six foot five with an afro that was picked and puffed out, making him appear even taller. At five-eight, Bledsoe always felt like he was talking to Kearney's collarbone.

"Sir, a question."

"James, call me Paul. I know you're a brand spanking new detective, but we're colleagues."

"Yes, sir. Paul."

"Let me see your badge."

"My—"

"Just let me see it."

Kearney dug into his deep pants pocket and held up the metal.

"Whoa, buddy. That's too friggin' bright. You need to tarnish it a bit. People'll think you just got it."

"I did just get it."

"You and I know that, but better if others don't."

"You're joking, right?"

"Yes, James. I'm joking. What'd you want?"

"Caught this case. Not sure what to make of it. I mean—I know what to make of it, but I think it sounds like a case Detective Argus handled."

"And?"

"He's retired, so I can't ask him."

"Okay, let's hear it."

"Well, we got a 911 call that a woman went missing. It's only been a few hours, but the lieutenant said I should look into it instead of waiting the forty-eight hours."

"I don't deal with missing persons cases, so if that's what the lew wants—"

"No, I mean I don't think it's just a missing persons case."

"Argus didn't work missing persons either. So you're thinking this is a homicide? That the woman has been murdered?"

"Yeah."

"Anything to back that up?"

"Nothing except, well, a feeling."

Bledsoe nodded slowly. "Sometimes that's all we've got." Bledsoe's neck was killing him from craning it back so far to see Kearney's face. He gestured to the chair at the adjacent desk. "Grab that seat. Tell me what you're thinking."

"So if I remember Argus's case, it was that serial killer, Stephen Raye Vaughn."

Bledsoe nodded. "I know a fair amount about that one."

"I was told you were friends with Detective Argus."

"Still am. But yeah, we tossed shit out about our cases all the time. Ran stuff off each other. Theories, that kind of thing. Like we're doing now."

Kearney scratched the back of his head. "So I'm thinking, what if this missing persons case is really a Vaughn case?"

"Vaughn is in a max security facility. Death Row. Ain't him."

"No, no. I realize it's not him, but—"

"Let's take a step back. Is there *any* proof at all that a murder's been committed?"

"No. It's just—"

"A feeling. Right. Okay, go on." Bledsoe normally would have blown the guy off, told him he's wishing too hard for a big case to cut his teeth on, that this is probably just a garden variety missing persons case—and the woman will show up in a couple of days. But he did not want to shake the new detective's confidence.

He was not going to give him a free ride, either.

"Yeah, so the woman left her kid in their car and went to get some groceries at the SmartLots center in Bethesda."

"SmartLots. That's where Vaughn shopped for his vics. Uh—no pun intended."

"Happened around the same time of day as Vaughn abducted his vics, too."

Bledsoe squinted in thought. "Go on."

"Woman was around the same age. I mean she's brunette and most of Vaughn's were blonde, but let's put that aside for a moment."

"Consider it on the side."

Kearney hesitated, then realized Bledsoe was making a joke. "Right," he said with a quick nod. "Okay, so that's a lot of coincidence."

Bledsoe waited, but Kearney sat there, then shrugged. "That's it? Same age woman, goes missing from the same kind of parking lot—"

"No, the *same* SmartLots center that Vaughn got his second victim."

"Same one?"

"Yes, sir. Paul."

Bledsoe pursed his lips and bobbed his head left and right. "Could mean nothing. I already told you, can't be Vaughn."

"What if it's a copycat?"

Bledsoe leaned forward in his creaky desk chair. "Can't rule it out—except we don't even know if anyone's abducted her. She just went missing. Right?"

"Yeah, but…her kid was left in the car. Alone."

"How old's the kid?"

"Twelve."

"Did they have a good relationship?"

"Just starting to work up the case, but according to Taylor, yeah. He said they were starting to argue a little more the last few months. But she's a good mom. He's a good student. Doesn't do drugs. Not a problem kid."

"So it doesn't make sense she'd just disappear on him. Willingly."

"My point."

"What about other stresses in her life? Husband?"

"Deceased. Some kind of medical issue. Died suddenly. Unexpectedly."

"Suspicious?"

"No, nothing like that. Something with his brain."

"The mom. On medication? Psychiatric issues?"

"She's young. Thirty-seven. Healthy. There's no reason for her to walk off on her own and disappear."

"That you know of."

"Right. So far. It's just that, in Vaughn's case, he didn't keep the women around very long before killing them."

Bledsoe grunted. "Less than 24 hours."

"Which is why I don't want to wait."

"You know how to work a homicide case?" Bledsoe held out a hand, stopping Kearney's mouth half-opened. "That was rhetorical. Tell you what, let me talk with the lew, see if he'll let me spend a few days on it with you, see where it takes us."

"I'd like that."

"Caught yourself a good first case, James."

"Guess so." He clapped his hands on his knees. "So now what?"

"You're gonna try to get hold of all security footage in the area of that SmartLots parking lot. I'm gonna call someone who knows more about the Vaughn case than I do."

"Detective Argus?"

"Nope. He's on vacation in Greece. The FBI profiler who consulted on the case with him."

Karen Vail was staring out the passenger window, thinking about Stephen Raye Vaughn, when her phone rang. Since she and her fiancé, Roberto Umberto Enrique Hernandez, were driving in her car, the Bluetooth speaker automatically took the call.

"Bledsoe. What's up?"

"Missed your voice."

"Oh yeah? You're on speaker. Robby's driving."

"Hey big guy. How's DEA treating you?"

"Treating me great. It's the cartels I seem to have problems with."

Bledsoe chuckled. "How's your knee, Karen?"

"Healing. Itches. Pain's almost gone, except when I run."

"This soon after surgery? You're allowed to run?"

"Of course not."

"I guess I missed more than your voice. You crack me up."

"She cracks herself up, too," Robby said. "She's a terrible patient, you know that."

Bledsoe laughed. "Terrible profiler, terrible patient. Nothing surprises me."

Vail frowned. "You realize I'm still on the call?"

"I do."

"It was minor arthroscopic surgery to clean things up from my last operation. Scar tissue, some frayed cartilage. I'll be fine."

"Good. 'Cause I got a case here. Not mine, exactly. I'm helping out on it for a few days. Rookie detective caught the case. He's convinced his missing woman is the victim of an abduction, possibly a copycat."

"Who's he copying?"

"Stephen Raye Vaughn."

"No shit."

"Well, too soon to say. I mean, really too soon." Bledsoe briefed her on Kearney's theory.

"And yet," Vail said, "you called me."

"I didn't want to shut him down. Kearney's got promise

and—well, you and I have had 'feelings' about things in the past. Sometimes they turn out to be right."

"One thing that's not right is we're now finding that 'copycat' is a misleading term. They're not copying per se but looking to successful killers for inspiration and guidance. Some serials—Dennis Rader was one—research other killers who've been caught. They don't duplicate everything because they don't want to go to prison. So they pattern themselves after a particular killer—but modify certain things to avoid the same fate."

"Improve on the crime?"

"Yes—and making it their own to stand out. Some admit they were inspired by others. Some deny it, even though it's clear they chose a specific offender as a role model. Keyes read true crime books about Bundy and avoided the mistakes Bundy made that led to his capture."

"Okay, so Debra Mead's kidnapper. He may be patterning himself after Vaughn. We should crack open his file in case there're some details we don't remember. Go through the media reports. Talk to Vaughn. Before he bites the dust."

"He's being executed in less than two hours."

"You kidding me? I knew it was soon, like sometime in the next month or so, but…shit. Two hours?"

"I'm on my way over there right now with Robby to witness it. I'll see if I can get in to talk with him."

Bledsoe groaned. "Jesus Christ."

"Hey, at least there's a shot. He hasn't been euthanized yet."

"Euthanized?"

"He's being put out of our misery."

There was silence.

Robby gave Vail a scrunched face look—conveying something like, "Probably don't want to repeat that again. Ever. To anyone."

"Uh, Karen?" Bledsoe asked. "You sure you're up to questioning him? I mean, you're not still on narcotics, are you?"

"Never was. Motrin first day, then gutted it out. Go do your thing. Don't worry about me."

"I always worry about you."

"You mean you always worry about me screwing up your case."

Bledsoe laughed—as did Robby—but neither refuted her assertion.

"You want me to find out if he has any connection to a potential copycat killer," Vail finally said. "Whether or not he was grooming someone else."

"Exactly."

"I'll do my best."

"Let's hope you can make him talk before he fries like an egg on an iron skillet."

"He's being lethally injected," Vail said, "not electrocuted. I thought we just covered that. Get your metaphors straight, will ya?"

"He does paint a picture," Robby said.

"That he does." She scrunched her nose. "I don't think I'm going to eat a fried egg ever again. Thanks so much, Bledsoe."

"Any time."

"So while we cozy up to Vaughn," Robby said, "what are *you* doing tonight?"

Bledsoe snorted. "I'm grabbing a beer, frying up an egg, then getting some sleep."

Vail rolled her eyes and shook her head dismissively. Robby chuckled.

"Hey Paul," Robby said, "you want to meet us at Phelps Correctional?"

"Nope."

Vail slumped in her seat. "Really?"

"Really. I'm tired. It's late."

"What if I can get something out of Vaughn? He didn't keep his vics around very long."

"I remember."

"So if we get some actionable intel, it would be a time saver if you're there, coordinate—"

"Shit, Karen. Robby, she did it to me again."

Robby glanced at Vail. "Did what?"

"Guilted me into changing my mind. Not easy to do."

"Maybe because she's right," Robby said.

"You both suck," Bledsoe said. "I'll text Robby when I get there, in case you're in with Vaughn. Meantime, I've gotta see if there's a chopper that can take me over to Phelps."

After hanging up, Vail turned to Robby. "You better step on it. If I'm going to talk with him, we're gonna need more time."

Robby accelerated slowly but steadily. Because it was so late, traffic was light.

"Crap," Vail said. "I forgot the popcorn."

"Popcorn?"

"For the show."

"Not funny."

"To be clear, I *do* take the death penalty very seriously. But when it comes to scum like Vaughn—who's guilty *way* beyond a reasonable doubt—I feel like justice is being served. That we got this one right. We caught him and he's not out killing others."

"I'll never forget the look of profound sadness and pain on the faces of the victims' families."

"The ones with the deer-in-headlights look get to me more," Vail said. "They know what's going to happen but they can't process the emotions. Should they be happy that the scum who took their loved one from them is finally going to get what he deserves? Or should they feel sad that we're forced to take the life of a person to exact justice?"

"No matter what happens, their loved ones aren't coming back."

"But it does help them sleep a bit easier knowing there was a tangible price to pay. Not closure per se, because I don't think there's really ever closure, but the daily pain of knowing the killer is still alive and breathing, getting three meals a day, *that* pain eases and eventually goes away. It restores some degree of faith in humanity, that you pay a heavy price for taking a life."

"I get it," Robby said. "But do you enjoy seeing one of these heinous individuals put to death?"

Vail chewed on that a bit.

Do I enjoy it?

"Before I answer, I should call Phelps, see if I can get the warden to squeeze me in."

"Don't get your hopes up."

"Especially since Doheny hates my guts."

Robby laughed. "Then maybe I should slow down to the speed limit. Fat chance you're gonna get in to see Vaughn."

"You're my fiancé and you don't know me by now?"

"What do you mean?"

"Never count me out."

Five minutes later, Vail hung up.

"I'm impressed," Robby said.

"Because I got him to agree to let me talk with Vaughn?"

"No, because you were pleasant and conciliatory and tactful."

"Ouch. That hurts. My own fiancé thinks I'm usually unpleasant, antagonistic, and indiscreet."

"Well," Robby said, no doubt realizing he had better choose his words carefully. "Not *usually*."

Vail shook her head. "Wrong answer."

"So to get back to my original question…"

"You're changing the subject."

"No, I'm going back to the *original* subject."

"Which was?"

"Do you enjoy seeing a serial killer executed?"

Vail leaned her head against the chilled passenger window. "Not sure I'd say *enjoy*. I'm not a masochist. But I do get satisfaction in seeing one die. I feel…well, relief, when they pronounce him dead. I mean, I know how these guys are wired. They can't be rehabilitated. We can't ever release them and expect they're going to refrain from committing murder again. They'll never be a contributing member to society.

"So yeah, when their hearts stop, I feel like I've made a difference in helping get them off the street—and ridding the human race of such deep evil, of cleansing the gene pool of that abhorrent—and aberrant—behavior. And that's how I'll feel when Vaughn's heart stops."

"What was his MO? How'd he select his vics?"

Vail sat back in her seat and absentmindedly scratched her knee with a fingernail, encircling the surgical site. "He wasn't a planner. He had his hunting places and waited for the right woman to enter his sphere. He's a very patient guy. He'd park in a shopping center lot and sit in his van and watch in the side-view mirror. When a young woman that interested him would cut down the aisle alongside his vehicle, he'd slide the door open. Grab her as she passed, slam her in the head with a mallet to knock her out, then slide the door closed. We figure it took no more than five seconds from the time he opened it to the moment it clicked closed."

"The women never had a chance."

"Then he'd bind their wrists and ankles with duct tape and tie a rag around their necks so they couldn't close their jaws. When they woke up, they couldn't talk, couldn't even scream. But by then they'd be on their way to his killing place, an old barn in the boonies of the Virginia countryside. When they got there, he'd tell them he wasn't going to hurt them, he just needed their help with something. That he'd take them back home when they were done."

"Buying their cooperation. How long would he keep them alive?"

"He never told us, but we estimated at most twenty-four hours."

"So how do we know so much about his MO? He admitted to the murders?"

Vail chuckled. "He admitted to *one*. But he wouldn't even tell us how he did that one. And he only admitted to that one because we had his DNA on the body. We didn't need his account, though. One of his vics escaped. Tenicia Jones. She told us everything."

"How'd she escape?"

"One part luck. One part 'never say die' personality. One part intelligence. And one part sheer determination to get back to her young son and husband. When Vaughn got her to his killing barn, he left her alone while he went to pee. She feigned unconsciousness, hoping she'd have a better opportunity to escape if he thought she was asleep."

"Smart."

"That was the one part intelligence."

"Yeah," Robby said with a chuckle. "I got that."

"So he figured she wasn't going anywhere."

"But she was still tied up."

"There were rusty tools and tractor parts against a wall. She squirmed over and cut through the duct tape on her ankles. And ran."

"He didn't go after her?"

"Sure did. Tenicia had no idea where she was, so she just kept running. About an hour later, it was pitch black out. She didn't stop. And neither did Vaughn."

"That's the 'never say die' part."

"Yep. That, and the fact he kept after her for two days. She didn't even stop to pee, just wet her pants. But no way was she going to relinquish any ground."

"And?"

Vail stared out the windshield at the headlight-illuminated countryside for a moment. "Fighting exhaustion and thirst, she finally found a road the next night. She knew Vaughn wasn't far off because she'd occasionally hear a twig break."

"Could've been a deer or some kind of large animal."

"She saw him. Once. She slowed to catch her breath and looked over her shoulder. Caught a glimpse of his jeans and blue sweatshirt."

"Can't believe she was able to keep at it for two days."

"When she found that road, she ran along it until a car showed up. Then she waited as long as she could before jumping out in front of it."

"Suicide? After all that?"

"No. She didn't want to give the driver a chance to drive past her. Some people are afraid and won't stop for anything—or anyone. She forced him to slam on his brakes. She could barely speak, her throat was so dry. All she said was, 'Help. Need police. Hurry. He's after me.'"

Robby glanced at Vail. "He let her in?"

"Yep. She jumped into the backseat and the guy peeled away, took her to the nearest PD. New Kent County Sheriff's Office."

"So Vaughn went hunting in suburbia and he killed them in rural Virginia?"

"Probably wanted to keep the dirty work far away from his house in case we caught on to who he was, keep us from amassing evidence that would lead law enforcement to his doorstep."

"I thought you had DNA."

Vail looked at Robby and let a smile thin her lips. "But *he* didn't know that. No one did. We kept it out of the press."

"Did you ever find his barn?"

"We did. But we couldn't connect him to it. He didn't own the property. And his murders were bloodless. Strangulation. So his DNA wasn't anywhere in the shack. Then he dumped the bodies in one of four nearby counties. And we never found his van."

"So where'd you get the DNA?"

"Under three of Tenicia's fingernails. She didn't go down right away after he got her in the van and smashed her in the head. Clawed him a bit on the forearm. Just enough to get some skin cells. And *that* DNA is what connected him to the other victim, the one he went to death row for. She also took a piece of him with her." Vail yawned loudly.

Robby held up his watch and caught the headlights of a car behind them. "You need to wake yourself up. Take a swig of coffee."

He didn't need to tell her twice.

Bledsoe dialed Vail's number. It connected on the second ring.

"Miss me already?" Vail asked. "It's only been ten minutes."

"I'm on the helipad. The chopper will be here in five."

"Awesome. Also, I was talking with Robby, telling him about the Vaughn case. Thought of something to look into. We never found his white panel van that Argus theorized was used in a lot of the murders. An old Chevy. It was seen in the vicinity in around half the cases. When I asked him about it during interrogation, I could tell he was holding back. There was something about it. Like he had some secret he wasn't telling me."

"We got the security footage from the parking lot, but I didn't see anything unusual other than Debra Mead starting to walk toward her car. Then we lose her. No van."

"Check again. For an old white panel van."

"You think it's related in some way to *this* kidnapping? I mean, what's Vaughn got to do with this knucklehead?"

"Don't know. But unless you have an abundance of leads to

track down, I've just given you something that could bear fruit. Check the footage of area cams, not just the ones in the parking lot, for an old Chevy van approaching, entering or exiting."

"How long till you get to the prison?"

She checked the GPS. "Half hour, maybe less. You?"

"Probably around the same. X-ray—the pilot—told me twenty minutes, depending on how fast he flies."

"X-ray?"

"Got the name flying Black Hawks in Iraq. Sees real good at night."

"You gonna be able to check the footage while en route?" Robby asked.

"I'm not flying the bird," Bledsoe said. "Hell yes."

Debra awoke in stages. She was aware of a darkness around her, of a musty odor that irritated her nose. Then the hard ground. Moist dirt. Pain in her wrists, shoulders, ankles. Her knees burned. And—

The van.

Oh my God.

She tried to sit up and realized her arms and legs were bound and something was shoved in her mouth, preventing her jaw from closing—or opening.

I'm in trouble.

She wanted to scream. But then she felt her tongue, drawn back against the cloth, which was pulled tight across her dry palate. No, not dry. Parched. She moaned.

"Oh—Debra. Hello there. Sorry, I've been an awful host. Let me introduce myself."

Debra's gaze darted left and right, up and down. She could not make out where the voice was coming from. And then a face appeared, lit from below with a flashlight.

It made her startle.

"Who are you?" she managed to say. It was formed as words in her mind but sounded like gibberish when it escaped her mouth.

"I'm Harrison." He clenched his jaw, then forced a smile. "Good to meet you."

She responded with a garbled, "Why are you doing this to

me?"

That was apparently too difficult for him to guess at, so he leaned closer and pulled out a knife. The polished stainless blade glinted in the light.

Debra moaned—more like a freaked-out scream, though it didn't come out as intended—and he pushed the blunt end against her cheek and pulled. The cotton parted like a shaft of asparagus and she felt instant relief in her jaw. She spit out the cloth fragments and repeated her question.

"Isn't it obvious?" Harrison laughed. "Because I can. Because I want to."

"Those aren't reasons."

Harrison studied her face. "Absolutely they are. Just not what you wanted to hear."

"I *want* to go home."

"I understand. We'll head back in two hours. Okay? Can you wait that long?"

She nodded, studying his eyes, which were mirror-black with deep brown, cocoa colored swirls. Was he telling her the truth?

He looked at his watch.

"Then why are we here? Why'd you kidnap me?"

"I need help with something. Didn't think you'd do it unless I, well, forced you. Will you? Help me?"

She nodded animatedly. "Yes, yes. Whatever. Just take me home."

"Of course," Harrison said.

And then the flashlight went off. She was left in darkness.

Bledsoe squinted at his iPhone screen and replayed the SmartLots video…for the sixth time.

He watched the cars driving into and out of their spots. He moved the device away from his face to get some perspective.

It ended and he played it a seventh time. He used his finger to speed up the recording and then slow it down. "There."

"There what?" X-ray asked over their headsets.

"Sorry," Bledsoe said. "Wasn't talking to you." He used his fingers to zoom in and found what he was looking for—off to the right and only half visible.

An old, white Chevy van.

He watched as the vehicle sat there in the lot. Finally, it rocked from side to side and the side door appeared to open. Because of the angle of the camera, he could not make anything out, but the top of the Chevy noticeably shifted—probably indicating something heavy moving within. "Damnit," he said under his breath.

He kept with that camera until, fifteen point three seconds later, the van pulled from its spot. He had no view of the driver as it turned right, out of the frame.

"Where's the angle that shows me the exit?"

"Not talking to me again, are you?" X-ray said.

"Nope. Sorry."

Bledsoe opened another file Kearney had sent. "Hmm. The exit closest to where that van was." He slowed the playback speed again, zoomed, and moved it around. This distorted the image, making it less clear and more pixelated in the fading light.

"C'mon, you bastard. Where are you?"

He saw something at the right bottom edge of the screen. He dragged the image left and found the van, then followed it another few seconds.

"Crap. We lose it on Jefferson."

He pulled out his phone and texted Kearney.

> i need all available footage
> include traffic cams
> for jefferson and mansen
> covering all exits of smartlots center
> headed east looking for a 1970s
> white chevy panel van

Kearney replied immediately.

> you think thats the killers ride
> old white chevy van

Bledsoe told him that's exactly what he thought, then related what he had seen on the traffic footage.

> and tell lenny to get the dmv
> registration history for sr vaughn
> see if he owned a chevy van
> and who owns it now

Kearney didn't waste any time:

> so you think i was right
> vaughns involved

Bledsoe groaned—eliciting a glance from X-ray.

> told you
> aint vaughn
> now hurry and get that info

"Detective," X-ray said over his headset, "we'll be landing in six minutes."

"Ten-four." Bledsoe checked his watch and began viewing the video footage yet again.

With sixty seconds to go before touchdown, Bledsoe felt his phone vibrate. He swiped away from the video and read the text from Kearney:

> case reports say multiple witnesses
> saw a 77 chevy van but
> no dmv record of vaughn ownership
> disposition unknown
> whereabouts unknown

Bledsoe texted Vail, then called Kearney, despite the difficulty of speaking over the rotor noise.

"So looks like our kidnapper—and Vaughn—used a 70s era white van."

"Coincidence?" Kearney asked.

"Definitely not. Get the Phelps visitor logs for Vaughn. Go back a couple of years. Email it to me and Agent Vail. Vaughn could've passed a message to someone."

"Even if that happened, the visitor may not even know who it was that they passed the location to."

"Worry about that later. Right now, get us the logs."

"Copy that."

Bledsoe felt the rapid descent of the bird and then saw the approaching prison yard lights.

PHELPS CORRECTIONAL CENTER

Vail did not win any points with the corrections staff, showing up in the eleventh hour to meet with a man due to be put to death.

She read their faces but decided to rise above their dirty looks. She owed them no explanations and expected them to do as the warden instructed.

Six minutes later—three of which she figured were unnecessary other than making them feel good because they had made her job more difficult—she was led to Stephen Raye Vaughn's cell.

He was haggard, a great deal thinner than when she had last seen him. Perhaps depression finally got to him…the stress of waiting, trying to remain hopeful during a hopeless time.

Or perhaps she was reading into it.

The officer opened the door. She gave Vaughn a terse nod but was not interested in exchanging pleasantries. Besides, what could she possibly say? *How've you been, Steve? Looking forward to Christmas? How 'bout them Nats?*

Vaughn was not a pleasant guy, and Vail certainly was not in a pleasant mood. She wanted to get right to business. Time was short.

For her. For Debra Mead. And, obviously, for Vaughn.

She cut right to the heart of the matter: the one thing that likely connected him to the unknown subject who had taken Debra Mead.

Vaughn was not biting. He denied knowing what she was talking about.

Internally, the seconds were ticking by in her head…an annoying metronome reminding her of the most valuable commodity humans could own, the one thing that money could not buy.

"Stephen. Think about what the news reports would be like if the cops find that van. Your van."

Vaughn snickered. "So what?"

Vail leaned forward and harrumphed, a mocking laugh that said, "You dimwit. You're smarter than that." She waited, but he did not bite. "Think about what would happen to it."

"No idea," Vaughn said with a shrug. "Stored in evidence? Sent to a junkyard?" He chuckled. "Sold to China for scrap?"

"C'mon, Stephen. You used that brain of yours to outwit and murder sixteen women. Now use it creatively."

He sat there staring at her. Blank eyes. "Still got nothing."

Vail glanced behind him, at the clock…where the second hand ratcheted around the dial. "You remember Ted Kaczynski?"

"That Unabomber dude."

"Yep. He didn't use a car to kill. But he lived in the middle of bumfuck nowhere in a cabin. That's where he constructed his bombs. Know what happened to that cabin?"

"Demolished. No, wait. Somebody charges admission to see it."

Vail nodded slowly. "Now you're getting it. They trucked it out to a museum. It's on display in a goddamn museum in Washington, DC. Part of American history."

Vaughn's face was stoic. "Uh huh."

"That car the DC Sniper used. The 1990 Caprice. You know about the DC Sniper, right?"

"'Course."

"John Allen Muhammad and his buddy hid in the back seat and shot their rifle out of a hole in the back of the trunk. Know where that car is now?"

"In a museum."

"Right. A floor directly above the cabin. Muhammad's car

and Kaczynski's cabin, both immortalized forever. Hundreds of thousands of people reading big plaques telling their story." She considered Vaughn's expression. He was getting it. "Once they find your van, where do you think it'll go?"

"In that museum."

"If you want, I'll make sure it goes on the same floor as the DC Sniper's car."

"No. I want Kaczynski. The Unabomber's cabin. That floor."

Vail feigned frustration—as if this were a real negotiation—then said, "Fine. Same floor as Kaczynski. I'll make it happen."

Vaughn looked at her. "Now why would you do that for me?"

"Because *you're* going to do something for *me*."

"I'm in a fuckin' prison cell on death row, Vail. About to die. What can I possibly do for you?"

"Excuse me," the corrections officer said. "Agent Vail, it's time."

"Five minutes. I need five more minutes."

The man shook his head. "No can do. Already gave you more time than I was s'posed to."

"But—"

"Not my decision. These things are timed. It's all set up. State law. No one wants to be responsible for prolonging this, if you get my drift."

Yeah, give anyone a chance for second thoughts, another appeal to the governor.

Vail turned to Vaughn. "Stephen, it's now or never. Tell me who has your van."

"What makes you think I know?"

"Because you groomed someone to take over for you. It took him some time, but he's now killing."

"So why should I give you his name?"

"Because he's stealing your thunder. They're gonna forget you. He's doing it better than you did. *He's* the one they're gonna remember, not you. But if we find your van, it goes in the museum. It'll be you who's memorialized. And your protégé will be nothing more than a footnote. At best."

"Okay, that's it," the officer said.

She had reached the end. She had to take a flyer. "Is the

39

protégé—is it Harrison, your son?"

Poker face. "Don't know what he's up to. He visits but he don't say much. I know one thing—doesn't seem to be interested in women."

"That doesn't mean anything. You know that."

Vaughn shrugged. "He's not your guy."

"Agent Vail, it's time. The death warrant has to be read to him and Mr. Vaughn's attorney and spiritual advisor are waiting for him. Follow Jack here. He'll escort you out."

He knows who it is, I can feel it.

"Stephen," Vail said. "If it's not Harrison, who is it? I need the name."

Vaughn closed his eyes. The officers walked to his side and pulled him up.

"Agent Vail." Jack gestured with his chin. "This way."

Vail accompanied Jack up to the locked gate. Buzzers sounded, metal clanked, and all Vail could think about was that she had failed. She wanted to smash her fist against the nearby bars.

As she walked down the corridor, she glanced back over her shoulder at Vaughn, who was being led through a door in the opposite direction.

Vail joined Bledsoe in a small administrative area.

"Well?"

"Close. No cigar."

"Shit." He looked away. "How close?"

"I needed another few minutes."

"You kidding me?"

"Nope."

"They wouldn't give it to you?"

"Already gave me extra time," Vail said. "This thing…it's a highly orchestrated event."

"It is, but still. Lives are on the line. A young woman—"

"I know, Bledsoe. I know." She turned to the guard behind the glass. "Can you have someone take us to the witness gallery?"

The man radioed for assistance.

"Let's have Kearney check on Vaughn's son, Harrison."

Bledsoe nodded. "Yeah. He'd be, what, early thirties now?"

"Could be our offender. Vaughn denied it, but let's find him and put him in a room, get an alibi. If he was anywhere near that SmartLots—"

"I'm on it," Bledsoe said as he pulled out his phone.

Seconds later, an escort led them down a few short hallways walking in a three-sided square. Apparently, they had been relatively close to the execution chamber all along.

Vail figured the holding cell where she had met with Vaughn was purposely adjacent to the chamber to reduce the chances of anything going wrong in the last minutes. With things so tightly managed, there was no time to deal with unforeseen occurrences.

11:57 PM

They entered the semi-circular witness gallery, a few rows of stadium-style seats rimming a glass-enclosed theatre of death. White walls and sparse stainless steel stared back at them.

The room was small; although the theater had some width, it was only a few rows deep. All attendees were afforded a close-up view of what would transpire.

A gurney sat close to the window, no more than ten feet from where Vail and Bledsoe were sitting. A red wall-mounted telephone—a direct line to the governor—sat unused in its receiver.

Also unused—but soon to be deployed—was a trio of rubber surgical tubes protruding from a short divider and snaking up to the gurney. Virginia followed a three-drug execution procedure. The first rendered the inmate unconscious, the second caused paralysis, and the third stopped the heart. Two of them—midazolam and potassium chloride—were made by a nearby compounding pharmacy. Vaughn was the first prisoner to use this form of midazolam, so the weeks during the run-up to his date of reckoning were not without handwringing controversy.

A door opened on the left side of the execution chamber and two burly guards entered, followed by the star of the show, Stephen Raye Vaughn, and another two imposing corrections officers.

41

Vaughn's face harbored a look of hatred and contempt as he gazed out at the glass that separated him from his witnesses. Vail knew it was a two-way pane that permitted them to see Vaughn, but the prisoner was merely staring at a reflected image of himself.

Vaughn was led to a gurney with crisp white linens. He sat down and laid back, two guards fastening thick leather straps to his limbs.

A curtain was drawn across the viewing window. Regardless, Vail knew that intravenous lines were being inserted into his heavily tattooed arms. She pictured Vaughn staring blankly at the ceiling, a feeling of helplessness enveloping his soul as reality struck him in the head like the mallet he had used on his victims' skulls.

Vail looked at the wall-mounted clock. It was black and white, like justice is supposed to be. Good and bad. Truth and lies. She watched the hand jerk along the hashmarks painted on the clock face. One second at a time.

And one minute to go.

"You did the best you could," Bledsoe said, settling himself into his seat.

Vail fell into hers. "For what that's worth."

"Déjà vu all over again."

"How so?"

"Richard Singletary. Tried to get him to talk, give up info on the Dead Eyes killer. How could you forget?"

"Forget?" Vail snorted. "Never. I just try not to think about it."

The curtain was pulled aside and the prisoner was once again visible.

"Stephen Raye Vaughn," Warden Doheny said, his voice sounding loud, but tinny, through the speakers. "You've been sentenced to death for your crimes. Do you have any final words?"

Vail squeezed her eyelids shut tightly.

C'mon, asshole. Give us the name.

Vaughn was silent.

Just like Singletary. When am I gonna learn?

"I wanna kill him," Bledsoe whispered.

"The state's going to do that in less than a minute."

"Too late, if you asked me."

"Decades too late."

"He's gonna take the name to his grave, isn't he?"

Vail sighed. "Looks that way."

"Yeah," Vaughn said. "I got something to say. Agent Vail out there?"

"I'm here," Vail said, rising from her seat and waving her hands at the glass. She realized that was unnecessary. The warden knew she was present.

"She's here," Doheny said.

"Tell her the van's license plates begin with a W T F. Don't remember the rest of it."

"That it?" Doheny asked.

"I want it in that museum," Vaughn said. "Near the Unabomber."

Fat chance of that happening. After forensics is done with it, it's going straight to the scrap heap. And I'm driving it there.

"That right?" Bledsoe said, nudging Vail with his elbow and starting to type on his phone.

"No. He's fucking with us. W T F, Bledsoe?"

He looked up from his screen. "Oh."

"The killer's name is," Vaughn said through the speakers—"is Agent Vail listening?"

Doheny turned toward the viewing gallery, even though he could not see those in attendance. "She's listening, Mr. Vaughn."

There was a long moment of silence. The warden looked down at Vaughn and waited, then said, "Mr. Vaughn? What's the name you want to give Agent Vail?"

Vaughn lay there a long moment.

"Mr. Vaughn," Doheny said, "I'm gonna need you to finish that sentence. Time's up."

Vaughn chuckled sardonically. "Time *is* up warden. Not just for me. It's up for the kidnapped woman, too. Tell Vail the name of the killer is John Q. Public."

Doheny frowned and looked out at the glass, as if knowing Vail was thinking about putting her fist through the large pane—and hoping she waited until Vaughn's heart had stopped beating.

Doheny shook his head and nodded to a guard five feet to his left. "Let's do it." He looked down at Vaughn, leaned in closer and said, "Have a good trip to hell, sir."

A smile flitted across Vaughn's lips.

Vail sat heavily and canted forward, leaning both elbows on her knees and burying her face in her palms.

Bledsoe placed a hand on her back. "I'm sorry, Karen. You tried."

Vail sat up, tears filling the lower lids of her eyes. One spilled over its threshold and raced down her cheek.

The tubes protruding from the divider jiggled a bit, one more than the others, and Vaughn's eyes began blinking rapidly. He took a few deep breaths, his eyes fluttered and slowly closed, as if he were falling asleep. In fact, he was. But this was one nap he would not wake up from.

His chest continued to rise and fall—and then it ceased to move.

Doheny summoned the doctor over. He put a stethoscope to Vaughn's chest, nodded, and then backed away.

"Time of death," Doheny said, looking at the wall clock, "12:01 AM."

Vail leaned back in her chair, neck fully extended, eyes examining the plain ceiling.

As they exited the penitentiary, Vail was uncommonly quiet.

"You should be happy. I mean, I know he didn't give it up, but—"

"He smiled, Bledsoe."

"Smiled? What are you talkin' about?"

"Vaughn," Vail said. "Before they injected him. After he told us to fuck off with that John Q. Public bullshit, he grinned."

"I didn't see a grin."

"I'm telling you, he smiled." She stopped and heaved a mouthful of vapor into the night chill. "What the hell was it for? They were about to inject him. His life's over. What's so funny about that?"

Bledsoe shrugged. "He didn't give up the name. We were there, waiting for something he was never gonna give up. Joke was on us."

Vail considered that, replayed it in her mind. "No, it's more than that. Like he knew something we don't know."

Bledsoe snorted. "Here we go again. You're reading into it."

"Maybe. But my intuition is usually semi-accurate."

"This time it's wrong."

"Hey," Robby called as he trotted over to them. "Get what you came for?"

"I got closure on my old case," Vail said. "I didn't get the name of the offender who kidnapped the kid. On balance, it was not a good evening."

"Sorry."

"And there's something else. And it's bugging me."

"What is it?"

"Nothing," Bledsoe said. "She's reading into things. Manufacturing something where there's nothing."

Robby looked at Vail. "Not so sure, Paul. You know Karen."

Bledsoe's phone buzzed. He pulled it out and glanced at the device. "Got the roster of visitors who came to see Vaughn. There were a bunch."

"Such a friggin' celebrity," Vail said. "And?"

"Kearney did his homework," he said, scrolling down the document. "Backgrounds and bios on all of them. Wanna take a look? Maybe one will jump out at you."

"He jumps out at me, he better be prepared for a swift kick in the balls."

"Just texted it to you."

Her phone rumbled and seconds later she began reading while Bledsoe and Robby huddled together to share Bledsoe's screen.

Finally, Vail spoke up. "This one. Vincent Caruthers. Herndon."

"You sure?"

Vail looked at Bledsoe. It was a look that spoke volumes.

"Okay, I get it. An educated guess."

"An educated guess. Best I can do right now. No crime scenes, no behaviors to analyze."

"Understood. Let's roll."

As they began walking, Bledsoe grabbed Vail's arm. "I still got the chopper here. It's hot. Much faster."

Vail turned to Robby. Her face probably said all he needed to know.

"Meet you at home," he said.

She nodded. "Don't wait up."

"Really, Karen? I've learned that's a losing proposition."

Vail and Bledsoe jogged toward the helipad.

"You shouldn't be running," Bledsoe shouted, the noise building as they neared the whipping rotors.

"Yeah, I know."

They got into the chopper and put on their headsets. X-ray raised the collective and they lifted off into the midnight sky.

"Swat is en route," Bledsoe said. "Detective Kearney's gonna meet us there, too."

"Looking forward to meeting him," Vail said absentmindedly, her attention on her Samsung's screen, going through the list of individuals who had visited Vaughn over the years.

She recognized a number of national journalists, which was not surprising. Vaughn liked the attention and the media loved running stories on depraved minds who killed gobs of people. It was a match made in Internet eyeball click-bait heaven.

But then a name caught her gaze.

"Hang on a second. Bledsoe, look at this."

He leaned over and snatched a look at her phone. "Lots of names there. Can you be more specific?"

"Here." She zoomed the screen on Harrison Vaughn.

"So? It's his son. Besides, you asked Vaughn about him. Didn't get anything."

Vail replayed that exchange.

"You ever talk to him when you were doing your victimology on Vaughn?"

"Of course. Family history's important. Never married, no girlfriends. Menial labor. Not as sharp as dad and didn't seem to exhibit psychopathic tendencies. But I eliminated him as an accomplice with the few facts we had. Tenicia was a big part of that. She said it was just Vaughn. Which made sense because if he had help, no way she would've escaped alive."

"So he visited Vaughn in prison. How many times?"

Vail scanned the document. "Pretty regularly."

She looked up. "We need Harrison's address."

"But you said Caruthers—"

"SWAT's en route. Let them handle Caruthers. Could be our offender. But Harrison…I've got a feeling about him."

"Christ," he said as he pulled out his phone. "Another one of your intuition things?" He tapped out a quick text and hit send as the helicopter banked slightly to the right.

"What if I was right about the smile?" Vail said. "What if Vaughn was laughing at us because he knew his son was carrying on in his footsteps?"

"He didn't smile."

Vail shook her head. "I know what I saw."

"Why can't it be a regular old copycat? Excuse me, a guy *patterning* him—"

"Copycat's fine. Just wanted to make sure you knew it's more like inspiration, rather than duplication, of what the killer did."

"So why can't it be a copycat?"

"They can only emulate those things the killer's done that are written in a book or news article. No one's written a book about Vaughn yet. And we withheld certain things from the media—including the white 70s Chevy panel van. So the only way he'd be able to 'copy' such things is if he—"

"Knows the killer."

"Right. And I'm betting it's more than that. It's personal. Vaughn coached him. Personally mentored him."

"But Harrison was only eighteen when Vaughn was arrested. You're saying he taught his son how to kill when the kid was young. A minor. So Harrison knew what his dad was doing and how he was doing it." Bledsoe shuddered. "That's friggin' awful."

"Let's assume Harrison hasn't offended until now. If Vaughn desensitized his son when he was young and impressionable, maybe he reinforced it when meeting with him in prison over the years. When he felt Harrison was ready he egged him on, pumped him up."

Bledsoe stared out the window a long moment, then nodded.

"If true, that'd mean he hasn't done this before. Makes sense. But why hasn't he acted until now?"

"Maybe he's been afraid to. The visits with his father could've served as encouragement, like you said." Vail turned her attention back to the phone and scrolled to the far right of Harrison's name. "He visited Vaughn several times recently. Last time was—" She looked at Bledsoe. "A week ago."

"When you visited Vaughn and asked for his help, he knew his son had finally done it."

Vail clenched her jaw. "I inadvertently told him junior had pulled the trigger. Made his day, I'm sure. That's what the smile was about." She looked out the side window, peering into the darkness of the Virginia countryside. They were over Caruthers' home. The top of the parked assault vehicle was barely visible in the moonlight, but she did not see the deployed officers. "Hover here a minute."

"Copy that," X-ray said.

"What do you think?" Bledsoe asked.

"I think we let SWAT do their thing and we go check out Harrison."

Bledsoe thought a moment, then his phone buzzed. He looked at the display, then nodded. "Let's do it. X-ray, change of plans. Got a new address for you."

They approached the home of Harrison Vaughn twenty minutes later, located in a dark, sparsely populated area of Charlottesville, Virginia.

Vail adjusted the headset mic in front of her mouth. "X-ray, sitrep from SWAT?"

"Negative. Stand by, I'll check." A moment passed. "Suspect Caruthers wasn't home. In process of clearing house. No sign of Debra Mead or indications she, or any other woman, has been held there. Over."

"Copy that," Vail said.

"Could be he has another place where he's planning to off her," Bledsoe said.

"Or he's not our guy."

They were now within view of the house—which was more like a home-built cabin in the middle of an evergreen thicket.

"I'll approach slowly, give you a 360 sweep of the perimeter so you can get a lay of the land."

"Copy that," Bledsoe said.

Vail nudged Bledsoe. "If he's not already awake, we're gonna announce ourselves."

"If he tries to leave, we should see him from up here. In fact, that might be the better call. We don't know what structures are down there. We're going in blind."

"I'm trying to remedy that," X-ray said. "Coming in from the north, then we'll go clockwise in a circle. You want, there are IR monocles in that kit by your feet."

"I want," Vail said, leaning forward to rummage in the bag. "Got it." She pulled it over her face, removing the headset first to seat it properly. Bledsoe did the same, and then they began scanning the countryside.

"Not seeing anything," X-ray said as he completed the second sweep. "Taking you down. Any preference? North, south, e—"

"Hang on a second," Bledsoe said. "Nine o'clock. That cloud of dust."

X-ray craned his neck and nodded. "10-4."

"Where?" Vail asked, looking past Bledsoe's left shoulder.

"Someone heading away from the property. In a big hurry, kickin' up a dirt storm."

X-ray pushed the cyclic forward to give them a better look. "It's a van, headed south."

"Got it," Vail said. "Can you head him off?"

"Working on it," X-ray said, swinging the chopper starboard and swooping toward the treetops. "How aggressive you want me to be?"

"What do you think?" Bledsoe asked. "Is Harrison the kind of guy who'd be armed or unarmed?"

"If he's our guy, we're assuming he kills with the same MO as his father—choking them and then carving them up—but we don't even know if he's murdered anyone yet. We don't even know if this is our guy."

49

"He's driving pretty damn fast from his shack after seeing a chopper doing a flyover."

"You're making some assumptions here, Bledsoe."

Bledsoe kept his eyes on the fleeing van. "He's running from the police. Looks guilty to me."

"Guilty—of what? Maybe he's got a warrant out on him for unpaid child support and he freaked out. Or it could be overdue parking tickets. Or he's a survivalist who thinks jack-booted government agents are coming to get him. Who the hell knows?"

"He's driving an old van."

"So do a lot of people in Virginia. I'm not saying he isn't our offender. But we could be wrong about this. Do we really want to go in hot and heavy without knowing for sure what we're doing?"

"What is this, role reversal? You're the one usually advocating a balls-to-the-wall approach."

"So you're saying I'm usually the one with the balls."

"Well, not in so—"

"That's okay. I'll accept that characterization. I'm trying to be a little more reserved. By the book."

Bledsoe chuckled. "Now's as good as any time to start, I guess. But in *my* book, a guy running from the cops because of late alimony or overdue parking tickets will surrender when confronted. If he doesn't surrender, whatever he's done is more serious." He tapped X-ray on the left shoulder. "Close on him."

2:03 AM

Bledsoe radioed his dispatcher and asked for them to coordinate with the local sheriff to get a car to Harrison Vaughn's cabin ASAP. If he was their killer, and if he did have Debra Mead inside, they needed to ascertain her status and render emergency medical care if necessary.

"Can we get a heat signature on the van?" Vail asked.

"Tried," X-ray said. "Not getting anything."

She snorted. "Well I'm pretty sure that old clunker isn't an autonomous vehicle. And it's not being driven by an android."

X-ray peered forward into the dark landscape ahead. "He's a cold-blooded killer, right? Maybe my infrared cam can't pick him up."

Yeah, that's it. Why didn't I think of that?

"Where the hell's he going?" Vail asked.

Bledsoe leaned his head against the window, careful not to strike his monocle on the glass. "Somewhere that we're not." He leaned back and pulled out his phone. "Text from Kearney."

"And?"

"A lot here. Gimme a minute. Gotta take the monocle off or I'll blow out my night vision."

"Tree cover makes it impossible for us to get any lower," X-ray said.

"So follow him until we *can* get lower," Vail said.

"Except that we have limited fuel."

Of course we do.

"I'll let you know when we've got ten minutes left. So far we're okay, but we should get some cars on the ground to intercept up ahead."

Bledsoe looked up from his screen. "We can have them lay down a spike strip."

Vail nodded. "Sounds like a good plan. Do it."

While Bledsoe made the request, Harrison emerged from the tree cover and entered a freeway.

"He's picking up speed," X-ray said.

Bledsoe grabbed the back of the pilot's seat as X-ray matched the van's acceleration. "Stay with him. I'm radioing our position."

At the moment Bledsoe finished, the van slowed and he made a sharp exit into downtown Charlottesville.

"What's his endgame?" X-ray asked.

"Maybe he's running out of gas," Bledsoe said. "Like us. Those tin cans got horrible mileage. He probably wasn't prepared to engage in a high-speed pursuit."

"At best a dozen miles per gallon when new," X-ray said. "At fifty years? Who knows. Ten? You could be right."

"It's been known to happen."

Vail fought off a smile. "Stay sharp. He may be getting ready to ditch the van, try to lose us somewhere."

"Yeah," Bledsoe said, "but where?"

"Someplace he knows well."

"And that is?"

Vail snorted into the mic, which came across as loud crackling. "I'll let you know the minute we find out."

605 E MAIN STREET
CHARLOTTESVILLE, VIRGINIA

They found out moments later, as the Chevy van drew to a stop at the end of the road—in the middle of it, actually. Perhaps Bledsoe's low fuel theory was right.

"Getting a heat signature," X-ray said. "Only one."

Vail sat forward to look at the screen. "So Debra Mead isn't with him."

"Let's just say, if she's *alive*, she's not with him."

Wiseguy.

"What street is that?" Bledsoe asked.

X-ray thought a second. "Looks like, um, Market. No—he *was* on Market, he stopped on Seventh. Right near that big tented structure, the pavilion next to the visitors center."

"I know the area." Bledsoe keyed his radio and relayed their location to local law enforcement. "By that freedom of speech blackboard."

"Did he get out of the van?" Vail asked. "Haven't seen any movement."

Bledsoe cupped the window to get a better view. "Door's opening. He's on foot."

"X-ray, can you get us down there?"

"You serious? It's a downtown, where do you suggest—wait, the top level of that parking structure. You'll have to run down a few flights of stairs, but—"

"Fine, just put us on the ground. Keep an eye on him from the air."

"Copy that."

"He's headed down the mall," Vail said, "east."

Seconds later, X-ray was setting the chopper atop a large, multistory cement monstrosity. "I'll circle overhead and relay his position. Won't be easy without a radio."

"Twenty-first century," Bledsoe said. "You'll figure it out, buddy."

They climbed out of the helicopter and ran toward the exit to street level, coming out near a historical landmark-style sign that read, THREE NOTCH'D ROAD. Behind it, a small multi-colored children's Merry-Go-Round was gated off by wrought iron fencing.

"I'm turned around," Vail said. "Which way?"

Bledsoe, SIG Sauer pistol in hand, headed past the storefronts on both sides of the open-air brick-paver mall, which featured restaurant dining tables sectioned off in the center of the breezeway.

"C'mon, X-ray," Vail said. "Give us some idea of where he is."

"You know he can't hear you."

"I'm sending the message telepathically."

Their phones buzzed. Vail checked hers.

> passing atlantic union bank
> coming up on urban outfitters

Bledsoe harrumphed. "Your message was obviously received."

"Harrison doesn't strike me as the type to shop at Urban Outfitters."

"You see him?"

Vail peered into the darkness. The mall area was lit by low wattage four-bulb ornamental light fixtures every few dozen feet. "I see some homeless guys down the cross-streets. But not Harrison."

Another text:

> coming up on the escape room

"Is that a joke?"

Bledsoe gestured at the storefront's sign, a good distance away. "Nope. But like everything else, I'm sure it's closed." Bledsoe

53

elbowed her to the right, closer to the Lynne Goldman shop. "I think I see him."

She squinted into the darkness. "Uh, yeah. Got him."

"Why come here? Everything's closed."

"Did you finish reading the background Kearney sent?"

"Shit, no."

"Give me your phone. Keep an eye on Harrison." Vail scanned the notes, which looked to be a copy/paste conglomeration of disembodied facts in different fonts. She figured Kearney had someone drive him to the Caruthers residence while he worked on the dossier.

She instinctively followed Bledsoe, who was slowly heading toward Harrison, taking care to keep out of his sightline.

"I know where he's going."

Bledsoe stopped. "Where?"

"Up ahead. The Paramount Theater."

"That's good because I lost him."

Another text:

> no eyes on
> hope you see him

"Probably went into the theater," Vail said, reading the background document. "Vaughn worked there after it reopened about fifteen years ago."

She snapped her fingers. "That's right. That's where he was employed before changing careers."

"Changing careers?"

"From veteran light board operator to professional serial killer."

"Why would his son be going there now?"

"I never got to ask Vaughn about his work at the theater," Vail said. "When I interviewed him, I focused on his childhood and teen years. And then one day he decided to stop meeting with me."

"Not even an educated guess?"

"Vaughn probably took Harrison there when he was young. Could be the only place they got to spend time together. Probably helped his dad with the lights during rehearsals or shows."

"So it's a safe place."

"Maybe in more ways than one. If we didn't have this info from Kearney, we might not have found him." She handed Bledsoe back his phone.

"So now what? Hang here until we can get some deputies onsite?"

"Yeah—call in the cavalry," Vail said. "But no. I'm not waiting to go in."

"Of course you're not. Because you have a death wish."

"Semantics. You call it a death wish, I call it a deep commitment to my job."

"You can't see me in the darkness, Karen, but I'm rolling my eyes."

"Laugh all you want."

"What happened to the more reserved, by-the-book approach?"

"That was then," Vail said. "This is now."

"Huh?"

"Don't live in the past. Only look forward."

"I'm looking forward to working with a normal partner again."

Vail led the way toward the theater. Its Greek Revival portico was lit up brightly, the vertical art-deco PARAMOUNT blade sign drawing attention to the false brick façade, which provided the illusion of height and importance.

Harkening back to its roots as a 1930s movie venue, an elaborate landmark marquis extended out from the building, rows of light bulbs hanging from its belly and illuminating the grand entrance—where Vail and Bledsoe now stood.

"What do you think?" Bledsoe asked.

Vail advanced on the six French doors ahead of them. "He probably forced one open. We go in the way he did."

"There are other ways in. Box office. Or the 'blacks-only' doors on the Third Street side used back when segregation was still a thing in the south."

"I'm not gonna try every freakin' door. None of these are open, I'm breaking the glass and going in."

"Quietly."

Vail looked at him. "How do you break glass quietly?"

They pulled on the various handles—until one gave way.

"No need." Bledsoe gestured at the lock. "Looks jimmied. Let's go."

Only a few accent lights were on in the dark theater, so Vail used her phone for illumination. But its carrying distance was limited. "Split up?"

"Works for me."

"Hang on. Let's be smart about this. He's come here for a reason—other than to hide or hopefully escape. He knows the place. And my guess is he had a good relationship with his father."

"Who just happened to be executed tonight."

"Exactly," Vail said. "That could've been a trigger. I overlooked that earlier. My bad."

"But now that we thought of it, what does it mean?"

"Comfort. He came here to remember him. In fact, if Debra Mead is his first kill—or hopefully *attempted* kill—it might be because it's the day his father was going to be executed."

"Shit or get off the pot?"

Vail scrunched her face. "Not the way I'd put it, but yeah."

"Makes sense. So…where to?"

"They control stage lighting from specific rooms in theaters, right?"

"Do I look like a guy who goes to the theater? Other than the movie theater, I mean."

"I knew what you meant," Vail said. "I've never gone behind the scenes, but there are always lights mounted above the stage and also in the back, above the balcony. I know there are sound boards for sound engineers, so I'm guessing there's something like that for lighting engineers. Or technicians. Or operators. Whatever they're called."

"Again, makes sense."

"Head to the stage, give me a global view. In case I flush him out, you'll be able to see where he goes."

"What about you?"

"I'm betting there's a room above the balcony, dead central, where both the sound and lighting techs work during the show. That's where Harrison will be. I'm gonna find my way there."

"How sure are you that's where Harrison will be?"

"Not sure at all. Why?"

"How about I go find the lighting room and you go to the stage?"

"Because I'm a woman?"

Bledsoe hesitated. "Because of your knee."

"Nice save. But I can handle myself."

Someday I'll have to tell him about my badass work with OPSIG Team Black. But then I'd have to kill him.

"Still. Be careful, Karen. Robby'll be real pissed at me if you get killed."

Moments later, Bledsoe stood behind the orchestra pit, in the center of the stage, looking out at the empty, octagonal theater. Dim lights demarcated the end of each row of seats. Best he could tell in the near darkness the audience chamber was grand, with gold leaf moldings, ornate woodwork carved into the ceiling, and two humongous near floor-to-ceiling paintings on each side.

Bledsoe strained to see across the room, above the balcony level, where there were four large windows and a rig of hefty spotlight-style fixtures trained on the stage.

He canted his head ceiling-ward, and—as Vail had surmised—an array of luminaires hung there, too.

He continued moving his gaze left to right, looking for Vail… or better yet, Harrison Vaughn.

Vail climbed a few steps and came to a closed door. It was dark and she wanted her eyes to acclimate, so she was no longer using her phone light.

Glock in hand, she cautiously turned the knob, then pushed slowly. Fortunately, the hinges did not creak.

She slipped inside, careful not to trip on a box of unseen equipment. The room was about twenty-five feet wide but only eight or so deep.

Power flowed through what she surmised were control boards.

Small lights poked out from the blackness, along with cabling, sliding dimmers, instrumentation, and controllers of various types.

The hum and white noise of electrical gear and their fans droned in the background, serving as a buffer to any noise she might make.

I hope.

A wall of equipment switches and sliders stood to her left, two Duracell PROCELL batteries serving as some sort of backup.

Directly ahead of her were four large panes of windows, which she figured looked out onto the seating and stage. Somewhere beyond that stood Bledsoe, though it was too dark to make him out—which meant Harrison could not see him, either.

The faint glow from the instrumentation provided too little illumination for Vail to see well. If Harrison was like his father, he was a hefty guy—so going toe to toe with him was likely not to her advantage.

Right now, brains—and her 9mm pistol—will have to beat brawn.

She could have pulled back and waited, but she did not relish the thought of being so close—and having to retreat. She wanted Harrison Vaughn in handcuffs, on the way to the Adult Detention Center for booking. Tonight. Or—rather, this morning.

Enough groping around in the dark. Vail had no idea where the wall switch was—ironic, given that she was in the room that controlled thousands? Hundreds of thousands? of watts of lighting.

And she couldn't even find a single bulb to turn on.

Fumbling with her phone was not an option. She wanted both hands free for her Glock.

She figured there had to be a small, focused lamp of some kind by the technicians' workstations. How else would they be able to see what they were doing during the performance?

Vail moved her left hand in a circle and her index finger brushed against something that telescoped vertically. She followed it down to a base—and flipped a rocker switch. It flooded the desktop with a small, but powerful halogen light.

Sitting ten feet to her right was Harrison Vaughn.

He yelled.

She yelled.

But they were saying different things.

Harrison: "Ahhh!"

Vail: "Don't move. FBI!"

Harrison made like most criminals—and ignored Vail's admonition.

He scrambled away on his knees to the right, around a bend and, as she learned, out the side door.

Vail followed—and heard Bledsoe calling out instructions to their fleeing suspect.

Man, the acoustics in here are great.

"Get down! The theater's surrounded. There's no place to run."

Have the deputies arrived? Or is he bluffing?

Vail emerged behind Harrison. Bledsoe was advancing on him, coming up the left aisle, his SIG steady and menacing.

"Down on the ground," Vail added, letting Harrison know she was there—and that he had no viable way out.

Rather than getting on his knees, he decided to protest. "What's this about? I didn't do anything."

"Debra Mead may have something to say about that," Vail said. "If you haven't killed her yet."

"Debra who?"

"The woman you kidnapped in the SmartLots parking lot."

"Don't know what you're talking about."

"We've got you on security camera footage. Those cameras were installed after your dad started abducting women. Ironic, isn't it, Detective?"

"How so?" Bledsoe asked.

"Vaughn taught his son how to kidnap and murder women, but one thing he didn't teach him about was how not to get caught."

Vail advanced on Harrison and handcuffed him.

"Where's Debra Mead?" Bledsoe asked. "And don't give me any bullshit like you don't know what we're talking about."

"I don't know who that is."

Vail twisted him to face her. "Look, asshole. If she's still alive, you'd better tell us where she is. It's cold out there. She's diabetic and if she doesn't get her medication"—she glanced at her watch—"in the next thirty minutes, she's gonna die. Then it won't just be reckless endangerment. You'll be tried for murder. Unlike the feds, Virginia puts its convicted killers to death."

More complicated than that, and Mead isn't diabetic—but what the hell.

"Yeah," Bledsoe said, getting in his face. "Like your daddy tonight. We were there. Saw him take his last breath."

Harrison narrowed his crooked right eye.

"The way she'd been taken," Bledsoe said, "we knew it was someone he'd coached. So we asked him who took her. Right before they injected him, that's when he gave you up." He paused to let that sink in. "We compared your DMV photo to our video clip in the parking lot, and bang. There you were. We put a name with a face."

"And here we are," Vail said. "Case is open and shut. You help us find Debra Mead, we'll recommend that the prosecutor cut you a good deal."

Harrison twisted his lips as he thought.

"Twenty-nine minutes left," Vail said. "Then Debra dies. Her diabetes medication—"

"She's in an abandoned shack in Hill County."

"Address?"

"Don't know. House is owned by a guy named Ed Malicki."

Vail got on the phone to X-ray and told him to head toward Hill County and mobilize deputies to the property of Ed Malicki.

She flicked Harrison on his left cheek. "Ed help you out?"

"He don't know anything. I just borrow his shack. Store stuff. He never asked what I put there."

"You know what, Harrison?" Bledsoe yanked him back to face him. "You're a piece of shit like your father."

Harrison spit in Bledsoe's face.

Vail stuck her hand on Bledsoe's fist and stopped him before he brought it forward into Harrison's nose. "He'll get his time, just like Vaughn."

Bledsoe groaned, then shrugged his jacket back into place. "I'm not good with delayed gratification."

"Let's get him outa here," Vail said, grabbing Harrison's left arm.

"You—you're gonna recommend the deal, right? To the prosecutor?"

Vail feigned surprise. "Of course I'll recommend the deal. Just like I said, Harrison. I'm a woman of my word. But the prosecutor, she hates my guts. Never takes my advice. Does the opposite, usually."

They pushed through the doors to the outside, where the air was bone-chilling cold.

Bledsoe blew on his left fist. "Temperature dropped about ten degrees while we were in there."

He sat Harrison on one of the metal chairs in the center of the breezeway in front of the theater, then double handcuffed him to the table while they waited.

Vail pulled out her phone.

"Who you calling?"

"With X-ray looking for Debra Mead, we don't have a ride. I'm getting an Uber."

Bledsoe gave her a look of consternation. "We can't transport a prisoner in—"

"Relax. I'm calling a local deputy I know, see if he'll come pick us up."

Minutes after loading Harrison into the rear of one of the responding police cruisers, their phones buzzed simultaneously. A text from X-ray:

> meads alive
> medics got a pulse
> weak thready
> but shes alive
> airlifting to hosp
> catch you latuh
> running on fumes
> sipping fuel

"Thank God," Vail said.

"Your vic's gonna be okay?" the deputy asked.

"Looks like it."

"You lucked out," Bledsoe said, elbowing the prisoner seated to his right. "Hear that, Harrison? You got lucky. Twenty-five to life instead of death row."

Harrison did not respond. By now he probably figured he had been played.

Bledsoe turned to Vail. "Maybe it was us who lucked out. We got to Debra Mead just in time."

"Luck? Skill? Who cares. Sometimes our job's a mix of both. I'm just glad that Stephen Raye Vaughn is a footnote in American history. And his son's gonna be behind bars before he could do too much damage."

Bledsoe sighed heavily, then looked out the window at the pitch blackness, pinpricks of stars winking back at them. "Bastard was one bad dude."

"Congrats. You win the award for understatement of the year."

Bledsoe stole a look at his watch. "Damn, it's friggin' late. Why is it that the dregs of society come out when everyone else is asleep?"

Vail shrugged. "Better time to ply their trade."

"Yeah, well, in my experience, nothing good happens after midnight."

"And yet," Vail said with a grunt, "tonight it did. Twice."

* * *

CELL PHONE INTOLERANT

KEVIN O'BRIEN

Ed McKinnon was pee-shy. No help was the fact that, at age fifty-nine, his prostate was about the size of a bowling ball. He hated using public restrooms. But sometimes it became necessary—as it did on that December evening, in the middle of Christmas shopping at the downtown Seattle Nordstrom.

Usually, he took care of these things before leaving the house. But the shopping expedition dragged on longer than he'd anticipated—what with the endless lines and cashiers who didn't know how to send gifts. Most of Ed's purchases were going to his brother's family in Phoenix, and he always sent his ex-wife Fran something, too. She lived in San Francisco. One of the cashiers had mentioned that he might find it easier to shop and send gifts online. Ed had told the woman that he wanted to support the brick and mortar stores. But considering how much his send-purchases seemed to piss off the clerks—as well as the customers waiting behind him—he figured he'd shop online next year. Then he wouldn't have to deal with all the obnoxious shoppers—like the ones who stood side by side on the escalators, blithely blocking everyone in back of them; or the idiots who decided to stop and text someone at the top or bottom of the escalators, creating more blockage; or the moron who thought bringing her dog (on a ten foot leash, no less) into Nordstrom during the Christmas rush was a brilliant idea. No one had "situational awareness" these days; most people were totally oblivious to everything and everyone else around them.

Ed lived alone in a three-bedroom house in Seattle's trendy Capitol Hill neighborhood. It had been his home for over two decades. The house was currently decked out for Christmas, very tastefully, too. He took pride in the place, and kept it immaculate inside and out. He led an orderly life. A dripping faucet was cause for alarm. But he easily repaired things like that. Ed was mechanically inclined. He worked for thirty-two years in the Union Pacific Railroad car repair shop, and took an early retirement last year. He kept active with bi-weekly visits to the gym, and spent hours every night in his basement "lab" tinkering with various inventions. He held thirteen different patents, but nothing he'd invented had taken off yet. He'd come really close with his idea for a touch-activated faucet, but somebody beat him to the punch.

One of his ex's major gripes was that he'd spent too much time down in their basement with his "mad scientist's projects." Fran also claimed he was kind of a control freak. Ed knew he was guilty on both counts. He certainly liked to be in control of things.

He just wished he had a bit more control of his bladder right now. And he wished every other man in Nordstrom hadn't suddenly decided to use the restroom the same time as him. Both stalls were occupied with two customers waiting; and both urinals were in use—with a guy and his toddler son in line ahead of him. It was a pee-shy sufferer's nightmare.

Ed would have preferred a stall. But things naturally moved faster at the two urinals. The dad and son didn't waste any time. So, reluctantly, Ed took one of the urinals.

At least he didn't have to pee standing next to anyone. But he felt pressured to hurry up and go while he was still there alone. He played a mind game that sometimes helped him get started, reciting in his head: "You're a two, you're a four, you're a six, urinate..." But it didn't work. He heard all this activity behind him as toilets flushed and the guys waiting for the stalls took their turns. The two other guys washed their hands and left. There was a hush. Then, by some Christmas miracle, Ed started to pee.

"I'm serious, I've been invited to five Christmas parties this weekend!" someone announced as he breezed into the men's room. The guy was right behind Ed when he spoke.

Ed was so startled, he stopped peeing in mid-stream.

The man stepped up to the urinal beside Ed's. He spoke so loud, his voice seemed to echo off the bathroom tiles. "The way I figure, I'll just Uber the whole night, because I'll be so wasted by the last party..."

Ed stole a glance at the man. He wondered who the hell this

clown was talking to. Was there someone in back of them?

No. The guy was on his goddamn phone.

This is why I hate people, thought Ed. He still needed to pee, but he'd temporarily gone bone dry.

"Well, Lloyd's is B-Y-O-B, but I'm not bringing anything. I won't be there very long," the guy said—over the loud drone of his stream hitting the plastic pad for the urinal cake. Obviously, he had no pee-shy issues. With his baseball cap on backwards, he looked like a cocky jerk. He was in his late thirties and had a slight resemblance to Jason Priestley—if someone had taken a bicycle pump to Jason Priestley and inflated him. Ed figured he was a jock gone to seed.

Ed heard a woman murmur something on the other end of the line.

He gave up trying to pee. He couldn't take any more of this.

"Oh, yeah?" the guy said into his phone. "Well, three guesses how I feel about that."

Ed zipped up and flushed. "SERIOUSLY?" he said loudly. "DOES THE WOMAN YOU'RE TALKING TO KNOW YOU'RE PISSING IN A PUBLIC RESTROOM RIGHT NOW?"

Rude Jason Priestley squinted at him. "What's your problem, man?"

"You are! You're my problem! I'm trying to take a pee here, and you're carrying on a phone conversation! Could you *be* any ruder?" Ed swiveled around and saw some twenty-something guy had just stepped into the restroom. The young man stared at him as if he were completely insane.

"No, it's nobody," Rude Jason said into his phone. "Some crazy guy here in Nordstrom. No, I'm not in the restroom. I'm in Men's Shoes..." He headed for the door.

"HE DIDN'T FLUSH AND HE DIDN'T WASH HIS HANDS AFTER HE PEED!" Ed announced loudly, so the guy's girlfriend could hear.

With the phone to his ear, Jason flipped him off as he left the restroom.

Ed was livid. He still needed to pee, but knew he couldn't. And both stalls were still occupied. Besides, he didn't want to hang around the men's room any longer than he had to. He hated confrontations. And nowadays, the least little conflict could end up in a mass shooting. Rude Jason could be lying in wait for him outside the restroom.

So Ed made a beeline from the men's room to the exit doors.

All the way home on the light rail, he was seething. He couldn't help notice how everyone around him was wrapped up in their mobile devices. It was a crowded car, and he found only two other people—a couple—who weren't focused on their phones. But they had their phones in their hands. Before Ed got off at his stop on Capitol Hill, he saw those last two holdouts start to check their mobile devices, too.

Walking home, he realized practically everyone he passed on the street—couples, people walking alone, people in groups—they were all on their phones. Ed felt like he was in some kind of Orwellian nightmare. He was the only person in the vicinity not on a phone or wearing some kind of head-phone device. Most of these people seemed ready to walk right into him if he didn't step aside. People with dogs were the worst. They were supposed to love their dogs, yet during the one time they did something for their pet, they were on the phone, ignoring the poor animal—and taking up the entire sidewalk, too.

He figured maybe this was a Seattle thing—especially in his neighborhood, populated with so many young tech types. Or was it like this everywhere?

As an inventor, he used to think cell phones were a modern age marvel. But when they first started to get popular in the nineties, Ed noticed the people who used them seemed like self-important assholes. *Look at me, I have a cell phone*, they seemed to say. He remembered the ones in his local video store, browsing the new releases and chatting loudly on their mobile devices—annoying everyone else in the store.

For a while, people on cell phones were like smokers. They were annoying, but they were a minority. Now everyone had a phone. There was no escaping them. Even when people weren't supposed to use their phones—at the movies, while driving their cars, in locker rooms or bathrooms—they still used them anyway.

It was like the rules didn't apply to them.

As far as Ed was concerned, cell phones should have stayed something that people used only for emergencies. They shouldn't have become a way of life.

He wished he could invent some device to discourage people from using their phones, at least in situations where it was inappropriate. Maybe he could come up with a remote control mechanism that would scramble the phone signal. But would that really stop all the rude, phone-obsessed people out there?

"Ed, you're certifiable," claimed his friend, George. Another divorced retiree from the railroads, George was one of those gray-haired ponytail guys. They'd been best friends for twenty years. George lived on a houseboat on Lake Union.

It was late February, and George sat on a step-stool in Ed's paneled basement "lab." After weeks of trial, error and experimentation, Ed was ready to test his cell phone "Intruder," a small gadget he'd fashioned to look like a remote keyless device for a car. Ed made himself the Guinea pig. He had four different brands and models of phones on the table in front of him. On each one, he would call his home number (Ed still had a landline—with an answering machine from the nineties). And while Ed was on the phone, George would click the device at him. Then they'd see what happened.

"I don't feel good about this," George said, frowning at the gizmo in his hand. "When did you come up with this little gem? Three in the morning? Nothing good ever happens after midnight, my friend. You were probably half-asleep when you put this together. I know it's just supposed to scramble the signal, but what if something goes wrong?"

"That's why we're doing this—to make sure nothing goes wrong when I actually use it," Ed explained. He picked up the Samsung. "And I do my best work after midnight. Remember, you're sworn to secrecy about this. I really appreciate it, buddy. Afterwards, I'll take you out for pizza and beers—on me."

"If you're still alive," George said. "Remember a few years ago, those cell phones caught on fire because of the lithium batteries?

What if something like that happens? I could blow your goddamn hand off or something. Or I might be sending out some radioactive signals..."

"Nothing like that is going to happen," Ed assured his friend—and himself. The truth was the scrambling signal might end up doing just about anything to the phone—and the person holding it. That was why he needed to be the Guinea pig with this experiment. He might have wanted to screw with some of the phone-obsessed jerks out there, but he didn't want to hurt anybody.

Ed didn't want to get hurt either. So, despite how he acted with George, he was skittish about this experiment and the unknown results.

He clutched the Samsung in his left hand and punched in his home number. He heard it ring upstairs. Extending his left arm, Ed held the phone as far away as possible. "Okay," he said, wincing. "Go ahead."

The machine answered. He could hear his recorded voice talking over the connection.

The Intruder device in his hand, George shook his head. "I can't! What if I end up killing you?"

"For God's sake, press the button!" Ed yelled. His hand was shaking. He wondered if this was the last time he'd have all his fingers. "Go ahead! Do it!"

His answering machine greeting was still going.

George grimaced. "Here goes..."

Nothing happened.

"Did you press the button?" Ed asked.

"Yeah..."

Ed went back to the drawing board.

A week later, he and George tried again. The experiment was another failure. Ed took him out for pizza anyway.

Five weeks and five pizzas later, Ed gave up. Not that he blamed George, but his friend had hardly been encouraging. He'd said again and again, it was a lousy idea that would end up getting him into trouble. And he was probably right.

Ed had no rational reason for taking the Intruder with him when he went shopping that Saturday afternoon in late April. The damn thing didn't work, but he thought he'd engage in a bit of whimsy, pressing it whenever he saw a rude texter or someone texting and driving. Maybe pressing the Intruder button would be good therapy for him—like squeezing one of those stress-relief balls.

He ambled down Broadway, the main drag of Capitol Hill, with the Intruder in his pocket. He kept passing so many Intruder-worthy candidates—most of them texters not looking where they were going. With each idiot he passed, Ed pressed the button on the device, but of course, nothing happened. And it was no fun merely pretending to screw up their phones.

Just ahead of him, Ed spotted a skinny young woman with corkscrew black hair wandering across the street—against the light. She wore earphones and worked her thumbs over her phone screen. A car with the right of way screeched to a halt as she mindlessly stepped in front of it. The driver honked. The girl didn't even look up or quicken her pace. She casually flipped off the driver and went back to texting.

It reminded Ed so much of Rude Jason, flipping him the bird. This woman probably gave people the finger all the time. Could she possibly be any more of a jerk? He wanted to yell at her, but of course, she wouldn't hear him.

Instead, Ed took the Intruder out of his pocket, aimed it at her and pressed it three times in a row.

The girl suddenly stopped dead and shrieked. The phone flew out of her hand, sailing up over her head. With a clatter, it landed behind her in the middle of the street.

The driver of the car revved his engine and zoomed past her, running over the mobile device. Ed heard it crunch under the tire.

Screaming hysterically, the young woman gaped down at the flattened, broken phone on the pavement. She acted like someone had mowed down her dog. At the same time, she kept wringing her hand and massaging it. Passersby looked at her as if she were crazy. Others didn't even notice her, because they wore earphones or they were too busy on their own phones.

She held up traffic again, crying and cursing at cars swerving around her as she frantically gathered up the pieces of her shattered phone. She set the shards in her claw-like left hand.

Ed knew it was horrible, but he couldn't help smiling.

He wondered what exactly had happened to make her throw the phone in the air like that.

He found out that evening, in his backyard with George during a final "test run."

Rolling his eyes, his friend wondered out loud why Ed had resurrected his lame-brained "Intruder" invention. "You and your After-Midnight Specials," he complained. "Nothing good is going to come from this…"

Ed hadn't told him about the incident with the jaywalking texter.

Once again, he was the Guinea pig. With his friend standing by the garden on the other side of the yard, Ed called his home line. He'd instructed George to wait for his cue and then press the button on the Intruder three times in rapid succession.

Ed heard his voice on the answering machine. He was about to brace himself and nod at his friend. But George jumped the gun.

"Here goes," George called out. He jabbed the button three times.

Ed wasn't ready for the jolt of electricity that surged through his hand—like a hundred fiery needles. He let out a howl and dropped the phone. Stunned, he rubbed his throbbing, tingling hand. He was so rattled that he could hardly get a breath.

"What happened?" George asked. "Did you get a shock?"

"Um, a—a little one," Ed lied. His heart was still racing. "Just a little one…"

He started to get the feeling back in his hand. With trepidation, he reached down and touched his phone. He didn't get another shock. He picked it up off the lawn and listened. The line was dead. He switched it on and off again, but nothing happened. The phone had short-circuited.

"Well, it looks like I screwed the pooch again," Ed heard himself say.

But it was another lie. Actually, he considered the experiment a major success. He just didn't want his friend to know, because George would only try to talk him out of ever using the Intruder again.

So, when they went out for pizza and beer afterwards, Ed talked about how he would abandon the project. But all the while, he thought of Rude Jason in Nordstrom's bathroom—and all the others like him. Armed with the Intruder, Ed wouldn't have to put up with them anymore.

The following day, when he walked down Broadway, Ed felt like Charles Bronson in *Death Wish*. He was just looking for trouble. The Intruder in his pocket gave him an intoxicating sense of power. Broadway was like Cell Phone Central. It stood to reason, that for every ten phone users, at least one was rude about it. So, with all the techies and millennials on Broadway, Ed figured he'd come across at least three Intruder-worthy candidates on every block.

He passed one person after another on their phones—texting, talking or scrolling while they walked. Hardly any of them bothered to look where they were going. After a while, Ed didn't even need to conceal the Intruder, because no one noticed him. He was over fifty. He may as well have been invisible. His thumb hovered over the Intruder button. He could have pressed it at any time. He must have seen at least a dozen idiots who deserved to get zapped. But none of them seemed quite rude enough. So he took mercy on them.

Or maybe he was just scared to use the device now that he knew what it could do.

Giving up, Ed felt deflated as he wandered into the QFC for some groceries. The supermarket was lousy with people on their phones blocking the aisles. As always, at least two or three morons had brought their dogs into the store—despite the signs saying pets weren't allowed.

Ed ignored them as he picked up stuff for dinner. Then he went to the checkout line. He didn't use the U-scan, because he wanted to keep the checkers employed. He got behind some nicely-dressed, forty-something guy who didn't bother to unload his handcart. He just set it on the conveyer belt and let the cashier unload the cart for him. He was too busy talking on his phone.

A couple of shoppers got in line behind Ed.

With fascination and mounting contempt, he watched the man carry on his phone conversation while the cashier rang up his groceries. "Do you have a QFC card?" the young woman asked him. "Sir?"

He kept talking. Barely looking at her, he held up his index finger as if to indicate that he'd acknowledge her in a minute. She'd finished ringing up his items, but he hadn't even reached for his wallet yet. Ed wondered what the guy was discussing on his phone that was so important. Did it really warrant holding up all the other customers in line behind him? Ed could see the cashier was getting exasperated with the guy. He wanted to tell him off. But he hated confrontations.

Then he remembered.

He had the Intruder.

Taking it out of his pocket, Ed pressed the button three times.

"Shit!" the guy bellowed, suddenly pitching his phone behind the counter. He shook his hand over and over as if he'd burned his fingers. "Goddamn it!"

The cashier thought he'd thrown his phone at her, and she laid into the guy: "Hey, what do you think you're doing?"

He screamed back at her that his Smartphone had just given him a shock. He held up the checkout line even longer while he retrieved the phone and then threw a fit over the fact that it was now dead.

"That's not my problem," the cashier told him. "Are you going to pay for your items or what?"

The guy stormed out of the store without his groceries.

Ed couldn't help smiling. It was a beautiful thing to see.

From then on, using the Intruder was easy—and so gratifying. It was like a triumph over rude, inconsiderate, self-important assholes everywhere.

It seemed the city was swarming with Intruder-worthy jerks. One of the sweetest victories for Ed was the encounter with a woman taking up the entire sidewalk with her Labrador retriever on a long leash. The dog crapped on the parkway. But the woman was too busy texting to stop and pick it up.

Ed even gave her a chance to redeem herself by politely

inquiring: "Aren't you going to clean up after your dog?"

She gave him a flutter of her hand as if to say "shoo," and went back to texting.

Zapping her felt so good.

The phone seemed to leap from her grasp, and she let out a scream that sent her dog into a barking fit. Her phone landed in a pile of some other dog's shit.

As Ed walked away, he heard her cursing furiously and the lab barking.

He also zapped four texters in a movie theater. The commotion he started was a lot more distracting than those glowing little screens in the darkened movie theater that always annoyed him. But in this case, the movie was only so-so; and it was utterly satisfying to watch each zapper-victim react. They jumped up from their seats. Drinks were spilled. Popcorn flew in the air.

Ed didn't feel a bit sorry for them. They'd been told before the movie—during the previews—to turn off their cell phones. But did they pay attention? No.

The gym was a goldmine of Intruder-worthy self-involved creeps, especially those guys who remained on the weight machines like squatters, taking five or ten minute breaks while they texted or scrolled between reps. Ed really enjoyed zapping them. He got five people in a row—all lazily sitting or laying on the mats, focused on their phones. None of them had been stretching or exercising. Meanwhile, people like him were waiting for space to do their sit-ups. He zapped three more in the locker room—two texters and one fully-dressed clown who stood by his locker, talking on his phone, spitting distance from the sign that showed a cell phone inside a circle with a slash through it. They all had it coming. No one dared to shower at his gym anymore because of these cell phone jerks and guys taking selfies in the locker room. Ed felt like a freak every time he undressed to take a shower.

He returned to the gym two days later, and zapped sixteen more people.

Two days after that, on his next trip to the gym, Ed noticed someone on the staff had posted a hand-written sign at the check-in desk:

WARNING TO CELL PHONE USERS

Several members have reported getting shocked while using their phones in the workout areas and locker room. Phones have short-circuited. Management is investigating the problem & assumes no responsibility. USE YOUR PHONES AT YOUR OWN RISK! Use of electronic devices in the locker rooms is strictly prohibited.

But people didn't pay attention to signs anymore. So there were still plenty of phone abusers in the gym—and two more in the locker room. Ed zapped them all.

The next time he went to the gym, the sign was printed up and laminated. The guy at the check-in desk was collecting phones, then tagging and bagging them. Too many gym members had complained or threatened to sue.

Ed noticed a similar sign posted at his neighborhood QFC—right by the one saying that pets weren't allowed. He hadn't realized just how many people he'd zapped in the supermarket, but apparently the number was significant. He noticed less people using their phones while shopping. People in the checkout lines were actually talking to each other—or to the cashiers.

After a while, at the gym, he found he didn't have to wait to use the machines or the exercise mats.

Now he didn't hesitate to zap the phone-abusers he encountered on the sidewalk—that included anyone not looking where they were going while texting; people on their phones walking their dogs; texting jaywalkers; and people texting while driving. He'd almost caused a few car accidents among the last group—or more accurately, the texting drivers almost caused the accidents. Didn't they know it was against the law?

After two weeks, the local TV news reported on the "cell phone malfunctions" that plagued Seattle's Capitol Hill neighborhood—along with some isolated incidents downtown, in Queen Anne, Ballard and Fremont. Cell phones were recalled and phone towers were tested. An article about it even popped up on page one of *The*

Seattle Times.

Ed felt compelled to write *The Times* an email:

To the Editor:

Regarding those cell phone malfunctions reported by your newspaper. If you're looking for a common link to all the instances of phones short-circuiting and shocking their users, don't look at the phone brand or models or the signal towers. Look at the phone users. Ask them what they were doing when their phones malfunctioned. Ask them if they were using their phones in movie theaters or locker rooms or bathrooms or while driving. Ask them if they were being rude or obnoxious when they were on their phones. Ask them if they were ignoring the people around them or their own children or their dogs, because they couldn't tear themselves away from their precious phones for a few minutes. The common link among all the reported 'malfunction' cases is that these scumbags all deserved what happened to them and their stupid phones. As long as there are inconsiderate phone users here in Seattle, phones will keep 'malfunctioning.' I promise you.

Sincerely,
Ed

He sent the email from a computer in the Ballard Public Library so it couldn't be traced to him.

But as soon as he sent the damn thing, Ed regretted it. He'd just admitted to *The Seattle Times* that he was behind all these people getting hurt and all that property damage. Were there cameras inside or outside the Ballard Public Library? Could the police track him down as the "Ed" who had written the email?

He suddenly felt like a hunted man—and they hadn't even published the email yet. He wondered if they would. Maybe *The Seattle Times* would assume he was a crank and simply ignore the letter.

Two days later, his note was printed on the newspaper's

front page under the headline: *"Anti-Phone Zealot 'Ed' Claims Responsibility for Series of Phone Malfunctions: Hero or Terrorist?"*

Ed suddenly felt like the Zodiac Killer or the Unabomber. Portions of his email were read on TV—and not just the local news, but national news, too. He was all over the Internet. Some people thought he was absolutely nuts. But others spoke out against phone-abusers—or to quote Ed, "cell phone scum." And to them, he was a hero, a crusader.

A follow-up article appeared a few days later. It cited the benefits to the "cell phone scare." Movie attendance in Seattle had gone up by twelve percent. Washington State Highway Patrol reported accidents due to distracted drivers were down by twenty-one percent. The Seattle Humane Society issued a statement that dogs were "healthier and happier" now that less and less dog owners talked on their phone or texted while walking their pets.

Ed's friend, George, was off the current events grid. He never turned on the TV or read a newspaper. So Ed didn't have to worry about George finding out. But it was weird to have created such a stir and not talk with anyone about it. Nobody knew he was famous. He couldn't help feeling lonely, but not quite as alone and isolated as he used to feel walking down the Seattle streets full of phone-focused people.

He couldn't use the Intruder quite so freely anymore. He found out the hard way—on the bus. The number of people texting or talking on their phones while riding had definitely decreased. It was quiet, except for one twenty-something guy talking loudly on his phone, laughing and casually cursing a lot too. His favorite modifier was "fucking." He used the word in practically every other sentence. After a while, it became annoying as hell. Ed could see he wasn't the only one. Other passengers on the bus were bothered by the guy, too.

So Ed subtly took out the Intruder and zapped him.

The guy howled and dropped his phone. "My fucking phone just fucking shocked me! Fuck!" The whole bus heard him.

A few people applauded. Ed suppressed a smile.

"Oh my God, Ed's on the bus!" another passenger declared.

"Ed, where are you?" someone else called. "Stand up!"

A couple of people started chanting his name, like he was a football star or something.

"Shut up!" yelled one man near the back of the bus. "That guy's nothing less than a criminal! He's a self-appointed vigilante. He's killed people!"

That was a boldface lie, but Ed wasn't about to say anything.

The guy he'd zapped was seething and out for blood. "Where's this Ed guy? He's gonna fucking pay for my fucking phone!"

Ed quietly slinked off the bus at the next stop—even though it wasn't his.

During the long walk home, he decided to retire the Intruder for a while. He'd become too famous to use it.

But then something happened, something he had no control over.

People started getting attacked while using their phones in public. It started out with texters and callers being doused with water, sodas or Slurpees—and in one noteworthy case, hot coffee. When the coffee-pitcher was arrested, he claimed, "The cell phone scum had it coming!" The victim, who suffered second degree burns, had merely been standing at a bus stop, texting a friend.

Incidents of people on phones being attacked went on the rise in several cities across the country. They were punched, pushed, and in some cases, even stabbed or shot.

When Ed read about the first fatality, he was sick with guilt. He knew it wasn't really his responsibility, but he'd started the trend. Some people even referred to the attacks on Smartphone users as "ripping an Ed."

It only got worse during the summer. Drive-by shootings were reported, with phone users as the targets. Road rage against texting drivers turned even more lethal with the phone users getting shot at or run off the roads and highways.

Everyone seemed to blame the elusive, mysterious "Ed" for all the carnage. *The Seattle Times* reported that the police manhunt for him had intensified.

But no one was getting shocked anymore. They were getting killed.

Ed wanted to write another letter to the newspaper saying he'd stopped zapping phone-abusers months ago, and he disavowed all the violence. But he decided he was better off maintaining a low profile.

Meanwhile, it got so nobody felt safe using their phone in public anymore. Phone booths started popping up again in various cities, but now the glass was bulletproof.

By October, the violent aggression against phone users was on the wane. On the streets, in the stores, and on public transportation, people still weren't using their phones. Instead, they talked to each other, read books or just seemed to notice things around them. Every once in a while, Ed would see someone furtively pulling out their phone in public, and they'd check something. Then, right away, the phone would go back in their pocket or their purse.

Ed still carried the Intruder around, like some people carry a rabbit's foot. He had it with him a week before Halloween when he went downtown to Nordstrom to buy George a pair of sneakers for his birthday. But Ed had had too much coffee that morning, and before browsing Men's Shoes, he ducked into the restroom. There was an open stall, and he grabbed it.

"You're a two…you're a four…you're a six…" he murmured to himself as he stood in front of the toilet. Then he peed right on cue. He flushed the toilet and stepped out of the stall. He was about to wash his hands at the sink when another man stepped into the restroom.

What were the odds?

It was Rude Jason again, still sporting the backward baseball cap look, and once more, on his phone. "Yeah, yeah, I know. Well, he's bluffing…" he said into his phone as he headed to the urinals. He unzipped with his free hand before he even reached his destination.

Agog, Ed stared at him. Despite everything that had transpired in the last ten months, this rude, self-important, phone-obsessed asshole was still a rude, self-important, phone-obsessed asshole.

Ed quickly washed and dried his hands. Then he reached into his pocket. He had to take the Intruder out of retirement just this once. He wasn't even sure if the device still worked, it had been so long since he'd used it.

He stared at Rude Jason's back while the guy continued his phone conversation at the urinal. With a smile, Ed pressed the Intruder button three times in rapid succession.

"Son of a bitch!" Rude Jason wailed. His voice echoed off the bathroom tiles. He dropped his phone in the urinal and staggered back. He was still peeing. The yellow stream shot around the men's room—all over the floor. Ed almost got squirted.

Wincing, the guy crazily shook and waved his hand as if his sleeve was on fire. He finally turned to the urinal to finish peeing and then zipped up. But obviously, he was still frazzled. He kept wringing his hand as he stepped back from the urinal. Then he slipped in a puddle of his own urine.

Agog, Ed watched Rude Jason's legs slip out from under him. He flipped back and landed on the floor. His head hit the tiles with a horrible crack.

His baseball cap askew, he was sprawled on the washroom floor, perfectly still. Beneath his head, a crimson pool began to bloom on the gray tiles.

"Oh, Jesus," Ed murmured. He stuffed the Intruder back into his pocket, and quickly took out his cell phone. "Hang in there, buddy!" he called to the man, who didn't respond at all.

Ed dialed 911. He kept thinking there might be a doctor somewhere in the store. With the phone to his ear, he hurried out of the men's room. He almost ran into a short, pale man with a thin mustache. He wore an army camouflage jacket. The man glared at him.

"Nine-one-one," Ed heard the operator answer. "What's your emergency?"

But Ed didn't reply. He froze in his tracks.

The man in front of him pulled a gun out from inside his camouflage jacket. "Cell phone scum!" he declared, raising the weapon.

The last thing Ed heard was the gunshot.

Then…nothing.

The shooter was an unemployed thirty-seven-year-old named Ronald Jarvis Barr. A security guard at Nordstrom tackled him at the exit as he tried to flee the store. No one else was hurt.

Ed was rushed to Swedish Hospital—along with Turner Pollard, 34, who had been discovered in the men's room. Turner had suffered a mild concussion, took four stitches in his head, and was released later that night.

Ed was lucky in many ways. The bullet that had passed through his gut didn't hit any vital organs. Moreover, the police and paramedics didn't make any connection between him and the notorious "Ed" who had started the anti-phone-abuse trend. Turner's memory was blurry, and he didn't recall getting shocked. His phone had been found in the urinal. The police assumed he'd panicked after dropping the mobile device and slipped on his own pee.

They also must have assumed the Intruder found in Ed's pocket was the remote keyless device for his car.

Ed decided that once they released him and he got home, he'd destroy the Intruder. He never wanted to use it again.

Ed had to stay in the hospital a couple of nights. On his second day there, he was still unsteady on his feet. But he wanted some exercise, so they gave him a walker to get around. He made sure his gown was closed in back as he feebly hobbled down the hospital corridor with some help from the walker. His stomach felt like it was on fire. But the doctor had told him that was normal in his circumstances. Still, Ed stayed slightly hunched over as he navigated the hallway.

Just ahead, he saw a thirty-something woman leaning against the wall, her hip pressed against the handrail. Her back was to him. "Oh, I'll be here again tomorrow—and probably the next couple of days," she said—apparently to no one.

As Ed passed her, he saw she was talking on her Smartphone. He also saw, on the wall directly across from her, a sign with a cell phone inside a circle with a line through it and the words: NO CELL PHONES ALLOWED.

"I think I'm just going home and making an omelet," she was saying into her phone. "Probably Tex-Mex..."

Ed stopped and stared at her until her eyes finally met his. "I hate people," he whispered, smiling.

The woman gazed at him as if he were crazy.
Ed nodded, then turned and slowly shuffled down the hallway.

* * *

ALL ABOARD

HANK PHILLIPPI RYAN

The Orient Express it wasn't. But I knew that when I'd booked my tickets on the sleeper car from my meeting in Chicago back home to Boston. It would be efficient, traveling overnight. A twenty-three hour adventure. A vacation. Sort of. My client was paying the fare, and they'd encouraged me to go for it. "All aboard," my client had said.

The glossy online brochure for the trip on the Lake Shore Limited had looked cozy, if not glamorous, and the idea of a separate compartment, just for me, all private and serene, might even give me a chance to catch up on work without interruption. And, imagine, even get some sleep. And arrive in Boston ready to wrangle some new business.

Now, as I attempted to punch my pillow-ish thing back into some semblance of pillowness, I wondered why no one had told me about the downsides of an overnight train.

The sound of the clackety wheels over the speed rails, I knew I could get used to that, it was train white noise, I figured, and had—sort of—expected it. But my luxury bedroom was not honestly luxurious. It tried, but it was a train. Three stems of stubby alstroemeria were stuck into a tiny glass vase perched, precariously, on a narrow metal shelf next to a cello-wrapped chocolate. A chair like a train seat, nubby tweedy blue upholstery, which didn't recline. My bed, a bunk, took up most of the cubicle. I'd chosen the lower out of the deep and powerful belief that anyone on top would certainly fall off and tumble to the floor. That floor was clammy, with carpet so thin you could feel the metal beneath it, and the shower was tiny, so tiny that I'd just wait until I got home, and the loo was in plain sight. No one was with me, but still, it felt—exposed. And speaking of exposed.

Although the porter had promised that the wide glass windows were one way, so that no matter what I was wearing in my sleeper compartment (or not wearing) no one in stations along the way could look in, I wasn't completely sure I believed that. As I stared at the bottom of the bunk thing above me, all coiled springs and twisted wires, I still feared that when we stopped—at Utica or Schenectady or Elyria—curious passengers on the platform would peer in to observe my insomniac self. Like a caged zoo animal on display.

See Cady Armistead in her traveling habitat, the sign on the outside of the train car might proclaim. "*Will Cady succeed in the cutthroat world of public relations? Or will she get devoured by the bigger animals?*"

Problem was, I thought, as I propped my head up on one elbow and watched the night go by, there was no way to tell how my life would go until the time came. Outside, the world was all in fast forward. It would have been fun to see in the daylight, maybe Ohio cornfields, if they had cornfields, or forests of upstate New York. At one point the dense darkness was slashed by bands of light; streetlights, I supposed. The train slowed, and I glimpsed a tiny town's stoplights all go red, and lighted billboards that flashed by too quickly to read. Kind of like life, I thought, sometimes moments happen, but so quickly they're uncapturable. My life as a public relations specialist—a fixer, as Hadley likes to call me— seemed to be rushing toward something, just like this train. But we can never know if the destinations we hope for will actually be on our life maps.

Or whatever. I just wanted to succeed. I'm good at fixing things, I do know that. Clients made miserable by snoopy and big-mouthed reporters, youthful indiscretions threatening to be headlines, time-bomb emails, college love affairs hanging like water balloons over a politician's head. My job is to fend them off, calm the waters, soothe the savage whatevers, and let my clients succeed. All without anyone realizing I'd had a hand in it.

At least two CEOs and an internationally famed art dealer owe me their reputations, although I could never reveal who. One called me his hired gun. But there are never actual guns involved, of course. Power and money and control and reputation—and the potential loss of them—are equally effective weaponry. Anonymity, too, is a successful tool. My anonymity.

I flinched, startled, as another fast-moving train careened past us, whistle screaming, racing west. Our windows seemed so close. And yet, no way to see who was traveling the other way, speeding toward the unknown.

I'd indulged in a late night last-call glass of drinkable-enough cabernet from the café car, read toward the end of my novel, chomped the last of the Doritos, and felt, actually, proud of myself. Content. Safe. Burrowing down in my pillow now, I thought, well, okay. Time to sleep.

And then I heard the voice.

I sat up in bed, so quickly I almost bumped my head on the bunk above. The voice was as clear as if it had been in the next room, and I guess it was. I was in sleeper car "A" and, calculating, I figured the head of my little bunk was adjacent to the head of a similar bunk in sleeper car "B" next door. It had to be, because I was hearing as definitively as if I'd been using my earbuds to listen to a podcast on my iPhone. We might as well have been in the same room.

"Sweetie, sweetie," the voice—a woman's—was saying. "That's cart before the horse. It was a real failure, right? I mean—three people in Sarasota?"

Horses? Sarasota? I admit I had a moment of trying to figure out what she might be talking about in that imperious voice, but it was now pushing 1:30 in the morning, and my get-some-rest efficiency was not being helped by the interruption. It was possible that my neighbor did not know how beautifully her voice carried. But this would be over soon. No one would be so rude as to continue a long conversation at this time of the night. Morning.

Wrong.

"My point is, there are no options," she was saying now. "He is not a process guy. We need to focus our efforts on hitting goal, and not be distracted with noise."

Not be distracted with noise? That was actually pretty funny. I leaped up, grabbed the pillow from the top bunk, slid myself back under the thin, pale blue blanket, and put the borrowed pillow over my face. Tried to block out the sound. That succeeded in making me unable to breathe. But not unable to hear.

"It's gonna be fun," I heard her say. "I'm telling me as much as I'm telling you. But I'm his right hand person at Rotherwood, so it's *so* not a problem. Clear sailing. We'll keep it clean. She'll be done."

Nice, I thought. *Charming*. And wondered who was on the other end. Whose right hand? Rotherwood, I knew, was a fancy prep school on Beacon Hill, a row of three story brownstones with historically genteel facades. What did they have to "keep clean?" As the CEO, and only O of Cady Armistead Enterprises, I was used to negotiations. Making things right, was how I explained what I did. Spinning my clients' sides of the story. It was funny to think that I succeeded when someone else had a problem, but that's how the world works. Checks and balances, all leading to equilibrium. I have to admit, as I listened, because how could I help it, to one end of the discussion-next-door, it sounded like someone indeed had a problem.

Whoever was about to be "done." Whatever that meant. "Done" didn't sound good, but it was none of my business.

My cell phone glowed on the floor, since I needed it near me, sadly, in case a client had an emergency. *Damn it*. Damn my curiosity. I grabbed up the phone, googled Rotherwood, looked up "contact us." Clicked. Contact at Rotherwood dot edu, so went the address. I clicked on "Our Staff." An array of women and men, diverse and professional in gray lapels and appropriate jewelry. I picked one at random. The email ended with Rotherwood dot edu.

We'll keep it clean, she'd said. Keep what clean?

But again, none of my business, and I would never know. I clicked off my phone, trying to quiet my inquisitive brain. The woman's voice had softened to a murmur, and for a moment I felt a twinge of disappointment. Something was going on in her world, and part of my job—and my passion, I admit—was to be curious. So I kind of wanted to hear the rest. But sleep was more important. I heard the loo flush in her room, had a moment of realization that if I could hear hers, she could hear mine. Then I heard water gushing in her aluminum sink. Mine was aluminum at least.

Mumble mumble, I heard. Time for me to sleep.

Outside the world was impenetrable, a dense July night, and staring, sleepless, out the window into nothingness, I imagined all the invisible dramas underway out there. The overnight hours, the time so many of us spend in suspension, our bodies recharging and our brains at rest. Or busy only in dreams. But there are those who are awake and active during that span of quiet. And some people live in different time zones, I reminded myself, so who even knew who Ms. Chit-chat next door was talking to. Still talking to.

"I'll shoot off an email to Shay," the woman was saying. "She's the one who got the directive. I'll cc you. But you minimize your contact, and then I'll swoop in."

Shay? I thought. Or Shea? Or Shaie? Ms. Shay? Mrs. Shay? Directive? Swoop?

Swoop?

My phone was a tempting rectangular glow on the thin gray carpet. *No*, I ordered myself. *Go to sleep.*

It only took me about four seconds to search Rotherwood for Shay. And Shea. And for good measure, Gray. And Bray. But nothing.

"Sweetie…sweetie, sweetie." The woman was now obviously cajoling someone. I envisioned those cartoons my sister and I used to watch on Saturday mornings, where some animated character would hold a wineglass against the wall to eavesdrop on the animated character next door. Nina and I had tried it, and it didn't work, we couldn't hear a thing, and decided it only worked in cartoons. But what I was hearing was as clear as it had been in Looney Tunes. And maybe just as looney.

"The board has no idea, you know that. He's a lush, a total lush. The wife's a basket case," the woman pronounced. "Ellen has disappointed me from the outset, so we can't rely on her at all. Its two t's right, in Pattillo? But if someone wants to commit career suicide, sweetie, who are we to stand in the way? Ha, ha, I mean."

I clutched my phone to my chest. Even in bed I was still wearing my little navy jersey travel bathrobe, and socks. The socks because the floor was iffy, and the robe in case the porter

91

had been lying about the windows. I thought about the people who'd shared the train with me before we all went off to our separate little compartments. You can't really look at your fellow passengers, even as you stagger down the aisle to the bathroom or the café car and back, balancing your wine or soda against the lurching train. That would be rude. And replaying the faces of my travelling companions only offered me half-memories of newspaper barriers, and earbuds, eyes focused on glowing screens, on a man with his head plastered against the wide glass window, dead asleep. A woman with a—I stared at the bunk above me, as if the video of the train car was replaying. A woman with steely hair, with sunglasses on her head, and earrings. Big earrings. Was she the one plotting something in the room next door?

Since Ms. Chit-chat was in a sleeper car, she'd boarded the train with me in Chicago, at the lofty-arched and elegant Union Station, where the roasty smell of the Nuts on Clark mixed with fragrant coffee and wafts of yeast-pungent beer from happy travelers in the Great Hall. We'd all trooped down the chilly dank platform, pulling our black roller bags and tote bags. A few travelers had been lugging pillows, which I had thought, at the time, was odd. Now I know why they had them. Which passenger was in the room beside mine? Our heads together, Pyramus and Thisbe, without her knowing?

Should I ring for the porter? Ask him to intervene on behalf of sleepy passengers everywhere?

Maybe I should pretend to call someone, speaking really loudly, and then when she hears me, she'll put two and two together, realize I can hear her, and shut up.

Or I could simply tap on her door and warn her. "I can hear everything you say," I'd sheepishly reveal. Or maybe I could just indicate how I could kind of hear, so she wouldn't be embarrassed, but so that she would stop the hell talking. We'd arrive in Boston's South Station at 9:50 am.

She'd probably still be talking.

"My firm intuition, my *firm* intuition, is that come next week, after she walks across that stage, that's the last we'll hear of her."

The last we'll hear of her. And after that line, I counted my blessings that I did not have to deal with someone like this in my own office. I had one assistant, the woefully underpaid Hadley who could find anything on the computer, break any password, track down any elusive source, get a reporter's private cell number or a police detective's home address. Hadley, unfortunately, was on vacation in some paradise with white sand and no internet. And probably good pillows. People said provocative stuff like that, though, without meaning it. *I'm going insane, I'm going to blow this place up, I'm gonna kill you.* Hyperbole. Exaggeration for effect. Everyone on the planet does it.

I heard brittle laughter through our wall. "Bye bye, Shayla Miller, right, sweetie? And then the next steps are ours. And I *know* you are, my dear. I do know. And I cannot wait to hear all about it. Sure, I'll hold on."

If I sat up in bed, put my feet on the ground and twisted my shoulder a bit, I could plant my ear flat up against the wall. I felt the ridged wallpaper, the chill of what the wallpaper covered—metal? drywall?—and heard my new friend continue her conversation. She hadn't—that I'd heard at least—apologized for the late hour, which told me she was the alpha in the convo, or her listener was in a different time zone. Or was just as invested in "getting it done" and "bye bye Shayla" as she was.

With a sigh and a glance heavenward, I gave up. I grabbed my little red notebook from my totebag, and scribbled down what I remembered. Rotherwood. Shayla Miller. Pattillo with 2 T's, she'd said. The board doesn't know. The board of Rotherwood? Doesn't know. Doesn't know—someone is a lush. Well, welcome to the real world.

Too bad this Shayla doesn't have me to help her. *Next week,* I wrote. What this woman was planning would come to fruition next week. But no one can fix everything, I thought, closing my notebook and snapping the red elastic to keep it closed, and the stories of our lives have their own tracks. Separate tracks. I hope Shayla deserved it, whatever 'it' was, because it certainly was coming.

I guess Cruella, as I'd decided to call her, was still on hold, or had paced to the other side of her roomette, because I could no longer hear her. I settled back in, closed my eyes, and tried to imagine Shayla. What had she done, poor innocent thing, to incur the wrath of this viper next door? Was it an *All About Eve* thing, where Cru was worried the gorgeous and duplicitous Shayla was angling to take her place? I pictured Bette Davis, and who was the ingenue? Anne Baxter.

Or was Shayla a big shot? Even nastier than Cru, maybe, demanding and unreasonable, and covering up for her protector, the secret-drinking lush? Maybe Cruella was a good person, good with an unfortunate voice, but simply trying to make her way in the cutthroat world of academia where there were knives out around every corner. Maybe Shayla had it out for her, too.

I was only hearing one side of the story.

Damn it.

I grabbed my phone, googled Shayla Miller Rotherwood. Nothing. Shayla Miller Boston. Nothing. Shae Miller, nope. Shay Miller. About a million women are named Shay Miller. So much for that idea. Shay Pattillo? I rolled my eyes at myself for doing this, an insane example of spiraling curiosity that even if it went somewhere, would never go anywhere. There weren't any helpful listings, anyway. My phone battery was on the verge of being under fifty percent, which makes me terrified, so I unplugged the lamp to make room and plugged it into the wall outlet. You'd think they'd have more plugs in these roomettes.

Somewhere in Pennsylvania, I figured, as the green numbers on the bedside clock radio thing reorganized their little lines into two zero zero. If I had simply flown, like a normal person, I'd be home, long ago, with Dickens snuffling for food and in my comfy slippers and watching the last episode of the new Stephen King. But no, I wanted an adventure, a time to think and plan and be by myself. I'd told people I'd be off the grid, which is absurd, you never really are, but it was meant to be an excuse for why I wasn't answering texts and emails.

The light changed outside, not that it got lighter, but somehow—darker. Wrapping my blue bathrobe more tightly around me, I got up to consult the framed route map displayed on the roomette's wall. Lake Erie? Which might have been fun to see in the daylight.

Which was approaching more and more quickly.

Cruella was talking again. Ooh. Better than Stephen King. I hustled back to my listening spot on the bed, ear to the wall.

"My mother-in-law is dying, thanks for asking," she was saying. "But that's a sidebar. Otherwise, life is good."

"Well lovely," I muttered to myself. "There's an interesting life attitude." But then I thought—*mother-in-law*. She's married. Somehow it had to be that she was the bad guy, and Shayla the target. Well, Shayla was the target, for sure. But did she deserve targeting?

"Dud, dun, duuh," I said out loud, imitating an old-time radio show.

The train lurched, with a yank and a stutter and a grabbing of the brakes on the rails so intense I felt my entire body clench in response. The clackety sound of the wheels stopped, a silence as intense as the noise had been only seconds before. Maybe we'd pulled into a station, my brain reassured me, maybe we were in Erie, like the dot on the map indicated, and maybe I'd be able to see if anyone was looking in. I peered out the window—but there was only darkness.

And then there was noise. Earsplitting, shrieking noise, like the scraping of ten million fingernails on ten million blackboards, the kind of high-pitched piercing whistle that had me clamping my hands over my ears and leaping up so fast I almost hit my head on the bottom of the upper bunk again.

"This is a fire alarm," a weird disembodied robo-voice announced over a scratchy public address system. "Message 524. This is a fire alarm. All passengers must evacuate. All passengers must follow the signs to the closest fire exit."

Kidding me? I thought. I sniffed, without thinking, as the voice continued to bellow instructions, and smelled nothing, and again rued my impetuous decision to take the train. How many false alarms must there be? When we had them in office buildings where I'd worked, first we'd always ignored it, figuring since it was surely a false alarm and the darn thing would stop, we'd think, so we'd amble our way toward the exit, dragging our feet, muttering about how annoying it was to have our work interrupted. I'd always take my laptop and phone, though, and handbag, just in case.

The robo-voice did not stop. I yanked down the heavy metal handle of my compartment door, and used all my strength to slide it open. The corridors were full of disheveled and bathrobed passengers, forced to march single file down the narrow space of the sleeper car hallway. They were all going the same direction, to my right.

"Anyone know anything?" I asked the passing group in general. The alarm interrupted my every word. "Is this a real—?"

"Ma'am?" A tall woman in a navy blue uniform and billed cap motioned me out of my room. "Right now, please, there's a fire alarm. We must exit the train right now. Ma'am?"

She must have seen my reluctant expression, and my motion to go back in to get my stuff.

"No time for that," she yelled over the still-demanding alarm.

I looked both ways as roomette doors slid open and more people filled the corridor. The passengers must have been coming from other cars, too, since there were way more people than the sleepers could have accommodated.

"Okay," I yelled in reply, pretending acquiescence but turning back into my room. I still didn't smell smoke. "But I have to get my—"

"Now, ma'am," the woman ordered, and eased me out the door. As I took two steps down the hall, she vanished, probably to roust any other reluctant occupants.

To my right, an open door. Cruella's door. The roomette was empty. It crossed my mind to go in, like, really fast, look around, see what I could see, and go. Maybe—take her phone? But the pulsing clamor of the passengers behind me propelled me away from answers (and burglary) and down the corridor. Another porter was stationed at the open door of the train, helping bewildered and annoyed passengers clamber down the pull-out metal steps to the gravel below.

"What's the—"

"Please keep moving, ma'am," he said, as he released my elbow. "Please continue walking across the grass and over at least as far as the trees over there."

Lights from the train—emergency lights, I guessed—illuminated the way in front of us, and somehow someone had made a path of blue train blankets across the grass. Good thing. Even though the summer night was mild, starlit, and with only the softest of summer breezes, many of the people I saw had bare feet, or like lucky me, only socks.

I needed my phone. I needed my *phone.* If that train burned up and my phone was on it I would be so mad. Silly, but that's what I thought.

We all padded toward the stand of trees, looming dark and fairytale-like ahead of us. Two little kids, both in white terry bathrobes and slippers that made their feet look enormous, clung to the hands of a woman in what looked like a knee-length sweatshirt. Men in shorts and tank tops, a few in jeans and unbuttoned shirts, stood in clumps, arms crossed in front of them. Everyone stared at the train. We could see the engine, and a few cars, but the rest of the train was hidden in darkness down the tracks.

No smoke, no fire, no anything. I took a deep breath, smelling pine, and the loamy softness of a summer night in the woods. I was grateful for the blankets on the ground, imagining all kinds of mud and bugs and creepy things underfoot. Woods were not my favorite. But, I figured, I'd have a good story to tell, and as long as the train didn't explode or go up in flames, and as long as we got back onto the train, and as long as we got back to Boston, it would just be part of my impetuous adventure.

"Where are we, anyway?" I asked a twenty-something guy wearing sweatpants and a backwards UMass ballcap.

"Lake Erie over there," he said, pointing. "See down there, just past the front of the locomotive? On the same side of the tracks as us, not too far away. And I know we already passed Erie, the city, and Buffalo is next, so, we're like somewhere between there. Middle-a-nowhere."

"Lovely," I said.

"You think there's a fire? Million bucks says no." He cocked his head toward the darkened train. All we could see was the open doors, and inside, bobbing lights—maybe people with flashlights?—moving across the windows.

"Hope you're right," I said. "Looks like there's not much activity. Or any flames."

"Or phone servers," he held up his cell. "My phone's a brick. Looks like everyone else's, too. Can't even tweet."

Many of the passengers, I could see by the emergency lights flicking shadows over their faces, were realizing they were cut off from civilization. Some people wandered farther away, holding their cells high in the air, as if somehow a signal would drop from the wispy clouds streaking the night sky above. Maybe they'd gone down to look at the lake. Chittering sounds came from the woods behind me, squirrels maybe, or birds, or some predatory creatures I'd rather not imagine. Looking at stranded us, and thinking: *dinner*.

"Excuse me."

I'd know that voice anywhere. But Cruella was not talking to me.

"Do you have service?" She gestured her phone toward ballcap guy. It was the woman with the steely hair, now pulled back in a ponytail, her face difficult to describe in the mottled light, but she looked super thin, especially in black yoga pants, a black tank top and flipflops. *Ninja bitch*, the unworthy thought went through my mind. Not exactly Bette Davis-looking, but who knows what the modern Bette would wear? She didn't acknowledge phoneless me. Clearly I knew nothing and could not help her.

"No bars," the guy said. "You?"

"This is unacceptable," she said. As if the universe cared what she thought or wanted. "I'm going to—" She paused, conjuring. "Ask for my money back."

Conversation starter. "Yes," I said, and then added, to show how much I admired her, "That's brilliant."

She eyed me up then down, assessing, dismissing, then defeated. "All my belongings are inside. Can you imagine? Our doors are open? What if there's a...a...someone. Who robs us? Maybe this is a planned robbery, there's no real fire, and it's all a set-up to get us out here, in the middle of hellish nowhere, and distract us, and all the while, inside, they're going through everything that..."

Good story, I had to admit. "I'm sure it's fine," I said. "You have a vivid imagination. But it seems a bit—elaborate, doesn't it?"

"How would they get away?" Ballcap had been listening to this with some interest. Then shook his head, deciding. "Nope. Probably some jerk smoking dope in the bathroom. Probably dumped his doobie in the trash, forgot to put it all the way out. Smoke alarm goes off, everyone goes nuts."

"Probably," I said. Wondering if Ballcap was "some guy." His eyes were red, and he did smell kind of like pot. But maybe there was a skunk back in the woods. And none of my business, anyway. "At least it's not raining or snowing. Right? And we'll be all aboard and underway soon."

"I'm gonna check out the woods," the guy said. And he ambled off into the trees.

"Are you from Boston?" I asked Cruella, just making polite conversation in the middle of the night on the edge of a forest in wherever Pennsylvania. "Or going there to visit?"

"I work there," she said.

"I do, too," I said. "I'm an actuary." I'd just read a thriller where someone said that was the profession you should choose if you didn't want to talk about what you did. No one thinks an actuary is interesting. "How about you?"

"I'm a school administrator," she told me. She addressed the train instead of me, but that was fine.

"Oh, such a small world," I said, so chatty. "My little daughter, Tassie, she's quite the student, and a piano prodigy, and well, we're just ready to look into schools. Walter and I are thinking private. And there are so many *fabulous* ones in Boston. Her trust fund of course will pay for all of it, so we're—"

"Clarissa Madison," she said. She had turned, and was now looking at me in a different way.

"Oh, is that the name of a school?" I pretended to misunderstand.

"No dear, that's my name," she said. "And you are?"

"Looking for a private school." I pretended to misunderstand again.

"Ladies and gentlemen!" A man's voice interrupted my

playacting. A stocky guy in a blue uniform—how many of those were on this train?—clapped his hands out in front of him, trying to get the passengers' attention. By this time, some had scattered off the blankets, probably the ones with shoes, and strayed farther into the woods or drifted along the length of the train, curious or frightened or bored. Or looking for phone signals.

The alarm from the train had stopped. *Good.*

I gestured toward the porter. "This sounds promising," I said.

"Better be," Cru—I guess, Clarissa, said.

I chortled to myself. I'd been close on the name.

Those of us who responded to him moved closer, a huddled group of displaced bleary-eyed passengers in various rumpled stages of haphazard clothing and bedhead hair. People mostly keep to themselves on trains, knowing if you strike up a conversation with the wrong person, they'll talk your ear off from here to Peoria. And too much physical scrutiny is rude, and likely to get you an accusatory look in return. But here we all were, this random pod of passengers or, what Kurt Vonnegut might have called a granfalloon—a group of people connected by a thing that doesn't really matter. We'd all go home, sooner or later, and this would be a hazy memory, an adventure in some of the retellings, fraught and dangerous. In others, an amusing entr'acte, an unexpected but insignificant detour.

"Ladies and gentlemen!" the porter called out again. We looked at him, I at least was, trying to make sense of this all, suddenly in the woods, strangers on a train, immersed in this shared experience. Blah, blah, the porter said, please be patient, we're checking, making sure, all fine.

Bottom line, fifteen minutes.

The crowd dispersed like Brownian molecules, aimless and adrift. Not me. I stuck by Cruella. I'd considered a plan, actually thought it through, that I would casually suggest we take a walk to see the lake. Why not on a summer night, we'd never get to see it otherwise. We'd talk about my (imaginary) Tassie and her trust fund and then I'd get her to spill about the turmoil at Rotherwood, and then I'd get some nugget of usable info and call Shayla when I got back to Boston. Maybe even anonymously.

I was just tired enough, I thought, as we stood there, silent in the throng, to imagine I could also lure her to the lake, knock her out, push her in the water, like, forever, and then pretend I'd never seen her. Would they even do a head count before the train pulled away? And even if they did, how could it be my fault? Poor Clarissa, must have lost her way in the dark.

And Shayla would be saved by the vagaries of mortality.

That plan did have a few complications, morality for one. And the law. And the unlikelihood of murder being the most reasonable solution to save a person I didn't even know.

"You know, Clarissa," I finally said. "I'm not really an actuary."

"Oh?" She seemed infinitely uninterested in that. Apparently not being an actuary is just as boring as being one.

"Yeah," I said. "I'm actually, well, what my staff calls a fixer."

"I see," she said, which from her tone I was obviously supposed to translate to *I don't care.* Then she did. "Why did you tell me about—do you really have a daughter?"

I took another deep breath, spooled it out. "I'm so embarrassed. No. That was a lie."

I went on, not looking at her, but we were both observing the random walks of the passengers, who now reminded me of those zombie movies, faceless pale creatures in tattered clothing, lurching through the forest on the determined hunt for brains. Or in this case, trains.

"I'm actually a public relations person, someone who can help harried executives when they have a particularly thorny issue in their office, something they'd like to get accomplished without letting the public know they had a hand in it. All very confidential, of course, but sometimes, things being how they are, there needs to be a fine hand making sure things go as they…should."

Oh, so now she was interested. Tentatively, carefully, interested, just a quarter turn toward me.

"I see," she said.

The lights on the train all came back on with a flare and a loud hum of power. The crowd cheered, inspired to delight by the promise of bathrooms and light and shoes, and maybe a massive glass of wine. Of cell service, and internet, and normalcy.

And the light dimmed again, and the crowd sighed, as one, and stood staring at the train, as if their collective longing would power it up again.

I pursed my lips, seeming to make a momentous decision, even though it was almost too dark to see each other clearly. "So, Clarissa, I'm embarrassed to tell you this. But—here we are, and it doesn't seem fair if I keep this a secret." I added some optimistic enthusiasm to my voice. "And maybe this is all for the best. If not for this apparently false alarm, we'd probably never have met."

"You've lost me," she said. She looked at the screen of her phone, still an opaque black rectangle, then stashed it into the waistband of her yoga pants.

"Clarissa? Full disclosure. My roomette is next to yours, and apparently you were on the phone this evening. Tonight? Before the alarm?"

Oh, yeah. Now I had her full attention.

"And?"

"And I heard every word."

"You listened to—"

"It was impossible not to, I'm afraid. The walls must be—well, who knows, but yes. 'The board doesn't know'? And 'he's a lush,' and well." I shrugged. "'Shayla.'"

It would have been funny, really, if it hadn't been the middle of the night in the woods outside of wherever Pennsylvania, with a massive broken train in front of us and a scatter of zombies loitering around us. I guess it was still funny.

Her chin came up, and even in the gloom I could see her wheels turning.

"I can help you," I said. "As a professional, I can tell you it's silly, and even—and this is just between us, trust me—misguided for you to take matters into your own hands. Whatever the matters are. Why get your hands dirty? Tell me the situation. I'll make it all work. And you, with a clear conscience, can go on with your life. Without Shayla in the way."

Her eyes got wide, then narrow. Strange to watch her think, in the random half-light of the emergency lighting and the occasional bloom of moonlight from behind the drifting clouds.

"Do I sound melodramatic? I apologize," I said. "It's not like you're planning, you know," I paused. "To actually harm her. Physically."

"Of course not," she said.

"Okay, then. You'd simply like her to do whatever she does, shall we say, somewhere else. Just guessing here. She's good at it, maybe too good?"

Clarissa nodded.

"And— to give you deniability, don't say anything—it doesn't appear that whoever is protecting her—the lush? Has any inclination to change the situation himself."

She nodded again.

I shifted on the blanket. My socks were damp from standing in the same place. I chose a drier spot. "So here's the thing. I could tell from the call—"

"I still can't believe you heard all that."

"Oh, I'm certain not *all* of it," I reassured her. "But I assume you're a busy woman, who only has the best of intentions, maybe…" I paused. "Fundraising for the school? Perhaps higher salaries for administrators like you, more perks, more recognition, a bit more prominence, some changes in the—"

"Yes." She cut me off. "Exactly."

"And this Shayla…wants your job? And you're thinking there might be a way to—embarrass? Or—"

"Can we not go into that?" She shook her head, as if shaking off cobwebs of temptation. "You eavesdropped, that's unacceptable. Shall we just pretend this never happened?"

"Of course." I agreed instantly. That's how you reel in a fish, let them think they're off the hook. I laughed. "My entire business model is 'this never happened.'"

She nodded. Looked down at the soggy blanket. The hum of the crowd surrounded us, and from time to time a clanging of train doors, or a random night bird. I waited. Public relations, I'd reminded myself, was all about helping whoever needed help. Not about sentimentality or Lifetime movies or damsels in distress. My clients were not always paragons of moral virtue, but they always needed me. Sometimes I had to allow them to realize that.

"It's like three in the morning," I said, looking at my Fitbit. "Wow."

"Her name is Shayla Miller," Clarissa said. "But you know that."

I nodded.

"Her phone number is—" She pulled out her phone, saw it was still a brick, put it back. She told me a number. "Can you remember that? And her email is at Rotherwood dot edu. You won't find her on the website. She's just moved to Boston."

"Got it," I said. And I did.

"I don't want to know," Clarissa said. "What'll happen and when."

"Goes without saying."

"You're not going to hurt her? I mean—physically? I want to be clear about—you're not going to k—"

"Please." I put up both palms, stopping her. "This isn't the movies. This is business. Civilized business."

"And—if it's not indelicate…" She glanced around. We were as alone as we could be.

"How will I pay you?"

I shrugged, as if it wasn't about the money. Which, I realized, it wasn't. It was about the balance of power. "Invite me to some event at Rotherwood, we'll talk. After it's over. And let me reassure you again, this is absolutely confidential. I will never ever say we'd worked together. Never. I'll never say I've talked to you, or know you. No matter what the circumstances."

"But what if—"

I gestured to our surroundings. "There's no what-if. There's no one who can put us together, not it any way. Maybe the pothead kid with the hat," I dismissed him with a flip of my hand. "Otherwise, you and I never met."

She laced her fingers together, put them under her chin. "I'm so—relieved. We were going to—"

I smiled, approving, letting her know we were comrades. And that she should continue.

"We were going to send emails from her computer," she went on. "With certain pretty compromising pictures we were having made, and then it would all get out, and she'd have to resign, and then we'd be back on track. The headmaster, well, he does drink a bit. But that makes our lives so much easier."

I frowned, emphatically so she could see, even in the gloom, how serious I was. "Can of *worms*," I said. "IP addresses, email chains, metadata, back and forths, the forensics people can find absolutely anything anywhere. You cannot send emails, Clarissa, it's like putting a spotlight on yourself. No, seriously, you leave Shayla alone. Pull way back. Let go. You were—and forgive me— saying something about walking across the stage?"

"Awards ceremony," Clarissa said. "She getting some national honor for—"

"Let her accept it," I said. "You join in the celebration. Encourage her, befriend her. Applaud her. The key is, you can't know when I'm going to do what I'm going to do. You have to be genuinely surprised. In a way, you know, your idea is perfect, subtle but devastating. But it has to be done the right way. I know how to hide the tracks, and no one will ever know, and think of how much easier your life will be."

"No violence." She held up a finger.

"Never," I said. "There are other ways to end people's lives; professional lives, at least. After we're back on board? Have a glass of wine, go to sleep, forget about this. It never happened."

A piercing whistle cut through the night, so surprising I clutched at my bathrobe. Clarissa, startled, grabbed my arm. All the lights in the train flared into brightness, and a rumble sounded from the massive locomotive on the tracks across the blanketed grass.

A blue-uniformed conductor climbed the three metal steps to the now-open doorway where many of us had disembarked more than an hour ago. "Ladies and gentlemen?" He called out again, and once again we all surged forward to hear him.

"Ladies and gentlemen, we are so sorry, this was a false alarm. We have gone through our checklist, and checked again, and our fire crew has discovered there was apparently someone smoking in the café car restroom, and they failed to extinguish their smoking materials before they were placed in the trash bin. Once again, ladies and gentlemen, smoking on the train is prohibited by law."

The crowd grumbled, a murmur of disapproval for this flouting of the social contract.

"Idiot," Clarissa whispered.

"But we certainly appreciate your patience," the conductor went on from above us, "and your cooperation, so we'll be offering each passenger a voucher for future travel on the Lake Shore Limited, or any trains in our system. And now, with your continued cooperation, we'll be underway as soon as the engineer signals."

As we clambered back aboard, I let Clarissa go first, leaving at least ten people buffering between us, making sure no one ever connected us, or could put us in the same place. Sure, if someone really delved into it, for some reason, they might find we'd been on the same train, but who would get that far?

Her door was already closed by the time I got to my roomette. Without even closing mine, I scurried to the listening spot. She was already on the phone.

"You won't believe what happened, sweetie," she said. "But I've been thinking. Let's let it go. We're bigger than this, are we not? We'll rise above it, and simply put our conversations down to a few too many glasses of wine. I'm out, sweetie. Let's let Shayla be. And let the chips fall where they may."

I got out my own phone, draped my earbuds around my neck, all of a sudden not feeling one bit tired. Now that we were back on the train's wi-fi, I had three internet bars, but I wasn't naïve enough to google Clarissa's name. Or her headshots. Which I would ask Hadley, in due time, to attach to various kinky clothing-free bodies, thereby creating certain gasp-worthy photos that might not make our Clarissa too happy. I mean, it wasn't my idea. But if it was good enough for Clarissa to do to Shayla, it was good enough for me to do to Clarissa.

But no one would know where the compromising photos came from. As I'd said, I knew what I was doing.

And maybe, if Clarissa Madison kept her part of the leave-Shayla-alone bargain, I wouldn't have to do anything at all.

I put in one earbud, ready to block out the noises the rest of the night had in store for me. It was time to sleep, peacefully sleep, knowing that starting tomorrow morning, when the Lake Shore Limited arrived in Boston, Shayla Miller's life would be different. And she'd never know why, never know she had me as her own personal public relations fixer. All of us women, starting in our careers, need all the help we can get.

I slid under the covers again, thinking about power and justice and sisterhood.

The whistle sounded, piercing the night, doors slammed, and a grumbling under my feet announced our journey was once again about to be underway.

"All aboard!" The conductor called.

* * *

GONE FOREVER

A *Lassiter/Martinez* Short Story

JOSEPH BADAL

The images of the dead…the carnage, flashed like dry lightning before Detective Barbara Lassiter's eyes. She blinked and shook her head, as though to clear her mind. *Hell of a thing*, she thought, *a homicide detective who has a problem holding it together at the sight of dead bodies.*

"You okay?" her partner Susan Martinez asked.

"Yeah."

"You want me to take the priest?" Susan said, as Barbara watched Father Michael Doherty through the open door of his office at the back of the church in Albuquerque's Near Northeast Heights. The man's haggard appearance had only worsened as the hours went by. Between consoling parishioners and fielding questions from detectives, Doherty seemed to have aged ten years in a few hours. Now, at 1:00 a.m., he looked as though he might collapse.

"No, I got it. We'll play it like we discussed. You go to Lucas Brennan's place. We still have someone at his apartment?"

"There's a deputy outside the place. Are you afraid he might 'rabbit' on us?"

Barbara remembered their initial interview with Brennan here at the church. The young man had a deer-in-the-headlights look. His eyes wide with shock. She'd thought that if he hadn't been so distressed, he would have been uncommonly good-looking. But his blue eyes and sensual mouth seemed to have been distorted with grief and trauma.

"No," Barbara said. "I'm more worried about his mental state. He was as distraught as any person I've ever seen when we questioned him earlier. I was afraid he was going to lose it. I didn't have the heart to make him hang around here while we processed the scene."

Susan said, "I called a grief counsellor and asked her to go to his place. I'll get over there as soon as I can."

Barbara took a deep breath, let it out slowly, and entered the priest's office. He half-rose from his chair as she offered him her hand. He took it with a brief, limp, damp grip, then dropped back into his desk chair.

"I need to go to the hospital to visit those who were injured." He swallowed hard. "And the families of those who were murdered." His voice was high-pitched, with a barely noticeable lilt of Ireland. "My...parishioners need me."

Barbara, at five feet nine inches tall, towered over the diminutive priest, who looked to be about sixty years old. His skin was pink but creased. His black shirt was wrinkled, and his white collar appeared to be at least two sizes too big. Earlier, she'd noticed dark spots on his shoes, which she knew was blood. She wondered if he was aware of it as she tried to make eye contact with him, but his eyes ping-ponged everywhere except at her.

"Are you up to answering more questions?"

He finally looked at her and nodded.

After placing her cell phone on the front edge of the man's desk, she told him she planned to record their conversation, which he agreed to. Then she recited the time, his and her names, and their location. She said, "I apologize for keeping you here at such a late hour, but it's important that we get a clear and complete picture of what happened. You being at the front of the sanctuary gave you the best view of...events."

Barbara waited for Doherty to respond. He'd dropped his gaze to the desktop between them and covered his face with his hands. He made a sound that was both groan and whimper. She prompted him again. "Can you tell me when you first noticed the man with the machete?"

He dropped his hands to his lap and raised his head. His eyes seemed to have homed in on a spot just below her chin. "Dear God, it was horrific." The lilt of Ireland had transformed into a full-blown brogue.

Barbara gave him a sympathetic smile. "I'm sure, Father. But the more detail you can remember, the better able we will be to proceed with our investigation."

"What's there to investigate, Detective? A madman came into my church with a weapon and slaughtered seven of my parishioners." He muttered something unintelligible and then added, "Another ten are in the hospital." A keening noise that sounded as though it came from his soul startled Barbara.

"Are you okay, Father?" she asked.

He waved away her concern. "Think of the children. They'll never forget what they saw."

Barbara took a moment to slow her breathing, to control her growing feeling of frustration with the priest, who didn't seem to want to focus on her question. "Just tell me what you remember, Father. Can you do that?"

Doherty expelled an exasperated sigh, closed his eyes for a moment, then looked her straight in the eyes. "I was close to completing the service when I saw a man stand in a row near the back of the sanctuary. He shouted in what sounded like a foreign language—maybe Arabic—raised a machete, swung at the people in the row in front of him, then stepped into the center aisle. He marched up the aisle and..."

After a long beat, Barbara said, "Please go on, Father."

"It was demonic, Detective. He moved so slowly, so methodically. Chopping to his left, then moving to the pews on his right. Then left again. Back and forth." He swallowed, then cleared his throat. "I was paralyzed. I didn't know what to do."

Barbara saw a glint of shame in the man's glistening eyes. He quickly wiped away a tear with his hand. She waited.

"I saw the man advancing." After another pause, Doherty added, "There was...joy, yes, that's what it was. Joy showing on his face. He smiled as though he was ecstatic as he came toward me. I remember dropping the aspergillum and—"

"Aspergillum?" Barbara asked.

"The instrument to sprinkle Holy Water. It has a long wood handle with a silver ball at the end."

"Thank you. Please continue."

"It took only seconds for the man to reach the front of the sanctuary. People were screaming and scattering in all directions." He visibly shuddered. "There was blood everywhere. I saw Peter

Brennan step into the aisle as the killer moved toward his daughter."

"The young woman in the white gown? Lois Brennan?"

"Yes." Doherty's voice broke as he said, "She took her vows last evening. That's why we were all there. Lois Brennan had just become a nun."

Barbara hesitated a few seconds to allow Doherty to collect himself. Then she said, "Do you remember what happened then?"

"The man swung the machete at Mr. Brennan. It was awful. I can remember the sound the weapon made when it hit his chest. I never heard anything like it before. Mr. Brennan cried out and dropped to the floor." Tears now fell from the priest's eyes, over his sallow cheeks, and onto his hands still resting in his lap. He ignored them.

Doherty took a shuddering breath. "Lois Brennan was kneeling in front of the altar. Her eyes were closed, and her lips moved in prayer. It shocked me. Here was this mayhem going on behind her and she never moved." After a second, he said, "She was one of the most devout women I have ever known. She would have become a wonderful nun." Another pause. "She's with our Lord Jesus now." The priest's eyes widened when he added, "The killer stood behind Lois, shouted something, and struck her again and again and again."

Doherty's eyes seemed to go out of focus for a couple seconds.

"It was as though he had come to the church primarily to attack *her*." Then he repeated the keening noise, which went on for several seconds. His face seemed to have sagged even more as he reached behind him and took a water bottle off a credenza. He unscrewed the cap and took a long drink. After he put down the bottle on his desk, he took a handkerchief from a pants pocket and wiped perspiration from his forehead. After a long beat, he said, "Where was I?"

Barbara could now smell the odor of sour perspiration coming from the priest. His sparse, white hair was plastered to his scalp. "You said you thought the killer might have targeted Lois Brennan. Why do you think that?"

"He moved quickly through the sanctuary, swinging wildly, haphazardly at people, striking each of his targets with one blow.

But he spent time over Lois. One strike didn't satisfy him. As I said before, he struck her repeatedly. She was covered in blood. Oh, my Lord. Her white gown was…." He let the thought hang in the air, incomplete. When he gathered himself, he added, "It was as though Lois symbolized everything he hated." His tears began again.

"Do you need a moment, Father?" Barbara asked.

Doherty shook his head and blew out a loud breath.

"What happened after that?"

"There were children in the first pew. The killer turned right toward them. That's when Lois's brother, Lucas, ran into the aisle, picked up the aspergillum, and went after the killer. He swung at him and hit the back of the man's head. But the man spun around and stepped toward Lucas, his arm raised high in the air. I thought that he was about to kill Lucas. I'll never forget it. But Lucas hit him again. I heard something crack when the aspergillum hit the man's face and he fell to the floor. Then Lucas hit him over, and over, and over again. He seemed possessed. He didn't stop until I went over to him and grabbed his arm."

"You know the Brennan family well?"

"Oh, yes. Quite well. They've been members of my parish for decades." He tried to say something else, but nothing came out.

Barbara had half-a-mind to terminate the interview, but she knew that the best time to get information from a witness was as soon as possible after a crime had been committed. She also wanted to query the priest more about his comment that the killer seemed to have specifically targeted Lois Brennan. She didn't want to leave the church without some idea about the motive for the slaughter.

"What can you tell me about them?"

It took Doherty a minute to collect himself. For a few seconds more, he seemed to reflect on Barbara's question, and then finally said, "That poor family has been through a lot. This might take a few minutes."

"That's okay," she said.

"I met Peter and Mary Brennan when they first moved to my parish. They were a handsome couple, anticipating their first child. Completely committed to the church. I christened all three of their children. Lucas, Edward, and Lois. They attended mass regularly."

The priest smiled and said, "The first time I had a conversation with Lucas was when he was about seven or eight. He was attending catechism class and seemed disturbed about something one day. When I asked him what was wrong, he told me he had seen a story on television about a man who killed several people. The story had shocked him and left him feeling out of sorts. He couldn't assimilate the concept of how one person could kill another.

" 'Why would someone do that, Father?' he asked me. I told him there were bad people in the world and that I hated for children to hear about such things.

" 'But why would someone do that?' he asked me again.

"I remember what I said as though it were yesterday." Doherty looked away, seemingly recalling the conversation. "I told him some people kill because they have been corrupted by Satan. They don't think the way we do. They're pure evil.

" 'Like crazy people?' he asked.

"Yes, like crazy people, I said."

Doherty again wiped his forehead. "I told him people sometimes kill because of bad things in their lives and they can't see any other way to react. But he didn't understand. Then I told him that people sometimes kill to protect their families.

" 'Do you think my father would kill someone if they attacked my brother or sister?' he said.

"If that was his only choice, I suspect he would. I think your father would do whatever it takes to protect you, your brother and sister, and your mother.

"He then asked me if I could kill someone. I told him I could never take someone's life."

A sad expression came over Doherty's face. "I'll never forget what he then told me: 'I could never do such a horrible thing.' I patted him on the shoulder and said I hoped he would never be faced with a situation that would cause him to even consider committing murder." Doherty's voice suddenly became husky. "All that changed here just a few hours ago."

"You said the Brennans have been through a lot. What were you referring to?"

"Until Lucas's fourteenth year, his life could have been described as one based on faith and love and on the belief that good always triumphed over evil. In a sense, he had lived a charmed life. Raised by loving parents and taught to have faith in his family, his God, and his fellow man. But then events seemed to conspire to undermine his love for those institutions or his faith in their integrity, their steadfastness, their everlasting goodness. But, still, Lucas's beliefs prevailed. He had been taught well. He was an unshakeable true believer."

Barbara shifted in her chair. She was about to interrupt the priest because she couldn't see where his tale was heading and how it would help her investigation. But she decided to remain silent for the moment.

"Even after his mother, Mary, died of cancer when Lucas was fifteen, after she suffered interminably for six months, and his father subsequently devolved into an emotional basket case, seeking solace in alcohol, Lucas's beliefs sustained him. He didn't complain about taking on an after-school and weekend job as a busboy at a local restaurant. He didn't blame God for the loss of his mother or for the precipitous emotional deconstruction of the father he had admired and looked up to. As the eldest of three children, he accepted responsibility for their well-being."

"Sounds like a good kid," Barbara said.

"The best," Doherty answered. He chuckled in sort of a deprecating way and said, "I considered talking to his father about Lucas going into seminary to become a priest, but I put it off because the family needed him so badly." Doherty sighed, then continued: "After a two-year period of alcohol-induced self-abasement, which brought the Brennans to the edge of financial ruin, Lucas's father rallied. He found a construction job with a friend's company. But the work seemed to be the only form of expression for Peter's energies and emotions. After exhausting days on the job, the old man had nothing left to give to his children.

"But Lucas remained committed to his values regarding family, God, and mankind. There was a strength in the young man that anyone who knew him found extraordinary. Neighbors, schoolmates, teachers, and co-workers admired him. That boy had more character than ten grown men.

"The Albuquerque neighborhood where the Brennans lived is cheek-to-jowl with the area called the *War Zone*. Near the State Fair Grounds. It isn't the safest part of the city."

Barbara said, "I know. My partner and I spend more time in that part of the city than we like. There's a tenuous peace that hovers over that neighborhood, like a storm cloud that perpetually threatens to unleash a downpour. Usually, the threat acts only as a tension creator. All residents are wary; many are frightened. Crime is intermittent and unpredictable. Generally, different ethnic groups barely get along. They seem to have little tolerance for one another."

Doherty nodded. "In contrast, tolerance is a key to the Brennan family ethic. Racial, ethnic, and religious slurs, as far as I know, are non-existent in their home. Lucas was raised to believe that others would treat him as he treated them. So, when a group of teenagers who were affiliated with a California-exported gang set upon him one night after he'd finished a late shift at the restaurant and stepped off a bus, he didn't change his mind, as many would have, about an ethnic group because of the behavior of a few. Sure, he was surprised and terribly distressed by what had happened to him, and it took weeks for his body to heal, but he went on about his life. He didn't lose faith. His beliefs were rock-solid."

The kid sounds like a saint, Barbara thought. "Did he go to college?" she asked.

The priest slowly wagged his head. "Lucas badly wanted to attend college. He graduated near the top of his high school class and received several scholarship offers. But, in his mind, he couldn't justify accepting any of those because he had obligations to his brother and sister. He took a job with the same construction company his father worked for. Eddie, the second of the Brennan children, was one year younger than Lucas and immediately after high school graduation enlisted in the Army. One year later, Lois entered a convent."

"That must have relieved some of their financial stress,"

Barbara said.

Doherty shrugged. "Of course. But it wasn't that the Brennan household was now absent stress. Eddie had been shipped off to Afghanistan and had told Lucas that the situation there was worse than he had imagined. The brothers exchanged emails quite frequently. Apparently, Eddie shared graphic stories with Lucas. I had several conversations with Lucas about his concerns for his brother. He experienced terrible tension headaches because of his worry about Eddie being over there. He confided in me that he prayed every day that God would protect his brother and would influence the leaders in Washington to bring the troops home. His confidence that his fellow man would do the right thing continued unabated.

"Nearly two years had passed with Lucas and his father working together. They'd pooled their earnings and built up a savings account that, along with a new mortgage, finally made it feasible for them to make significant repairs to their home."

"Sounds like things were going well for them," Barbara said.

"Yeah, until the economy weakened. The construction company Peter and Lucas worked for initially laid off employees as things slowed down. Finally, it closed its doors. Peter and Lucas couldn't make enough money doing part-time jobs to stay current on the mortgage. When they became six months delinquent, the lender foreclosed on the property. They lost their home about a month ago."

Doherty stopped at that point and just stared at Barbara.

"Is there anything else you would like to tell me?" she asked.

Doherty fluttered his hands and barely shook his head.

And the kid has now lost his father and sister, Barbara thought. She thanked Father Doherty for his time and let him escort her out to the sanctuary. Although the bodies had long since been removed, there was plenty of evidence that a ghastly event had occurred there. *Stains in the carpet*, the coppery odor of blood, the stench of other body fluids, the floor and pews littered with parishioners' personal effects. The room was cold because someone had left the front doors of the church open—maybe to vent some of the smells. Barbara looked out through the open doors and saw snow flurries falling, blown around in an anarchical pattern by gusts of wind.

Great, snow in Albuquerque, she thought. *A perfect addition to an already crappy day.*

"When will you be finished with"—Doherty waved his hands around to indicate the large space—"all of this?"

She didn't want to describe the church as a crime scene that needed to be processed. Instead, she said, "I'll do everything in my power to expedite the investigation."

After Father Doherty left her, Barbara went outside to her unmarked vehicle and drove to the Bernalillo County Sheriff's Office headquarters in downtown Albuquerque. In the Detective Squad Room, she called Susan. "You with the Brennan kid?"

"I'm just a couple blocks away. I got hung up on a phone call from the lieutenant. You finished with the priest?"

"Yeah," Barbara said. "He's pretty torn up. You can imagine. He saw it all happen. He had a front row seat through the entire attack. Probably wondering how he escaped injury. Call me when you leave the Brennan apartment. I'll meet you somewhere for an early breakfast."

"I'll be glad to get this over with," Susan said. "That poor kid is probably suffering something awful." Then, as an afterthought, she said, "I hope he can take some satisfaction from taking down the guy with the machete. Lucas Brennan probably saved a lot of lives."

Lucas had been trying to mentally and emotionally process the events of the past few hours. Like a terrible dream, everything that had happened seemed surreal. He checked his cell phone and noted the time: 2:00 a.m. He walked around the rundown second floor apartment he and his father had shared for the past month. The brown stains on the ceiling from roof leaks, the threadbare soiled carpet, the cracked paint on the walls, the dated kitchen appliances, the rust stains in the sinks and the shower sickened him. He moved to the front window and parted the curtains. The deputy who had driven him home was still posted outside in his cruiser. A detective had, at first, wanted him to go to the sheriff's department to be questioned, but she'd changed her mind when he'd asked to be allowed to go home. She'd agreed if a deputy accompanied him.

He was aware of shouting coming from the apartment next door—a regular occurrence at all hours of the night—but ignored it the way one ignores—even becomes inured to—the hum of an air conditioner or the vibrations from and sounds of passing traffic. But exhaustion had set in and he finally collapsed on the saggy couch they'd salvaged from a thrift shop. He barely remembered a call that had come in from one of the female detectives a few minutes earlier. She'd told him she would be by in a little while. *What more can I tell her than I already did at the church?* he wondered. He looked around the living room and felt a crushing sadness.

"What did faith in God and in your fellow man get you, Dad?" he whispered. "It's just Eddie and me now." A sudden and brief sob broke from his throat. Then his cell phone rang, startling him. He was about to ignore it but sneaked a peek at the screen and saw that the caller was someone named Stanley Wisniewski. At first, the name didn't resonate. But then he remembered that Eddie had mentioned Wisniewski. How the two had met in Afghanistan and become fast friends.

He answered the call. "This is Lucas Brennan."

"Lucas, it's Stan Wisniewski. I'm a friend of your brother, Eddie. I'm call—"

Wisniewski's voice cracked. Then he choked out a sob.

Lucas's breath caught in his chest; he couldn't seem to breathe. He finally expelled the air in his lungs. "Stan, what's happened?"

Wisniewski coughed, paused a couple seconds, then said in a heavy, raspy voice, "Eddie and I have been best friends since we shipped over here." Another pause, then: "We agreed to notify our families if something happened to either one of us. I'm sorry to have to tell you that…Eddie was shot in a fire fight today."

Lucas felt icy fingers penetrate his skull, cascade through his chest, and down into his gut. His whole body was suddenly cramped.

"Is Eddie okay? Is he going to be all right?"

"He didn't make it, Lucas."

Wisniewski broke down and cried. He sounded inconsolable. His words were incomprehensible. Lucas's eyes welled with tears, which rolled down his cheeks. His throat felt tight and dry. He didn't have the strength to move.

"The Army will officially notify you about what happened," Wisniewski continued in a hoarse voice that was now little more than a whisper. "I'm sorry to be the one to have to bring you this news. I know what your family meant to him. How close you and Eddie were." He stopped for several seconds this time, then said, "I'm so sorry, Lucas. I'm going to miss Eddie so much."

Lucas felt as though his insides had been invaded by creatures trying to bore their way out. His hands shook and he had to squeeze the cell phone to keep from dropping it. He tried to thank Wisniewski for calling but couldn't get the words out. He mumbled something but wasn't certain what. He felt as though he was going to scream, but suddenly focused on how he would tell Lois and his father about Eddie. Then he shook his head. Momentarily, he'd put aside what had happened to them. But then the realization of his father's and sister's deaths struck him like a lightning bolt. There was no one left with whom he could share his losses. His family was gone. God and man had abandoned him. Tears continued to cloud his vision as he stood and flung his phone against the wall.

A banshee-like wail reverberated off the walls and ceiling of the apartment. The sound made Lucas feel as though he'd been transported to an unearthly place. It wasn't until he'd grasped that the noise had come from him that his sorrow turned to an all-encompassing anger, and then that anger turned to rage. Everything he had loved and believed in was gone. Gone forever.

And, in that very moment, his mind seemed to come apart and then repair itself. Like pieces of a puzzle that fit together perfectly before and, despite a completely different design, fit together again. He felt transformed. The memory of how he'd attacked the killer in the church flooded his brain. Images of his hand holding the heavy object that the priest had dropped flashed before his eyes. As though watching a slow-motion movie, he saw his arm repeatedly rise and fall as he struck the killer in his face, turning the man's features into a ghastly mess. A warm rush flowed through his body and he suddenly felt at peace.

Then, with single-minded purpose, he decided that evildoers had to pay for the deaths of his father, his sister, and his brother. He made a mental list of those satanic acolytes who brought misery on people. The politicians who supported war; the bankers who took away peoples' homes; the terrorists and mass murderers who killed the innocent.

Yes, the evildoers must be punished, he thought. *And I will be the hand of God who will make them pay.*

* * *

NIGHT SHIFT

LINWOOD BARCLAY

It's 12:35 a.m. and the retired newspaperman, Larry, looks at his watch and says to the guy sitting on the barstool next to him, "I should probably get home. Looks like my buddy's not gonna make it."

The other guy, who introduced himself as Frank when he sat down next to Larry more than an hour ago, says, "Well, it's been a pleasure talking to you. You sure have some good stories. I had a friend, worked for a big paper like yours, he had no end of great stories. And he wasn't even a reporter. He was an editor. But he still had his share of tales."

"Same here. I was an editor most of my time at the paper. Started as a reporter. Most everyone does. But ended up working on the desk. City desk, mostly. Did some time on foreign, too."

"This friend," Frank says, "was so tired half the time. He worked the overnight shift."

"That's the worst."

"But he said some pretty weird stuff could happen in the middle of the night."

"Yeah, well, the real struggle can be staying awake," Larry says. "I worked overnights for a couple of years straight. Don't know how I survived it, but I was a young man, could take the abuse. Coming in at eleven, driving home at six in the morning. Nearly ran off the road a couple of times. But if something happens, that can get the adrenaline flowing. Keeps you awake."

"All the nutcases come out at night, I bet," Frank says.

"No shit. Sometimes they'd wander right into the newsroom. Come into the building, head up the elevator. This was back in the eighties, before everyone started tightening up security. Had a guy come in once, wielding a shock absorber. Swear to God. Started swinging it around like a baseball bat. Cops came in and got him. And the switchboard would shut down at midnight, so anyone who phoned the paper, the call went right to the newsroom, so I'd be at

my desk, editing a story, writing a headline for something that was to go into the morning edition, which closed at one-thirty, and the phone'd ring, and it'd be some guy complaining that his paper was late."

Frank laughs. "Who calls in the middle of the night about a late paper?"

Larry shakes his head. "Exactly."

"What was the weirdest thing that ever happened to you on overnights?"

Larry thinks a moment. "Oh, here's an interesting one." He glances at his watch again. "What the hell. Oh, and keep in mind, this was before caller ID and call display and all that stuff."

"Okay," says Frank.

"Let me get another beer."

And this is the story Larry tells:

* * *

The guy who said he was going to kill as many people as possible the following day called into the newsroom at five minutes past one.

Larry, the overnight city editor, had arrived two hours earlier, relieving Charlene from her duties on the desk. She'd just overseen the production of the metro pages, all the local news, and was in the process of typing up a turnover note that included a list of things that might need to be checked on over the next several hours, or followed up on the next day.

"Mikey's at a late night city council meeting where they might vote on putting in bike lanes on Connor Street," she told Larry. "So he might file a top to his story. But if nothing new happens, you won't hear from him. Oh, and there was a house fire on Wilton. Heard about it on the scanner. Just a one-alarm, doesn't look huge, but sent Guffman in case it's worth a pic. Otherwise, things couldn't be deader. National had the big story tonight. You'll have an easy shift."

"Don't say that," Larry said. "Last time you said that, three minutes after you left they found that kid's body in the attic."

Charlene smiled. "Over to you. Oh, and you've got Jeff in the radio room. Harvey booked off sick so Jeff's doing a double."

"Anybody call Melanie to come in early so Jeff doesn't have to stay until six?"

"Tried. She must have left the phone off the hook. She's no fool."

Charlene took off and Larry got settled into his seat on the city desk. Got signed onto the newsroom computer system, checked for any personal inter-office messages. He'd asked for the second week of August off and wondered if the city editor had gotten back to him. She had not.

About fifteen minutes into the shift, the early copies of the first edition to roll off the presses were delivered to the newsroom by the copy boy. He dumped a stack of them on the city desk, then continued to distribute them to various offices.

Larry unfolded the paper so he could see the entire front page. Most of it was devoted to an event on the other side of the country. A man with a high-powered rifle had gone into a fast-food joint near Monterey and started picking off people one by one. Twenty dead, fifteen injured. A police sniper took out the shooter. The only other story on the front was an update on a local highway expansion. The massacre turned inside to four clear pages of sidebars.

Larry scanned the headlines, looking for glaring typos. Nothing jumped out at him, so he turned inside, had a look at pages two and three. This was followed by a quick sweep through the main section. A fast read of headlines, and a read of Charlene's note, brought him up to speed on everything he was going to need to know. The city council bike path story, the one that might need updating, was on page six.

He got out of his seat and strolled across the newsroom to the glass room-within-a-room that was known as the radio room. It was filled with radio scanners that picked up chatter on all the police and fire channels. If a reporter heard something that sounded like a story, he could head out, or alert the city desk, and they'd despatch someone.

Sitting in the chair tonight was Jeff. If something happened, he'd be the one who was despatched. He was the entire reporting staff on the graveyard shift.

"How's it going?" Larry asked.

Jeff shrugged. He had one ear for Larry, the other on the constant stream of static and chatter coming from the radios. There was always talk going on. What you listened for was a change in tone. Cops or firefighters raising their voices, talking hurriedly. That was when you knew something was up.

"Got stuck doing a double?"

Jeff said, "This is the third time Harvey's done this to me, and it's always on a Sunday night, when I know he's in Boston, where he's got this new girlfriend. He wants a three-day weekend with her, the asshole. So while I'm sittin' here, trying to keep my fucking eyes open, he's gettin' his knob polished."

"Looks quiet, anyway," Larry said.

Jeff shrugged again. "Who knows."

"Want a coffee? I'm going down to the caf."

"Please." Jeff went to dig some change out of his pocket but Larry raised a hand.

"I got it."

Larry departed. Jeff folded his arms on the desk to make a pillow and slowly lowered his head onto them. He was still like that when Larry came back with the coffee.

"You nod off?"

"Nope," Jeff lied. He knew, even if he was asleep, urgent-sounding voices on the radios would have brought him around.

The phone rang.

Jeff sighed and reached for it. "Newsroom," he said.

"I'm sick and tired of you sons of bitches," a man on the other end said. "You liberal fucking rag. Bunch of commies is what you are."

"I know this voice," Jeff said. "You called here the other night. I'm gonna give you a little warning. You call one more time, and I'm going to report you to the circulation department and they're going to cancel your subscription." He slammed the phone down, chuckled to himself. "I wonder if we could really do that?"

"I wish," Larry said.

"You put sugar in this?"

Larry tossed a couple of packets at him. "Enjoy," he said.

Jeff adjusted the volume on some of the radios, bringing up a couple, turning down a couple of others. Finding just the right balance of mayhem between fire and police.

The phone rang again.

"Newsroom," he said.

"Are you the person my husband was talking to?" a woman asked.

"I don't know," Jeff said wearily.

"He just called and said some mean things about your paper."

"Oh, yeah, him."

"Please, please don't cancel our subscription! I love the crossword. If I didn't get my daily crossword and horoscope I'd go out of my mind. I promise he won't call again."

"I'll think about it," Jeff said, and hung up.

About half an hour later, shortly after one, the phone rang again. Jeff sighed and picked up. "Newsroom," he said.

"Did you see that story?" a man asked.

"What story was that, sir?" Jeff said.

"In California. The guy who went in and shot everybody."

Jeff glanced over at the early edition the copy boy had left for him. He hadn't opened it, but the shooting story was above the fold.

"Yeah, I saw that."

"That was wild, wasn't it?" the man said.

"Is there something I can help you with?" Jeff asked.

"I just wanted to tell you, that's gonna happen here. Tomorrow. Well, later today, I guess, since it's already tomorrow."

Jeff sat up a little straighter in his seat, turned down a radio that was putting out a lot of static. "How would you know something like that, sir?" Jeff asked.

"Because I'm going to do it."

"You? You're going to go into a restaurant and shoot a bunch of people?"

"I've been thinking about doing something like that for a long time. Then this guy did it. If he can do it, I can do it. I'm ready."

"Who am I talking to?" Jeff asked.

"My name's Tim," he said.

131

"How you doing, Tim. I'm Jeff."

"Hello, Jeff."

The guy sounded so fucking calm, Jeff thought. He grabbed his pen and started making notes in the spiral notebook he always kept on hand.

"What's your last name, Tim?" he asked, feeling his pulse slowly quicken.

"I don't think I should give you that."

"Okay, that's fine. I get that. So, this thing in California. That didn't exactly work out well for the shooter, you know. He's dead. If you decide to do what he did, you know, you're probably going to end up the same way."

"I know."

"So, if you want my opinion," Jeff said, and uttered a nervous laugh, "I'd reconsider." There was a pause at the other end of the line. "You there, Tim?"

"I'm here."

"You heard what I said?"

"I did. But I'm going to do it anyway. I don't care what happens to me."

Jeff looked through the glass. Fifty feet away, Larry was sitting at his computer terminal, tapping away. Jeff started waving, trying to get his attention.

"Nothing really matters anymore," Tim said.

"Don't say that," Jeff said, still waving. He stood, banged lightly on the glass. Not so loud that the caller would hear, but loud enough, he hoped, that he could get Larry's attention.

Take your eyes off the fucking screen, Jeff thought.

"Why's that?" Jeff asked. "Why would you say nothing matters?"

Larry noticed movement in the corner of his eye, stopped looking at the screen, and glanced Jeff's way. Jeff waved him in urgently. Larry pushed his chair back, stood, and started walking toward the radio room at a leisurely pace.

Could you walk a little slower maybe? Jeff thought.

"My marriage broke up, for one thing," Tim said. "I never should have gotten married in the first place. We weren't right together. It was a mistake. I thought I'd got her pregnant, and I guess I did. But then she lost the baby before the wedding date, but I didn't feel I could back out then. You know, sometimes you feel talked into these things, there's nothing you can do to get out of it, and then it's too late."

"Yeah, sure, I hear ya," Jeff said as Larry stepped into the room. "What's going—"

Jeff put his finger to his lips. He started writing a note, in block letters, on his notepad. He tore it off and handed it to Larry while he kept listening to Tim.

CALL COPS. GUY NAMED TIM SAYS HES GOING TO SHOOT BUNCH OF PEOPLE TODAY.

It took Larry half a second to read the note. He mouthed two words: "Tim who?"

Jeff shook his head quickly, said, "Yeah, marriage. You never know how that's going to work out. I've never been married. Thought about it once or twice, but then the women came to their senses."

Larry ran back to his desk, dropped into his chair, looked at the list of contact numbers taped next to the phone, dialed the police non-emergency line, which connected him to a desk sergeant. He quickly identified himself to the woman who answered.

"What's going on?" she asked.

"My reporter is talking to a guy on the phone who says he's going to shoot a whole bunch of people later today."

"What else can you tell me?"

"Not much. His name's Tim. Other than that, I got no idea."

"I'm going to put you through to a detective. Hold. I'm gonna brief him before I connect you."

"Okay."

Larry waited. About thirty seconds went by before a man came on the line and said, "Durkin here. Who's this?"

Larry told him, then filled him in on what little he knew.

"Is it this thing in California?" Durkin asked. "Got him all inspired?"

"Maybe."

"Okay, I'm going to give you my direct line. I'll be here all night.

This is what I want you to tell—what's your reporter's name?"

"Jeff."

"This is what I want you to tell Jeff."

Larry scribbled, then signed off with Durkin. He ran back to the radio room, where Jeff was still on the phone. Larry handed him the note.

COPS SAY KEEP HIM ON LINE.

When Jeff got that far, he gave Larry a look that said, "Really? Never would have thought of that."

The rest of the note read: GET FULL NAME, ANYTHING ABOUT HIM. ADDRESS.

Jeff rolled his eyes, tossed the note back, gave Larry a thumbs-up, mouthed "Brilliant." Then said, into the phone, "We've all been there, I know."

Jeff had taken more notes while Larry was on the phone with the police. He handed them over.

MARRIAGE BROKE UP. LOST JOB. WONT SAY WHERE HE WORKED. BIT OF ACCENT, THINK MAYBE PA.

Larry pointed to the last word. Jeff mouthed "Pennsylvania." Then shrugged, suggesting he might be wrong. Larry nodded, then ran back to his desk to make another call.

Tim said, "I hope I'm not keeping you from something."

Jeff said, "No problem. I'm just on the graveyard shift, killing time." Soon as he said the words *graveyard* and *killing* he wondered if he should be choosing his words more carefully.

"You always have to work these kinds of hours?" Tim asked.

"I haven't done this shift for a while. I'm doing a double."

"A double?"

"A double shift. I was supposed to be off at eleven, but the guy who was supposed to relieve me booked off sick, so I'm here till six."

"Nice guy."

"Yeah, that's what I was thinking. Right now some girl's rockin' his world. So what kind of work did you do? What'd you get laid off from?"

"Retail," he said. "A mall job. Laid off makes it sound like they were cutting back. It wasn't exactly like that for me."

"What happened?"

"I talked back to a rude customer. Got fired."

"What'd you do, exactly?" Jeff asked.

"Someone was trying to return something without a receipt. I think they actually stole it from another store and brought it to us for a refund. Happens all the time. Sometimes right in the store. They find something on the rack, tear off the tags, come up asking for their money back. I told her to take a hike and she complained to the manager and I got fired."

"Sounds like you were trying to do the right thing."

"I don't know. If I'd just given her the refund there wouldn't have been all the fuss. Store doesn't want bad publicity, customers bad-mouthing the place. But people are so dishonest. People are awful."

"Yeah, well, we've got a few subscribers call in and they're not so nice, either. So…what store was this?"

"Just a store. Doesn't matter." He paused. "It's nice talking to you."

"Yeah, you too," Jeff said. "You sound like a nice guy."

"Thanks." Another pause. "I guess they won't be saying that, this time tomorrow. After I've done it."

Their conversation became long and meandering. Small talk. Jeff telling him where he'd gone on his last vacation—it was a fishing trip and he'd caught a muskellunge that was nearly four feet—the first paper he worked for, a girl he once dated whose father was in a TV series. Anything to keep the guy on the line.

Back at his desk, Larry had been telling Durkin that the guy on the phone with Jeff just lost his job, and his wife, and he might be from Pennsylvania, although that was just a guess.

"That's not a lot to work with," Durkin said.

"I know. It's all Jeff's got right now. Can't you just trace the line?"

"That's not as simple to set up as they make it look on TV. Be a lot easier if your guy could just get us a name. Get Jeff to be his friend."

"He's doing that."

"Yeah, well, tell him to stick with it. Really sympathize. His name's Tim, right? Tell him to use his name a lot."

So Larry wrote another note to Jeff that said COPS REALLY NEED NAME and CALL HIM TIM A LOT and BE LIKE A FRIEND. He knew that was only going to prompt Jeff to roll his eyes again, like he couldn't figure out this shit on his own.

Larry looked back at the radio room, saw Jeff still on the phone. He ran back, tossed the note in front of Jeff, and shrugged, as if to say, "I know."

To Tim, Jeff said, "I guess I don't see how killing a bunch of people is going to make any difference, Tim."

"It'll make a difference," Tim said.

"Yeah, but how? You walk in, start shooting all over the place, you're probably going to hit some kids and moms and stuff. How's that making your situation any better?"

"It makes an impact," he said. "It makes a statement."

"What if you end up shooting *me*? I mean, here we are talking, we're making a connection. We're getting to be friends over the phone, and then tomorrow, I'll go into some place to get a burger and fries and you'll walk in and shoot me."

"Where do you usually go?" Tim asked. "I'll pick a different place so it won't be you. Or maybe you should just stay home tomorrow."

"You're missing my point, Tim. If it's not me, it could be someone else you know. Some acquaintance. Maybe some friend you had in school, you walk in and end up killing his mother or his sister or something. You don't want to do that."

Tim went quiet, as if considering what Jeff had to say. "That's kind of what my psychiatrist says."

"Well, there you go," Jeff said. "I don't even have a degree or anything in psychiatry and I'm as smart as your shrink." He tried another laugh. "Pretty good, huh? Maybe I should be charging you for this call. That's a joke."

"I guess what you're saying is common sense."

"I mean, Tim, come on. Why'd you phone in? Why'd you call into the newsroom to tell me this?"

"I guess...I don't know."

"I think you do. Come on. Think harder. You called the

newsroom, didn't know who you'd get, but you got me, and we're talking, and you know why you did this?"

"You tell me," Tim said.

"You wanted me to talk you out of it. That's why you called. You wanted whoever picked up the phone to talk you out of it."

Jeff glanced at the row of clocks that hung high on the newsroom wall. There was half a dozen of them, showing the correct time in London and Munich and Jerusalem and Beijing and Los Angeles. The sixth one was local time, and it read 3:14 a.m. Jesus, Jeff thought. He'd been on the phone with this guy for more than two hours. And that coffee Larry'd bought him was already looking for a way to escape. What was it they said about coffee? You only rented it? Jeff really needed to take a piss, but there was no way he could end this call and go strolling off to the bathroom.

He eyed the trash can under the desk. If he had to, he'd take a piss in that.

Jeff wrote down more notes on his pad, then waved at Larry. This time, Larry was already looking in his direction. He sprinted across the newsroom.

Jeff's note read: WORKED RETAIL. WONT SAY WHERE. SAYS HE'S STILL GOING TO DO IT. SEEING A SHRINK. SOUNDS LIKE MAYBE HE'LL DO IT AT LUNCH TIME WHEN PLACES BUSY.

Larry read the note, nodded, went back to his desk.

He placed another call to Durkin, read him Jeff's note.

Durkin said, "What was that part about a shrink?"

"Just what I said. Seeing a shrink. So I guess Tim is seeing a psychiatrist. Sounds like the kind of guy who *should* be seeing a psychiatrist."

"We need that shrink's name. Tell Jeff to ask him what his psychiatrist's name is."

Larry scribbled GET PSYCH'S NAME, ended the call, and ran back to the radio room. He handed the slip of paper to Jeff, who glanced at it, nodded, tossed it aside.

"This is for all the people who've cheated me and betrayed me," Tim said. "Like my wife and my manager and everyone. My parents, too. They were never there for me when I needed them. My father, he never gave me credit for anything. He was ashamed of me. He was this big college football star. I was never any good at sports."

"Me, neither," Jeff said. He told a story about how, of all the things he had to do in phys ed, he was the absolute worst at lacrosse. "They wanted me to catch a tiny little ball in a tiny little net at the end of a fucking stick. Was not going to happen."

"I hated all of it. I've never been very coordinated. Whenever they'd pick teams, like in gym, I would always be picked last."

"I hear ya," Jeff said. "I like to joke that when they got to me, they'd see if they could get someone from *another* school."

That actually prompted a chuckle from Tim.

"You know what?" Jeff said. "Here's an idea. Why don't you come down here, to the paper, for when I get off at six? We'll go get some breakfast, talk this out. There's a really good diner close to the paper, open twenty-four hours. They do a great omelet. My treat."

"Oh, I couldn't do that."

"Why not?"

"It'd be a trap."

"What?"

"A trap. You'd tell the police and they'd come and get me."

"No, man, it'd just be to talk. How long have we been talking? I feel like we've developed a level of trust between us. Look, I won't lie to you. I don't want you to go into a burger joint today and shoot a whole bunch of people to death. So, yeah, I got an agenda. But that's it."

"I don't think so. I have to do what I have to do."

"Okay, so, you know what I *would* have to do."

"What?"

"Soon as you get off the line, we'd have to put out a warning. Tell everybody not to go to their favorite restaurant today because we got a tip someone was going to walk in and start shooting. So, even if you were still going to do this, there wouldn't be anyone to shoot. Everyone would be on guard, you know what I'm saying?"

"I guess you would have to do that," he said. "I wouldn't blame you for doing that."

"Thanks."

"So I'd just have to make it another day. Maybe next week."

"No, no. You'd have to call the whole thing off."

"I have the guns," Tim said.

"Yeah?"

"Like, more than one. So if I run out of bullets with the first one, I can switch to the other. It'll take the police a while to get there. I think I can kill a lot of people by then."

"Jesus, Tim, if I can't talk you out of this, think what it's going to do to my conscience." Jeff paused, thinking. "I'm gonna have a lot to unload on my *own* psychiatrist next time I go."

"You're seeing someone, too?"

"I thought everybody had a shrink," Jeff said. "Who isn't fucked up, you know what I mean?"

"Yeah, we all got problems."

"Be a small world if we were both seeing the same head shrinker," Jeff said. He grabbed a section of newspaper at random, scanned the page for a name, any name. He spotted an entertainment piece about that sitcom that takes place in a Boston bar. "I'm seeing Dr. Danson. Any chance that's who you're seeing?"

"No, I'm seeing Dr. Willoughby," he said. "He's nice, but I don't think he's really doing anything for me."

Jeff wrote DR. WILLOUGHBY on his notepad and started waving it in front of the glass. Larry came running, ripped the note from Jeff's pad, ran back to his desk and dialed.

"Durkin."

"I got a name," Larry said. "The psychiatrist. The one Tim's seeing."

"Fire away."

"Willoughby. I'm not sure of the spelling. I've got a phone book right in front of me. Hang on."

Larry dropped the receiver, dragged over the thick yellow pages directory, and opened it to psychiatrists. "Willoughby. Willoughby. Yes!" He grabbed the receiver. "I've found a listing for a doctor with that name. I've got an address and a phone number."

"Office address?" asked Durkin.

"I guess."

"Not going to do a lot of fucking good at four in the morning. I need a residence. We gotta wake this doc up and talk to him. We've got our own resources."

Larry heard Durkin put the phone down at his end. He had to wait for more than a minute before Durkin came back.

"Okay, thanks," he said, and ended the call.

Larry put the receiver back on the base and said, "You're welcome."

He wrote GAVE COPS NAME on a slip of paper and delivered it to Jeff, who gave him a thumbs-up.

"Maybe I should do it sooner," Tim said. "Find a breakfast place."

"Aw, come on, Tim."

"If you're going to get the word out, I need to act sooner. Gotta get this done before you can issue a warning."

"Okay, okay, listen, let's talk about this. Let's talk about—let's talk about your family. Things didn't work out with your wife, but…what about kids? You got kids?"

"No. I told you. She lost the baby before we got married. Aren't you listening?"

"Yeah, but I thought maybe you had another one. What about parents? I know you said your dad was a shit, I heard the college football stuff, but what about your mom? She still with us?"

"Yeah. She is. But she's in a nursing home."

"She got all her marbles?"

"Yeah."

"So what's she going to say?"

"Huh?"

"When she turns on the news and finds out her son shot a whole bunch of people? How's she supposed to go on after that? Everyone pointing to her on the street, saying, 'See that lady? It was *her* son that killed all those people.' Is it fair to do that to her?"

Tim didn't say anything for a moment. "I don't care."

"Come on. She's your *mom*."

"I want her to know. I want her to have to deal with this. She's got it coming."

Jeff couldn't hold it any longer. He pulled the wastepaper basket out from under the desk, stood, unzipped and let loose, just as Larry stepped into the room.

"Shit, sorry," he whispered and stepped back.

Jeff shook his head tiredly. When he was done, he tucked himself back in place as best he could with one hand still holding the phone, listening to Tim the entire time. He sat back down and pushed the can back under the desk.

Larry re-entered the room, scribbled on Jeff's pad NO NEWS. ANYTHING I CAN DO?

Jeff managed a grin, pointed to the can. Larry declined the offer to take it to the men's room to empty it and instead went back to his desk. Along the way, he glanced at the wall clock. It was nearly four-thirty.

Thank God, he thought, *nothing else happened tonight.* The fire turned out to be nothing, and Mike had never filed a new top to the bike lane story. Council must not have come to a decision. Had there been some overnight development, there was no way he could have pulled Jeff off that phone call to deal with it. Not with God knew how many lives at stake.

His phone rang.

"Hello?"

"Durkin. Just thought I'd let you know. We found the psychiatrist. Sent a car over to his house, woke him up. They asked him, you got a patient who might be inclined to go into a crowded place and shoot up a whole bunch of people? Oh no, he says. I know just who that would be."

"He told them? He gave you guys a name?"

"In this kind of circumstance? Yeah, he gave us a name. Tell your reporter to keep him on the line just a little while longer."

"I will."

"And there's something I want to talk to you about after," Durkin said.

"I'm here till six."

"Okay."

The detective ended the call. Larry ran back to Jeff with one last note: KEEP HIM TALKING LITTLE WHILE LONGER.

Jeff nodded.

Tim was saying, "Maybe not a place where people go to eat. I got a better idea. Maybe the subway. There'll be hundreds of people down on the platform. Just before the train comes in, I can jump on the tracks. I think that'd be a good way to go out."

"I went to one of those once," Jeff said.

"One of what?"

"Jumper, in the subway. Man, that is *not* the way you want to go out. He was in pieces."

"But it'll be fast," Tim said.

"They'll be looking all over the place to find all your bits," Jeff said.

"You're not scaring me. But I appreciate you talking to me. I'm gonna go now."

"No man, hang on. Let's keep talking. Can I tell you something?"

"What?"

"I just took a piss in a trash can."

"You didn't."

"I did. Whipped it out, took a whiz right here at my work station. Good thing you called in the middle of the night. Doing that in the day, women around, that could get me in a little trouble with personnel, you know?"

Tim chuckled. "That is pretty—hang on."

"What?"

"There's someone knocking at my door. Let me just see who it is."

Jeff could hear Tim put the phone down. In the distance, some indistinct talking. And then, fumbling, someone picking up the phone.

A different voice. Female. She said, "It's over. Thanks for your help."

And then she hung up.

That was it.

Jeff put down the phone. "Jesus," he said, putting his head down on the table.

Larry saw him hang up and ran over.

"What happened?" he asked.

"I guess it was the cops. They knocked, he answered, it's over. Christ, I'm shaking."

Larry found that he was, too. "Man, what a night. Holy shit. You know what you did? Do you know?"

Jeff looked at him blankly. "If you mean taking a piss right here, yeah, I can kinda smell it."

"You fuckin' just saved a whole bunch of people's lives."

Jeff offered another one of his familiar shrugs. "I don't know. Fuck. I am totally wired." He ran his fingers through his hair.

The phone on Larry's desk was ringing. Larry ran back, snatched the receiver up.

"It's done," Durkin said. "Just wanted to thank you guys, and ask you a favor."

"What's that?"

"Sit on this one for a bit? I mean, I know I can't tell you what to print and not to print, but this guy, he got inspired by that mass shooting, and you wonder how many others might be feeling the same way. Just…sit on it. Talk to your dayside editor. This guy's probably going to be taken for psychiatric assessment. He's probably suicidal."

"I'll leave something in my turnover note," Larry said.

"You guys did good. You did *real* good. I might actually stop hating your paper so much for how you cover the cops." He paused. "Nah, I'll still hate ya. Gotta go."

Durkin ended the call.

Larry realized Jeff was standing right there next to him.

"Where the fuck do you get a drink at five-thirty in the morning?" he asked.

"I happen to know where the photogs keep a bottle in the darkroom."

"Lead the way."

* * *

"And that's what happened," Larry said. "A crazy night. Jesus, look at the time."

"Did you ever find out what happened to the guy?" Frank asked, still sitting on the stool next to him.

Larry shook his head. "No, never did. We ended up not doing a story on it. Partly, we thought it would be blowing our own horn too much. 'Paper saves city from massacre.' Nah, this was one of those times when we went along with what the cops wanted."

"What do you think happened?"

Larry tried to get the last drop out of his beer glass. "I don't know. Maybe he got the help he needed, turned his life around. Or maybe he had just one fuckup after another. Someone like that, who knows. Do they get their life together, or do they get worse and worse?"

"You know what I think happened?" Frank said. "I think that arrest, it was like the first domino. He got dragged into the system, never got the help he wanted. Things got worse and worse for him over the years. In and out of institutions, maybe some time in jail. My guess is, he was having a bad night, that he never would have gone and killed all those people, that he just needed someone to talk to, and he happened to connect with this Jeff guy, started to think he really was a friend, that he honest-to-God actually gave a shit about him, and had no idea that he and his editor were working behind the scenes with the cops to get him, to betray his sorry ass."

Larry, slightly glassy-eyed, took a closer look at his drinking partner.

"And by the way, my name's not Frank," Tim said. "And Jeff asked me to pass on his regrets about not being able to make it tonight. Took a long time to track down the two of you."

And that was when Tim reached inside his jacket for something.

Larry said, "Son of a—"

* * *

MIDNIGHT IN THE GARDEN OF DEATH

HEATHER GRAHAM

"They say she came to life each night after midnight; she traveled like the wind, coming back into town, feeding upon a new person each night. Then, they would awaken in the morning, spitting blood, choking on that blood…dying, in a pool of their own blood!" Marcy announced.

Hayley listened to her cousin, silently shaking her head as she and their friends stood in the old cemetery, staring at the vault that held the remains of the local "vampire," Elizabeth Barclay.

Those remains were, not surprisingly, in the Barclay Cemetery.

Hayley knew the legend, too. She'd grown up here—or partially grown up here. Her parents had moved a bit east to New Orleans when she'd been twelve. But Marcy's father, Hayley's uncle, was the manager and groundskeeper of the small cemetery, and Marcy had spent all seventeen years of her life living in a home that bordered the cemetery.

And she loved the legends—and doing her best to scare others, boys especially.

The wind seemed to breathe out a rush of cold air as Marcy's words settled on their small crowd. The trees in the center lane of the "city of the dead" where vault after vault arose in majestic lichen-covered splendor rustled, as if someone moved around them.

Yes, Marcy was good.

But her cousin smiled then, saying, "The townspeople found a way to end the horror! They marched to the cemetery with torches. They broke the gate to the vault and battered down the old wooden door. They broke open her tomb and wrenched the coffin from the vault, dragging it back outside. And there, while her poor mother watched and screamed and cried, they opened her coffin. Horrible scratch marks ripped through the lid of the coffin, revealing what was inside. There she lay! Elizabeth, fresh as the day they had buried her weeks before, her beautiful face a soft shade of alabaster, eyes sweetly closed—and blood, yes, blood, a trickle of it, running from her ruby red lips!"

Marcy paused again for effect.

Her little crowd was silent at first; Mary Boucher, pretty and petite, seemed to be shivering, though it was a warm Louisiana night. Tommy Hilliard, captain of the football team, had a crooked smile on his face, but Hayley wondered if even he might be a little bit unnerved. Next to him were Frank Legrand and Art Richard, also on the football team.

Tonight, Marcy's guests were the cream of the crop of the local high school. She had three of the best players on the football team, and the guest list rounded out with little Mary Boucher—captain of the cheerleaders—and, of course, Hayley.

Marcy wasn't always in the elite group, though she had managed to stay on the edge of it—and tonight, of course, she'd been able to come up with a great play to get such an illustrious group together—her father was out of town. She'd invited them all on a bit of a dare and an adventure that might not come their way again.

She'd had a crush on Tommy Hilliard forever, and he'd recently broken up with his girlfriend, Tiffany Myers.

Tiffany hadn't been invited. But just as Marcy had pined for Tommy Hilliard forever, she had hated Tiffany. But then, to be fair, it had always seemed to Hayley that Tiffany had gone out of her way to be cruel to Marcy, mocking her as the "grave-digger's dirty daughter" and other such names.

Tiffany hadn't been nice to anyone, really. She was rich and—in her mind, at least—entitled. It wasn't being rich, Hayley had decided, since she knew other rich kids were darn decent and good to others. It was the way that Tiffany had of mocking anyone poor, anyone with a handicap—anyone she didn't like or want in her circle.

Hayley had heard Tommy talking earlier; he'd told Frank and Art that he'd probably wind up back with Tiffany. In truth, Tiffany was a stunning blue-eyed blonde with a perfect body that didn't stop—Tiffany worked hard to keep it that way. Her legs were legendary.

As Tommy told his friends, "She could wrap those legs around a man in a way that couldn't even be imagined."

Hayley had tried very hard to explain this to Marcy, but Marcy was convinced that she had her chance. Tiffany was a silly, shrieking shrew—while she had at least some semblance of decency and intelligence. Tommy would see that.

And he hadn't even suggested Tiffany be invited that night. That was a sign, as far as Marcy was concerned.

Marcy's father was out of town. She was about to graduate; she was an adult, eighteen in a month, and he could trust her, of course. And Marcy was responsible. Usually. She'd even told her dad about having a slumber party. She just hadn't told him she was hosting a slumber party that wouldn't be in the house—she'd have it in the cemetery.

Marcy swung around to look at Hayley, grinning with triumph. "Hayley, finish the story."

Hayley smiled weakly. "They thought poor Elizabeth was a vampire. They dragged her from the coffin, cut out her heart, and burned it—before her poor mother's eyes." She hesitated. Mary Boucher looked really frightened. Hayley chanced her cousin's wrath by continuing with, "Of course, the poor young woman had suffered from 'consumption,' or tuberculosis, a disease which couldn't be cured at the time. The saddest part of the story is they weren't always embalming people back then and it's most likely that she was buried alive. The disease had spread, causing others to contract it and those people might well awake spitting blood. And the scratch marks on the coffin...I can only think how horrible that must have been, except, hopefully, she was barely conscious in there, or...died quickly without even being aware how desperately she'd scratched against the coffin to get out."

Marcy gave her a stern frown. She was supposed to be scaring people—not reassuring them.

"Yes! Imagine! Being buried alive in Louisiana in such a vault where, they say, in just a year and a day the sun will burn down, scorch, and bring flesh and blood and bone truly back to basics, nothing but man—or woman—as dust and ash!"

"Good story," Tommy Hilliard said, pretending to suppress a yawn.

"Shush," Marcy said suddenly.

"Why? What? A zombie is coming?" Tommy asked, laughing. He was almost eighteen—solid as a rock and inching over six-feet tall. He had already been recruited by a dozen colleges.

"No," Marcy said, grinning. "Officer Claymore—hurry, let's get back into the house—he always comes by here right at midnight, making sure no vandals are running around."

They headed quickly through the small open gate which led to the rear of Marcy's house. Her yard was enclosed as well with the same brickwork that surrounded the cemetery, except that, in most areas of the cemetery, the wall was only about two-and-a-half feet tall.

The doorbell rang just as they came in. Marcy murmured something and hurried to it, smiling sweetly as she opened it.

It was indeed Officer Claymore. "You all right, Marcy?" he asked, looking beyond her to the group inside.

"Fine, Officer Claymore—and thank you."

"Yeah, I heard your dad is out of town," Claymore said. He was a middle-aged man with something of a round look. He tended to smile—but Marcy had seen him in action when a couple of thugs had tried to rob a local bakery.

He was pudgy maybe, but he could be damned fierce.

"My friends are keeping me company tonight," Marcy said.

"Good." He looked around at the group.

"There's a strange man hanging around town," Claymore told them. "From what I hear, sounds like a harmless fellow, carries a sign that he's a veteran and needs help. Scruffy-looking fellow, long, unkempt hair, big coat."

"We won't bother him if we see him," Marcy said.

Claymore grinned and shrugged. "Either that—I mean he's a harmless old guy—or he's the ghost of Ethan Fray, fellow shot down and killed in the streets *after* he got back from active military duty. I've heard he runs around attacking people in the shadows."

"Funny, funny," Marcy said softly, smiling. "You trying to scare us, Officer Claymore?"

Claymore suddenly drew serious, frowning. "Kids, you have to be smart and careful. Keep doors locked. This is serious. They had a couple of murders in New Orleans in the last weeks. They think there may be a serial killer loose—he slices up his victims and leaves them displayed bizarrely. They're calling him the City Slicer. So, yeah, I'm serious."

"New Orleans," Art said. "All the crazies go to New Orleans. We're, like, more real out here in the bayou country."

"Please, we're good kids, honest," Marcy said.

"Okay, so we're not New Orleans. That doesn't make us safe. I'm hoping you're all smart enough to be careful, not scared," Claymore said. "You see a ghost—well, scream like hell. You see a poor fellow down and out who needs help—well, leave him be. I say, if you see him trying to sleep by one of the tombs, leave him alone—good idea if he's a ghost or a real man, right? You should never be in that cemetery at night, anyway. If you see anything—"

"Like the City Slicer?" Art asked.

"Scream blue blazes and run like hell. Look, yes, any city seems to draw more crazies. That doesn't mean that weird or bad things can't happen here."

Tommy Hilliard barely suppressed a laugh. "Like a ghost—or a vampire rising?" he asked.

Officer Claymore looked at him. "Who knows about Ethan Fray, hmm? But I guess it was before your day, Tommy Hilliard. While legends may be legends, what people do with them can be bad. Trust me—nothing good happens after midnight in that cemetery."

Art let out a soft laugh. "Ah, come on, Officer Claymore! No disrespect intended, sir—but it's a cemetery." Art was getting tall, too, but he had a lean build. He could run like a rabbit, and he had done the community proud with many an amazing touchdown.

"Right," Frank Legrand said. "The dead don't really come back to life."

"No?" Claymore asked, smiling slightly. "There's been a saying for years—don't go into the old cemetery after midnight."

"Someone cursed it, right?" Mary asked nervously.

"Of course!" Marcy said.

"Ah, come on," Art said. "Every good cemetery should have a curse. Even an 'after midnight' curse. I mean, we're all creeped out by death."

"Mr. Richard—" Claymore began, using the customary pronunciation of the name.

"*Ree-chard*," Art corrected. "Old Cajun family," he told Claymore, shaking his head and looking around. "Not Art Richard. Art *Ree-chard*."

Claymore nodded. "All right, Mr. *Ree-chard*. The curse supposedly came with our famous vampire, Elizabeth Barclay. She supposedly came back to life—even with her heart cut out and burned—and warned people to stay out of the cemetery after midnight. And in 1923, cops back then found a pair of lovers with their throats slit in front of the Barclay vault on a fine, sunny morning—they'd last told friends they were heading into the cemetery for real privacy."

"A century ago," Frank murmured. He smiled. "But that's cool, Officer. We're here to just have a slumber party in the parlor—you know we all graduate and go off soon, and this is…well, you know, we're going to just kind of have some quality time before going in different directions."

"1950," Officer Claymore continued. "Someone strung up a man like a scarecrow—on the side of the Barclay vault. And in 1980—not long after the vampire craze hit New Orleans and surrounding areas—we found an unidentified woman drained of blood and left…left right by the gate to this house. Maybe she was trying to escape the cemetery and the curse and just didn't make it. She wasn't found in the yard—her body was in the cemetery. So, hey, I'm a logical man. But I still say, don't go fooling around in the cemetery now. Is the cemetery cursed, or do crazy killers just like cemeteries? I don't know. Just watch out now because it *is* after midnight."

"Thank you so much, Officer Claymore," Marcy said. She smiled brightly. "We're all in for the night."

He nodded to them briefly and turned to go.

Marcy closed the door and leaned against it. "At last! Give him ten minutes and then we can go out and set up our little tents and tell more tall tales."

"Maybe he's right," Hayley said. "Marcy, maybe we should just stay in."

Frank made a squawking sound and acted like a chicken.

"Hey!" Mary protested.

"Ah, come on," Art said. "Claymore was making fun of all of us—he's probably laughing his ass off right now, thinking he's scared the shit out of us and we'll just stay here, quaking or running on home. Let's do what we came to do—sleep in the cemetery!"

"Let's do it," Frank said. He smiled and headed to the back of the house; the canvas sacks containing their sleeping bags and two pop-up tents they'd acquired from an on-line shopping source waited there, out of sight from the front of the house.

"He's right. Let's do this," Tommy said, striding after Frank.

"I don't...I don't like it," Mary said.

"You can go home," Art suggested. "I mean...we're all here, but if you're afraid in a group of six, well..."

Mary shook her head. "No, I want to be with you all, but... okay, let's go." She looked at Hayley, maybe hoping that Hayley would protest.

"There are six of us," Hayley said.

She wasn't sure why she had an uneasy feeling. But then, she'd thought it a strange thing to do from the get-go. Even after moving to New Orleans, she'd come back frequently to spend the weekend with her cousin.

She'd grown up with the cemetery as part of her family life.

Maybe she was just being like Mary—spooked by the legends, or by Officer Claymore. She knew, of course, that the things he had told them were true. Her uncle knew, too, but he didn't believe in curses—he believed in bad people doing bad things.

As she followed the others out, she looked up to the sky. There was no rain forecast; it was spring, and the night was just right, hovering around seventy degrees. Here, even the nights could sometimes be sticky hot once summer was in full bloom, but tonight...

The temperature was beautiful; there was a light stir of breeze in the air. And overhead...

It was a full moon. A shimmering, bright full moon. As beautiful as the weather, except…tonight, it made her shiver.

"A full moon!" Mary breathed, walking beside her.

Frank, just a bit ahead, heard her. "Hey, the place is cursed by a vampire, Mary, my love."

"Right," Tommy called. "Sorry, the place is home to no werewolves."

Hayley gasped suddenly, looking through the tombs in their neat rows, noting that the moon had certainly made the night brighter—but it had also allowed for strange shadows to form. And…

She thought she'd just seen a shadow move.

"What, what, what?" Mary asked worriedly.

Hayley laughed. "Sorry, I just…I think I dropped my ring. I'll be right back."

She was an idiot. No, she knew this place, had grown up knowing this place…

Still, dumb! It was after midnight!

What the hell am I doing? She asked herself.

Well, running through the vaults alone because you saw a shadow. Brilliant.

She'd only gone two rows in and stood in front of the McCafferty vault when she saw her "shadow."

The vault was unusual in that it had an open alcove, an area before the giant gated door that was covered and offered two benches in front of a statue of St. Francis. Hayley's history had taught her that Judith McCafferty had loved animals and brought about some of the first laws that punished human beings for cruelty to animals. She loved the vault; she sometimes brought flowers herself for the metal holders that held them while they were fresh and living and allowed them to be easily removed when they were not.

Her shadow was there; she thought at first she had come upon an unknown form of monster because she just saw a dark form seated on one of the tile benches. Then she realized it was just a man. A bearded and somewhat scraggly-looking man, slightly bowed as he sat, hands in prayer as she came upon him.

He looked up fast, as startled as she was.

"I—hi!" Hayley said.

She saw him wince, saw the weariness in his sad eyes—powder blue, she thought—as he looked at her.

"I'm sorry; I can get out. This alcove here…it shields you from the wind and rain. When there is rain. I know I can't be here. You're the caretaker's daughter."

"I'm his niece, but…no. You're fine there, sir. Please, feel free to rest." She hesitated and indicated the family tomb. "One of the ladies interred here was super kind to people—and, of course, animals." Hayley wasn't sure why, but she felt a tremendous empathy for the man. He was so down and out. So down and out that he had to sleep in a cemetery. "Please, I'll just slip away. And I'm sorry, my crazy cousin is having a slumber party, so there will be some noise."

She had an unopened water bottle stuffed in the pocket of her jacket. She pulled it out and set it at the end of the bench, smiling at him. "Have a nice night," she said. "And try to ignore us."

"Thank you," he said.

Hayley hurried back out to the main lane in the cemetery, ready to catch up with her friends as they set up for the night in front of the Barclay family mausoleum. Tommy was busy using the little plastic hammer that had come with one of the tents to get the stake to stay in the ground just off the gravel path.

Frank had come with a battery-operated "fire-log" and he was setting it up on the gravel. Marcy, giving instructions, was telling them tents would be on the grass next to the Barclay tomb, the fire "thingy" would be on the gravel, and whoever was telling the story would sit on a little mat by the light from the fire "thingy" and the others could lie on their sleeping bags in the tents.

She was just finishing her instructions when Mary, who had wandered a bit farther along the dirt and gravel central path, started to scream. Scream and scream.

"What the hell?" Tommy demanded. A stray cloud danced across the moon; what light they had paled—and the shadows seemed to darken and grow.

As he walked toward her, Mary turned and threw herself into

his arms, half screaming, half shouting out gibberish.

"What, please, Mary, what?" Tommy begged.

"Oh, God! Oh, God, oh God!" Frank breathed at his side, pointing.

The stray cloud covering the moon had moved on. And they could all see.

There was rigging between two tombs, ropes that stretched from one small family tomb to another.

They were tied to…

A corpse. One that was barely real…bones, bits of flesh, pieces of cloth, and a skull with hair and ravaged pieces of cheeks and lips still attached. Hayley stared, stunned.

Tommy Hilliard, tough Tommy Hilliard, let out a scream that might have wakened the dead.

Then they all turned to run; Tommy was so rattled he pushed away from Mary who had been leaning on him. Mary fell, Frank leaped over her.

Marcy still gaped; Hayley came to and rushed for the fallen Mary, along with Art, who had also retained some of his senses. But even as they helped Mary to her feet, Hayley could hear laughter—high-pitched, delighted feminine laughter.

She stood still.

Tiffany Myers, unable to control her amusement, walked out from behind one of the tombs from where the body had been hung. She tossed her long, blonde hair over her shoulder as she appeared, followed by Bobby McGill, who dressed as the "wolf" mascot for their high school games.

Bobby was a sweet guy, but always on the periphery. He hadn't made the team; he was a little bit pudgy and had never managed to clear up his acne.

And normally, Hayley thought, Tiffany wouldn't have given him the time of day.

"You, oh, my God! You, Tommy Hilliard! That was hysterical. All of you! Big, brave kids—going to spend the night in the cemetery. Wow. Thankfully, I have this all recorded on my phone. Oh, my God! It's going to be so wonderful!" She started to laugh again, and she turned and stared at Marcy, "Wow, honey, I guess your cemetery party is really—dead! You forgot to invite me but, hey, not to worry—I wouldn't really want to be in here with this group of silly cowards. Oh, lord, Marcy, you should have seen yourself. Some grave-digger's daughter *you* are."

"People are interred here, Tiffany. My dad has never dug a grave."

"Whatever. Oh, my God, that was too good. Bobby, come along now. You were a big help, but I have other things I need to do, other people to see…oh, that was too, too, funny!"

Shrieking with laughter, she started down the path that led to the main gates, followed by Bobby McGill.

Tommy started to go after her; Marcy caught his arm.

"Tommy—"

"Marcy, not to worry. That was sick; she's had it with me. Maybe we will all go into the house for the night. But I want her phone." He turned suddenly, wincing. "Mary, I am so sorry. I didn't mean to knock you down. I really did freak." He stared at the corpse. "And it's just a leftover Halloween decoration. I don't know why I didn't see that!"

"Guys," Hayley said. "I'll go after her. I'm not—well, you know. I'm not local anymore—I mean, I'm not in school with you guys. I'll see if I can reason with her before she gets out. If I need to, I'll threaten that I'm going to call Officer Claymore, or…I don't know. Let me try."

She hoped they listened to her—if Tommy accosted Tiffany, it might get nasty. Tiffany was in a mood.

Tommy was a big guy.

Hayley didn't want anyone getting hurt.

She heard footsteps behind her and swung around. It was Art.

"Hey, Hayley, I'm not going to speak, just follow, make sure you're alright, okay?"

"Sure. Thanks."

Hayley had followed a path that led straight to the main gates. But she'd been wrong, apparently. Tiffany didn't seem to be along the path anywhere. Hayley turned back to Art.

Art shook his head. "She really thinks she can do anything to anyone. I keep hoping that graduation will make a change—get

Tommy away from her. Tommy is really okay, you know?"

"I, um, I guess," Hayley told him. "I'm not in school, but...I mean, anyway—we need to find Tiffany. Right now, I want to deal with her and not Tommy."

"You know the place, right? Which way?" Art asked.

She hesitated. "She could have cut across to the entrance on Lafitte Court. There's no street that way, just an alley and then the back of some houses. But if her car is on the road—"

"She would just have to walk down the alley to reach it. Of course, she could crawl over the wall in some places," he said, pausing to grimace, "but she might break a nail."

Hayley smiled. "We can cut through here."

Barclay Cemetery was, from the air, laid out in a cross. There were two main paths through it—one with the center tomb being the Barclay tomb, and the one that crossed. Hayley led Art in a zigzag to reach that center path down from where Marcy and the others waited.

She didn't want to report failure yet.

The moon was riding high again. Hayley *had* known the cemetery forever, but she still noted, by the moonlight, the beauty of the tombs, built more like a Colonial or Victorian house than homes for the remains of the dead. Most of the vaults or mausoleums were clean and painted; on some, the owners were far away and long gone from the area. Hayley's uncle tried to keep up with them, but the space was large, and while there was only an occasional burial now and then, it was an active cemetery, and he tended to be a busy man.

Here and there, the tombs were covered with the darkness of age. Every now and then, a rusty old gate swung open on its hinges; weeds grew up around the tombs, and the atmosphere of death and decaying elegance was heavy. And still...

"She's done it again," Art said, shaking his head. "Bitch! She knew we'd come after her. Well, hell, I'm not screaming or staring like a fool again!"

Hayley stopped in her tracks. He was looking toward the gate. Between the last family tombs in the row, connecting ropes were stretched out again. Gargoyles, crosses, any piece of funerary art had been used for the anchors.

A body hung between them.

This one fresh.

"Oh, God—no, no! She's fooling around," Art said.

Hayley didn't think she was. Compelled, she moved forward, and as she did, a horrified scream froze in her throat.

It was Tiffany…the body was Tiffany. Her eyes were still open, but it seemed a river of blood poured from her throat and down her shirt and her jeans…still dripping to the ground. She was strung out with arms and legs fastened to the ropes, like a creature caught in a spider's web…

A creature with a gaping wound at the throat, so deep it almost severed her head from her body.

Hayley had the sense to shove her hand into her jeans for her cell phone.

"Oh, God! It's real this time!" Art breathed. "There, oh God, there…on the ground. There—it's Bobby McGill…on the ground, but not strung up yet, and…"

"We have to get him; he may not be dead."

"Oh, my God, oh, my God—"

"Stop!"

She wasn't sure if it was an instinct or something she had seen in a movie, but Hayley slapped him hard in the face, shoving her phone at him. "Dial 911 and get the others out! 911, now, and be coherent!"

"They won't believe—"

"When they hear the sirens, they will."

"He's still in here. Whoever did this, he's still in here!" Art whimpered.

"Go!" she snapped, and she hit him again. "Dial."

The second hit did it. Art dialed 911 as he walked, and then ran, away. Hayley barely noticed; she was staring ahead, but Bobby seemed to be alone on the ground.

Of course, shadows were everywhere.

It was after midnight in the Barclay Cemetery.

She moved forward, carefully at first, keeping her eyes on Bobby where he lay on the ground and not on Tiffany—where she remained in the air, dripping blood.

She reached Bobby. There was no blood on him; he just lay there, as if he had been hit.

"Bobby! Bobby!" she whispered fervently.

His eyes opened. He stared; then he screamed.

"Bobby, stop! He—whoever—they'll hear!"

"Dead, dead, dead, Tiffany…he slammed me on the head, he wrenched her away. I saw it while I was falling, oh, I saw it, saw him rip up her throat, oh, God, oh, God—"

"Bobby, get up. We need to get out of here. The cops will be here soon, but we must get out now, okay, come on, come on!"

"Out to your cousin's house, can't go that way!" Bobby said, indicating the closest exit. "I think he went that way, came in that way…has his stuff, his rope, whatever, that way. Oh, God, Tiffany!"

"Come on, Bobby, come on!"

Half-leading him, half-carrying him, Hayley got him to move. She headed straight down a path at first, moving fast.

But she sensed something, someone behind her.

She angled in among the tombs, taking a winding path, barely aware of the funerary art now—the angels and saints, guardian dogs, flower urns, and gargoyles.

Bobby started to trip in a nest of weeds; she straightened him and realized they were coming up on the Judith McCafferty family vault and she prayed silently the killer had not come upon the lowly veteran seeking shelter there.

She paused, gasping, leaning against the enclosure there for a minute. Bobby was heavy; he was trying to move, he was just staggering, probably from the knock on his head. She could see blood on him now; a thin trickle that fell from a big knot on his temple.

Bushes were rustling near them.

The killer, she thought, had discovered Bobby gone.

And he was coming.

She eased out carefully, and then she froze. He was there. Right there in front of her, just feet away from the plaque that honored Judith McCafferty.

She didn't know what she had expected. A human being, yes,

160

but one with jagged teeth and drool sliding from his lips. Ugly and frightening in appearance…

He wasn't ugly; he was just a man. Maybe six-feet-even, with brown hair now slightly askew over his forehead, light eyes, and an easy smile that seemed especially heinous as he was dotted in blood. His shirt was flannel; he wore jeans. He was perhaps twenty-something, maybe thirty…and, without the blood, he might have been appealing, charming even…someone Tiffany wouldn't have hesitated to speak with.

He carried a huge knife. The moonlight caught upon it, but it didn't shimmer.

It was covered in Tiffany's blood.

"Well, hello there," he said softly. "So, you're the one who stole chubby-boy from me while I was setting up my trap. Well, that means some really special care for you."

Bobby slumped in her arms.

She wasn't sure if it was his injury, or if he'd just passed out cold.

She stared at the man, the killer in her midst, torn.

Her desire to live was almost overwhelming. And yet somewhere inside she knew if she left Bobby to die, she might not ever be able to really live again.

"Hi there, yourself," she managed. "Sorry I stole fat boy. But, hey, not to worry—the cops are on their way. You might want some more fun, but you don't have time for any more fun. You need to run—now!"

"Leave this lovely cemetery?" he asked her. Then he laughed. "You really think any of your idiot friends managed to call the cops?"

"Yes," she said. "Now, I can see where you doubt that, but… really. You need to run."

He smiled. A deep, deep, self-pleased smile, and he took a step toward her. She backed against the wall of the tomb, unable to hold Bobby. She needed to run, run fast, but…

"Oh, I am going to have so much fun—"

He broke off abruptly. He just stood there; Hayley had heard something, but she didn't know what. Something, a strange sound, as if...

As if he had been the one struck on the head.

She stared at him, barely daring to blink. He suddenly fell forward, and in his place, she saw the shaggy homeless veteran she had spoken with earlier.

"Go! Grab your friend and go," he told her. "I don't know how long he'll be out."

"Thank you! Oh, thank you—"

"Go!"

She nodded and reached down for Bobby, determined she was going to get him to go on a diet. She slapped him—she was getting good at slapping—and he groggily came to.

"We have to go."

He nodded.

He got to his feet. And with him, Hayley ran the best she could. But as she reached the center of the "crossroad" in the cemetery and saw the gate to Marcy's backyard not far ahead, she heard sirens screeching through the air.

Art had managed to dial 911. Help was coming.

And even as she dragged Bobby forward, Tommy and Frank came running out of the yard, taking him from her, yelling that they needed to get in, lock the gate, lock the doors!

They did so, locking the back door just as the first police car ripped into the front yard.

* * *

It turned out their haste at that point hadn't mattered. The police had found their serial killer, Matthew Marin, back at the McCafferty vault, right where he had fallen.

He had been alone.

Hayley wanted to know where her homeless friend had gone. She explained over, and over again that he'd saved her and Bobby by cracking the killer over the head with something.

A piece of a broken gargoyle, fallen from the arch over the McCafferty vault.

There was no sign of anyone else in the cemetery. Police

combed the place—there was no homeless man.

She insisted that there had been. But they were all exhausted and reeling. Parents were on the way; the police had finished with the questioning; the medical examiner had to come, which somehow seemed like an oxymoron to Hayley—coming to a cemetery to do a preliminary examination on a corpse.

The corpse was Tiffany. No, they hadn't been friends. It was still tragic. Everyone had someone who loved them and the murder was horrible.

Marcy seemed to remain in shock. Hayley put blankets around her; she made her hot tea. Mary was oddly calmer now; the worst had passed.

The boys were quiet and thoughtful. She knew Tommy felt as if he had been a failure; he was ashamed of himself. They tried to assure him the shock of the situation had gotten to all of them.

Detectives were on the case, of course, but as time wore on, it was Officer Claymore who stayed with all of them, almost like a mother hen, watching them, helping with anything—coffee, water, tea, pillows, whatever.

"Water," Hayley told Claymore at one point. "The man in the cemetery—I gave him a bottle of water."

"We did find an empty water bottle," Claymore told her, but he still looked at her sadly.

"A real person drank it," she said.

"Maybe one of your friends, maybe Tiffany before…"

"Why can't you believe me? I wish I'd had the courage to stand up against such a monster, but I'm telling you—"

"Maybe there was a man who saved you. Maybe, in all the trauma, you don't know what really happened; Hayley, it doesn't matter. You couldn't have saved Tiffany; others are alive, you're alive!"

She knew that. She should just be grateful.

But she wanted to be grateful to the stranger.

Claymore stayed with Hayley and she sat with him while she waited; her father was on the way. He'd be taking her and Marcy with him back to New Orleans.

New Orleans would be fine now. The City Slicer had come

here. He had been taken away with a serious head injury; he might or might not live. Whether he did or didn't, he'd be safely locked away.

Claymore looked at her, smiling gently. "You're a strong one, Hayley."

She shook her head. "No. I'm not trying to be a pest, but I wish they could find him. I know that everyone questions me on whether he was real or not. I know that he was. Whoever he is, he saved our lives."

"Hayley, I'm afraid if he was there, he's disappeared."

"Well, I wish he hadn't disappeared," Hayley said.

"Are you *absolutely* sure you didn't throw that piece of gargoyle sculpture yourself?"

No, she hadn't. Or had she? Was she losing her mind?

No. She'd seen him, as clear as day. Even by moonlight. He'd been real; her savior had been real. He had spoken to her. She'd left him her bottle of water.

"He's gone now," Claymore said. He offered her a grimace. "Hey. Maybe you were saved by the ghost of Ethan Fray. Anyway, I thank God that with that madman loose here we only lost one; it could have been so much worse."

Hayley just gave him a weak smile. It was still sad; so tragic. Tiffany had been a jerk, but no one deserved what had happened to her.

And still, Claymore was right. It might have been so much worse.

She knew she was grateful to be alive. And eternally grateful to the man—living or dead—who had helped her.

She saw her father's car pulling into the front yard; saw his face—the love, the fear, and the concern.

She ran to be taken into his arms.

She knew only one thing.

Never again. She would never, *ever* be in that cemetery again after midnight.

Because she knew now that, curse or no, nothing good happened there after midnight.

No, nothing good happened after midnight. Even in a garden

of death.

* * *

THE SIXTH DECOY

An *Aristotle "Soc" Socarides*
Short Story

PAUL KEMPRECOS

Elmer Crowell had a sharp eye and a sharper blade. He could take a block of wood and cut away everything that didn't look like a bird, creating a masterpiece that looked as if it could quack, waddle or take flight. Some people say he was the best bird carver in the world.

Ol' Elmer was an authentic American genius, no doubt about it. He was also a humble man from what I've heard. He would have dropped his whittling knife if someone told him the carvings he turned out in his ramshackle shed would bring millions of dollars at auction. And his gentle soul would have been burdened if he knew the desire to possess the things of beauty that sprang from his mind and his hands could lead to bloodshed.

Crowell had been dead more than a half century before the golden, late fall day when I crossed paths with his ghost.

I had spent the morning scrubbing down the deck and cleaning out the galley of my charter fishing boat *Thalassa*. The rods and reels were stowed in the back of my pickup truck. I'd scheduled a forklift to raise the boat out of the water and lower it onto a wooden cradle to be tucked under a plastic blanket for a long winter's nap.

The fishing season had been as good as it gets. Nantucket Sound teemed with schools of hungry striped bass, and every one of them had a death wish. The skies were sunny, the seas gentle and the tips generous.

Hooking fish wasn't something I thought I'd be doing for a living, but as the ancient poet Homer once said, our destiny lies on the knees of the gods.

The Immortal in charge of my fate must have had restless leg syndrome, because I fell off his knee, cutting short my college education in philosophy for a lesson in life, and death, paid for by the U.S. Government in Vietnam.

After mustering out of the Marines, I became a cop and

worked my way up to detective in the Boston Police Department. I was engaged to be married to a beautiful and intelligent woman whose only blemish was her judgment in men.

I might have weathered a corruption scandal at the BPD if I kept true to the code of silence, but I lost my will when my fiancé died in a car accident.

After the funeral I got in my car and headed south from Boston with a bottle of vodka, driving until the road ended at a deserted Cape Cod beach. After a few slugs from the bottle, I fell asleep in the lee of a dune. I woke up to the cries of hovering gulls and the rustle of breaking waves. I staggered off the beach and was sobering up in a coffee shop when I met an old fisherman named Sam. He was looking for a crewman. I said I might be interested in the job.

Either Sam had been desperate, or he'd seen the desperation in my face, because he simply nodded and said, "Finestkind, Cap."

Fishing was tough, but cheaper than stretching out on a headshrinker's couch. More effective, too. Rolling out of bed at three in the morning to catch the tide, commuting twenty miles into the Atlantic Ocean and working a twelve-hour day forces your mind to ignore the little demons of regret tap-dancing in a corner of your brain.

The wind, and sun reflecting off the glassy sea had burned most of the sadness from my face and darkened my skin, hiding the lines of bitterness lurking at the corners of my mouth, even though they were still there. Sam accused me of going native when I went for the pirate look, with a gold earring, and a droopy mustache that decorated my upper lip.

More often than not my mouth was set in a grin as Sam gossiped about townspeople, fish, and the cooking prowess of his wife Mildred. When Sam retired I took over his boat, but couldn't cut it on my own. I cleaned up my act, mostly, and bought a charter fishing boat with a loan from my family.

Every day was an adventure. I had to make sure my clients didn't fall overboard or hook themselves instead of a fish—a state of alertness that had called for a higher degree of sobriety than I was used to. I'd been busy from sunup to sundown, subsisting on

Mountain Dew and peanut butter and jelly sandwiches.

In the off-season I'll earn a few bucks with an occasional commercial diving job. There's not much demand to go underwater during the winter. I've held onto the private detective license I got after leaving the Boston PD, but there's even less call for a PI.

With my boat coming out of the water, and no jobs in the works, money would soon be tight. I set a course across the marina parking lot for a waterfront bistro named Trader Ed's. I was thinking that a frosty beer might help me come up with an idea how to keep the boat loan payments to my family flowing during the lean months. I was about halfway to my bar stool when a silver Mercedes convertible pulled up beside me and braked to a stop. A woman wearing a dark gray pinstripe suit got out from behind the steering wheel.

"Excuse me," she said. "I'm looking for a boat captain named Aristotle Socarides. The harbor master pointed you out."

"That's me," I said. "How can I help you?"

"I'd like to retain your services."

"Sorry," I said, shaking my head. "I'm done fishing for the year. My boat will be out of the water in the next day or so."

"That's not a problem." She removed her sunglasses to reveal coral-colored eyes under arching brows. "My name is Bridget Callahan. I'm an attorney. I know that you're a retired police officer and that in addition to running a charter boat, you sometimes take on cases as a private detective."

"Word gets around."

"Thanks to modern communications technology."

She held up a cellphone. On the small screen was the face I see in the mirror during the morning shave. The earring and mustache of my pirate days were gone. I was now a serious businessman. The photo of me at the wheel of the *Thalassa* was from the business section of the *Cape Cod Times*. The headline was: "Former Cop, Charter Captain Moonlights as Private Eye."

"I mentioned the private eye thing to the reporter as an aside," I said. "I don't have a lot of clients."

"All the better. You'll have time to take a case for a client of mine."

"Depends, Ms. Callahan. I don't do divorce investigations. They're too dangerous."

"Nothing like that. My client would like to recover some valuable property."

She tucked the phone in her pocketbook and handed me a business card. The words embossed on the card in gold told me that Bridget Callahan was a partner in a Boston law firm that had more ethnic names than the United Nations.

"Big legal powerhouse, as I recall," I said. "Making partner couldn't have been easy."

"It wasn't. It took talent, hard work and a willingness to deal with difficult clients."

"Congratulations. Does this case involve one of those difficult clients?"

She nodded.

"Why come to me? My last big case had to do with oyster poachers. Your firm must have staff investigators."

"We do. One of them gave us your name. He said you'd be perfect for this job. That you take unusual cases."

She mentioned a retired detective I knew from the BPD.

"He's a good cop," I said. "What makes this so unusual he can't handle it?"

"The client is a bit eccentric."

"In what way?"

"He's a collector," she said, as if that explained everything.

"Does this eccentric collector have a name?"

"His name is Merriwhether Ruskin the 3rd. He wants to meet you."

"Send him over. I'll be here for at least another hour."

She brushed a curl of silver and auburn hair back from her face as she collected her thoughts. "Mr. Ruskin doesn't get out much. He has, um, peculiar health issues. It's hard to describe. He'd like to talk to you in person."

I glanced up at the clear blue autumn sky. The raw north winds and slag gray clouds of winter seemed far away, but it would be spring before I earned another paycheck. Meanwhile, the boat loan statements would arrive with the regularity of waves breaking

172

on the shore. A job for a rich client would get me through a few months, maybe longer.

Trader Ed's would have to wait. "I'm ready when you are," I said.

"Wonderful," she said. "Let's go for a ride."

Bridget's client lived twenty minutes from the marina on the shores of Nantucket Sound, in a gated community of sprawling silver-shingled houses hidden behind tall hedges that protected their owners' privacy as effectively as castle ramparts. The only things missing were moats and drawbridges. A long gravel driveway led to a two-story mansion surrounded by manicured lawns of impossible green. A white-trimmed porch bordered with hydrangeas ran along the full length of the house.

On the drive over, Bridget talked about growing up in the gritty working class enclave of South Boston, making her Harvard law degree even more impressive. I talked about my roots in the former factory city of Lowell and my stint in the Marines. We were chatting like old friends by the time we got to the house. She snapped the switch into business mode as soon as she parked behind a black Cadillac sedan in the circular driveway.

"This is it," she said.

This was a mega mansion that looked to be at least ten-thousand square feet in size. I had to crane my neck to take in the whole length of the front porch and the three-story height.

"Nice little shack. What does Mr. Ruskin do to pay the lighting and heating bills in this place?"

"He doesn't have to do anything. He comes from an old New England family that made its fortune years ago in labor procurement, energy and pharmaceuticals."

Bridget answered the question with a straight face, but the airy lilt in her voice sent me a different message. "I get it. The skeletons in the closet of many a respectable Yankee family. Slavery, whale butchery and the opium trade, in other words."

"Yes. In other words. Mr. Ruskin currently dabbles in nation-building."

I had to think about that. "Gun running?"

"Guns, missiles and bombs. And people to use them." She cocked her head. "I think I like you, Mr. Socarides."

"Soc. My friends call me Soc."

"Very well, Soc. I answer to Bridge. Shall we?"

The slightly stooped man who answered the front doorbell looked like the greeter in a funeral parlor. Gray hair, grayer face and matching four-button suit, all the color of fog. Speaking softly in an undertaker's voice, he said, "Follow me to the visitation room."

He led the way down a long hallway, opened a door and ushered us into a rectangular space around twenty feet square. Three walls were plain. The fourth was covered by a hanging tapestry that showed a medieval hunting scene of sharp-toothed dogs taking down a unicorn. The fact that the victim was an animal that never existed did little to ease its pain at being ripped apart.

The gray man pressed a wall button. The tapestry slid silently aside to reveal a glass window. He pointed to a leather sofa facing the window, then left us alone.

The lights on the other side of the window went on seconds after we had taken our seats. We were looking into a big room. Directly in front of us was a metal and plastic desk and chair.

The room was a zoo of the dead. Animal heads of every kind festooned the walls. Their eyes were glassy and their expressions far from happy. Antelope, mountain goats, bear, some big cats.

Bridget was silent.

"You've seen this before?" I said.

"Yes," she said. "I think it's kind of creepy."

"Ever wondered what hunters do with the rest of the animal?"

"That's even creepier."

"What is this place?" I asked.

Before she could answer, a door swung open between a pair of tusked boar heads at the far end of the room. A ghost-like apparition entered the room, made its way in our direction, and stopped next to the desk. It wore a hooded white suit, like the kind worn to protect against hazardous materials. A white gauze mask covered the lower part of the face. The feet were encased in fabric pull-ons.

"You're right; Ruskin is eccentric," I murmured.

"That's not him," Bridget said. "That's his valet." She put her finger to her lips, then glanced at a red plastic globe on the wall above the window. "That's a camera and a microphone that is very, very sensitive."

The door opened again. Another man entered, leisurely walked the length of the room, and stood next to the figure in white.

"Ruskin?" I whispered.

Bridget nodded.

I'd pictured Ruskin as a raw-boned flinty-eyed Yankee with a mouth full of horse teeth, mop of unruly hair and a profile that looked as if it had been carved from a granite quarry. Bad call. Ruskin was as bald as a bullet, had a neck that belonged on a cartoon bully and looked as if he chewed steroids as candy. He was wearing a snug T-shirt and shorts that showed off a buff physique. His hands looked as if they could hurt someone.

He said, "Thank you for coming, Mr. Socarides. Please pardon the unusual meeting arrangements. This is a protected environment. I suffer from a number of acute allergies, all potentially life-threatening. It's a rare, progressive affliction particular to the Ruskin family. This gentleman is an employee of mine. The suit he has on is to protect me from outside allergens that would cause a severe reaction."

Despite his mauler looks, Ruskin spoke with a cultured accent that carried echoes of an English boarding school.

"No different than talking over the phone," I said, although it was a lot different. "Ms. Callahan said you need a private detective to recover some valuable property."

"Correct. Tell me, are you familiar with the work of Elmer Crowell?"

"The bird-carver?"

"That's right, although he was much more than that. Allen Elmer Crowell is considered the Father of American Bird Carving. He was the master of a unique form of American art who has been called the Cezanne of waterfowl carvers. Another question. Have you heard of Viktor Orloff?"

I would have to have been stuck in a cave not to know about

Orloff. His face had been in all the papers and on TV. "Sure. Orloff was the financial guy who conned his clients out of millions of dollars. Were you one of them?"

Ruskin's lips twitched in an almost-smile.

"I knew better than to invest money with that slimy old grifter. We had a business arrangement. He had agreed to sell me a preening merganser."

"Come again?"

"It was a carving, part of a set of six half-scale models that Crowell had carved for special friends. I own the other five. I paid Orloff for the decoy, but before I could pick it up he was arrested and put in jail. The judge denied bail because Orloff was a flight risk. His house was sealed with all its contents."

"Including the bird?"

He nodded. "As you probably know, Orloff was convicted and went to prison. He had my money but I didn't have the decoy."

"No chance of getting your money back through legal channels?"

"Unlikely. Even if I could dig it out of whatever black hole Orloff had hidden it in."

"I see the problem. There must have been a long line of people trying to get their investments back."

"I wasn't an investor. I could prove that I owned the bird. I didn't *want* my money. I wanted the decoy to complete the set. An intact set of Crowell decoys would be worth millions, but the bird was desirable to me as a collector."

"Any chance you could get the house unsealed?"

"Yes, under ordinary circumstances, but the house burned down before my lawyers could file a claim. Cause of the fire is still unknown. Then Orloff died in prison of a heart attack, which surprised many people who didn't think he had a heart."

"The decoy?"

"It supposedly went up in flames."

"You sound like you have doubts."

Ruskin whispered to the man in the white suit, who went to a wall cabinet and slid open a glass door. He reached inside and came out with a large plastic cube. He carried it back to Ruskin who set

176

the container on the desk, flipped the lid back, took something out and held it above his head like an offering to the gods.

The carved bird in his hands was around half the size of a real one. Its copper-colored head was turned back in a graceful curve with the long, sharp beak pointed at the tail. The gray and white feathers painted on the wooden wings looked so real they could have riffled in the breeze.

"The preening merganser has everything Crowell was famous for," Ruskin said, lowering his arms. "Attention to detail, accuracy, and beauty."

"You're confusing me, Mr. Ruskin. You said the merganser is missing, presumably burned."

"It *is*."

He turned the bird over and brought it to the window, close enough for me to see the black oval sticker on the bottom. Printed on the sticker in silver letters were the words: "Copy of A. E. Crowell Preening Merganser. Product of China."

"A Chinese rip-off?" I said.

"Yes. A well-done fake, but still a fake."

"What does it have to do with the missing bird?"

"*Every*thing, Mr. Socarides. Only someone with access to the Crowell carving could have made a reproduction that is so accurate in every respect to the original."

"Not sure I understand."

"Ms. Callahan?" Ruskin said.

Bridget explained.

"The reproduction was advertised for sale in a collectors' publication. It was purchased for a hundred and fifty dollars. My firm's investigators traced the bird to a manufacturer in Hunan province, China, which specializes in making wooden reproductions of all kinds. The original piece is scanned digitally and the data fed into computer-guided laser carving machines. Skilled craftsmen do the final detailing."

"That would mean the Chinese had access to the original?"

"Indirectly," she said. "A company in upstate New York does the scanning and transmits the data to China."

Ruskin rejoined the discussion. "And I believe the American

and Chinese companies used the real decoy to manufacture the fake."

"Do you know who contracted for the work?"

"No. Someone dropped the carving off, waited while it was scanned and picked it up. Payment was in cash."

"Could they have copied it from a photo?"

"Yes. But not as accurately as this," Ruskin answered. "Crowell knew bird anatomy from years as a professional hunter, and his birds were accurate in every detail. Moreover, he imbued his models with life. This is good for a fake, but without the hand of the master it is just a prettied up piece of wood."

"Have you been able to run a trace on the magazine ad?"

He put the carving back into the case, closed the cover, and handed the container to his valet, who carried it from the room. Ruskin lowered his athletic body into the swivel chair, leaned his elbows on the desktop and tented his fingers.

"The ad was placed by something called Elmer's Workshop. No email address. Orders went through PayPal. The ad listed a post office box in the town of Harwich, Massachusetts where, coincidentally, Crowell lived and worked."

"Any idea who rents the P.O. Box?"

"No. It's since been closed."

"Any chance the reproduction was made *before* the fire?"

"The records at the New York and Chinese operations show that the reproduction was made after the fire, indicating that the original survived the blaze."

"What would you like me to do, Mr. Ruskin?"

"I believe finding the source of the fake will lead you to my property. You may have some contacts locally. Having city detectives poking around would attract unwanted attention. You understand the need to be discreet, of course."

The job seemed like an uncomplicated one, except for the Orloff angle. The charming old bandit had left suicides, divorces, and bankruptcies in the wake of his stealing spree. And his greedy fingers were still reaching from the grave. Ruskin was unsavory, but he wouldn't be the first client of dubious character that I'd worked for. Any doubts I might have entertained went up in smoke when Bridget handed me a check made out in an amount triple what I would have charged.

I rubbed the check lightly between my thumb and forefinger. "I'll see what I can do."

"Good," Ruskin said. "Let me know as soon as you hear something."

He rose from his chair and, without another word, headed for the door.

Hiring interview was over.

Seconds after Ruskin left the room, the old gray man showed up and pushed the wall button. As the unicorn tapestry slid across the window, he handed me a cardboard box.

"Mr. Ruskin thought this might assist you in your work," he said. "He wants it returned when you are through. It is not to be taken from its protective container."

He led us back the way we came. We stepped onto the porch and the door clicked shut behind us.

"Was that for real?" I asked, taking a breath of fresh air. "That stuff with the allergies?"

"Mr. Ruskin could be a hypochondriac, I suppose, but he's gone through a lot of unnecessary trouble and expense modifying this house if he's simply imagining his allergies. All his food is prepared in accordance with his allergy issues. The butler is a bit of a gossip. He told me Ruskin is allergic to everything you can think of."

"Does he ever leave the house?"

"Not very often, the butler says; only for urgent matters, and when he does he wears a hazmat suit. He usually goes out only at night."

I set the cardboard box down on the porch and peeled off the sealing tape. Then I lifted out the transparent plastic container that held the reproduction decoy Ruskin had shown me. The lid was secured with a padlock.

I jiggled the lock. "Ruskin is very protective of his property."

"Mr. Ruskin is deathly afraid of contaminated things or people coming into the main house. When it comes back this box will go through a clean room where it will be wiped down and sterilized. Anyone coming into the living quarters from the outside has to wear a throw-away suit."

"Like the valet?"

"Yes. His name is Dudley. That's all I know."

I put the bird container into the cardboard box and Bridget gave me a ride back to the marina.

There wasn't much small talk. I was thinking about Ruskin's strange request. She was probably mind-counting her retainer. She dropped me off in the parking lot. When I got out of the car, she handed me a brown, eight-by-ten envelope.

"This report was prepared by our staff investigators. I'll call you at some point to see how things are going. Mr. Ruskin's phone number is inside. He has asked that you contact him directly as the investigation moves along. I'll be in touch."

She put the car into gear and left me standing at about the same spot she stopped my trek to Trader Ed's. This time I made it all the way to a bar stool. My personal alcohol meter was on empty, but I decided to stay sober. Sipping on a club soda with cranberry juice and lime, I went through the papers inside the envelope Bridget had given me.

I skimmed a history of the Crowell decoys and read that his workshop was still standing. It had been moved from the original site to the property of the Harwich Historical Society at Brooks Academy, which was a short drive from where I was sitting.

Seemed like a logical place to start. I tucked the papers back into the envelope, slid off the bar stool and headed for my pickup truck with the cardboard box tucked under my arm.

If you looked at a map of Cape Cod you'd see that the town of Harwich is near where the elbow would be on the peninsula, which curls out into the Atlantic like a bent arm. Harwich is an old seafaring town with Nantucket Sound at its doorstep, so it's no surprise that it once had a school of navigation.

The school was housed in a graceful, 19th century Greek-revival building named Brooks Academy that had been turned into a museum run by the Harwich Historical Society. I parked behind the academy and walked across the parking lot to a low shingled building.

Hanging over a sliding barn door was a black quarter board with the words "A. E. Crowell, Bird Carvings" in white letters. On a shelf above the door to the shop was a carving of a Canada goose. The workshop was closed, but a pleasant, middle-aged woman working in the museum opened it up for me. She accidentally set off an alarm and had to shut it off. I stepped through the entrance to the workshop and into a room with wall displays that told about Crowell and his work.

I tossed a couple of bills into the donation box and said I carved birds for a hobby. I jokingly asked if the Canada goose was a Crowell. She laughed. "It wouldn't be out there if it were."

The museum had a few Crowell decoys in its collection, she said, but nothing like the carvings that were bringing a million dollars.

The shop contained a workbench, wood-working tools, a pot-bellied stove, and what looked like an antique sander and band saw. A half-dozen miniature bird models with minimalist details sat on a shelf.

A carving on a work bench caught my eye. It looked identical to the fake bird sitting in the box on the front seat of my truck. I asked where it came from.

"A bird carver named Mike Murphy donated the reproduction. We had it in the museum where it would be more secure, but since it's only a reproduction someone suggested we put it out here. As you may have noticed, we have a burglar alarm in the barn, but there's nothing in the workshop that's really valuable. Even the tools are borrowed."

I thanked her, put another couple of bills in the donation box and walked back to my truck. I leafed through the folder Bridget had given me and re-read the investigation report where they interviewed someone named Mike Murphy.

A guy with the same name had been the caretaker of the Orloff mansion. He told the investigators he had seen the merganser in Orloff's study. The bird was there when the marshals sealed the place. He assumed it had been burned in the fire. He couldn't say for sure because he got to the fire after the house had burned down. Someone at the fire department had called him.

The investigators left it at that. I might have done the same thing, except for Murphy's donation to the historical society. It suggested that he had more than a casual interest in the preening merganser, fake or not. And I wanted to know why.

Murphy lived in a one-story ranch house in a working-class neighborhood that was probably never fashionable, nor ever would be. I parked in the driveway behind a beige Toyota Camry and knocked on the front door. The stocky man who answered the door stared at me with inquisitive blue eyes.

"Can I help you?" he said.

"My name is Socarides." I pointed to the *Thalassa* logo on my blue polo shirt. "I run a charter boat out of Hyannis. I'm also an ex-Boston cop and I pick up a few bucks on the side as a private investigator for insurance companies. I wonder if I could ask you a few questions about Viktor Orloff."

He gave a weary shake of his head. "Orloff is the gift that keeps on giving. Wish I never heard of the guy."

"From what I know of Orloff, you have a lot of company."

Murphy grinned. He had a wide jaw cradling a mouth filled with white even teeth.

"Come on in," he said with a sigh.

Before I accepted his invitation I went to the truck and got the cardboard box. He gave the carton a curious glance, then ushered me into a living room paneled in knotty pine. He shooed away a long gray-haired cat from a wood-framed chair and told me to take a seat.

He sat on a sofa, picked the cat up and stroked its head.

"This is Gus," he said. "Gotta keep him inside because coyotes come through the yard once in a while, but he doesn't seem to mind being a house cat."

Gus looked as if he didn't mind anything. I glanced around the living room. There was art on every wall, most of it prints of waterfowl. Wooden decoys were scattered on shelves and tables around the room.

"Quite the collection," I said.

"Thanks," Murphy said. Then he crossed his arms and gazed at me. "How can I help you?"

"My client is a rich guy named Ruskin. He bought a Crowell decoy called the preening merganser from Orloff, and paid a lot of money for it, but the law took your former boss off to the clink before he could make good. Then Orloff died in prison and his house burned down, along with the decoy."

Murphy nodded. "I already talked to the cops. What does your client want to know that isn't in the record?"

"He thinks maybe the merganser didn't burn up."

Murphy scoffed. "That's because he didn't see the fire."

"You did?" I remembered from the file that Murphy told the interviewer he lost his job when Orloff was arrested and hadn't been back to the house since it was sealed.

"I didn't see the actual fire," he said, catching himself. "I saw the TV stuff and came by the house later. It went up quick, like it had been set."

"The investigation didn't say anything about arson."

"A guy like Orloff would know people who could do a smart job. Everything had been reduced to cinders. *Everything*. I don't know where Ruskin would get the idea that the bird wasn't burned up."

"From this." I opened the carton, extracted the plastic case, and set it on the coffee table. "Made in China. Ruskin saw an ad in a magazine and ordered this Crowell reproduction."

"Chinese are pretty clever at copying stuff," he said.

"Ruskin says a copy this good could only have been made from the original. Which means the authentic Crowell didn't burn up."

"Orloff could have had the fake made before the real bird got burned."

"That's not what the record shows. The repro was made *after* the house fire."

He shrugged. "Can I take a look?"

I handed him the encased bird model. He ran his fingers over the plastic surface of the box.

"Where did you get this?"

"Probably the same place you got the one you gave to the museum."

"You stopped by the museum?"

I pointed to a photo of the Crowell workshop that hung over the fireplace mantle.

"They moved the decoy to the woodworking barn," I said.

His hand stopped stroking the box. "No kidding. Why did they do that?" He sounded almost startled.

"Thought it would add to the workshop's authenticity. The lady at the museum said you were a bird carver."

"I carved most of the birds in the house, but I'm no Elmer Crowell. I've taken a few courses and have the tools."

"That makes you an expert compared to me. How does the mail order repro stack up against the original?"

"Technically, it's very good, but it doesn't have the soul you'd see in a Crowell. I figured I'd never own a real one, so I bought the reproduction. I must have seen the same ad as Ruskin. I ordered one just to see what they'd done."

He put the box down on the coffee table, which is when I noticed the blurry blue tattoo on his forearm. I could still make out the eagle, globe, and anchor of the Marine insignia. That explained the military buzz cut of his white hair.

"Semper fi," I said, and pushed my sleeve up to show him a smaller version of the EGA on the top of my arm near the shoulder.

"I'll be damned," he said. "Where'd you serve?"

"Up by the border mostly. You?"

"I spent a lot of time around Pleiku. Got a Purple Heart. What about you?"

I shook my head. "Only wounds I got were psychological. Worst one was when a village got shelled after I told everyone they were safe. Now I think real hard before I make a promise."

A knowing smile came to his lips. "Sometimes you don't see the forest for the trees."

Murphy seemed more relaxed. He told me that after the Marines he had married and gone into the postal service like a lot of vets, retired early after his wife got a bad disease that eventually killed her, and started a small company keeping an eye on summer houses when their owners weren't around. That's how he met Orloff, and went to work for him as a full-time caretaker until the time his boss got arrested.

"Did he cheat you?" I asked.

"He owed me a month's salary. They say he only went after big accounts. But he stiffed little guys like me. He even cheated a fund for handicapped kids that didn't know he was handling its money. He was like somebody's uncle, people trusted him right to the end."

"Speaking of the end, this looks like a dead one," I said. I gave him my business card. "Let me know if you remember anything else."

"I'll keep my eyes and ears open. Come by to see me anytime. I don't go out much and stay up late. Maybe I'll hear something from the bird carver crowd. You never know."

"That's right," I said, getting up from the couch to shake hands. "You never do."

The investigative report said the fake decoys had been mailed from Harwich. I stopped by the post office, went up to the desk and asked the postal clerk what the cheapest rate would be for sending out a box like the one in my hands.

"Depends on weight, of course. Parcel post is the cheapest, but it's also the slowest," she said.

"I was talking to a friend named Mike Murphy. He's got a P.O. Box here and sends out a lot of packages, but I don't remember what rate he used."

"We've got a few Murphys. I don't recall anyone doing a lot of shipping."

"I'll talk to him and get back to you."

I remembered that there was more than one post office in town. I got back in my truck and drove a few miles to the pint-sized West Harwich post office. I went through the same routine with the postmistress, and this time I struck gold.

"Mike uses straight parcel post to send boxes that look just like that," she said. "Haven't seen him for a while, though. Not since he closed his box."

"I'll tell Mike you miss seeing him," I said.

Twenty minutes later I drove down the pot-holed dirt driveway that leads to the converted boathouse I call home. *Chez* Socarides was part of an old estate when I bought it and rebuilt it into a year-round residence. The place is still just short of ramshackle, but it's got a million dollar water view of a big bay and distant barrier beach.

My cat Kojak ambushed me as soon as I stepped inside. I poured him some dry food, grabbed the phone, went out on the deck, and tucked the box with the fake bird under a chair. Then I dialed the number for Ruskin. He answered right away.

I told him about my talk with Mike Murphy, his connection with Orloff, and the visit to the post office.

"Do you suspect Murphy knows more about my decoy than what he's saying?"

"Yes, I do, which is why I want to go back to talk to him again."

"When you do, tell him he'd better say where it is, or else."

"Or else what, Mr. Ruskin?"

"I'll leave that to your imagination."

I didn't like what I was imagining. Ruskin was suggesting that I threaten Murphy.

"I don't work that way, Mr. Ruskin."

"Well, I do," he said. "And I have found my methods extremely persuasive."

"I can tear up your check or send it back to you, Mr. Ruskin. Your call."

There was a pause on the other end of the line, then Ruskin laughed.

"No need to do either. You don't think I'm serious. I've decided to offer a reward."

I should have been suspicious at Ruskin's fast turnaround. But I was put off by his conciliatory change of tone.

"It's worth a try. How much of a reward?"

"Oh, I don't know. How about ten thousand dollars?"

"That will definitely get his interest. I'll go see Murphy tomorrow and make the offer."

"Yes," Ruskin said, after a pause. "That should work."

He hung up. I went back into the house and came out onto the deck with a can of Cape Cod Red beer. I popped the top and took a slurp, thinking about my conversation with Ruskin. He said his rash suggestion to lean on Murphy was a joke, but I wasn't so sure. I sipped my beer, letting my mind zone out as the late afternoon sun painted the bay and beach in autumn pastels.

After the beer can went dry, I went back into the house. I pulled together a Greek salad for dinner, then worked a few hours on some paperwork for the charter operation. The figures looked so good that I decided to call my family in the morning to tell them about my accounting.

My eyes were tired from looking at numbers. I had another beer, then I stretched out on the couch and fell asleep. The chirp of my phone woke me up. I groped for the phone, stuck it in my ear and came out with a groggy "hello." I heard a wet gargle on the other end and a second later the phone went dead. The caller ID said Mike Murphy had called. I hit the redial button and got a busy signal.

The phone's time display said it was after midnight.

I splashed cold water on my face and headed for the door.

Murphy's house was in darkness. I parked in the driveway behind the Toyota Camry, went up to the front door and knocked. No answer. I knocked again, louder this time. No one came to the door. I rang the doorbell. No one answered the ring, but something brushed up against my leg.

I looked down at Murphy's cat, Gus. Funny. Murphy said Gus stayed indoors because of the danger from coyotes.

I tried the knob. The door was unlocked. As I opened the door Gus scuttled past me into the darkness. I stepped inside and called Murphy's name. No answer. I tried again. This time I heard a low moan. I felt for the wall switch and flicked on the lights.

Murphy was stretched out on the couch, one arm dangling limply toward the floor. The lower part of his face looked as if it had been smeared with ketchup.

I snatched a phone from the floor next to the couch and called 911. I said I was Mike's neighbor and that he needed medical help.

Then I knelt next to Murphy. I put my face close to his, and said, "You're going to be okay, Mike. Rescue squad is on its way."

He opened his mouth and I got a knot in the pit of my stomach when I saw that his beautiful Irish smile had been ruined. Something or someone had hit him in the jaw with a force powerful enough to knock out his front teeth. There were bruises on his left cheek. I guessed he'd been worked over with a blackjack.

Anger welled in my chest.

"Who did this to you, Mike?"

He tried to talk. The best he could manage was a wet gurgle similar to the one I had heard over the phone. I asked him again. This time he said what sounded like *goats*. I tried again. The same answer. His dazed eyes looked past my shoulder. I turned and saw he had fixed his gaze on the fireplace photo of the Crowell barn. Then, mercifully, he passed out.

I had done all I could for Mike. I didn't want to explain to the police who I was and why I was there. I went outside, got in the pickup, drove half a block and parked where I could see the house. Minutes later, I saw the flashing lights of an ambulance coming down the street.

It was clear to me who'd worked Mike over. Ruskin made no secret that he would crack heads if necessary to get his hands on the decoy. Thanks to my big fat Greek mouth, he knew Murphy held the key to its whereabouts. I had handed Mike on a platter to a dangerous man.

Maybe I should tell the cops what I knew. Lousy idea. Ruskin had the money to hire a team of lawyers who would say that there was no evidence. And Ruskin had the perfect alibi. He never left the house because of his acute allergies, poor guy.

I watched the rescue squad bring Mike out on a stretcher and put him in the ambulance. I followed the ambulance to the hospital emergency entrance. I waited outside a few minutes, but there was nothing I could do while Mike was in the ER, so I drove home.

When I drove up to my house I saw I had company. A black Cadillac was parked in front. I pulled up next to the car and got out of the truck. The caddy's door opened and a tall man emerged from the car. His silver hair was combed back from a broad forehead. He had a sharp-jawed face with a chin like a shelf. He stood there with his arms folded.

"Ruskin sent me," he said. He had an accent that was neither English nor Irish. I figured him for Australian.

The black running suit didn't hide his broad-shouldered physique any better than the white coverall did when I first saw him in the trophy room. "You're his valet. Dudley."

If he was surprised I knew his name he didn't show it. His expression looked as if it had been carved in ice.

"Yeah, that's me. How'd you know my name?"

"Ruskin's butler."

"He talks to much."

"I almost didn't recognize you without your hazmat outfit."

"What? Oh yeah. The spook suit. I put it on after I've been out of the house. Ruskin worries about bringing in bad stuff."

"I'd ask you in for a cup of tea, Dudley, but the place is a mess. What brings you by this time of night?"

"Mr. Ruskin wanted me to tell you you're off the case. He doesn't need you anymore."

"Funny, he didn't say anything about firing me when I talked to him a few hours ago. He suggested I offer a reward to a source who might be able to lead him to the decoy."

"Save your energy. You're done."

"Does that mean he's found the decoy?"

"He knows where it is. You're out of the picture."

"He paid me a lot of money to snoop around."

He sneered. "Don't bother cashing the check. He's going to put a stop payment on it."

"Mr. Ruskin is stiffing me?"

"You didn't find the bird. That was the deal. He had to take matters into his own hands. I'm here to pick up the fake bird."

"It's a fake. What's the hurry?"

"Mr. Ruskin doesn't like other people to have his property."

"People like Mike Murphy?"

"Whaddya talking about?"

"I told Ruskin that Murphy might know where the decoy was. A few hours later someone put him in the hospital."

Dudley smiled. "So?"

"So maybe the police might like to know the connection between your boss and Murphy getting beat up."

"That would be stupid on your part."

"Tell Ruskin I'll drop the duck off tomorrow. Maybe we can talk about my paycheck then. Thanks for coming by, Dud."

Calling him Dud was my first mistake. Turning away from a violent thug was my second. He moved in, and I saw him unfold his arms from across his chest a second before something hard slammed into the side of my head. My legs turned to rubber and I went over like a fallen oak.

I didn't even have the chance to yell, "Timber!"

A groan woke me up, which wasn't surprising because it was coming from my throat.

I pushed myself onto my elbows, then onto my knees, got my legs under me and staggered into the boathouse. The right side of my head was on fire. I had trouble focusing, but I saw that the inside of the house looked as if a bulldozer had gone through it. Only not as neat.

I called Kojak's name and sighed with relief when he sauntered out of the bedroom. I splashed cold water on my face for the second time that night, put ice in a dish towel and held it tenderly against my head where it helped numb the pain.

I went out on the deck. The box was where I left it, behind the chair. The bird container was still inside.

Dudley said his boss knew where to find the Crowell decoy. I stood on the deck and recalled my conversation with Murphy, and the startled look on his face when I told him his gift to the museum had been moved to the barn.

I remembered, too, the way he had stared at the Crowell barn photo when I found him with his teeth smashed in. It was a deliberate gesture that must have caused him some pain but he did it anyhow.

Sometimes you don't see the forest for the trees.

You can get so involved in the details, you can't see the whole picture.

Whether he intended to or not, Mike's wry comment told me he had found a safe place for the original Crowell. Right in the open, where no one would suspect it to be.

It was a short drive from my house to Brooks Academy. The black Cadillac was parked on a side road in the shadow of some trees.

I dug a filleting knife out of its case, snuck over to the car and stuck the blade into all four tires. The car slowly slumped onto its rims. About then, I heard the sound of an alarm from the workshop. Dudley was making his move. I got back in my truck and drove to the police station around a half mile away. I went in the front door and hurried up to the dispatcher's desk.

"I just went by Brooks Academy and heard an alarm going off," I said. "There's a car parked nearby. Looked kinda suspicious."

The dispatcher thanked me, and while she got on the phone I slipped out of the police station. I sat in my truck and saw a cruiser drive away from the station toward the museum. A minute later another patrol car raced past, going in the same direction.

I waited ten minutes, then drove by the museum. Four cruisers with roof lights flashing were parked near the museum. Some police officers were talking to a tall man. He had his back to me so I couldn't see his face, but his hair looked even more silvery in the harsh beam of headlights.

On the way home I stopped by the bank ATM and deposited the check from Ruskin. The transaction went through, thanks to the warning from Dudley.

I was still thinking about Dudley when I stepped into the boathouse. He'd probably say he got drunk and broke into the workshop by mistake. Ruskin would spring him from jail before the arresting officers got off their shifts.

A guy like Dudley doesn't make his way through life without leaving tracks. I called the best tracker I knew. If John Flagg was surprised to hear from me at three o'clock in the morning, he didn't show it. He simply said, "Hello, Soc. Been a while. What's up?"

Flagg seems to function without sleep. Which may have something to do with his job as a troubleshooter for an ultra-secret government unit. We'd met in Vietnam and bonded over our New England heritage. He was a Wampanoag Indian from Martha's Vineyard whose ancestors had been around for thousands of years. My parents came to Massachusetts from the ancient land of Greece.

"Ever heard of a guy named Merriwhether Ruskin the 3rd?"

"Sure. He runs one of the biggest mercenary ops in the world. Bigger than the armies of lots of countries. Why do you ask?"

"He hired me for a job."

"Never figured you for a soldier of fortune, Soc."

"Me neither. That's why I'm no longer on his payroll. Ruskin has another guy working for him. First name is Dudley. Maybe Australian. I know that isn't much."

"Give me a minute. I'll look in the bad guy database." He hung up. I could imagine him tapping into the vast intelligence network he had at his fingertips. He called back after three minutes. "He's an Aussie named Dudley Wormsley, AKA 'The Worm.' Interpol has a pile of warrants out for him."

"I thought as much. Wonder if there is any way to let the FBI know that 'The Worm' is sitting in the Harwich, Massachusetts police station, under arrest for breaking and entering."

"I'll take care of it. When we going fishing?"

"Charter boat's coming out of the water, but there's my dinghy. As you know, I don't bait my hooks."

"Suits me," Flagg said.

I hung up and thought about Mike. He said he'd been attacked by *goats*. Dudley had referred to the hazmat suit as a *spook* suit. Spooks equal ghosts. Which meant plural. Which meant he wasn't alone. Which meant the second ghost was Ruskin.

With Dudley out of the way, Ruskin was an open target, if I could get to him, although that was unlikely given the air-tight fortress he lived in. When I got home I retrieved the box from the deck and brought it inside. I took out the plastic case protecting the merganser, put it on the kitchen table and stared at it, taking in the graceful lines of the bird's body and neck.

"Talk to me," I said.

Early the next morning I got up, poured some coffee into a travel mug, and called Ruskin's number. The butler answered the phone and said his boss was busy. I said that was all right. I merely wanted to drop off Mr. Ruskin's decoy. He said to leave it at the gatehouse.

After hanging up, I got a small leather case out of a duffle bag I keep in my bedroom closet. Inside the case was a full range of lock picks. After a few tries, I popped the padlock and lifted the box lid back on its hinges. I remembered how Ruskin had reached into the box for the carving and lifted it above his head.

Then I took the decoy out of the box, put it in the sink and got a jar of peanut butter out of the refrigerator. I spooned some butter out of the jar onto the bird carving and smeared it all over the wooden feathers with my hands. Then I nestled the glistening fake bird back into its fake nest. I padlocked the box again and carried it out to the truck.

As I drove away from the gatehouse after dropping the box off for Mr. Ruskin, I thought what I'd done was rather sneaky and not very nice. Maybe Ruskin was allergic to peanuts. Maybe not. But I didn't like being played for a patsy, especially when innocent people are hurt. It happened at a village in Vietnam, and with Murphy. It wasn't going to happen again.

I stopped by the hospital on the way home. Mike was out of the ICU and sleeping. The nurse in charge said he was doing fine.

Bridget called me that night to say that she had been trying to reach Ruskin, but his butler said he wasn't available. She said she would keep me posted. I didn't know what Ruskin was allergic to when I returned his decoy. Maybe I just got lucky.

Mike got out of the hospital a few days later. I drove him home and checked in on him while he healed and popped painkillers. When I asked why he had called me instead of 911, he said it was because Marines stick together.

Once he was able to talk at length we discussed what to do about the Crowell decoy.

He confessed that he'd taken it from the Orloff mansion for payment of back wages. When he found out the bird was worth maybe a million dollars, he knew he couldn't sell it. He read about Chinese reproductions somewhere and went into the fake decoy business for himself. He had the original scanned in New York and made in China. He sold out the first batch except for the one he kept. But he started to get nervous about attracting attention to himself and wanted the Crowell bird out of the house. He hid it in plain sight at the historical society museum, never figuring they'd put it in the Crowell barn.

"Legally speaking, the bird belongs to Ruskin," I said. "He told me that he paid Orloff for the merganser, but I have only his word for that. It's quite possible no money exchanged hands, which means that the sale never went through. In that case, Orloff was still the owner. Did he have any heirs?"

"None that I know of. He left lots of folks holding the bag. Including me. But if I admit I took it from the house, I could get into trouble."

Mike was right. He'd removed the bird without permission. His sticky fingers saved the carving, but it was still grand larceny. If the debtors heard about the bird, they'd want it put up for auction so they could get a cut, no matter how small.

I thought about it for a minute. "You mentioned a fund for handicapped children that Orloff cheated," I said.

"Big time. They'll never recover."

"They might," I said. "Suppose we contact their lawyers and say we have the bird. Tell them that Orloff felt remorse over cheating the fund, and he wanted to donate proceeds from the sale of the Crowell at auction."

"Great, but how does that explain me having the bird?"

"You're a bird carver. Orloff let you take the bird so you could prepare a prospectus at auction. When he went to jail and the house was sealed, you didn't know what to do. Orloff called and told you he wanted to move ahead with the sale, then he died."

"That old bastard never said that. Never would."

"Maybe, but that's the way you understood it. It makes him look good, and helps a bunch of kids who need it. Splitting it among the debtors would only make the lawyers rich. Look at it this way: the Marines have landed and the situation is well in hand. Semper fi."

Mike shook my hand with a lobster grip.

"Semper fi."

Mike's new implants look like the real thing. They should. I used Ruskin's check to help pay for them. It was the least I could do, but left me with nothing for the boat loan. I was drowning my sorrows in a beer at Trader Ed's one night when another boat captain offered me a job crewing on a charter boat in the Florida Keys. I said I'd take it. The timing was good. Bridget called the other day to let me know the Ruskin job was permanently off.

Sometimes I wonder what Crowell would have made of the whole affair. He'd be puzzled at all the fuss over one of his birds, but I think he'd be pleased how things turned out with the preening merganser.

The knees of the gods, as Homer said.

Or my partner Sam used to say after a good day of fishing: "Finestkind, Cap."

* * *

A CREATIVE DEFENSE

JEFFERY DEAVER

She hadn't wanted to go.

Though she was an academic at a school with a "fine fine-arts program," as she joked, classical music wasn't really Beth Tollner's thing.

Pop, sure. Jazz. Even soft rap, a phrase she coined herself.

Musicals, of course.

Wicked, In the Heights, Hamilton....

She and Robert were, after all, only in their late twenties. Wasn't classical for fogies?

Then she'd reflected: That wasn't fair to those of middling age. Most classical was just boring.

But Robert had been given a couple of tickets from one of the partners at the firm where he was a young associate, and he thought it would be political to attend and report back to his boss how much they liked the performance.

Beth had thought: What the hell? Why not get a little culture?

And nothing wrong with dressing up a bit more than you would to see Van Halen or Lady Gaga. She pinned her blonde hair up and picked a black pant suit—Robert wore navy, lawyer attire *sans* tie. Quite the handsome couple, she thought, catching a glimpse of themselves in the mirror.

The venue was an old monastery on the edge of their small town, Westfield, Connecticut. The place had been renovated but maintained much of the gothic atmosphere it would have had when it housed a functioning religious order. Much of the chill, too; the November cold seeped in through a dozen crevices. Beth supposed that the music she and Robert were about to listen to had echoed around these stone walls long, long ago; the Salem Chamber Players, out of Massachusetts, would be playing music from the 18th and 19th centuries tonight.

The half dozen musicians were dressed in dark slacks or skirts and white shirts, and were led by a lean, balding conductor in a black suit. The concert began at eight and they worked through some pieces that were vaguely familiar and some that were not. Having had a glass of wine before they left, and another at intermission, she struggled to stay awake. (Robert made the wise choice of going with coffee.)

But there was no risk of nodding off during the last piece on the program.

The *Midnight Sonatina*, the notes reported, was rarely performed, the Salem Players being perhaps the only group in the country that had the piece in its repertoire.

Beth was curious why.

She soon learned.

The conductor gestured to the lead violinist, an attractive young woman with a tangle of red hair, which sported a distinctive white streak. She rose and, with understated accompaniment from the others, launched into the lightning fast piece. It was wildly complicated, richly melodic at times, eerily discordant at others. Beth, Robert—the whole audience—sat frozen in place, mesmerized during the five or six minute performance.

"My," she found herself whispering. Robert's handsome face was frozen, his mouth agape. No wonder it wasn't played much; few would have the technical skill to master it.

When they finished, the sultry violinist, her narrow face dotted with sweat, strands of hair plastered to her forehead and cheeks, stood with her eyes closed, breathing hard from the effort.

The audience rose to their feet and applauded hard and cheered and fired off dozens of "Bravas!"

As they drove home, on the dark hilly country roads, twice their Acura sedan strayed onto the shoulder. The night was windy but that didn't seem to be the problem for the low-slung vehicle. The third time the car lurched to the side Beth glanced at her husband. He seemed lost in thought.

"Honey?" she asked.

At first he didn't appear to hear her. He kept staring straight ahead, at the wisps of ghostly fog which the car sped through.

Beth repeated, "Honey? Something wrong?"

He blinked. "Fine. Maybe a little tired is all." Robert's firm was miles from their home and he had to be awake at 5:30 or so to beat rush-hour traffic.

"I'll drive."

"No, I'm fine. Really."

But farther down the road he nearly missed a turn.

"Robert!"

He blinked, gasped and skidded the car to a stop. They'd narrowly missed slamming into a road sign.

"What happened?" she asked urgently. "You fall asleep?"

"I… No…. I don't know. It's too foggy. And…I zoned out, or something."

"Zoned out?"

He shrugged, nodded at the wheel. "Maybe you better."

They swapped places and in twenty uneventful minutes they were home.

Beth parked in the driveway and they walked into the house. Robert almost seemed to be sleepwalking.

"Are you sick?" she asked.

He looked at her with a blank expression.

"Robert. Are you sick?"

"I'm going to bed."

He didn't shower or brush his teeth. He just changed into his pajamas and lay down on the bed, not even climbing under the blankets. He stared at the ceiling. His body, Beth noted, didn't seem relaxed.

"The flu?" she asked.

"What?"

"You have a bug or something?" She felt his forehead. He was chill to the touch.

But then suddenly he grew relaxed. He squinted and seemed to notice his wife sitting on the bedside. "Weird dream," he said, then smiled, rolled over and fell asleep in seconds.

Dream? Beth thought. Hadn't he been wide awake?

* * *

At three a.m. Beth was startled awake. What? A noise, a motion?

She looked over at Robert's side of the bed. He wasn't there.

Alarmed, thinking about his odd behavior, she rose, pulled on her bathrobe and walked into the hallway. There she paused and listened. A faint humming was coming from downstairs. She continued to the first floor and there she found her husband, in the living room, staring out the window. There wasn't much to see, just the neighbors' house, the Altman's place, fifty feet away. They were the neighbors from hell; Robert and Fred had been feuding for years over petty but irritating things. Beth tried to remain above it, but she joined the fray occasionally. Sandra could be an utter bitch.

Robert was staring at the glaring yellow clapboard (the color being one of the sources of dispute; Robert was sure they'd picked the hue just to spite the Tollners). Robert was humming. The sound was very quiet. Four notes over and over again. If they were from a tune, she didn't know what it might be.

Was he asleep?

What was that rule? Never wake somebody up when they are sleepwalking?

But she was alarmed. "Robert? Honey?"

No response.

"Honey? Is that a song? What is it?"

Maybe from an ad? From a movie? If so, and she could learn the name, maybe she could get through to him.

She got her phone and ran her name-that-tune app. It returned no titles, other than the pitch of the notes: *A-D-D-E.*

"Robert?"

Eventually the humming stopped but he kept staring out the window. She walked up to him and put her arm around his shoulder. His muscles were hard as a bag of concrete, his skin still chill. She pulled her hand away, alarmed.

The humming resumed.

At six a.m. she called the ambulance.

* * *

"He's responsive now. Vitals are good. MRI and CT are normal. To be honest, we have no diagnosis at this point." The psychiatrist told her this as he sat across from Beth in the Westfield Hospital waiting room.

A slow-speaking man, with a faintly Southern accent, he continued, "Robert was in some kind of a fugue state. Like he was hypnotized." The lean doctor, in a well-worn light blue jacket, consulted a chart. "I was just speaking to him earlier and he said he hasn't been taking any drugs. Nothing showed up in the preliminary bloodwork but we've sent samples to New Haven for some other tests. I wanted to ask you."

"No, nothing," she said, her voice ragged—from exhaustion.

"Has he ever taken any psychedelics?"

"Lord, no." Neither of them had done anything more than smoke a little pot and not for a year or so.

He jotted a note then looked up. "Anything unusual happen last night, prior to the event? Traumatic?"

"We went to a concert." She told the doctor about the drive home. How he "zoned out."

Another look at the chart. "And no occurrences in the past like this?"

She shook her head.

"Has he ever seen a psychiatrist before?"

Her pause got the man's attention and he cocked his head.

"We've been to a counselor, the two of us. He has…Robert has some anger issues. We worked it out. But, no, he's never seen a doctor for anything like this."

She thought he'd leap on that fact but he wasn't interested. Anger was boring maybe, compared with Robert's bizarre fugue state.

"Do you have any idea what the humming was about?" he asked.

"No."

Since Robert was not considered a danger to himself or anyone else and seemed fully cognizant, the doctor said he could go home. If anything troubling was revealed in the new bloodwork someone would call.

To her relief, Robert recognized her instantly; she wasn't sure he would. He rose from the wheelchair and hugged her hard.

He said, "Hey… Don't know what happened. Just…too much crap at work. Too long hours."

The partners worked the younger lawyers half to death, especially those like Robert, who represented some massive hedge funds based in the state.

They walked to the car. On the drive home he pulled down the visor to examine his face and finger-brushed his mussed, brown hair.

The radio was on, music softly playing. Robert shut it off. An awkward silence descended.

"Nice place, the hospital," he said.

"It is. Staff's friendly."

"Décor's good."

"Landscaping's nice. Are you hungry?"

He thought for a moment. "No."

There followed a dozen other deflecting questions and answers.

"I don't think you should go in to work today."

"No. I shouldn't."

Beth was relieved; she'd been worried that he'd insist.

"You don't remember last night?"

"Well, the first part of the concert. Not the last. And not driving home." A frown. "Did I drive?"

"I did." She didn't want to mention the near accident.

He took this in and fell silent.

Soon, they arrived and pulled into the driveway. She climbed out and stepped around the car to open the door for him.

But he lifted a hand, gave a laugh and said, "I'm good, m'lady," in a bizarre British accent.

He got out and hugged her. Robert was back. This was confirmed when he shot a scowl at the Altman's house. The color was the gaudiest shade of yellow you could imagine. "Bile," he called it. "I'm writing another letter."

The last letter of complaint to the homeowners' association had infuriated the Altmans, and shortly afterward the Tollners found dog crap dotting their front yard. Their neighbors owned a pit-bull mix that was as obnoxious as its owners.

Inside, he went to the bedroom and changed into jeans and a

gray UConn sweatshirt.

Robert had apparently changed his mind about his appetite and decided to eat something.

"I'm totally famished." He devoured half of the tuna salad sandwich she made, then the other. Sipped coffee.

She said, "I should get to the school for about an hour. Are you...?"

"Oh, sure, honey. I'll be fine. Give me a chance to catch up on my games."

He certainly did love video games. He'd had to give them up almost entirely, though, because of the long hours at work.

She hugged him again, and he kissed the top of her head. She could smell his sweat; it was strong. He didn't seem to notice his own odor. She thought about telling him a shower might make him feel better but wasn't sure what his reaction would be.

* * *

Beth drove to her office at the private college where she was a professor of sociology. She finished a departmental report and graded a dozen papers. These tasks took longer than they should have because her mind kept jumping back to last night: Seeing her husband's glazed face. Feeling his taut muscles and cold skin.

Zoned out...

It was then that the doctor's question about drugs came back to her. No, he didn't do recreational drugs and, at the moment, no prescription ones.

But what if he *had* ingested something that affected him? After all, the final blood workup wasn't in yet. Food? They'd had the same casserole at dinner and Beth was fine, but at the intermission of the concert, he'd had that coffee with milk. He'd eaten something too. Cookies, she believed. And they were homemade, baked by the friends of the chamber group or of the performing arts venue. Could the milk or the pastry have been tainted?

Beth pulled her laptop closer, went online and looked up the local newspaper, to see if anyone else had gotten sick after the venue.

No, no one had been. Or, if so, the malady hadn't made the

news.

Her search had also turned up a review of the concert. It was favorable and, as she expected, the notice centered on the *Midnight Sonatina*, the mesmerizing violin solo.

The reviewer wrote that he had never heard of the piece but, upon research, learned several things: one, it was so difficult to play that it was rarely performed—as the program notes had reported; and, two, the piece had a connection to several crimes. A link sent her to another article: "The Curse of the *Midnight Sonatina*."

She gave a soft laugh and went to the site on which the story was posted, a history journal she'd never heard of.

The first of the crimes surrounding the Midnight *involved the creator of the piece himself.*

Italian composer Luigi Scavello, 1801-1842, was known to be eccentric and would wander by himself through the hills outside of Florence, disappearing for days at a time. It was then that he did much of his composing. He said the earth and animals and sky and rocks gave him the inspiration for the songs he wrote. He usually returned from his hiking wild-eyed and disheveled. He studied with the famed Paganini, whose difficult compositions he would have no trouble performing— one of the master's few students to be able to summon the skills required.

But Scavello soon quit his studies and grew more and more reclusive.

In 1841, he vanished for three days and when he emerged he reported that he'd spent the time in a cave in the Tuscan hills. It was there that he'd written what he considered his masterpiece, Sonatina in E Minor for Violin *(the "*Midnight*"). He'd composed the piece over the course of a single day and night, he claimed. Fellow musicians didn't know what to make of the sonatina, as it was well beyond the ability of most violinists.*

The first performance was a chamber concert in a church near Chianti. Scavello played the piece himself. By all accounts, the sonatina mesmerized the audience—moving them to tears in some instances, to shock in others. A few actually collapsed with emotion.

A week after the performance Scavello went mad and murdered a local priest, then cut his own throat, bleeding to death in the middle of the square outside the church.

All word of the Midnight Sonatina *was lost and there's no record of its having been played again, until decades later, when a British musicologist doing research in Italy discovered the piece. The professor returned to London, where a chamber group there added the sonatina to their repertoire. It was at one of their concerts that the sonatina was associated with yet another horrific crime.*

Beth was interrupted when her phone hummed. She glanced at the number.

She frowned. It was the mobile of Sandra Altman, from next door.

Neighbors from hell...

"Sandra."

"Look, I don't know what your husband's up to but you better tell him to stop it."

"What're you talking about?" Beth asked.

"He's at your living room window. He's been there for an hour, staring at us. Glaring. It's very upsetting. We tried calling the house but he's not picking up. If he doesn't stop, Fred's going to call the police."

Beth's heart sank. Robert had relapsed into his odd behavior of last night.

She said stiffly, "He hasn't been feeling well."

"Feeling well? He's sick, all right. Sick in the head. I've always known it."

Coming from the woman who would steal their newspaper and refused to trim trees whose branches fell onto their property.

Not to mention dog shit.

"I'll give him a call. And—"

But then the woman was talking to someone else; her husband, Beth supposed. "Where are you going?"

"To tell him to stop," came the man's distant voice.

Then there was a pause. "Fred, no! He's in the front yard. He's got a knife! Get back here. Fred? Now!"

Beth heard a shrill scream. The line went silent.

* * *

The police were at the house when she arrived. Beth skidded the car to a stop, half in the driveway, half on the lawn.

Two men—both pale-complexioned, one round, the other tall and balding—were on her doorstep. They wore nearly identical suits, navy blue, and white shirts. Gold badges rested on their belts. She jogged to them, breathless from the run and breathless from the shock of what she'd learned had happened.

She stared at the Altman house. The medical examiner was wheeling one body out. That would be Sandra's; Fred had been slashed to death in the front yard.

Crying softly, Beth asked the stocky detective where her husband was, and how was he?

"He's in custody, Mrs. Tollner. We found him walking down the street, about three blocks from here."

"He was holding the knife. The murder weapon."

She dabbed her eyes and thought of the people she'd have to notify: her parents, Robert's. His sister, too, and her husband, Joanne and Edward, the only relatives who lived nearby.

"Is he—was he hurt when you arrested him?"

"No," the tall officer said. "Looks like, according to the arresting officers, it was like he was sleepwalking. Muttering and humming to himself. He was read his rights but he didn't acknowledge understanding them."

His partner: "Mrs. Tollner, does your husband have any history of mental illness?"

Through her mind streamed images of the incident from last night, her discussion with the psychiatrist. It occurred to her that maybe she shouldn't be answering their questions. Wasn't there something about a privilege between husbands and wives?

"I think I'll talk to our attorney," Beth said evenly.

"This is a very serious crime," the heavy-set officer said.

Her look was essentially: And you need to remind me why?

"It'll go a long way for Robert, if we get cooperation. From *all* parties." That was from his partner.

Was this good cop/bad cop? Beth knew all about that; she had watched many of the true-crime TV shows.

"I'm going to talk to a lawyer." She looked defiantly from one to the other.

"That's your right." This was from the one she thought was the bad cop. Maybe they had swapped parts.

When they were gone, she went inside and stepped into the kitchen to make some coffee. She stopped abruptly. Robert had removed four sharp knives from the wooden blocks and arranged them carefully on the green granite island. They appeared to make a pattern but she couldn't find any meaning.

She started to put them away but then thought maybe the police would get a warrant or ask her if she'd moved anything. She left the blades where they were.

In the spacious living room, Beth dropped onto the couch and placed a call to a man named Julian Kramer. He was a criminal lawyer with one of the biggest firms in southern Connecticut, and she'd been given his name by Robert's sister, Joanne, who like her brother was also an attorney, though the woman did no criminal work.

Kramer had been expecting the call. He listened patiently and told her his fee structure, which she instantly agreed to. He asked a number of questions. She sifted his words for clues as to whether or not he was hopeful for Robert, but she spotted no tell.

Then thought to herself: given the facts, how much hope could he offer?

Was there any doubt her husband had stabbed to death two people he despised?

"Give me the names of the detectives," the lawyer said. I'll call and see what the booking plans are. If he's in an unstable mental state, there'll be a different set of procedures."

She did this then hesitated. What did she want to say? Do your best. Please help. You have to understand he'd never do anything like this.

Except he had.

"Anything else, Mrs. Tollner?"

"Does it look hopeless?"

Now the lawyer was the one pausing. "We'll probably need to be creative in crafting our defense. I'll be in touch."

Creative. What did that mean?

She then took a deep breath and began making calls to the family.

They were, of course, difficult—impossible conversations, largely because she had no answers to the rapid fire and frantic questions friends and family and co-workers of Robert asked.

She then called the jail and learned that Robert was still in the prison hospital. He remained unresponsive. He wasn't able to talk to anyone. He was, however, still compulsively humming.

Beth disconnected and slumped on the couch. A moment later she sat up, as if jolted from a nightmare.

She'd been thinking of the four notes Robert had been humming in repetition. She realized she'd gotten the order of them wrong, starting with what would have been the third, not the first note. Not A-D-D-E.

What Robert was really humming was "D-E-A-D."

* * *

The bell rang and Beth opened the door to admit Joanne Post.

In the driveway her husband, Edward, a lean, handsome man of around forty, sat in his work truck, *JP Designs* stenciled on the side. He owned a landscaping company.

Beth waved to him. The couples had been close for the past year, ever since Joanne and Ed had moved here from Virginia. He waved back.

She closed the door and the two women walked into the living room. Robert's sister was a tall, lanky woman, a lawyer for a firm that did environmental law. Her salt and pepper hair was cropped short. Joanne was an avid runner and today she wore orange athletic shoes, as well as jeans and a navy sweatshirt.

The women embraced and Joanne wiped a tear with her index finger.

Beth adjusted a log in the fireplace—she'd found fires comforted her at frantic times like this. Joanne sat on the couch next to the crackling blaze and warmed her hands. Beth brought in mugs of coffee.

The sister asked, "How is he?"

"The doctor, from the jail? He called. He was nicer than I thought he'd be, I mean, he's also a guard, when you think about it. He said Robert's still in some kind of fugue state. He told me they don't use the word 'breakdown' anymore—it's not specific enough—but it fits in Robert's case since there's no particular category they can put him in.

"What do you know about the insanity defense?"

"I do real estate," Joanne said, shrugging.

"But from law school? You must remember something."

Joanne looked off. "I think it's that you can't be tried if you didn't understand the nature of what you did. Or if you can't participate in your defense."

She added there would be motions for a mental evaluation. A doctor picked by them, one picked by the prosecution, and a judge-appointed third psychiatrist. This would take some time. "Are you thinking of insanity for Robert?"

"This is going to sound strange at first, but hear me out."

She told Robert's sister about the curse of the *Midnight Sonatina*—the composer's murder of the priest and his suicide.

She then went online and found the article she'd been reading earlier, when she got the call from Sandra Altman. The women sat next to each other and read:

> *The professor returned to London, where a chamber group there added the* Midnight Sonatina *to their repertoire. It was at one of their concerts that the sonatina was associated with yet another horrific crime.*
>
> *After the premier performance, one of the concert goers, upon returning home, began acting strangely: it was reported that the man simply stared at his wife for minutes on end and when, unnerved, she summoned friends over, the man went into a rage and he stabbed her to death. He'd complained to*

friends earlier that he suspected his wife was having an affair.

The man's lawyer presented a novel defense to the court—that he'd been driven momentarily mad by the sonatina. Upon examining him, physicians disagreed over the diagnosis. Some reported that he was indeed moved to temporary madness by the piece, while others asserted that he was feigning.

A renowned physician testified on his behalf, stating that if music has the power to move us to joy and sorrow, why cannot a piece move us to rage and even murder—beyond our control?

The judge found him guilty, but, because the doctor's argument was persuasive, spared the defendant from hanging.

Joanne said, "What, claim that he was possessed by a piece of music? You know that can't happen."

Beth was an academic and approached life according to the scientific method. Of course there was no such thing as a curse. The supernatural did not exist.

But she said, "Hypnosis is real. What if, instead of a swinging watch, a string of notes could put you under, let you act out your impulses?"

"Claiming he was hypnotized into delusion?"

Beth nodded and added about his humming the four notes. What they spelled.

"Jesus," Joanne whispered.

"The lawyer said we needed a creative defense."

"That's pretty damn creative." Joanne thought for a moment. "Maybe there *is* some basis for it. What if it happened other times? Somebody hearing music and losing their mind temporarily."

"If it *is* temporary." Beth choked on a sob.

Joanne took her hand. "He'll get better. We'll get the best doctors we can."

Beth wiped the tears. "Let's get to work."

Sitting, hunched forward at the glass-topped coffee table, each looked over her own laptop.

"First," Beth said, "let's go the broadest we can: Sound inducing impulsive behavior. Not necessarily music."

It was possible, they learned, to, yes, induce hypnosis via sounds, though it seemed generally to be true, too, that being hypnotized could not turn otherwise upstanding people into criminals.

"It's something," Joanne said. She jotted references and websites on a legal pad. "What about military marches?" she suggested.

Nothing, though, suggested that martial music affected the psychology of soldiers, other than inspiring them into battle.

Discouraging.

Joanne kept searching. "Here's a YouTube video of the Salem Players. I want to see if anybody commented on it." The piece played softly. Given the computer's tiny speakers, it didn't sound nearly as eerie as it had last night.

"And?" Beth asked.

"Nothing helpful. Just like 'Cool Piece.' 'Where are you playing next?' 'Love your hair!' Stuff like that."

Beth watched the energetic performance for a moment and then had a thought. She placed a call to the venue and learned the musicians were at rehearsal, but were presently on a break. She was put through to the conductor.

"Hello?"

Beth identified herself and said, "I was at the concert last night. First, what an incredible performance."

"Why, thank you, Mrs. Tollner," the man said in his lilting British accent. He added modestly, "The hall is acoustically marvelous. How can I help you?"

"I'm a professor and I'm doing some research."

Both were true, in a way.

"I'm curious about the *Midnight Sonatina.*"

"Yes?"

"Do you know if anyone in the audience has ever had an odd reaction to the music?"

"Odd reaction… You mean those stories that it drove people mad?"

"Yes."

He chuckled. "Urban legend. It's probably driven some *violinists* mad when they tried to play it but that's because it's the

213

most difficult violin piece that's ever existed."

"But no one in the audience?"

"Never."

She thanked him and hung up.

The two women kept up the work at their respective laptops for another half hour before Joanne stretched and looked at her watch. It was nearly six in the evening. "You have any wine? I need something stronger than coffee."

"Sure. Fridge if you want white, cupboard to the left if you want red."

"You want some?"

"Not now." Beth returned to the computer and kept at the search.

Nothing…

But then she had a hit.

> *Murder at Boston Concert*
> *Man in Audience Goes Berserk*
> *Italian Piece Claimed to Send Him into Bloody Frenzy*

She'd missed the article in her earlier searches because the piece was not named, described merely as an Italian sonatina. It was the *Midnight*, though, because the composer was Luigi Scavello and the date of the composition was the same.

She read the article quickly. It was published in a Boston newspaper in 1923. Following a concert in a music college south of the Charles River, a member of the audience suddenly began ranting at a couple with whom he and his wife had attended the performance. He then drew a knife and stabbed the husband to death. He'd had no history of criminal activity, though the two men had quarreled over a business loan not long before.

The defendant's solicitor came up with a novel legal claim that he had grown temporarily deranged because of the piece of music.

> *The poor man's nature was given to sensitivity and listening to the hypnotic piece of music, the* Midnight Sonatina, *stole him of reason and caused him to act on his most base impulse.*

In short, my client was not himself.

The lawyer admitted that, yes, it was an extraordinary claim, but the medical testimony established that what had once been an intelligent functioning man was reduced to an animalistic state.

She called to Joanne: "I've got another one. And listen to this. The judge ruled the man was *not guilty* by reason of insanity. He was committed to a home and didn't have to go to prison."

So there was yet another instance of precedence for the argument for insanity.

A creative defense….

A moment later Beth heard a soft sound behind her.

Humming.

Gasping, Beth turned and, in shock, stared at Joanne, who was gazing at her sister-in-law. Her face had the same eerie, blank expression as Robert's.

And the humming, too, was the same as earlier, the notes her husband had hummed over and over again.

The notes that spelled *D-E-A-D*.

Beth realized that Joanne had just listened to the *Midnight Sonatina* on YouTube. And she, like her brother, had also been possessed by the bewitching tune.

Joanne grabbed Beth's hair and lifted the knife, the longest and sharpest of those that had been sitting on the island in the kitchen.

* * *

Edward Post, Joanne's husband, was finishing the interview with the detectives from the Westfield Police Department.

The town was generally idyllic and free of crime—*serious* crime, at least, so two knife-wielding psychotic attackers was a rarity, to put it mildly.

The odds that they'd be brother and sister? Nearly impossible.

But here they were.

The man stepped outside, stretched and walked to his Jeep. He climbed in and drove to his company, JP Designs. It was one of the more successful landscaping companies in South Central Connecticut.

In the back of the east lot was a large trailer, a nice one. Post would occasionally stay here if the hours were long and he didn't feel like tackling the long drive home.

He parked and then walked inside.

Beth Tollner walked forward and the two embraced.

They sat down on the couch. They were here because reporters were mobbing their houses.

"You can stay here for the time being." He nodded to a second bedroom in the rear of the trailer.

"I think I will. Thanks."

"How's Joanne?" Beth asked.

Edward answered, "Broken arm. Concussion. She's in the same prison hospital as Robert."

As Joanne had lifted the knife, Beth had reached behind her and grabbed the fireplace poker. She'd struck her sister-in-law a half-dozen times, and the woman collapsed on the floor. She remained conscious—and humming eerily—but didn't have the energy to rise and renew her attack.

"The physical stuff isn't that bad. But she's still in that weird state. Like sleepwalking."

Beth said, "I figured out the knives, the pattern."

"That he left on the kitchen island?"

"Right. Robert arranged them like they were notes on a musical staff. D-E-A-D."

Edward shook his head.

"That two people flew into murderous rages after listening to the music? That'll help the defense." She looked over at her brother-in-law. "I'll meet our lawyer tomorrow. I'm sure he can recommend somebody to represent Joanne. He can't handle her case too. There'd be a conflict."

"She did try to kill you, after all."

"No, she didn't. It was somebody—*something*—else." Beth nodded at her computer. "I want to give the lawyers as much information as we can about the sonatina."

She returned to the article she'd been reading—the account of the Boston concert attack in 1923.

The conductor of the chamber group, Sebastiano Matta, took strong umbrage at the suggestion that the piece of music they had played—everyone agreed, with consummate skill— was in any way responsible for the tragic event. "Music cannot cause any such mischief. We will not allow anyone to spread scandalous rumors about Señor Scavello's marvelous sonatina. No one will ever stop us from performing the piece."

Beth clicked forward and came to the last page.

A short scream shot from her mouth.

Edward spun and approached.

"No," Beth whispered.

"What is it? Tell me."

"They're the same," she whispered.

"Who?"

Beth was looking at a photograph of Matta, the conductor of the chamber group in Boston, where the murder had occurred in 1923. And beside him, the beautiful young violinist who'd performed the *Midnight Sonatina* that night.

They were identical to the conductor and principal violinist of the Salem Chamber Players from the concert yesterday evening.

Identical, right down to a scar on the conductor's jaw and a streak of white in the young woman's hair.

How could this be?

Then, with a shock, she remembered that she'd called the conductor, saying she was researching any odd incidents surrounding the sonatina. And given her name.

No one will ever stop us from performing the piece...

Just then Edward's phone rang. He glanced at the screen—she could see it read No Caller ID—and hit answer, held the unit up to his ear. "Hello?"

He frowned and glanced at Beth. "Odd. Nobody's there. Just some music."

The chill shot through her body like an electrical jolt. She whispered: "Put it on speaker."

He did, and a whirlwind of notes, like knives hissing through the air—the opening measures of the *Midnight Sonatina*—filled the trailer.

* * *

AFTER MIDNIGHT

Cinderella Then and Now

RHYS BOWEN

The palace clock was chiming midnight as she ran down the steps. Behind her she heard the prince calling, "Wait! Lovely maiden, please wait. Don't go. I don't even know your name." But she did not turn back, she kept on running. One of the glass slippers fell off on the steps, making her almost trip and fall, but she wrenched off the other one and kept going, barefoot. Ahead of her she could see the sparkle of the glass coach, the white horses chomping and ready to gallop away with her. She was vaguely aware of guards standing at the bottom of the steps, hearing the prince's voice, unsure whether to apprehend her or not. She brushed past them and climbed into the coach.

"Home, quickly," she commanded.

The coachman cracked his whip, the horses neighed, and she was flung back in her seat as they took off. Countryside flashed past in a blur until suddenly there was a flash, a crackle, and she found herself sitting on the road. She was no longer wearing the shimmering dress, but her old rags. A large pumpkin lay beside her. Mice scurried around, looking for places to hide, and the goose who had been her coachman honked forlornly.

"Oh no," she sighed. She was a long way from home. If her step-mother and sisters arrived home before her, she would be in awful trouble. "What do I do now, fairy godmother?" she called into the night.

There was no answer. Clearly the fairy godmother had done her one good deed and retreated into another realm. Cinderella was on her own, back in the harsh reality of a long walk through a dark forest. The mice scurried to her as she stood up. She scooped them up and tucked them into her pocket. She was not about to abandon them to be prey to forest beasts. Neither would she like to be prey herself, she thought.

"Fly home," she said to the goose. "I can't carry you and you'd be a tasty treat for a fox."

The goose took a few ungainly steps, wings flapping until it became airborne and flew off into the night. "If only I could fly away home," she thought, but then she realized that she had no place she could call home any longer. With a sigh she picked up the pumpkin and set off, wincing as her bare feet contacted the rocks in the unmade road.

She had not gone far when she heard the sound of hoofbeats behind her. She stepped off the track, blending into the darkness of the trees. Only brigands and robbers would be out at this time of night, she thought, unless it was a coach returning from the prince's ball. And the occupants of a grand coach were hardly likely to give a ride to someone who looked like a beggar girl. The thought crossed her mind that it might be her step-mother's coach. Could she think up a plausible reason to stop it and ask for a ride home? She tried to think of one, but lying did not come easily to her. If Step-mother arrived home first she would think that Cinderella had shirked her duties and gone to bed, and she would lock the big front door.

"I could say that I wanted to catch a glimpse of the ball gowns," she thought out loud. "She'd scold me and call me stupid, but surely she'd give me a ride home, or I might be too tired to make her breakfast in the morning."

The galloping hooves drew nearer. The shapes of horsemen loomed up. Not a coach in sight. She stood very still among the bushes as they passed. Suddenly one of them gave a shout. They wheeled around and were facing her.

"You, girl!" one of them shouted. "Have you seen a coach pass this way? A glass coach?"

"No, sir," Cinderella said. "No coach has passed this way since I've been on the road."

The lead horseman came closer. One of his fellows held a flaming torch above Cinderella's head.

"And what are you doing out in the forest alone, at this time of night? I'd like to know."

"I had to go to my relatives' house to fetch this pumpkin," she replied. "I had to pass the castle and I heard the music coming from the ball. I'm afraid I lingered too long, hoping to catch a glimpse of the beautiful dresses. Now I'll be in trouble if I'm not home soon."

"Where do you live?"

"At the tall white house on the far edge of the forest."

"You're a servant there?"

She hesitated and swallowed hard before saying, "Yes, I'm a servant."

"So you say no coach has come this way?"

"On my honor, sir, no coach has passed me."

One of the men laughed. "A servant's honor. That's funny."

"What about a horseman? People on foot?"

"Nobody, sir. I have passed no one."

"Perhaps she's one of them," the man with the torch said. "Disguised as a beggar."

The lead horseman dismounted and came toward her. "What's your name, girl?"

"Ella, sir. What is this about?" she asked. "Can't I please get on my way? I don't want to get into more trouble."

"It is about a jewel robbery," the man said, looming over her now and staring hard into her face. "A valuable ruby necklace was taken during the ball. The countess did not miss it until later and there was a frightful hue and cry. Then the guards mentioned that a young girl had run down the steps, not stopping when they told her to, jumped into a coach and galloped away. Nobody at the ball could identify her so it was assumed that she was the jewel thief. The prince was most upset."

"I'm afraid I can't help you, sir," she said. "As you can see, anyone dressed like me would not have been allowed near the palace."

"Perhaps she changed her clothes," one of them suggested.

"Pardon me, sir, but if I had been the girl who galloped away in the coach, why would I have discarded it, here in the darkest part of the forest, and changed into rags? If this girl was the robber she could have been far away by now."

Some of the men nodded, having no argument with this. But the one with the torch held it closer. "Maybe she's an accomplice.

The robber slipped the rubies to this girl as she went past, knowing she might be pursued."

"Search her!" one of the men urged.

"Oh no, please. I assure you..." Cinderella began, but the headman had already taken the pumpkin from her and was running his hands over her. He plunged his hand into one of her pockets and withdrew it, cursing. "What the devil?" he growled.

"Only my pet mice, sir. I take them with me because I don't trust my employer's cat."

"Pet mice! What next?"

He put his hand more cautiously into the other pocket and drew it out triumphantly. "And what have we here?"

He held the glass slipper up toward the light. "A pretty little item for a servant girl!"

"I can explain, sir," Cinderella said, her cheeks burning. Lying did not come easily to her. "I found it resting at the bottom of the palace steps. I looked around to see who had dropped it but there was nobody in sight. Since one shoe would be of no use to any of the ladies I thought I might keep it as a souvenir of the evening. I'm hardly ever allowed out, you know. And the shoe is so beautiful, is it not?"

The headman stared hard at her. "There's something about you that makes me uneasy. You speak like an educated woman and yet you are dressed in rags. Are the rags perhaps a disguise and you are the clever jewel thief who has hidden the necklace in a convenient hollow tree to be retrieved later?"

"I grew up as the daughter of gentlefolk. My parents both died and I am not treated well by the people I now live with. But I have nowhere else to go."

"So a priceless ruby necklace might come in handy," the man with the torch said.

"Where do you think I could sell this necklace?" Cinderella asked him. "If I went into a pawn shop, dressed as I am, the constabulary would be summoned immediately. And I give you my word that I am no thief. If I had found this necklace I would have returned it to its rightful owner. That was how I was raised by my parents."

"Perhaps she's hidden the jewels in the pumpkin!" one of the men suggested. "Perhaps it's a fake pumpkin." The headman drew his sword and sliced the pumpkin in half with one stroke. The rich vegetable smell rose up. "Only an ordinary pumpkin after all," he said in disappointment.

"And now I shall be scolded for damaging a good pumpkin that we were supposed to be using for a pie," Cinderella said, enjoying a brief moment of his embarrassment.

"Tall white house on the edge of the forest, eh?" The headman frowned, staring at her. "We may be paying a call on you tomorrow—after we've searched these woods for hiding places. But there's not much we can do in the dark. Go on, then. On your way."

They wheeled their horses around and galloped back the way they had come, leaving a cloud of dust behind them. Cinderella's heart was still beating fast. She retrieved the two halves of the pumpkin, put the slipper back in her pocket, and set off on her weary way.

She was relieved to arrive home before her step-mother and sisters and curled up in her narrow bed.

"I danced with a prince," she whispered to herself. "It wasn't a dream. It was real." If only the magic had lasted a little longer. And now she still might find herself accused of a robbery. How could she explain to her step-mother if the men came knocking at their door?

Her step-mother and step-sisters did not get home until after two. Cinderella heard them stomping up the stairs, arguing as usual.

"I am exhausted. I danced so much my feet are killing me."

"I don't know why. You hardly danced at all. You were sitting there nursing a glass of wine every time I saw you."

"Well, you only danced with that count who must have been close to a hundred years old. Certainly not with the prince."

"Well, neither did you."

Their conversation drifted out of hearing range. Cinderella fell asleep, awoke with the sun and went down to the kitchen, finding comfort in her usual tasks. Because the sisters had come home so late she let them sleep through most of the morning and only took up their morning tea when a bell rang furiously.

"And how was the ball?" she asked politely as she put down the tray between them.

"Delightful. So glamorous," Esmerelda said with a smirk.

"And the prince?"

"Not really handsome at all, was he, sissy?" Esmerelda said. "Rather pale and boring, if you want to know. And he only danced with an equally unattractive girl in an ostentatious blue dress."

"So you didn't have a good time?"

Cinderella glanced across at Ermintrude, her other step-sister.

"Oh yes, I had a good time," she said. "Now take my shoes and polish them. I stepped in a puddle last night."

"And take our wigs to be brushed and styled," Esmerelda snapped.

As Cinderella left the room something was troubling her, apart from the sisters' usual rudeness. Ermintrude's face. Something about the way she had looked when her sister mentioned wigs. Cinderella had seen that expression before. When Ermintrude had taken her sister's hair ribbon. When she had sneaked the last cake from the cake stand and tried to blame it on her sister. Guilt mixed with triumph. And a strange idea began to form in Cinderella's head. Esmerelda had said that her sister had sat nursing a glass of wine all evening. Cinderella could picture it now. Her sister sitting alone at a side table while the dancers twirled around her, with a glass of red wine in her hand. But she didn't drink red wine. It made her skin go blotchy and red. Why would she have risked that at a ball? And then she was still carrying that glass, undrunk, when she went to the powder room. Cinderella had not seen her return—she had been too busy dancing with the prince. But at a later glimpse there was something not quite right with her sister's wig. It sat a little too high on her forehead. It made her look rather comical, Cinderella had noted.

Cinderella polished the shoes and brushed the wigs. Sure enough there was a trace of red stain inside Ermintrude's. She waited until Ermintrude was alone, sitting at her dressing table. "Here are your shoes, sister."

"Put them in my closet." The step-sister waved her away.

"And I have your clean undergarments. Shall I put them in your drawer?"

"No. Leave them. Just go," Ermintrude snapped, reaching out a hand to prevent the drawer from being opened.

Still, Cinderella lingered.

"Just go. What are you waiting for?" Ermintrude said.

"I thought it only fair to warn you that a valuable necklace was stolen at the ball last night. We may have a visit today from palace guards who will search the house," she said.

"Why should that concern me?"

"Because they will certainly come into this room," Cinderella said. "Open all the drawers, rummage through your clothing."

"Why would they do that, pray? I am a gentlewoman. They would not dare." The step-sister's face had turned very red.

"Ah, but they would dare. And what would they find, dear sister?" Cinderella paused. "I know you stole the necklace."

"How dare you! What can you know about anything?"

"I know how you did it," Cinderella said. "I suspect the necklace slipped off a lady's neck while she was dancing. You saw it on the floor, picked it up and dropped it into a convenient glass of red wine, where rubies would be invisible. You held onto that red wine all evening until you realized you could not take the glass with you. So you went to the powder room and managed to tuck the necklace under your wig. It didn't quite sit properly after that."

Ermintrude was staring at her. "How could you possibly know any of this? It's all lies. You are insane."

"I just hope the men don't search the house too thoroughly, because if they find the necklace, it will be a lifetime in prison at the very best. Or even the noose."

The color had now drained from Ermintrude's face. "Why should they want to search this house? We are respectable people."

"I heard they will be searching everybody who was at the ball."

"And how could you possibly know any of this? A servant girl, sitting all alone by the fire?"

"Suffice it to say that I do know. Maybe I followed you to the ball last night. Maybe I watched you… And I will tell the truth if the men come. And they will search until they find the rubies. Even in among your undergarments."

Ermintrude's hand went to the drawer before she realized she was giving herself away.

"I'll bury them in the garden," she said, defiantly. "They will never find them."

"Oh, but I understand they will bring dogs with them. Dogs specially trained to sniff out jewels."

"Then what should I do?" The defiance had gone from her voice.

"I have a suggestion that will save you and the honor of this house," Cinderella said. "You will take the jewels and go straight to the palace. Tell them you found them lying in a puddle last night. You looked around but there was nobody to hand them to and your mother was anxious to go home, nervous about being out alone in the dark. So you had to wait until this morning to return them. You will receive their undying thanks, and there may even be a reward."

"Do you think so?" she asked in a small voice.

"Either way you will be seen in a favorable light by the palace. That is important, isn't it?"

"I suppose it is." She opened the drawer, tipped the rubies from a stocking and stood staring at them. They were indeed very beautiful. "I saw them on the floor. I grabbed them on impulse. I'll never own anything so lovely."

"I know how you feel. I felt the same way when you all left for the ball."

For a second the step-sister looked at her as if she was seeing a real person for the first time. "Why are you doing this for me?" she asked. "You could have kept quiet and let the guards find the rubies and arrest me."

"Because, dear sister, unlike you I was brought up to be a good person. Nothing can change that." She walked toward the door. "But I will warn you of one thing. I have my ways of knowing what you do. I saw you at the ball last night. And I may not always feel so generous toward you. So I'd like to be treated with a little more respect in future."

"All right."

Cinderella smiled to herself. She had only just gone down the stairs when there came a furious knocking at the front door. She went to open it, her heart beating fast. Ermintrude was now trapped in the house. But outside stood a man in magnificent clothing. "I have been sent at the order of the prince," he said. "To find the young lady who lost this glass slipper last night."

CINDERELLA 2

He came out of the bar just as the clock on a nearby church was striking midnight. A cold wind was swirling up from the desert to the south, making him button his jacket. He needed to get going if he wanted to make Tucson by morning. He was about to get into his car when he noticed the girl. She was sitting in the bus shelter hugging a guitar almost as big as she was.

Their eyes met. "Nice car," she said.

"Yes, isn't it? Latest model," he said with pride in his voice.

She continued to sit there, hugging her guitar to her body.

"You won't find a bus at this time of night," he said to her.

"I know that."

"Shouldn't you be at home, a girl of your age?"

"That's what I'm trying to do—get home," she said, defiantly.

"And where is that?"

"California."

He gave an incredulous laugh. "Then you are a long way from home."

"No kidding."

"What on earth are you doing out here in this God-forsaken place? Going to college?"

She gave a bitter laugh. "I wish." She paused. "I'm trying to get home from Nashville."

"Tennessee?"

"No, Nashville on the Moon. Of course Tennessee."

"You're a brittle little thing," he said.

"Yes, well, I haven't exactly had it as easy as you."

"What took you to Nashville? Dreams of becoming a country music star?"

"Why else does anyone go to Nashville?" she asked.

"And it didn't work out?"

"I learned all I needed to know about the music industry and what goes on in Nashville."

"And it wasn't for you?"

"There was nothing there for me." She hesitated. "Or at least I found out there was nothing there for me."

"So you're heading home. Have you hitchhiked this far?"

"No, I took the bus this far. But I'm running out of cash."

"I could give you a ride as far as Phoenix, if you like."

"That would be great."

"Come on then." He clicked open the car door. "Put your things on the back seat and let's get going."

She stood up, carefully laying her guitar on the back seat but keeping her small backpack with her in the front. The engine purred to life and the big car took off, leaving the lights of the city behind. There was an occasional truck on the road but otherwise they were driving through total darkness.

"So are you any good as a singer?"

"Not bad," she said.

"You want to sing something for me?"

"I'd rather not."

"Suit yourself, but you know I happen to be a big music producer."

"Really?"

"Really. I used to be in Nashville, years ago, but now I'm based in LA. I do more film music these days. Where the money is."

He had expected her to sing for him then, but she remained silent. After a while he asked, "What's your name?"

"Jolene Kent."

"Good name for a country singer." He chuckled, "Was it really your name, or did you make it up?"

"It's a real name."

"Jolene. I used to know a girl called Jolene, years ago. She was good. Great voice. Really cute too. Looked a bit like you."

"Really? What happened to her?"

"I don't know. It didn't quite work out for her. She got messed up. Drugs. It happens a lot in Nashville."

"What's your name?" She countered.

"Hal. Hal Benson."

"Is that your real name, or a made-up one?"

He had to laugh. "My real name is Harvey. Horrible name."

They drove on, the headlight beams cutting swathes of light through the darkness. The girl dozed off. He glanced at her from time to time, looking incredibly young with her long dark hair falling across her cheek, clutching her backpack as if it was a stuffed teddy bear. And for a moment he felt a tenderness toward her—the daughter he'd never had. He had never married. Too easy to find women without being tied down to one.

The first streaks of dawn were in the sky when he pulled off into a deserted rest area. The girl woke up as cold wind swept into the car.

"Where are we?" she asked.

"A couple of hours from Tucson, I think. Rest area. I need to visit the restroom. You might want to use it too."

"Okay." She got out, taking her backpack with her. He noticed she never said thank you. Badly raised, he thought.

When she returned from the restroom she stopped, finding a blanket on the ground beside the car. "What's this?"

He had a strange, predatory smile on his face. "You didn't think you'd get to ride with me without paying your fare, did you? Come on. You've done it before."

She took an involuntary step back. "I haven't, actually."

"A virgin. How delightful. That is a bonus. And you're going to thank me for it. I'm an expert, you know. It won't be with one of those clumsy and panting boys. Now take your jeans off."

"It's cold out here."

"Well, there's not enough room on the back seat. Come on. Let's do this before we freeze."

She looked around. He sensed her panic.

231

"I wouldn't think of running away. There's nothing for miles."

"I wouldn't leave my guitar, anyway." She started to unzip her jeans, then tried to pull them down. They were tight. "I usually have to sit on the ground to get them off," she said. "Aren't you going to take your clothes off too?"

"Like you said, it's cold."

"What if I refuse?"

"Simple. I drive on. Leave you here. Hope someone finds you before the coyotes. Or I get impatient and rape you."

She struggled with the last of the jeans. He sank to his knees on the rug beside her. In the first light of dawn his face was hard with desire. "You're wasting my time. Come here, you little bitch."

He grabbed at her ankles and brought her toppling down onto the blanket. He laughed as he tried to pin her in place. She grabbed his hand, sank her teeth into it. As he cried out, she scrambled to her feet.

"Oh, I love a good fight," he said, getting to his knees.

"Stop. You might want to hear this," she said.

He frowned. "No pleading to spare you because of your aged mother!" And he laughed.

"Not aged. Just dying." There was a sudden silence with only the whispering of the wind through sagebrush. "I didn't go to Nashville to be a music star," she said. "I went to find my mother. She dumped me with my grandma when I was born. I never met her. I was curious."

"Oh, spare me the sob story," he said.

"You need to hear this," she said. "I found her. She's pitiful. A heroin addict. Skin and bone. Stringy hair, hollow eyes. But she told me about you."

"Me?"

"How you promised to make her a star, then you got her hooked on drugs and then you got her pregnant. And you wanted nothing more to do with her. Denied I was your baby."

"You can't be serious."

"Her name is Jolene, not mine. I'm Carrie, actually. Remember that Jolene you knew? The one who was the good singer? Oh, I've been learning all about you. And I made it my mission to find you.

I've followed you this far. And I don't think you want to rape your daughter, do you, Daddy?"

"I don't believe a word of it," he said, but he sounded unsure.

"Why do you think I was sitting beside your car, waiting for you tonight? I wanted to see for myself if you were the rat my mother said you were. And you are."

"Now listen you little…" He was trying to get to his feet when she picked up a rock and brought it crashing down onto the back of his head. He gave a grunt and pitched forward. She stared at him, feeling horror mixed with triumph. Then she turned him over. He wasn't breathing. For a moment she had a wild fantasy about driving off in his car, leaving him for the vultures and coyotes. But decided against it. That would be stupid. They'd track her down and accuse her of murder. Instead she retrieved her jeans and put them on again, finding it hard with her hands shaking from cold and emotion. Then she turned her attention to him and carefully removed his trousers.

She took out her cellphone and was pleasantly surprised to find a signal.

"There's been a horrible accident," she gasped when the 911 operator answered. "A man gave me a ride in his car. He stopped and tried to rape me. I pushed him away. He tripped over a rock and fell and hit his head. I think he's dead."

The operator was kind and soothing. Carrie sat in the car until state troopers arrived half an hour later. They, too, were kind and understanding. They took in the sprawled body, his trousers lying neatly on the driver's seat. "Come on, honey. Let's get you home," one of them said.

She drove off in the squad car without looking back.

* * *

EASY PEASEY

JOHN LESCROART

Carrie McKay's cellphone alarm went off at midnight and after taking a moment trying to figure out where she was and what she'd set the darn thing for, she rolled over and killed the noise, which sounded far louder than it had ever sounded before in the daytime.

She lay back down, holding the now blessedly silent phone and listening for any other sounds it might have roused in the house. Her mom and dad were just across the hall in their bedroom, hopefully still deep in slumber. Her brother Kyle's room was adjacent to hers, with just the one wall separating them. But she knew that he usually slept like a rock and probably wouldn't have heard the alarm. Probably.

Still, she waited, listening, making sure.

After a minute that seemed like a half hour, she finally decided that the alarm hadn't awakened anyone. She threw back her covers, turned and sat up. Her stomach growled as though she was hungry; she put her hand flat on her belly and tried to breathe out the tension. But she knew that it wasn't lack of food roiling her insides.

It was nerves.

She was starting to realize, because she really wasn't cut out for it, that she never should have told Dawn and Emily that she'd be part of the raid to TP Jason Trent's house tonight. After all, he was Dawn's boyfriend. Carrie didn't think she'd ever even said hi to him. But you didn't say no to Dawn if she wanted you to do something with her. She was definitely the leader of the cool kids at school, and Carrie had been aching to be one of them herself, always just not quite making it.

She was afraid that she wasn't really a natural for something like this, actually sneaking out in the middle of the night. It had been bad enough when she went into Target two days ago to buy the Super-Size pack of twenty-four rolls of Charmin', waiting in the checkout line, hoping and praying that she wouldn't run into somebody she knew, especially one of her friend's mothers. But no big deal, she'd told herself. Everybody had to buy toilet paper. She could always say she was just running some errands for her mother. Nothing sinister going on. She was one of the good kids, after all, and nobody would think anything about it.

And in the end, nobody had seen her.

Hiding the actual package of rolls was another issue altogether. Carrie had to keep them out of sight somewhere for two days. Why had she gone down and bought it so early? What if her mother checked the car's trunk in the next two days and wanted to know what this cache of toilet paper was all about? There would be no guarantee that her mother wouldn't open the trunk, and no fooling her if she did. So Carrie couldn't put them there where her mom could find them.

Or, really, anywhere in her own house.

In a panic she'd called Emily from the Target parking lot, which she hated to do because she knew from TV that it would leave a telephonic record of when they'd talked. If anybody, like the police for example, did some kind of real investigation for this crime of trespass—or was it vandalism? Or both? …Whatever, they'd be able to put it together that she and Emily were planning something.

But what else could she do?

She had not planned on this degree of subterfuge holding onto the TP. She hadn't even thought of it as an issue. Before Emily picked up her own phone, Carrie actually considered throwing the evidence away in one of the dumpsters behind the Target. But if she couldn't even score and hold onto a few rolls of TP, that would surely betray her pathetic personality flaw.

Gutless and fearful, that's what they'd say about her.

There was a really thin line between being one of the good kids and one of the cool kids, and so far Carrie had managed to fool most everybody as fitting into both camps.

But Emily, like Dawn, was all the way cool. She actually thought that Carrie's worries about where to hide the toilet paper were legitimate. And Carrie's suggestion that they stow the TP in Emily's Tuff Shed in her backyard (which Emily's dad almost never used anymore) was actually a great hiding place and a pretty brilliant idea.

Sucking in a breath, pushing with the flat of her hand on the continual churning of her belly, Carrie stood up. She was still mostly dressed. She'd left her socks on and worn her jeans and her black high school logo sweatshirt to bed. It wasn't like her mom and dad came in every night to tuck her into bed anymore. The unspoken personal space barrier for the past year or so was her door: if closed, everything was fine and there was no need to come in and check on her. So tonight she had left it closed. Her parents trusted her and she was, here at home at least, definitely one of the good kids.

Using the flashlight from her phone, she found her tennis shoes and put them on. Then, with the flashlight still on, she crossed the room to the windows that faced out at the front of the house. Pulling open the plantation shutters, she unlocked and then raised the right-hand window, and stepped out into the night.

If the quiet in her room had been comforting, the quiet outside was all but terrifying. Standing on the dewy grass, she listened to nothing.

Then suddenly she realized that she still held the lit-up phone and that the window was open. She tip-toed back to the house, closed the window and turned off her light. Now it was pure dark. None of their neighbors even seemed to be watching television. There was no moon. She checked her phone; it was 12:08. She was seven minutes early. Squatting behind one of the low bushes that grew in the front of her house, she settled down to wait.

Seven minutes…yikes!

At last, at long last, car lights up at the corner turned onto her street. She checked her phone, exactly 12:15. Standing up from where she was hiding behind the bushes, she ran across the lawn and out to where Dawn's car was pulling over to the curb.

Dawn, driving, let her window down. "Hey," she whispered. "Way to go. Perfect. Hop in the back seat but don't close the door all the way. Just hold it. No noise."

Carrie, her heart beating so hard she was surprised that they couldn't hear it, followed these instructions to the letter. As soon as she was in, Dawn got the car rolling again and caught Carrie's eyes in the rearview mirror.

"Is this awesome, or what?" Dawn asked.

"Totally," Emily said from the front passenger seat.

Carrie wracked her brain searching for the right answer. "Easy peasey," she finally said in the calmest voice she should muster.

"Easy peasey, so cool. We knew you'd be down with us, Car," Dawn said, then giggled and added, "Jason's going to just shit."

* * *

For a while, Chris Duke believed that he was friends with Jason Trent. After all, they'd played on the same football teams for eight years, Pop Warner on up, with Trent always the quarterback and Chris usually a linebacker on the D-squad, although he'd had some luck last year transitioning to fullback and had even taken a few snaps at that position last Spring. Things had been looking up. Chris was large, strong and fast. Maybe he could become an impact player.

He and Jason had always gotten along well enough, not that they talked much or anything like that. But they were teammates and that's all that needed to be said. Then they became a little more than that after grades came out at the end of Chris's junior year and he hadn't made the academic cutoff with his 2.0 GPA, when he needed a 2.5 to stay on the team; he'd gotten a damn C-minus in geometry, like he was ever going to use geometry in real life.

But Jason—though himself not the sharpest tool in the shed—was in the summer school tutoring program and the two of them spent a couple of days a week at Jason's fancy house on the golf course trying to make sense out of triangles and circles, proofs and space, and the areas of figures. Total waste of time, Chris thought, since what was that stuff ever going to do with him? And ultimately he didn't understand it anyway.

But he and Jason had broken up the tedium and failure of the geometry lessons with computer games and working on Jason's passing and handoffs and Chris's receiving. They had laughed a lot. Jason was rich—well, his parents were—but basically he seemed like an okay guy. When they checked in back at summer camp, Chris knew that Jason put in a word to Coach to let him try out in the backfield again.

But then his final summer school grade, another C-minus, came in and the coach told him he had no choice. It wasn't his decision to make. Chris didn't make the academic cut and therefore he couldn't be on the team.

Jason, who went off to football practice after school every day like he always did, simply dropped out of Chris's universe. He obviously couldn't have cared less about whether or not Chris was still on the team. He'd given it his best shot to help him, sure, but now that was over. It hadn't worked, and the two guys had nothing left to say or to do with each other.

A couple of times, Chris had nodded to Jason passing in the hall and though he'd nodded back, it was obvious that his former tutor did not know for sure exactly who he was.

Jason probably meant no offense, of course, but life was life, fair was fair, and he was still the quarterback after all, while Chris was nothing.

Oh, except a loser.

He only accidentally heard about Jason's parents' vacation to Cabo when he'd been sitting at the next table in the cafeteria and heard Jason telling his current babe girlfriend Dawn that he'd be alone in the house starting Thursday and through the weekend, so she could come over any time and…

…and she'd stopped him there, although there had been a lot of laughing.

Now it was Friday morning, about twenty-five minutes after midnight, and Chris had made his way past the backs of four houses down the Sixth fairway, to Jason's place. Two houses in, there'd been some dim lights on inside, and across the fairway, a few more, but otherwise generally it was dark, dark, dark.

Chris was wearing jeans and a black t-shirt. The September night was warm. He hadn't figured out exactly what he was going to do or how he was going to do it, but the general idea was that he was going to even out the playing field of their lives, at least a little. The way it was now, Jason had everything and Chris had nothing. That just wasn't right.

Several times over the summer, Chris and Jason had taken the shortcut through the parent's bedroom on their way out to the pool, which was just a few steps outside the floor-to ceiling glass French doors. The room was about half the size of Chris's whole house, with a king-sized bed and a dresser on the top of which Cheryl Trent kept an enormous array of her jewelry, taking up almost the whole top of the dresser, neatly laid out or hanging on display—bracelets, necklaces, rings and earrings. Everything appeared to be made out of gold, diamonds, and other gemstones in every color and shape.

Chris didn't know the actual price of any of that stuff, but he couldn't imagine it would be less than fifteen or twenty thousand dollars. Maybe way more. As if that kind of money had any real meaning for him.

The plan to even things up was coming together.

How about if all that jewelry went missing when the Trents were on vacation down in Baja? First off, the parents were going to have to consider the possibility that their own dear son Jason was the thief. And even if they didn't go far down that road, their trust in him would have to be shaken, and they'd still be out all of that jewelry, stolen while Jason was supposed to be watching the house.

Nice job, kid. We thought you were responsible and could take care of things while we went away for a few days, but we guess not now. It's sad but there it is: we just can't trust you completely anymore.

But even without that, even if they bought Jason's story about his complete innocence, the house wouldn't feel safe and impregnable any longer. And that alone would be a huge payback.

Okay, Jason, Chris thought, welcome to my world. This is what it feels like when you get cut and your parents don't have money to bail you out and you're not important to anybody anymore. Get used to it. The rest of your life starts tonight.

* * *

Thunk.

Jason Trent woke with a start and sat up, fully awake.

What the hell was that?

His heart pounding, he swung his feet over and down and crossed his room in the dark to his closet where his jeans hung off the peg on the back of the door. Pulling them down and putting them on, stepping into his topsiders, he crossed back to the bed, moving as quietly as he could, the lights still off.

Feeling around, he opened the door to the bedside table where he'd stashed the gun he'd taken from his father's office after his parents had driven off to the airport.

He probably should have told them, or asked them about wanting to have the gun in his own room next to his bed, just in case something weird happened—which it never did, not in this Neighborhood Watch community—but he didn't want them to know that he was even a little tiny bit uncomfortable about staying alone in the house for the weekend.

Not terrified, really, just nervous.

But if he told them that he felt he needed the gun, they might—no, they *would*—start to curtail their traveling. And the two of them getting away alone, like with this trip to Baja, had only recently become something his parents were doing with regularity, leaving him alone at the house, often having Dawn over (and Shelley before her), or his teammates, or even just hanging out in his house alone, when he could sneak some alcohol—not so much that they would notice when they got back, but enough to get a little buzz.

So, bottom line, he'd waited until they'd driven away before he got the gun out and stored it next to his bed.

And now he had it in his hand, loaded, with the safety off, a round racked in the chamber. Ready for action.

Something had made that noise. He told himself that it was probably just an animal—raccoon, opossum, skunk—messing with the garbage cans, but he wanted to be sure.

His bedroom was on the second floor and he walked out into the hallway to the top of the stairs. Next, as quietly as possible, he started descending, slowly, a step at a time, listening.

And there it was, the unmistakable sound of a car door slamming out in the street. And then voices. Could it be laughter?

On the ground floor now, crossing the foyer in only a couple of steps, he got his hand on the knob and flung open the door. At least two figures were moving out on his front lawn, shadows in the dark. "Hey!" Turning on the light over the front door, he yelled, "Who's there? What's happening out here?"

But at the exact same moment, before there could be any response from the people on the lawn, came the unmistakable sound of glass breaking somewhere in the house, back toward his parents' bedroom.

Whatever was going on, they had him all but surrounded.

* * *

Chris realized, maybe a little too late, that he hadn't thought it through enough.

Of course the doors were going to be locked. Did he think he was just going to be able to stroll in and clear the jewelry off the dresser and then leave the way he'd come?

But he was already here at the goddamn back door to the bedroom. He'd crossed the whole backyard and come up around the pool, and when he realized that the door was locked, he slammed at the mullioned windows as hard as he could with his whole body. They were just windows. He couldn't believe they could be that tough to break.

But they didn't. And also the good deadbolt lock didn't give. Not an inch.

Still standing just outside the door, he considered that he should just give up and come back another night with a better plan, maybe bring some tools to help him break in. But abandoning the idea when he was this close just didn't sing for him. He could still get it done. He was right here, right now. He had to make it happen.

The house was dark and empty and silent. Slamming against the door didn't appear to have woken up Jason. Peering through the glass, he saw that there were no lights on inside.

He'd just have to blast his way in, then be fast and efficient. He knew exactly where the jewelry was. Just get in, he thought, and get out.

The Trents had large and decorative river stones that Chris remembered up by their house and now he grabbed one and slammed it against the window; it broke with a deafening crash next to the doorknob. Reaching through the opening, he found the deadbolt and gave it a turn, and when he pushed it, the door opened.

As he stepped in over the broken glass, a light in the hallway came on under the bedroom door. Jason was definitely up now. Chris heard him calling out to someone way down the hallway by the front door.

And then, clearly not out by the front door any longer, now coming Chris's way, Jason yelled again. "Hey! Whoever you are, get the hell out of here! I've got a gun and I'll shoot your fucking ass!"

There wasn't time for any reaction except for Chris to lunge at the hallway door to the bedroom, which had its own deadbolt. That door was already closed, but he had to make sure it was locked, so he flicked on the lights. He then tried the lock, and a good thing he did, because it turned and the bolt shot home.

It was just in time, as Jason threw himself up against the door. "God damn it. God damn it. Open up!"

Jason slammed his gun hand against the wood of the door, but it didn't budge. Not learning much from the experience, he tried doing the same thing again.

But this time, the damn gun went off with a resounding boom.

* * *

When Jason had first opened the front door and called out, turning on the light over the front door, Dawn went into ballistic mode and kept ordering her two companions to keep on with the job, to get as much TP as they could draped over the shrubs and hedges that bordered the yard and walkway.

Meanwhile, though she wasn't sure exactly how she was going to do it, she'd deal with Jason. Getting him under her control had never been a problem before. She'd figure something out. She knew she could distract him enough for Carrie and Emily to cover some more of the shrubbery with the TP rolls, and that pretty much directly related to how important her and Jason's relationship was to her. The more she trashed the front of his house, the more she loved him.

He'd get that. He was cool. He totally got the code and would understand the risk she was taking to proclaim her love and devotion.

But then, all of a sudden, just as the front porch light came on overhead, Jason turned and went off somewhere, out of sight, into the house.

And now a shot! It had to be a shot. What else could it be?

"Holy shit!" she screamed, rushing up to the front door. "Jason! Jason!"

There he was, off to her left, standing in the hallway (looking pretty darned awesome with no shirt on) with a gun in his hand by the door to his parents' room. Turning, he spread his hands. "Dawn! What the hell? What are you doing here? What's happening?"

She moved a couple of steps into the house toward him.

"What do you mean?"

"I mean, what are you doing? Who's in my parents' room?"

"I don't know. What are you talking about?"

"I'm talking about somebody's in there right now."

"You're kidding me?"

"Yeah, I'm fucking kidding you." He flat-handed his free hand at the door again, screaming at the closed door. "Get the fuck out!"

Dawn took another step toward him. "I heard a shot. Did somebody shoot at you? Are you okay?"

"Yeah." He held his gun out so she could see it. "This thing is my dad's and it just went off when I slammed it up against the door. I'm all right."

"You're sure?"

"I'm God damn sure, Dawn. What? I wouldn't know if I'm fucking shot?"

Dawn drew on a quick pout and spoke in her most authoritative voice. "You don't have to talk to me that way, Jason. You've got no reason to be mad at me. I'm only here to help you because I heard a shot from out there. Jesus."

"Well, help me by telling me who is in this room."

"I don't know. Some bad person. I don't know anything about that. How would I know that?" Another step toward him. "Whoever it is, Jason, we've got to get out of here. We can call the police from outside. Let them take care of it."

Jason threw a glance at his girlfriend, then slapped at his parents' door one last time. "Whoever you are…fuck you! Get out of my house!"

Dawn reached out, took his hand and began to pull him back down the hallway to the front door. "Come on, Jason. Come on."

* * *

Sheriff Deputies Greg Trudeaux and Paul Walker were almost terminally worn down from their shift so far tonight, which like so many other nights had entailed breaking up couples who were making out on the levee a couple of miles south of town. Typically, there was underage alcohol involved, to say nothing of underage girls, and most of the time Greg and Paul just gave everybody the relevant warnings, took and poured out their drinks, and told them to get on home.

Usually nobody was really drunk, but even when they were, the way it got handled was one of the deputies would drive the kids' car back to one of their parents' houses, where the parents could then deal with the problem. It was the kind of town that liked to pretend, against all evidence to the contrary, that it didn't have a teenage drinking problem, so the word from on high was at all costs to avoid writing anybody up so the DUI would not appear on the record of any of these good kids.

Both of the deputies thought this was a stupid policy, but what could they do? Still, it left them both perpetually on edge, frustrated about what lessons were being taught. Some of these so-called "good kids," they knew, were capable of some bad stuff. Nothing tonight, true, but every time they approached a parked and dark car down an abandoned levee road, there was a chance of something unexpected happening. And, in fact, these were not always "kids," good or otherwise. Some were a couple of years out of high school, unable to cut it in college or even in the minimum wage job market, and they were now unemployed and angry.

Every car a possible threat. And tonight they'd pulled up behind seven of them.

Wound up tight as a spring? You could say that.

In any event, when they got the call from dispatch about some kind of disturbance from one of the Troon Estates Neighborhood Watch people, they were ready to switch gears and roll. Even though it was probably as mundane as some girls TPing some guy's house—with school just starting, it was high season!—nevertheless, some other of the lower-rent parts of town had recently come under the apparent influence of wannabe gang members from the capitol just down the freeway. There had been an alarming rise in residential burglaries in the last year or two, especially in some of these seedier areas, although "seedy," like DUI, was a term best left unspoken.

Except for their black and white police car, the county road back was completely deserted. To recalibrate his and his partner's own respective equilibriums, Paul Walker was having some fun on the drive into town, pushing eighty miles an hour without his red and blue lights flashing and keeping his siren mute.

They just hit the city limit, maybe half a mile more before they'd get to their turn into the Estates proper, when dispatch came on again. "Car sixteen, do you copy?"

Greg picked up the dashboard microphone. "Car sixteen, copy."

The dispatcher, Davon White, was normally the soul of calm, but now there was a palpable sense of urgency in her pinched and no-nonsense voice. "We've got a ten seventy-one on the call to Country Club Court. Repeat, ten seventy-one. Other units will be responding."

"Ten seventy-one," Greg said. "Shots fired."

Paul threw a quick glance over to his partner. "I know what it means."

"You want to pull over? Wait for backup?"

"When something real is finally happening? In your dreams, Greg." He reached out and punched up his emergency lights and siren. Then, with his tires screeching, he took the right hand turn onto Country Club Drive.

* * *

Not even a minute after Carrie heard the shot, the siren's wail froze her where she stood in the middle of the lawn. Relatively close to the house, she was caught in the lights over the front porch. Dropping the last couple of rolls of toilet paper, her hands went to her mouth and, unable to control her reaction, she let out a scream.

From behind her, Emily yelled, "What is it? What is it?"

"Where's Dawn?"

"Inside. Still inside."

"Oh my God! We've got to get out of here."

"We can't just leave her. Anyway, she's got the keys. Jesus Christ. What are we going to do? We can't just..."

Emily turned away from Carrie as the police car skidded around the corner into the Court, catching her in its brights as it lurched to a stop, deputies coming out of both sides, their weapons out. Emily put her hands up over her head.

"Down," the driver said. "On the ground. Hands where I can see them. Down, I said!"

Carrie followed the movements of the other cop, who'd come out the passenger door, his gun also drawn. She didn't know how it happened, but her reactions did not seem to be under control and suddenly she had her own hands spread apart in the air over her head. "Don't shoot, don't shoot, don't shoot!" she wailed. "I'm sorry. I'm so sorry." Then she was on her knees, sobbing.

Both of their guns extended out before them, the deputies kept advancing toward the open front door, toward the light.

Then Carrie became suddenly aware of another movement around to her side, toward the house. She turned her head and saw Dawn come out through the doorway.

A couple of steps behind her, Jason followed, shading his eyes from the light above him, the gun in his other hand.

The deputy down by Emily called out. "Gun! Gun!"

And both cops opened fire.

* * *

The standard investigation into the officer-involved shootings came to an end in the week before Christmas vacation, with both deputies completely cleared of any misconduct. After all, they'd come in the middle of the night to the scene of what looked to be a burglary in progress. The apparent perpetrator, armed with a handgun, was a couple of steps behind a young woman who appeared to be involved in some kind of a possible hostage situation.

The deputies really had no other option. The investigation concluded that they had acted reasonably under the circumstances and undoubtedly had prevented further injury to the other young women who had been involved in what had started out as a TP hazing event and then somehow gotten out of control under many still-unexplained circumstances.

In the intervening months since the incident, Greg and Paul took a lot of grief among their law enforcement colleagues for their poor marksmanship, but the fact that they hadn't killed anyone had probably played some role in their exoneration.

Which is not to say that they hadn't done some damage. Jason Trent took four bullets, one in each extremity, and the injuries had made him miss the entire football season, although the prognosis was that he would probably be able to play in college if he so chose.

Dawn Halley was hit in the face by ricocheting marble from one of the columns by the Trent's front door and was looking at a further array of plastic surgery procedures to restore as much as possible to what had once been her angelic face.

The mystery of the person who had originally broken into the Trents' bedroom through the back door and dead bolted the door to the hallway remained just that. Whoever it had been—the prevailing theory favored one of the wannabe gangsters—he or she, probably scared off by the gunshots, took nothing and left no trace of evidence. (There were fingerprints from some of Jason's football teammates, but since the Trents' bedroom was a well-trod shortcut on the way to the swimming pool, these were discounted as easily explained and irrelevant.)

* * *

For a couple of weeks after the incident, Chris was consumed with guilt and fear: the former at what he'd actually done, the latter that someone would find out and charge him with something. Gradually, though, he settled on feeling most responsible for the injuries to Jason. After all, if Chris hadn't broken in, little or none of the events would have happened. And it wasn't the girls TPing the house that had made Jason break out his father's gun.

In any event, Chris came to the conclusion that, even if he wasn't going to do something stupid like confessing, he should at least try to do something to somehow make things better. Even if it was only symbolic, it seemed that it might be worth a try. After all, because of Chris's break-in at the Trents, the football team was also short one very important guy. If Chris could somehow make it back to the team and contribute...

So against all reason—and he'd already learned from geometry that logic was not his forte—he signed up for the tutorial workshop again. If he could get a C or better in geometry before the first quarter was over, he could still get some playing time and even make some small difference. Anyway, he thought, it was worth a try, maybe undo a little of the harm he'd done.

And the great bonus turned out to be his new tutor, Carrie McKay, one of the good kids and also one of the cool kids, maybe now the coolest since Dawn Halley was no longer in the running. In any event, Chris had always thought that Carrie was way out of his league. He couldn't believe how obvious and easy geometry turned out to be when the person tutoring him actually got it herself. Things made sense. A-squared plus B-squared equals C-squared.

Cake.

He wound up with a B+ and the week after Thanksgiving, he started at defensive safety—six tackles and two interceptions, thank you.

Also, Carrie was an amazing kisser.

* * *

TONIC

D. P. LYLE

"What you think he does with them?" Eddie Whitt asked his cousin.

Floyd Robinson rode shotgun in Eddie's old '49 Ford, black, dented, primer-coated left front fender, a jagged crack across the windshield. The tires weren't none too good neither. He twisted in his seat. "You ask me that ever time."

They had parked beneath a large oak tree, middle of a grassy field, protected by a small hillock from McFee Road, a rutted, asphalt ribbon that wound through trees and rich farmland. Far enough from the town of Pine Creek to avoid any unwanted attention. It was just past midnight, the sky black, dotted with stars, the moon a sliver, like a fingernail clipping.

Eddie's hands rested on the steering wheel, eyes straight ahead, cigarette dangling from his lip. It bobbed as he spoke. "And you never have no thoughts on the subject," he said.

"'Cause I don't care." Floyd gave him a glance. "Long as he pays, I don't give a big old hoo-ha what he does."

"Don't get all pissy. I was just wondering."

"Maybe you should wonder about something else. Like what he's going to say when he sees this one."

Eddie took a final drag from his cigarette and crushed the butt in the ashtray. "Won't be happy."

"Nope."

"And I bet we don't get two-fifty for it," Eddie said.

A pulse of light flashed over the tree. Then another. Eddie glanced over his shoulder. A pair of headlight beams bounced across the crest of the hillock and wound down toward them.

"Here he comes," Eddie said.

They climbed out as a brand new 1954 Chevy Bel Air jerked to a stop behind the Ford. Cream colored with a dark green top, white wall tires. Classy. The kind that told the world the driver had a wad of cash in his pocket.

Antoine Briscoe stepped out. Tall, lanky, black pants, white shirt, long black duster, what he always wore. "What you got for me?" His voice deep, smooth, almost lazy. A twinge of annoyance buried in there. Like he had better things to do. Or maybe didn't care too much for Eddie and Floyd. Which was true. Hell, a rickety, old, blind coon dog could see that.

Eddie popped the trunk. Antoine reached inside and pulled back the canvas. He tugged a flashlight from his duster's pocket, flicked it on, and aimed it inside. He shook his head, his long dark hair swaying just above his shoulders. "This ain't fresh."

"It's the best we could come up with," Eddie said.

Antoine flapped the covering back in place. "Won't do." He looked from Eddie to Floyd. "Won't do at all."

"Why don't you ask him?" Eddie said.

Antoine smiled. Not friendly, more a grimace. "And who might that be?"

"You know we don't know," Floyd said.

"And you never will." He nodded toward the trunk. "A hundred bucks."

Eddie twisted his neck, trying to work out a gathering crick. "Our agreement was two-fifty."

"Our agreement was for fresh product. Not this shit."

Eddie saw Floyd's jaw flex. Knew the sign. His cousin had a temper and when it started to rise, his jaw muscles would pump up. Get all big like a squirrel with a mess of hickory nuts stuffed in its cheeks. He laid a hand on Floyd's arm. "That'll do."

Antoine smiled. "Thought it might." He reached in his pants' pocket and pulled out a thick fold of bills, gripped by a silver clip. He tugged them free, peeled off a pair of fifties, and handed them over. He returned the clipped money to his pocket and walked to the rear of the Chevy, his duster flapping with each step.

He opened the trunk. And waited. Offering no help. As if it was beneath him. Or, as Eddie suspected, he didn't want to get his hands dirty.

The cousins awkwardly transported the bundle from one trunk to the other and folded it inside.

"There you go," Floyd said.

"Can I ask you something?" Eddie said.

Antoine offered a smirk. "You can ask."

"What's he do with them?"

"Don't see that that's any of your concern." He took a step forward, looking down on the cousins. "Who he is and what he does is not for you to know." He closed the trunk with a sharp click. "When can we expect another one?"

"When we get the opportunity," Eddie said. "Ain't like they grow on trees."

Antoine stared at him. "Make it soon. Demand is up and we're running low." His eyes narrowed. "Maybe expand your search area."

"We'll look into that," Floyd said.

"Do. Otherwise we'll have to find another source." Antoine walked to the driver's side door, pulled it open. "And make it fresh." He climbed in, cranked the engine, wheeled a U-turn, and drove away. A faintly visible dust trail blurred his taillights as he disappeared over the hill.

"I don't like him," Floyd said.

"He don't seem to like us much neither."

* * *

"What the heck does 'messed with' mean?" Sheriff Amos Dugan asked Travis Sutton, his best officer. Dugan glanced at the bedside clock. Five a.m.

Amos Dugan was the sheriff of Lee County. A pretty easy job most days since his jurisdiction was small, consisting of assorted farms and two small towns; Pine Creek, the county seat where his office was located, and Pine Valley, eight miles east over a few wrinkles in the farmland. That was it. Unless you wanted to count Harper's Crossroads, which he didn't. Not as a bona fide town. Only sixteen folks lived over there on old man Harper's land. Each resident a direct descendant. Except for the two boys who'd married Harper's daughters and gave him a passel of grandkids.

But, this day wasn't kicking off all that well. Not just Travis's call but last night's dinner over at Clay's Diner. It had seemed greasier than usual and he'd eaten too much, and too fast, his stomach now complaining. Had most of the night, making his sleep fitful at best.

Travis laid it out. "Just that. Someone messed with a grave over at the cemetery. Carl called me this morning. Maybe an hour ago. You know how he's always up before dawn and hankering to get to work. Anyway, he got over to the cemetery right early, even for him, and found someone had been digging around at Wilbert Fleming's grave. I drove over and had a look-see."

"And?"

"Sure enough. Looked like the soil had been disturbed."

"Of course it was disturbed. He was just buried yesterday."

"Yeah, but Carl said it'd been messed with."

"There you go again. Did someone just root around or did they dig up Wilbert? Is that what you're saying?"

"No, nothing like that. Didn't seem so anyway. Just looked like the dirt mound wasn't like it should be."

"According to who?"

"Carl. He should know. He's the one what dug the grave after all."

"Maybe dogs or something like that?" Dugan asked.

"I suspect it coulda been but it didn't really look that way. Carl wondered if he should dig it up and see if Wilbert's missing."

Dugan considered that but didn't much like the idea. "I'd have to get a warrant. Or Martha's permission." He sighed. "And I damn sure don't want to go over there this time of day and ask her if we can dig her husband up because someone might've stolen him." He stifled a yawn. "Why would someone do that in the first place?"

"Beats me."

"I'd bet on dogs," Dugan said. "Or maybe those feral pigs that've been roaming around causing mischief lately."

"What should I tell Carl?" Travis asked.

"Tell him not right now. But that I'm thinking on it."

* * *

Eddie was of the opinion that luck had always followed him. Floyd, too, for that matter. But mostly him. Hooking up with Antoine, and his mysterious boss, was an example. Easy money. But right now, he couldn't come up with a plan. The local newspaper obituaries offered no leads. Maybe they'd have to spread out a little bit. Check out a couple of the neighboring counties.

It was two days after their last meeting with Antoine and he and Floyd sat on stools at McGill's, their favorite bar. The clock had just rolled past midnight. The crowd had thinned a bit, but since it was Friday, or in actual fact Saturday now, still plenty of folks hanging around—some shooting pool, others simply drinking and swapping lies.

Then it happened. That stroke of luck that always seemed to come at the right time. From two guys a few stools down. He thought maybe he'd seen them there before, but couldn't be sure. What caught his ear was one of them saying, "You going to Jerry's visitation this afternoon?"

Eddie nudged Floyd. Nodded toward the men.

One was older, maybe fifty, heavy, and wore a blue work shirt; the other younger, skinnier, gray shirt, the one that asked the question.

Blue shirt: "Yeah. Four o'clock? Right?"

Gray shirt: "Yep. Over at Grace Funeral Home. Gloria and me'll be there."

Blue shirt: "What time's the funeral Sunday?"

Gray shirt: "Noon. Over at Pine Valley Cemetery."

Blue shirt: "Closed casket, I assume."

Gray shirt, nodding: "I hear his truck hit a tree. Tore his head all to hell."

Blue shirt: "Well, at least it was quick. That's a blessing."

Gray shirt: "He was only twenty-eight."

Blue shirt: "A pure-dee tragedy's what it is. He was a fine boy."

"Pardon," Eddie said, looking past his cousin. "I couldn't help overhearing what you was saying." Blue shirt looked at him. "He was only twenty-eight?"

"Sure was."

"What was his name?" Eddie asked.

Blue shirt hesitated, and then said, "Jerry Crabtree."

"From Pine Valley?"

"Yep. Why?"

"He a baseball player?" Eddie asked. "In high school?"

"Sure was. A good one."

Eddie nodded toward Floyd. "We played against him."

"You did?"

"He was a couple of years ahead of us but we remember him. First base. Could really hit."

"That's him." Gray shirt jumping in. "It's the rain what did it. I hear tell he lost control of his truck."

"That's awful," Eddie said, shaking his head, doing his best to sound concerned. "Maybe we'll come to the funeral."

Blue shirt nodded. "I suspect his family would like that."

* * *

"What the hell was that all about?" Floyd asked.

They had paid the bill and were now walking down the street toward their car.

"I got me an idea," Eddie said.

"What might that be?"

Eddie climbed behind the wheel and waited for Floyd to get in. "Better than all that digging."

"What on God's green earth are you jabbering about?"

Eddie pulled from the curb. "Let me noodle on it for a minute."

* * *

It was just over twenty-four hours later when they drove into Pine Valley.

The last couple hours had been busy. First a stop by McGill's for a beer and a chat with Wayne, the bartender. The only way they had to reach Antoine. Eddie motioned Wayne over. Eddie leaned on the bar, looked around, made sure no one was listening. "Need to get a message to Antoine."

"About what?"

"Tell him we got something for him. We'll meet him around two a.m. Usual place."

Wayne nodded, cracked open a couple of long-necks and slid them toward the cousins. "On the house. Be back in a minute."

Wayne disappeared down the hallway, toward his office.

"This better work," Floyd said. "If we bring Antoine out in the middle of the night and we ain't got nothing, he's gonna be pissed."

"It'll work."

Wayne returned. "All set."

Next stop, Pine Valley. Eight miles east along a winding, two-lane, asphalt county road. They saw only two cars, both zipping by the other way. Before heading into town, Eddie guided the car off onto a dirt road and then across a field where he parked near a stand of pines.

Eddie stepped out. "This'll work."

Floyd removed a pair of saws from the backseat and they went at it. Took half an hour to take the tree down and cut the trunk into five pieces, each about thirty pounds, figuring the sections all told weighed about as much as old Jerry. Close enough. They lugged them to the trunk and lifted them inside.

"Let's get this done," Floyd said.

Pine Valley wasn't much of a town and this time of night the streets were dark and deserted, only a couple of the bars showing any signs of life. Along the road that marked the north edge of the business district, if you could call it that, sat Grace Funeral Home. A wooded lot that backed up to a wad of trees, its front lawn and driveway sloping down toward the road. To the left of the low brick building sprawled the cemetery, dotted with a few trees and sprinkled with white headstones that seemed almost ghostly in the dark. They drove by, giving it the once-over before circling back. No lights on inside, no cars in the lot. Eddie switched off the headlamps, scooted up the drive, and whipped around behind the structure.

Getting in was easy. Floyd used a screwdriver to lever open the lock. In less than half a minute, they stepped inside, the odor of formaldehyde and death greeting them.

Eddie hated funeral homes. Never been in one, unless there was a visitation in progress. Those were all lit up and filled with people. Not like now where it was dark and spooky. The stillness was smothering, the echoes of their footsteps on the concrete floor unnerving.

"This place is creepy," Floyd said.

"That it is," Eddie said. "Let's get at it and get the hell out of here."

They found the cold storage area behind a metal door that grated and squeaked as they slid it open. Inside, the chilled air held a nauseating stench.

"Jesus," Floyd said. "How does anyone do this for a living?"

Inside were two caskets, each supported by a metal stand. One open and empty, the other closed. It was pewter colored and the lid heavy. Floyd directed his flashlight beam inside.

A corpse. Covered with a white cloth. Eddie peeled it back. They jumped in unison. Jerry Crabtree's body was wrapped in similar cloth, his exposed face a brownish, reddish mass of flesh.

Eddie felt his stomach lurch. He struggled not to vomit. "Good lord." He stepped back. "I don't know if I can do this."

"You can," Floyd said. "Think of it as two hundred and fifty bucks."

Eddie took a couple of deep breaths, settling things. He nodded.

Twenty minutes later they had removed the body, placed the five tree sections inside, closed the casket all nice and tight, and ferried Jerry's corpse to the trunk.

"What if they take a peek inside before the funeral?" Floyd asked.

"Don't see why they would."

"But if they do? What then?"

"No way they can connect this to us," Eddie said.

"We better hope not."

Eddie got in the car and sat behind the wheel. Sweat frosted his face and his stomach continued its protest.

"You okay?" Floyd asked as he climbed in the passenger seat.

"Mostly."

* * *

"Let's see what you got," Antoine said.

They stood near the Ford's trunk beneath the tree where they always made such exchanges. Eddie popped open the lid. Antoine peeled back the dingy canvas covering the corpse. He gave a start.

"What is this?" Antoine asked. "What the hell'd you do?"

"We didn't do nothing," Floyd said.

"He hit a tree," Eddie added. "All we did was snatch him from the funeral home."

Antoine looked at them. "You did what?"

"We figured it was better than digging him up tomorrow night," Eddie said. "And he's a day fresher."

Antoine shook his head. "Don't you think they'll miss him? At the funeral?"

Eddie explained the closed casket service, the logs they had slipped inside. He closed with, "Clean and simple."

Antoine smiled. Sort of. "That's actually pretty clever." He looked back at the corpse. "Not sure he can use this though."

"Sure he can. The rest of him's fine. Only twenty-eight and just forty-eight hours dead."

Antoine hesitated, and then said, "Okay, get it moved."

Again, he stood back and let Floyd and Eddie do the work. Once the transfer was completed, Antoine handed them the two-fifty, climbed in his car, and drove away.

Eddie followed him down the drive to the road. When Antoine turned right toward Pine Creek, Eddie went left. In the rearview mirror, he watched until Antoine's taillights disappeared around a curve, then swung onto the gravel shoulder and pulled a quick U-turn.

"What're you doing?" Floyd asked.

"I want to know where he's going. Who he's delivering the body to."

"You think that's wise? He might see us."

"Not if we're careful."

Eddie raced back up the county highway, until he saw Antoine's taillights disappear over a rise in the road. He flicked off the headlamps.

"I hope you know what you're doing," Floyd said. "And don't run into nothing."

Tailing Antoine was a snap. His was the only car on the road and once in town they could easily stay a couple of blocks back and follow his every turn. Just south of downtown, he climbed a steep drive to a massive antebellum home that possessed views over the town and the entire valley.

Eddie pulled to the side of the road. "What the hell?"

"Ain't that Dr. Bell's house?" Floyd asked.

"Sure is."

Eddie watched Antoine's car slide around the side of the mansion and toward the large white barn behind. The car came to a stop and the taillights went dark.

"What on earth does Dr. Bell need with a corpse?" Floyd asked.

Eddie thought about that but couldn't come up with a reasonable idea. "Let's go grab a beer and think on it."

* * *

"I ain't sure this is a good idea," Floyd said.

"Me neither," Eddie said. "But we got to know what's what."

"We do?"

"Ain't you curious?"

"Course I am. But I don't want to get caught neither."

"It's three in the morning. Ain't nobody up and about." Eddie motioned toward the mansion. "Not a light nowhere."

Over a few beers at Floyd's place they had decided that a look inside Dr. Bell's barn was in order. Took Eddie a while to convince Floyd but finally he gave in. He always did. They parked in McGill's lot, walked the two blocks to the edge of town, crossed the county road, and eased into the trees a couple of hundred yards from the Bell Mansion. They worked their way to the back side of the property, hopped the fence, and now stood near the barn's corner, the rear of the mansion in full view. Bell's Caddy sat near the back door.

"Now what?" Floyd asked.

"Find a way inside."

That proved easy. The large double doors were closed but the lock hung loosely and unlatched in the metal loop. The door squeaked softly as Floyd pushed it open, then closed, once they were inside. The air seemed musty and laced with a slightly sweet, almost medicinal odor.

Eddie swept the interior with his flashlight. One large room, no loft, a series of tables lined up cross-ways in the center. Open bins filled with plastic barrels and stacks of cardboard boxes, alternated with tall lockers along the left wall. To the right, a massive industrial mixer sat near a low gas stove topped with four metallic stock pots. Along the far wall, shelves held rows of Dr. Bell's Body Tonic.

"What the hell?" Eddie said.

"You don't think...?" Floyd fell silent as if he couldn't finish his thought.

Eddie walked among the tables. A few bone fragments and what looked like strips of leather lay on one. An electric meat grinder and two stainless steel blenders on another. A black plastic jar labeled "Bone Meal" caught Eddie's eye. He lifted it, shook it, spun the lid off. Floyd directed his flashlight beam inside. A fine, grayish-white powder.

"What the hell is all this?" Floyd asked.

Eddie did a slow three-sixty before responding. "Looks to me like old Doc Bell is grinding up bodies and putting them in his tonic."

Dr. Bell's Body Tonic was famous. The drug store downtown had an entire shelf devoted to the various mixtures. Each touted a specific health benefit. Printed right on the label in big, red letters. Some made your brain better; others built muscles or cleaned up your liver or kidneys. Still others were for fevers or bowel regularity or to build stronger bones. Dr. Bell's stuff could fix your whole damn body.

"Your mom used to give us that shit," Floyd said.

"I know." Eddie scratched an ear.

"What are we going to do?" Floyd asked.

"Ain't much we can do. I mean, we been stealing bodies. Not like we can tell another living soul."

"Exactly."

The voice came from behind them. The cousins spun that way. Dr. Thomas Bell and Antoine stood in the doorway. Eddie hadn't even heard it open.

"We was just curious," Eddie said.

"Like the cat?" Bell said. "Didn't work out well for him, did it?"

"We don't mean no harm," Floyd said. "And we ain't going to

say a word. We was just…" His voice trailed off.

"Just what?" Bell said.

Eddie stared at him, racking his brain for something to say, something that would get them out of this. He came up empty.

"Looks like we have ourselves a couple of fresh ones," Antoine said.

Eddie now noticed the gun Antoine held in his hand. "Look, we don't want no problems."

"Probably should've thought of that before you came snooping around," Antoine said.

Bell laid a hand on Antoine's arm. He waved his other toward the tables. "What do you think of all this?"

"I don't rightly know what to think," Eddie said. "This ain't what I expected."

Bell nodded. "It's really quite simple. My product, my tonic, is better than all the others because it contains what the body needs. The right mixture of proteins and minerals for good health."

"'Cause it contains body parts?" Eddie asked.

Bell smiled. "See, you do understand."

Eddie glanced at the jar of ground bones again. "I suppose."

"The only question is, what are you going to do?" Bell said. "Now that you possess this knowledge."

Eddie glanced at Floyd, getting a blank stare in return. "Ain't much we could do. Or would, for that matter." He shuffled his feet. "I mean the folks're already dead and gone. Ain't no harm in using them to make others better, I suspect. It's not like the dead would know."

Bell clapped his hands together. "That's exactly right. Death is always tragic and sad, but if we can help make others better, the loss is not in vain."

Eddie nodded.

"So can I be assured you two are okay with this?"

Floyd shrugged. "Ain't no skin off my nose."

"Mine neither," Eddie added.

"Good." Bell held their gaze for a moment. "The one you brought us tonight is exactly what I need. Young, muscular, and fairly fresh."

"What about his face being all stove in?" Eddie asked.

"No concern. You see, I dry them out. Sort of like making jerky. Then grind them up. The bones, too. Only need a tiny amount to make each bottle of tonic." He smiled. "So the only question I have is, how many can you supply?"

Eddie looked at him. "I guess that depends on how many folks pass. And how soon we can get to them."

Bell nodded. "Maybe expand your horizons to other counties."

"We're already thinking on that. It'd be a might trickier since we don't know those areas as well."

"And that's why I'm offering you a raise. Double. How does that sound?"

"Good." Eddie nodded. "Sounds real good."

"You see," Bell said, "I sell in four states right now but I see an opportunity to move into half a dozen others. Which requires growing the operation. And, in turn, more raw materials."

"Bodies?" Floyd asked.

"As many more as you can locate."

* * *

It was Sunday morning. Sheriff Amos Dugan sat in his front porch rocker, reading the newspaper, and finishing off a cup of coffee. He had another hour to kill before getting dressed for church. That's when a car pulled into his drive.

"Amos," Bill Grace said as he climbed out and walked toward the porch. "Sorry to bother you on a Sunday morning."

Dugan knew Grace, the funeral director over in Pine Valley. Fact was, they went way back. To grammar school.

"No problem, Bill." He folded the paper. "Can I get you a cup of coffee? Millie just made it fresh."

"Another time." Grace lowered himself into the adjacent rocker.

"What can I do for you?" Dugan asked.

"Got me a situation." Grace shook his head. "One hell of a situation."

"Sounds like I ain't gonna like it."

"Jerry Crabtree's body's gone missing."

Dugan rocked forward and stared at his friend. "Want to explain that?"

"His momma stopped by this morning. Early. Brought Jerry's Bible for me to slip in the casket." He stared off toward the peach tree in the yard, took a breath, and went on. "She'd of put it in herself, at the visitation yesterday, but it's a closed casket deal. The funeral's today. She wanted her boy buried with it."

"And he's gone?"

Grace nodded. "Someone replaced the body with chunks of tree trunk."

"Good lord." Dugan let out a sigh. "Sometime during the night?"

"Looks that way. I saw some scratching on the back door lock so I suspect that's the way they got in."

"What would someone want with Jerry's body?"

"Ain't got no idea."

"I'm here to tell you," Dugan said, "the world don't make no sense sometimes." He rubbed his chin. "You tell his momma yet?"

"Nope. Wanted to talk with you first. But she's my next stop."

Dugan stood, his knees protesting with a few creaks and pops. "I'll get dressed and tell Martha I ain't going to make church today. Then I'll meet you over at your funeral home. Say about an hour?"

"Sounds good."

Dugan watched his friend drive away, letting the news settle. This changed everything. The disturbed dirt over at Wilbert Fleming's grave took on a whole new meaning. Opening it up could no longer be avoided. If someone stole one body, why not two? He suddenly felt all of his sixty-two years.

* * *

Tuesday night around midnight found Eddie and Floyd at McGill's. Sitting on barstools, knocking back a few beers. They'd heard a few folks talking about the theft of Jerry Crabtree's body and someone digging up Wilbert Fleming, God rest their souls, but those conversations were short lived and quickly moved on to the weather, hunting, fishing, football. The usual topics.

Eddie was feeling good about things. Sure Jerry and Wilbert

going missing was creating a bit of a stir, but now three days later, he felt Floyd and him were in the clear.

That's when Antoine walked in. He didn't say a word, merely nodded toward the back as he walked by. Eddie and Floyd slid off their stools and followed him down the hall that led to the restrooms, past them, and out the rear door to the gravel parking lot over near the trash cans. Antoine turned, folded his arms across his chest, and glared at them.

"So much for your brilliant idea," Antoine said.

"What do you mean?" Eddie asked. "It worked."

"Did it?"

"Well now, we weren't thinking they'd ever know, but even if they do there's no way it comes back to us." He tapped his cousin's shoulder. "Or to you and Dr. Bell."

"Not yet."

"If they was going to, they already would of. Don't you think?"

"I think Dr. Bell ain't happy. I think I ain't happy. I think you two shouldn't think so much. You're not very good at it."

"It was a good plan," Eddie said. "How'd we know they was going to look inside? I mean, it being closed and all."

"But they did."

"It still ain't gonna cause us no grief."

"You better hope not." Antoine's eyes narrowed and his jaw muscles gave a couple of pumps. "No more stealing from funeral homes. Dig them up like you're supposed to. No one will look *after* they're buried."

Eddie nodded.

"And no more big ideas lest you run them by me first."

* * *

Thursday evening, Eddie and Floyd were again at McGill's. It was nearing two a.m., closing time, and only half a dozen people remained. A few stools down sat a visitor. Skinny guy from Maryland, on his way to New Orleans, stopping for the night. At least, that's what he jawed to Wayne the bartender about. He'd had more than a few beers and wobbled, even when planted firmly on a barstool.

"You sure about this?" Floyd asked, speaking just loud enough for Eddie to hear.

"Seems easy enough," Eddie said.

"Should we talk to Antoine first?"

"Screw him. He don't own us."

"But he's the guy who pays," Floyd said.

"Bell does that."

"Not directly."

"Maybe it's time to cut out the middleman."

"Bell won't like that," Floyd said.

Eddie cut his eyes toward his cousin. "He just might. One less mouth to feed. And we'll get more money." He nodded toward the visitor, leaned near Floyd. "Especially if we can bring him a *real* fresh one."

"I don't know. I ain't sure I like this."

Eddie smiled. "You never like what I think up. Until you dwell on it a spell. Then you see the wisdom. Way it always is." Another smile. "Besides, ain't nobody going to miss him."

"Someone will."

Eddie shrugged. "Not no one around here."

The guy dug in his pocket and pulled out a few wadded bills. "How much I owe you?" he asked.

"Make it seven even," Wayne said.

The man laid a five and three ones on the bar. "There's a dollar for you." He slid off the stool and shuffled toward the door.

Eddie paid their tab. Once on the street, they saw the guy. Half a block away, weaving his way down the sidewalk. The street was otherwise deserted. They caught up to him as he reached his car and struggled to unlock the door.

"Hey buddy," Eddie said. "You okay?"

The guy looked up, grinned. "If I can get this door unlocked I sure will be."

"Don't look like you're in any condition to drive. Can we help you? Where you going?"

The guy straightened up, wavered, caught the car roof to maintain his balance. "Bartender said there was a motel just down the road."

"There is," Eddie said. "Pretty nice one. Why don't we take you there?"

He seemed to consider that. "Can't leave my car here."

"No problem. My cousin'll drive you there and I'll follow along. That way you'll have your car in the morning."

"You'd do that?"

"Sure. We'd be obliged to."

* * *

Seven-thirty in the morning found Sheriff Amos Dugan behind his desk, staring at the nervous young couple before him. Robbie Peters, seventeen, high school junior, football player, and Betty Jane Marks, a sophomore who played clarinet in the band.

"What can I do for you youngsters?" Dugan asked.

Robbie glanced at Betty Jane. "We saw something the other night."

"Something like what?"

"It was last Saturday night. We'd gone to a movie over in Pine Valley. Then we…" again, he looked at Betty Jane.

"Just relax, son," Dugan said. "Tell me what you came here to say."

"We went parking for a while. Over in the cemetery."

Dugan laughed. "Me and the missus used to do that when we was your age."

That seemed to relax the couple.

"We like it because it's quiet," Robbie said.

Dugan nodded, laughed again. "It is that."

Robbie smiled. "Anyway, you know it's right next to the funeral home. Grace's." Dugan nodded so he continued. "We saw a car come up and park behind it."

Dugan sat straight up. "Go ahead on."

"Two guys went in the back. They had flashlights and seemed to be carrying stuff in and out for the better part of a half hour. Seemed odd."

"Any idea what they was up to?"

Robbie shook his head. "We was too far away to see good. And we were afraid to leave. Didn't want no one knowing we was there."

He glanced at Betty Jane again. "She missed her curfew 'cause we had to wait until they left."

"And my daddy wasn't happy," she said.

Dugan nodded and smiled. "Parents can be that way." He looked back at Robbie. "I take it you couldn't identify these guys?"

"Like I said, we was a good piece away and it was dark."

"Their car? What kind was it?"

Robbie smiled. "That I know. I like cars. It was a forty-nine Ford. Black."

"And it had that brown stuff on the fender," Betty Jane said.

"Primer?" Dugan asked.

"Yeah," Robbie answered.

"If it was dark how come you could see that?"

"When they left, they circled around by the cemetery. They was only maybe fifty feet from us. I was afraid they'd see us but they didn't. Anyway, we saw the fender then."

After the kids left, Dugan picked up the phone and buzzed his secretary, out front at the reception desk. "Clarice, you know where Travis is?"

"Sure do. He's standing right here, drinking coffee and looking like an idiot."

Dugan loved Clarice. Her irreverent sense of humor kept him and Travis on their toes. "Well, send the idiot back here."

Travis walked in. "What's up?"

Dugan told him the story.

"I know that car," Travis said. "Belongs to Eddie Whitt."

"You sure?"

"I'm sure he's got a forty-nine Ford with a stove-in left front fender."

Dugan nodded, then stood. "Maybe we should go have a talk with him."

"You thinking Eddie stole Jerry's body?"

"Looks that way." Dugan shook his head. "Means he's probably the one what dug up Wilbert Fleming, too."

* * *

Eddie turned up Dr. Bells' drive.

"I still think we should've talked to Antoine first."

"Don't you see his car? Up there by the barn?"

"Course I do. I just meant maybe we should've met him out at the usual place. Showing up here, Dr. Bell might not like it."

"He will when he sees what we got."

Eddie parked next to Antoine's Chevy. One of the large double barn doors was cracked open a couple of feet so they stepped inside. Dr. Bell and Antoine stood by one of the tables, mixing a pot of liquid with a large wooden paddle. It smelled almost like stew. Almost.

"Morning," Eddie said.

The two men whirled toward them, surprise on their faces.

"What the hell you doing here?" Antoine asked.

"Got a new one for you," Eddie said.

Antoine walked toward them, the scowl on his face deepening, "Didn't I tell you to never come here again? We got a place to do this. A private place."

Eddie nodded, smiled. "This one's so fresh I thought we'd get it to you right soon."

Dr. Bell approached. "Please tell me you didn't steal it from a funeral home again."

"Nope. He's just some guy. Passing through town."

"What happened to him?" Bell asked.

"I think he choked on something."

"What does that mean?"

Eddie laughed. "Let's just say he had trouble breathing."

* * *

Dugan and Travis scoured the town for Eddie's car. A visit to his house and then a quick stop by his momma's place turned up nothing. They then zig-zagged all over but saw no sign of the car. As they circled the county road on the edge of town, Dugan said, "Not sure where else to look."

"What about there?" Travis said. He pointed up the hillside toward Dr. Bell's mansion.

Dugan glanced that way. Eddie's car sat near the barn behind and to the left of the house. "Good eyes."

"Damn fine police work's what it was." Travis smiled.

"What the hell's he doing at Dr. Bell's place?"

"Don't know. But that's Antoine's car up there, too."

"Antoine Briscoe?"

"The one and only," Travis said.

Antoine was no stranger to Dugan. He'd arrested him more than once. Drinking and fighting mostly.

"Interesting group of folks," Dugan said.

"That'd be my assessment."

Dugan slowed, turned up the drive. "Maybe we should go have ourselves a chat."

He parked near the left front of the house, out of any sightline from the barn, and stepped out. He opened up the back door, grabbed his twelve-gauge LC Smith double-barreled shotgun. He cracked it open, saw the two 4-0 buckshot shells inside, and snapped it closed.

"You think you'll need that?" Travis asked.

"Can't hurt to have it."

* * *

With the stranger's body stretched out on the table, Dr. Bell cut away the clothing and began his examination. Head to foot. Eddie watched, wondering just what the hell he was doing. Bell seemed to focus on the dead guy's neck. Finally, he straightened and looked at the cousins.

"This man didn't choke. He was strangled."

"So?" Eddie asked.

"So? That's all you have to say?" Bell's face reddened, his jaw pulsed.

"You wanted fresh ones. We got you one. And it ain't even been embalmed or nothing."

Eddie felt the heat from Bell's glare.

"It's one thing to dig up dead bodies, even steal them from funeral homes, but this? Are you two mentally defective?"

Antoine's gun appeared, leveled at the cousins. Eddie took a step back, raising his hands.

"I was you, I'd put that gun down."

The voice came from behind him. Eddie whirled around. Sheriff Dugan and his sidekick Travis Sutton stood in the doorway, Dugan's double-barrel aimed at the group.

"Set it on the floor, Antoine," Dugan said. "And give it a kick over this way."

Antoine did, the gun skittering across the floor. Travis picked it up.

Dugan's gaze swept the room, the four men, the corpse, the stacked cases of Dr. Bell's Tonic. He gave a slow nod. "Looks like we all're gonna need to engage in some sort of discussion."

"I can explain," Bell said.

"Got my ears on," Dugan said.

Bell stood there, silently. Seemed to Eddie that he was figuring what to say. Probably running through his options but not finding a good one. Neither could Eddie. Not one that would explain away the dead guy on the table and all the bones and jars of tissue and organs waiting to be dealt with.

"What's the matter?" Travis asked. "Cat got your tongue?"

Bell sighed, then spelled it out. The corpse, the tonics, the entire operation.

Dugan's gaze hardened, but as Bell went on his face seemed to relax. When Bell finished his story, Dugan gave a slight nod, did a spin around the table, along the shelves, examining everything.

"And this is how you make all your money?" Dugan asked.

Bell nodded.

"How much we talking here?"

Bell shrugged. "You've seen my home." He waved a hand. "And the Caddy I drive."

Dugan propped the shotgun over one arm, the muzzle angled at the floor. "Why don't we go inside, grab some coffee, and you tell me more about how all this works?"

* * *

TONIGHT IS THE NIGHT

SHANNON KIRK

George Talent is going to do it tonight. He's sick of waiting, fretting for the right moment. The right words. Tonight is the night, dammit! Indeed, he says those words, "Tonight is the night, is the night, is the night," in his native New England accent, to his own ruby face and Santa-round nose and salt-n-pepper beard, right out-loud to himself in the rearview mirror of his Richard's Mountain company truck—the white one with the double cab, the one with chains on great snow tires. Well, the whole fleet has chains in this kind of blizzard.

Settled in his intentions, George turns off the crackly news, coming in on wonky radio waves tonight, given the weather. After the dread peddlers were done with their blizzard forecasts and dire warnings, as if a typical blizzard isn't just another groundhog's night in Vermont, a hyper-boy newscaster pitched high on another trauma going on in the mountain region: some weird-ass brutal murders. The newscaster even named what all presumed was a serial killer, "The Spine Ripper," based on the common style of the kills.

Flippin' psychos, more of 'em as time goes on and growing sicker, George thinks. *It's the damn internet giving crazy ideas. But who cares, got nothing to do with me. Tonight is the night, no matter what.*

George cranks off the ignition, pushes open the driver's door, and slides out. Standing in the open door, given the fast snow infiltrating his cab, he works quick to shove his keys with the *Strand Bookstore* keychain deep in his cavernous man-jean's pocket. He next grabs his camo-print Duck Hunters' Guild wallet from the center cubby and shoves it in an even-deeper butt pocket. He nods deference to an important book of brown leather he leaves in the center cubby, adjacent to his sheathed hunting knife.

"I do love you, Lady, but time's moving on. It has to be tonight.

You'll always, always be my girl. Tonight is the night," he says to the book.

Before back-stepping in the snow to shut his door, he checks the mini clock embedded in the dashboard. Noting it's 12:05 a.m., he resolves that his work day has near begun, shuts the door, and presses "lock" on the universal fob that works on all vehicles in the Richard's Mountain fleet of trucks. As he walks to tonight's first destination, he, like a carefree child, rakes four fingers through the snow-plastered decal on the side of his truck. Four thick lines now etch the decal's snow-capped peaks and evergreen base and *Richard's Mountain* in luscious red script on the top curve, and *99 trails, 99 dreams, 99 ways to fall in love* on the bottom curve.

It's true midnight now, meaning it's time for breakfast or a mid-drinking snack in the townie/mountain staff bar: Malforson's Bar & Grill. "Grill" being quite a euphemism, since there is no grill and only two items are on the flippin' menu.

But whatever, *whatever*, it'll do. *Always has.*

George makes his way towards the bar, which most passersby fail to see from this curvy mountain road. Set in a depression of land, only one story, and near-surrounded by snowy pines, it could be, on dark nights—especially stormy nights like tonight— just a roadside shadow. Up close, it appears as a cozy troll cottage baked of gingerbread, with its brown shingles, smoking chimney, and low-hung windows with drifts of snow in each pane. Amber battery candles sit on the sill of each window, firmly cementing the joint as one Santa's more jaded elves might frequent after a long night of making tinker toys and bobsleds.

Another mountain staffer ambles behind George, having locked his own company truck. George hears the beep of this worker's universal fob and twists to nod a hello. The co-worker, Kyle something or other, he's new, brand new, nods back.

Where'd Kyle whatshisface come in from? Colorado? Marquette? Who cares. Not tonight. Don't care.

"Hey there, George," Kyle New Boy says.

"Hey," says George, scrunching his eyes to avoid a deluge of snow from the sky.

George doesn't wait for Kyle, and this isn't George being rude.

This is him teaching new boy the ropes. There are rules, laws, amongst staff and townies in the hidden cocoon of Malforson's Bar and Grill. And one law is no talking outside. Another is no monopolizing a single-solitary person's short-time inside, before a mountain shift. One can talk to the whole bar, if the whole bar is listening, but one-on-one ear beatings are strictly banned. Kyle doesn't rush to catch up to George, so hopefully new boy gets it.

And so, the regular night routine clicks in to begin.

But this is no regular night. *No! I won't let another night pass. Tonight is the night.*

It is the beginning of the work day for the skeleton crew that grooms the slopes in the middle of profit-promising blizzards, such as tonight; and it's the middle of a drinking night for the Cliffs and Norms of the village. This is their *Cheers.* The binary menu fits both sides of the divide: eggs-n-bacon sandwiches in tinfoil, kept under a humming heat lamp is one choice; and palm-shaped sliders cooked in a toaster oven is the other. Mostly the sliders are meant to soak up the townies' constant rum and cokes and dozens of draws from the tap, and the egg-n-bacon hockey pucks are for mountain staff. Sometimes the staff and townies mix up the menu between themselves; a grease-dripping slider from the toaster before an all-nighter in a snowcat is a great way to start one's work-night. But no matter what, *no matter what*, there's not a damn fool townie who would take even a drop of drip coffee meant for the mountain's night staff. That would be sacrilege. Also sacrilege would be mountain staff taking a townie's designated seat at the bar. Coffee and stools are sacrosanct, the *détente* formed to accommodate the demilitarized zone of Malforson's.

These are the intricate, unstated but firm, *laws* of Malforson's: no ear-beatings, only communal talking if the community as a whole is listening, no coffee for townies, no designated bar stools for mountain staff. *Laws.*

Breaking any could lead to violence. Possibly justified homicide.

There are other laws, too.

Such as, one law, seems to George, is that not a mugger in here is permitted to believe any of George's amazing, and true dammit, tales. Nor do any of these fools believe he'll ever actually profess his love to Karen's face.

But dammit. *Tonight is the night* to profess his love. *Screw these muggers at the bar. Who cares what they believe.*

George, at six-foot-five and straight-up turned fifty this year, doesn't flinch under the sheets of snow layering him like fancy-pants buttercream on a normal-old cupcake. He doesn't sway a fraction from the frigid, whipping wind. Doesn't slip even a second on the black ice hidden under accumulating powder on the walkway from parking lot to black bar door. A long-term employee of Richard's Mountain, he's wearing his strap-on cleats over steel-toe boots. His internal temperature is a furnace anyway, so he's not cold, especially since he's in a Richard's Mountain, arctic-tundra, gortex, smoretex, whatever newfangled fabric coat. *Fine.*

Whatever, he thinks, while spiking into the black ice and pulling the black handle on the black door. *Big deal we got a storm. It doesn't matter. It's tonight. Tonight is the night. I'm talking to Karen if she's willing to listen. I hope I haven't waited too long.*

In a short mudroom of sorts, George takes off his coat in a way that shimmies any snow to the metal grate floor, meant to capture snow and send it to a well beneath. In hanging his coat on a wood peg, he slides out a thin empty thermos from an inner pocket. Next, he bends to remove the strap-on cleats from his boots and sets them in his regular cubby, one amongst a total of fifty, lining both sides of the bar's foyer. In behind him bustles new boy Kyle, who, breaking a Malforson's law, speaks.

"George, right? It's George?"

"Yeah."

"We have to take our spikes off here?"

"Yeah," George says, nods, and walks off.

Again, George isn't being rude, he just has to get this new kid to get it. He can't be seen being cornered into talking with some wolf pup. George is barely accepted, even after twenty years on the mountain, in this townie-dominant bar. He can't allow himself to be one of the staff the townies ask the owner to bounce. A terrible fate, for there's no other joint in Richard's Village open past ten p.m. for food, and eating in the resort bar at midnight means mingling with well-heeled skiers from New York City.

George doesn't like being reminded of New York City.

Ugh, he cringes, setting a hand to his heart to think of New York City.

But no! No more! No more wallowing on heartbreak of the past! *Tonight is the night.*

He's going to tell Karen during their night shift on the mountain. Even in this fog-out, blinding blizzard, which at the crack of dawn will bring all the gosh-damn city skiers. Yep, tonight's the night for love in Vermont, no matter how much snow-catting and limb trimming and lift clearing they need to do on every one of the 99 trails of dreams and ways to fall in love.

Tonight!

George makes his way to a non-designated middle stool at the bar. New boy Kyle sits two stools over, and the entire bar gasps. A woman at a table by a window with an amber candle says, "Oh shit, here we go."

George closes his eyes. Now he'll have to talk to Kyle. It's incumbent upon him to correct Kyle's gaffe, given that staff instructs staff and townie instructs townie. No other mountain staffers are present yet; George swivels to confirm. Not his beloved Karen, thank goodness. But she never comes to Malforson's anyway. And no annoying Bob yet. Not even ever-present Old Eli. So, dammit, George has got to do it.

"Look, kid. You can't sit there, right. That's Pete's chair. You best move before he…"

The bartender, named Kemper, with white rag in beer mug steps up and helps, "Before Pete gets back from his piss, yeah."

"Boy, you better hurry up," George says, trading an eyebrow-twitch with Kemper the bartender. This Kyle is in his thirties, George guesses, but George calls all of the newbies, "Boy," until they prove themselves worthy to have an actual name.

Kyle doesn't, as he should, immediately stand. He continues sitting, his lips pursed, looking at George as if evaluating.

"Right," Kyle says.

George squints an eye, wondering if he's going to have to

bulk up and fight. Wouldn't take much. George is a lumberjack of redwoods compared to Kyle's kindling-gathering frame. But George doesn't like violence. He especially doesn't want to fight tonight, tonight is a night for blizzard love.

Kyle breaks the gaze, stands, and says, "Well then. I'll move," not apologizing or noting any concession to established laws and norms as the new kid on the block.

As Kyle moves away from the stool, Pete rushes from the bathroom to reclaim his spot and shoots a glare at Kyle. Kyle raises his arms and says, "Settle old boy, no problem." To this shocking affront, Pete flares his nostrils at George and says, "You best get your boy in control."

George low-rumble groans. He can't disclaim Kyle just yet, for an unstated rule is that mountain staff must cover mountain staff. Never know if you get caught in a drift in a blizzard, on the cold side of Richard's, and need someone to race a tread patch to a shredded one on your snowcat before you freeze to death at 2:00 a.m.

"He'll get the hang of it. Won't you, Kyle?" George says.

"Sure, George, sure," Kyle says, eyes narrowed on him. "Hey, Bartender, how about the news instead of the game?"

George hangs his head between his shoulders, as if an exhausted parent to a never-ending shit stream of bad behavior from a toddler. It's like a rapid fire series of law breaking from this insolent Kyle. Nobody calls Kemper "Bartender." And nobody, absolutely nobody—not even the oldest townie—asks Kemper to change the channel.

"Look, Kyle," George intervenes before a townie steps up to face off with Kyle. That's how quick the violence rises over such infractions in Malforson's. The *détente* is actually a tinder box. "I'll spell it out. You're going to have to sit on over at that dark table by the bathrooms and keep your thoughts to yourself. See where nobody's sitting? That's for the new guys. You got some time there before you can get on up over here. K?"

"You know what?" Kemper the bartender says. "I'm in a good fuckin' mood, guy. How 'bout I welcome you with this one-time prize, yeah? Here ya' go." Kemper clicks away from a re-run of a famous Patriots' game over to the news. Immediately a weatherwoman with giant blonde hair is being tossed around on screen at the lakefront in Burlington. Wind, snow, typical blizzard words of hysteria and dire warnings to stay in and keep those generators ready. Hopes that people stocked up on milk and water and bread. *Typical*. None of the bar occupants, except maybe Kyle, listen to a word of it.

Kyle doesn't say thanks for the channel change. Doesn't smile. He walks backwards, nodding in turn at Pete and George and Kemper. He plucks at a phantom toothpick in his teeth with his tongue. George thinks he sees Kyle mouth the words "rude boy" to him, but George won't allow himself to think that's what Kyle said. A shiver runs down George's spine, thinking on a violent day in his past when those same words were said by a stranger. *No, no, he didn't. He couldn't have. I'm imagining things. Besides, don't escalate this.*

"Gotcha, cowboys. I'll sit here at the table in the dark then," Kyle says.

Kyle, tucked away at the least favorite table, sits tight. He accepts a black coffee from a waitress and catches an eggs-n-bacon hot disc tossed to him by Kemper. Otherwise, he disappears into the worst table's shadows. He glares at the TV news, or he could be glaring at George or Pete, given that they sit directly under it. Or maybe Kemper, who moves behind the bar, under the television.

George proceeds to order and dine on both a greasy slider and a bacon-n-cheese, partly to show his solidarity with both factions in the bar. And partly to abide his hungry nerves.

He's back to thinking on his plan with Karen.

"Tonight's the night," he says to Kemper.

"No shit," Kemper says.

"Hell yeah. I'm going to rip off the Band-Aid and declare my love. I got to."

"Big man like you, no way. Too chicken. Will never happen," Kemper says, in good cheer.

"Yeah, well," George says. "You're wrong. Throw me in another slider. Extra cheese. And more coffee."

Kemper goes about his work.

A number of townies and a couple more mountain staff have filtered in in the meantime. The entire while, Kyle has remained in shadow and silent. Now that the bar is more filled, people sitting at tables by the windows with candles, a few more at the bar, and a smattering few within the two green booths on a side wall, a bees' hum of voices is rising. As with most major weather events, especially a blizzard, the outside has pushed the dark matter between barflies tighter. So this will be a communal conversation night.

Townie Pete, next to George, kicks it off with his loud booming voice.

"Well, now, George. Ain't it was a night like this, what…seven, eight years ago? After you lost your Blessed Martha, bless her heart, may that good woman rest in peace." Pete pauses to make a sign of the cross. As if in rote-practice in a Catholic mass, the entire bar, but for new boy Kyle, says, in clunky unison, "Bless that Blessed Martha. May she rest in peace." George nods thanks to their deference for Martha.

"Anyway," Pete continues. "Wasn't it sometime years after, after Our Blessed Martha was stabbed by a, what you try to tell us? A robot?" The whole bar laughs, except for Kyle, who is still glaring at the TV or Kemper, or Pete or George. It's hard to tell the angle of Kyle's sightline, given the shadows of his exile.

George rolls his eyes. "Here we go. Go on then, get it over with. Go on with what you got to say, Pete." These muggers are never going to believe George's amazing true tales. And a robot did stab Martha. But *whatever*. "Whatever, Pete, whatever. Go on then."

Pete, chuckling, says, "Hold on, hold on," and takes a massive gulp of his rum and coke. It might be his tenth of the night. "Oh boy, George, you and your tales. So was after Blessed Martha, I know, but you come in a night after a blizzard just like this. And ho boy, did you lay one fresh pile of shit on us. I'll never forget. You ever gonna forget it, Kemper?"

"Hell no," Kemper yells, while setting down George's extra-cheese slider.

"You ever gonna forget, Sue?" Pete says, swiveling to see a woman, sitting at the end of the bar, her designated townie seat.

She has the frown lines of a lifelong smoker, and, incongruously to this deep dark forest of a troll bar, wears a shiny green sequined tank top.

"I ain't ever gonna forget it, Pete. Neva," Sue says. She tips her own rum and coke at George in salute. George tips back, even while he rolls his eyes, annoyed they don't believe his true tales, but also willing to take a ribbing. He is, after all, a lover in his hot-furnace lumberjack core. And what none of these muggers knows is, he can, when he tries, be an actual poet. But whatever. *Whatever.* Let them roast him. He can take it. Because tonight is the night for telling Karen, no matter what. Ten years he's been lonely, without his blessed Martha. It's time for love again.

"Hey, I know this tale, Pete. Let me tell it," annoying mountain staffer Bob interjects. Bob is sitting in one of the green booths. Kyle is still glaring at the news, or at Pete or at George or at Kemper, it is so hard to tell. George doesn't want to call Kyle out because that would only escalate whatever it was it seemed Kyle wanted to previously escalate. George thinks it's best to let the regulars roast him, finish his night breakfast, and get to the mountain.

In the background, the news has shifted from dystopia-level storm reports to the dominating news story of the last few weeks, the one George was listening to in his truck. All about some sick human-body filet artist that the authorities can't seem to identify or catch. "The Spine Ripper is believed responsible for an alarming eight unsolved murders this winter thus far," the newscaster says.

But the regulars are well into a communal story, and the news has to rise to the level of Mount Washington blowing and revealing herself to be a secret volcano for these muggers to quit a communal story.

"Go for it, Bob," Pete blesses, ignoring the news. "Go on, tell that wild George tale."

"Right, right. So, was a blizzard just like this," Bob says, picking up the thread. "George here, he had the cold side of the mountain that night. I had Front Face. Anyway, we all worked all night. The next night, we're back in here rearing up for another long night shift. George comes in. This George right here, you, George," Bob says, pointing at George.

"No shit, Bob. I'm George," George says, shaking his head to Townie Pete to indicate his opinion that co-worker Bob is daft.

"So, you, George, you're a friggin' kick. You pop in here, all big guy chest out, blustering about how on the cold side of the mountain, come 2:00 a.m. the night a'fore, a pack of coyotes comes up and surrounds your snowcat. Yipping and barking at you mad. And they're threatening and jumping up and snipping away at the door and all, so you're holding it tight." Bob stands from his green booth and reenacts George's first reenactment. Bob is pulling and pulling on air as if holding closed the door to a snowcat. "So, then, you say. Then, you notice that the alpha was standing directly in front of the point part of your plow blade, and under a full moon, which was blurry white, what with the snow. I remember you gave that detail, George. You're good, a good storyteller, yeah. Anyway, that alpha bitch coyote stared at you as if a snorting bull, getting ready to charge one of them there marionettes with the red cape."

"Oh my fucking hell, it's a matador, you idiot. Not a marionette," George says.

The bar laughs. But Bob is not derailed. He laughs himself and continues. "So anyway, Madam Coyote Bitch is about to charge and have her pack charge when a bark from behind her made her turn her head. Up steps Blessed Martha's hound Cope, you said. Her very dog who ran off to the woods when she was stabbed by a robot, oh my Lord in Heaven, that's what you claim. You hadn't seen Cope in years, until that night with the coyotes. Seeing Cope, you near passed out. You got out of your cab, threw Cope an eggs-n-bacon, because you say you always carry a "pocket snack" from the bar, and Cope, well Cope she damn well took it! Cope growled at the coyotes, who hurried up behind her and waited. Cope was always a smart hound. And then, snap, the pack fled, along with Cope. You said your Martha was looking out for you is what. Oh what wild bullshit, George. A hound and coyotes living together. What extraordinary bullshit, you blubbering romantic."

The entire bar is roaring now. Except for Kyle, who continues glaring on at the television, or at Pete or at George. Can't be Kemper this time; Kemper's shuttled to a somewhat hidden corner with the fireplace to add another log.

"Oh my God, George. Oh my God. And then, then, you say, up on a crest under the blurry moonlight, Old Cope, that magnificent hound, howls at the moon." Bob pauses to howl at a fake moon in the bar, "Awhoooo." He sits back down in his green booth, knuckles his table, and says, "Shit, George, it's amazing you survived. Good thing you can communicate with animals. Sure as fuck can't talk to a human woman no more. Amiright, y'all?"

"Hell right. How long you been crushin' on Karen, George," Kemper asks.

"Bite me," George says.

A log rolls in the fire and embers sizzle; the flames jump at the fresh air and lick high against the brick back of the fireplace.

George takes a moment to look around at the crowd as they break off in diminishing laughter. He notes Kyle still staring at him, or Pete or overhead to the TV. Not laughing along.

"There was that other time," Townie Pete says, twisting around in his bar stool to face the crowd, which causes all interior noise, except the crackling fire and the TV voices, to cease. Pete continues, "It was come this last here spring, what was it? This spring, I think. When the rivers were bloated and freezing ass cold. George comes in and says how he passed a bare-naked-ass man, bathing in the river, right off the main road. Great straight out in the open. Had himself a towel wrapped 'round his head like a lady out of the shower, was that it, George? And a body brush and all, scrubbing his pits. His dangler was free out in the freezing cool air."

Bob, the daft co-worker, rises again from his green booth, thrusts his groin forward, and wiggles his fingers over his crotch, pantomiming along to Pete's rendition of the story.

Pete chuckles at Bob and his finger dangler and continues his roast. "Everybody knows a fool would freeze his literal balls off in such arctic water. George gives us all these crazy details about how the dangler guy looked like a snowman, with a round bald head on a round neck on a round torso with round arms, round legs. 'He was a person made out of snowballs,' George here told us. Can't be true," Pete says. "Ain't nobody else report such an insane sighting."

"To Tall Tale George," Sue yells.

289

And the entire bar, except for Kyle, raises their beers and rums and cokes and coffees to George. "To Tall Tale George," they yell.

Except for Kyle. Kyle glares on in the same direction he's been glaring since he sat.

"Gruesome remains of Middle Tech college student, Christine Heilan, found this morning by Tyson's fishing hole. Her body had been, like others, split up the middle, her spine removed, and a fishing hook left in her lip," the news says.

"Why the fuck they give us these details?" Bob yells, flinging his arm in accusation at the television.

"Because it's after fucking midnight is why," Kemper says. "They give more after the babies are in bed. I'm putting the Pats back on."

And to this, the crowd cheers.

Kyle stands, throws cash on the least-favorite table, and walks out.

George waits several minutes for Kyle to leave and tilts his face to Kemper with a bemused look. "So the new guy's a bit of a… what would you call it?" George says.

"He's a stalka, that one, alright. I'd watch that one," says Sue, answering for Kemper. Sue's the Richard's Village townie who reads tarot cards for tourists. "He's not right in the noggin," she adds, tapping her temple. Sue's a New Englander through and through, several generations deep of Yankee blood, so thick, seven heirs more and living in Texas would still carry her accent of dropped r's and long a's. And like any soul stitched out of old Vermont sticks and true Vermont stones, Sue knows a thing or two or ten about witchcraft and judging who's worth your time and who can disappear down a running river. In fact, when Sue voices her opinion on anyone it's rare, but always right. And to her pronouncement about Kyle, several men in the bar say, "Ayup."

George considers Sue's words and nods a couple solemn beats at her. Her throat and chin are uplit in a tint of green from her sequined top, like she might, indeed, be a true witch.

He ticks his tongue as a way of saying he agrees with her.

"Alrighty then, I'm off. Big blizzard night. Gotta get em' powder perfect for the morning rush," George says, standing and extracting his Duck Hunters' Guild wallet. He throws a twenty to cover his $12.00 worth of finished food and coffee and a takeaway breakfast sandwich, which Kemper, without having to be asked, tosses to George. George pushes his thermos for filling, and Kemper obliges. George tells Kemper to keep the change.

Everyone quiets and stares at the screen when an alert sounds the "Breaking News" alarm—which must be fucking huge if the station would go so far as to interrupt this famous Pats' game. The newscaster narrates along to a sketch now being shown. "Just in. A woman who claims to have escaped a man who kidnapped her and her friend, and who she watched slice her friend on the bank of Poison River, in the manner we've previously reported on other victims, has provided this sketch."

"Oh my gawd," Sue says in a hush.

"What the fuck?" Bob says.

Kemper, who tends to be the most sane and most sober, and therefore generally regarded as the genius of the bar, looks to George and says, "Hold up, George," stopping George, who's standing now and about to push in his stool. "That your man? Your snowball man, bathing in the ice river?"

George looks up to see a sketch of a man with a round bald head, round neck, round torso, and round arms, just like he saw, the one bathing in the bloated spring river.

"Holy shit," George says. "That sure does look like him."

"You gotta call the Staties, George? Let 'em know?" Kemper says, but with questions littering his words.

Several people in the bar mutter, "What?" with scrunched brows, questioning whether any of George's tales could possibly have an ounce of truth.

"No fucking way that's George's phony bologna bare-ass snowman," Pete says, to which daft Bob scoffs and laughs, but with less assuredness than when he told his own George tale.

George considers their comments while looking at the screen. He takes his filled thermos as Kemper hands it to him, turns, and walks to the door. He knows he saw a bare-ass man made of a stack of circles bathing in the river this last spring, just like he said, but these muggers always make him question his own tales. *I know what I saw. Right?*

Anyway, whatever, *whatever!* He yells at his own mind. *You can think more on it as you snowcat tonight, don't listen to these muggers putting doubt in you. Focus on the plan with Karen. Tonight is the night no matter what!*

As George goes through the motions of slipping back into his spikes and Richard's Mountain coat, placing his eggs-n-bacon pocket snack and thermos in coat pockets, and walking to his truck, he sets his intention on Karen, but also on the lost love in his life. Ten years ago, George had love in his life. Ten years ago, in fact, he was with his beloved Martha, a fellow Vermont duck hunter who he'd met in the guild.

One day, after one year of dating and duck hunting together in Vermont, George bit his bottom lip, as Martha perused used copies of poetry books in New York City's Strand Bookstore, where they liked to go on mini-weekend vacations to browse poetry, for Martha, and mysteries and thrillers and fishing and hunting guides for George, and also for Martha. And sometimes historical fiction, if it involved tales of royalty. To them, amongst the "eighteen miles of books," as the Strand advertised, they felt they were in a "heavenly displacement." Yes, indeed, the Strand for them was a celestial atmosphere that allowed for a feeling of floating above the otherwise green-shining, leaf-littered, snow-packed, streams-rushing, beautiful but predictable, seasonal cycles of home-base Vermont.

On this day in the Strand with Martha, having near bit through his bottom lip, Martha pulled from a shelf a rough-leather copy of Emily Dickinson poems, which copy George knew she'd pull, for he'd planted it there. He'd previously rushed in ahead of her, saying he had to find a bathroom, and in the process and hurry he accidentally stomped another man's foot. He was so nervous and wanting to surprise Martha so bad, he simply couldn't stop to help or apologize. His entire attention became laser focused on his mission with Martha.

And there's something in George's subconscious about all of this, the rushing, the foot stomp, that has always been an unsettling undercurrent to him. For he shouldn't remember that part at all, but he does. And today, in walking in his spikes in a blizzard back toward his company truck, that beginning part, the rushing and colliding with another in the Strand, is strangely clear as a bell.

But George shakes away strange thinking and continues on in his remembrance of Martha. Steeped now within the outside world of the blizzard, a howl of wind greets him, or some howl. Cope? *Nahh, just the wind. It ain't Old Cope. Can't be still out in the world, no, not Cope. I miss you, Cope. I miss you, Martha.*

George walks on in the onslaught of snow. He walks slow, safe, in his grip shoes.

Back in that high emotion day in the Strand, as he knew she would, when Martha flipped to the copyright page to check the copyright date in the planted leather Dickinson, for she had a collection to curate, Martha gasped. Therein, written on Richard's Mountain letterhead, was this note:

Martha,

> *Live, extended*
> *in this heavenly displacement*
> *in this 99th way*
> *in this run of ducks;*
> *In our pages of,*
> *crimes of love*
> *tangled by, magnificent lies—*
> > *devil-tooth spies*
> > *slick guys and Queens.*
> *I love how you love them*
> *Hover above the tree lines*
> *and gorge streams;*
> *Rise beyond their laws and their lessons*
> *Engraved for those, stuck in snows,*
> *Hiding in grasses,*
> *deep treads in spring mud*
> *Float in our world of lawless reigns*
> *on page prints with cracked spines*
> *Our time or no time*
> *In book aisles,*
> *By wolf dens,*

Bar stools and dog walks
I ask thee,
    Please save me.
Marry me,
George

It might not have been worthy of Dickinson, but it was nature centered and spoke of the freeness that love brought. The protection. He'd wanted to throw into a magical maelstrom all the locations where they loved being together, Vermont, duck hunting, walking Cope on mountain trails, the Strand, in books about all kinds of tales, as if some gravity-free, magical heaven in which they lived, always in love's safety.

Anyway, this was his intention, a rather subjective inspiration he gleaned in sneaking reads of Martha's Dickinson collection, after Martha fell asleep at night. This proposal, this very poem, was a full year, night after night, in the planning and editing and fretting he'd be able to rise to the exalted pedestal Martha deserved.

He watched while she read, her eyes widening in surprise.

He held his breath.

Martha looked up, at first in a stare, no smile.

And then, Martha smiled. Martha broke down and cried. Martha said yes, and Martha gasped, and said *yes, yes, yes*, a gorgeous, unending song of yesses.

"This is the best poem ever written in the history of all poems," Martha said through yesses and tears.

They forehead-to-forehead rolled their heads together in the poetry section of the Strand; Martha clutching the proposal note to her heart, and George clutching the Dickinson to his heart. George swears that in memory of this moment, a blackness, or a presence, some something was watching them with evil eyes, in the shadows of the perpendicular stack. He swears he felt that evil presence exactly then, and not in retrospect, after what happened to Martha four hours later.

George is five feet off his truck now, and those four lines he drew on the side are all gone. The Richard's Mountain decal has been re-covered in side-swept sticky snow. Drifts of snow lean half-up the chained tires, and the white roof of the truck has its own flat hat of snow, as does the hood. So isn't it odd, George thinks, that his footsteps are still visible by his driver's door?

Those aren't my boot prints.

George quick presses the unlock button on his universal company fob, yanks open his door, and his heart fills with fire. Raging, wild, destructive fire.

The cubby is empty.

Martha's special leather Dickinson is gone.

So, too, is George's hunting knife.

George backs away from the door. Looks everywhere all over the parking lot, but it is hard to see. The snow is falling sideways, and seemingly, upside down in this wind. He sees no moving person. The howling wind further obscures his senses. He notes the outlines of cars and trucks in the parking lot. Kyle's is gone.

Had to be fucking Kyle, that prick. Bob, Eli, the others, they're still in the bar and wrapping up to come to shift. Kyle's got a universal fob. That prick.

George is alight now. He jumps his big body into the cab, yanks the door shut. He cranks on the engine and immediately heat blasts into the double cab and up on the windshield. He hits his powerful windshield wipers, which makes short life of the layer of snow that accumulated while he was inside.

He doesn't wait for the engine or cab to heat; he jams into reverse, rocks the tires back and forth a few times, and guns the gas to launch out of his parking space, swerving onto the mountain road, which, thanks to the Mountain's extra tax payments, has been plowed and salted ten times already tonight.

Richard's Mountain is the Vermont mountain that consistently holds the record for most open lift days with clearest access roads. And such aggressive maintenance means the mountain is always short on, and therefore, hiring staff. Always.

That bastard, Kyle! I'll knock him into next winter!

George's rage to get to the mountain and find Kyle, who surely took his knife and book, makes George feel he is driving through the thickest of road shadows, snagging his progress. He can't get there fast enough.

A fear tickles at the back of George's mind. He looks in his rearview mirror and sees headlights approaching. He thinks maybe the headlights approach too fast, but whoever is behind slows and keeps at a distance. In truth, although the roads are plowed and George thought he was gunning it, he crawls, as does whoever is behind him, at 20 m.p.h.

In looking again in his rearview mirror, a sudden recollection replays in his mind. That same day, the very day he proposed to Martha, they were driving home to Vermont. She was smiling in a cushiony happy way in the passenger's seat of George's civilian Volvo, as they crossed the Mid-Hudson Bridge. It was then that George, like tonight, had a creepy feeling on his neck when he looked in his rearview mirror. Tonight, as he does the same, he tells himself he is not seeing what he saw back then, again, now, tonight. Back then when he looked in the rearview on the Mid-Hudson, in broad daylight, there, in the car behind, the driver of a gray Ford four-door wore a robot head make out of a cardboard box. Two holes for eyes. Red balls, or suction cups, were glued on as buttons. And wires, maybe un-bent hangers, were antennas.

The robot waved at George through the rearview mirror.

Back then, George fluttered his eyelids, thinking he was hallucinating. He opened his eyes wide, and sure enough, still there. A man, George could tell from the hairy waving hand, with a cardboard-box robot head, was driving, riding up on George's bumper, as if following.

"I'm pulling off for gas in Poughkeepsie," George said to Martha.

"Maybe I'll get us some Combos and Cokes in the store then," Martha said. "And a bone to bring home to Cope."

"Sounds good," George said, distracted and keeping one eye on the still-waving robot behind. He didn't want to alarm Martha. Didn't point any of this out, which he might have normally, had he thought this to be some roadway stranger prank. George felt it was something different. He'd tell her once they were safe off the highway.

They pulled into the Poughkeepsie gas station. He remembers pumping the gas and feeling safe, for he didn't see the robot driver pull off behind them. Martha was in the store. There were no other customers. When done with the gas, George pulled up to the air machine on the side of the station to plump one of the Volvo's tires. Then, in a snap, as Martha came out and rounded the station's corner, the gray Ford pulled in fast, drove to the side of the station a half-length beyond George, who was busy with the air nozzle on the driver's side front tire. The man with a robot head sprung from his car, ran to Martha, stabbed her three deep times in the chest, and, later confirmed, *in* the heart, returned to his car and, before throwing his body back in to speed off, yelled to George, "Payback, rude boy."

It was three seconds and done. Martha died of blood loss and body trauma ten minutes later in George's arms. He cried to police that a man in a robot costume did it, had followed them over the bridge. Had called him "rude boy," and that this was "payback," but George had no clue what any of it was about. The police could only confirm, given the strangest angles of two separate exterior cameras at the station, that indeed a gray Ford with no plates pulled in, as George said, and a man, of whom all they could see were his legs and thrusting knife, stabbed Martha. They could see George fully, airing his tires, and caught unaware and in shock the full three seconds the murder took place.

When George got home, after all the official fuss, three days later, Cope sniffed Martha's dried blood on George's sweaty undershirt and fled into the Vermont mountains.

In looking through the rearview now, George calms a half fraction to realize he can't make out the driver behind, as it is too dark between snowfall and the driver's headlights colliding with George's taillights, and so, not much can be seen except a blur of black and white. So George cannot confirm, this way or that, whether a man dressed as a robot pursues him again. But he has that same prickling feeling.

Chill the fuck out and get to that asshole Kyle.

George pulls into staff parking at Richard's Mountain. He wastes not a second in parking, exiting, and shouting to the General Manager of the mountain, who's waiting on staff in the parking lot, wearing his multi-pocketed managerial coat.

"Where's Kyle?" George yells.

The General Manager walks up to George, looking up from a shielded clip-board and from under a wide brimmed hat. Snow falls between and on the two men. "Prick's gone, George. Just left. You seem about as pissed as I for that fucker."

"He just left the bar. He couldn't have gotten here more than ten minutes before me."

"Yeah, that's right. He got here about five minutes ago, and I was waiting for him. After he parked, I made him give me the keys, and told him to hike his sorry ass with security back to his staff cottage and clear out by 2:00 a.m."

"Holy shit. What the fuck did he do?"

"He ain't who he says he is. He started last week, yeah. Promises about referrals, all that shit. Well I let him start, dumb fucking me, while I wait on references and background to clear. His name sure as fuck isn't Kyle whateverthefuck he said his name was. When I faxed his picture to all the referrals, not a one knew who he was. So I have a cop buddy run his prints. This prick just got out of Rockingham Prison two weeks ago. He ain't no Kyle, he's some Brett Brickadick, whatever, asshole, who cares. Did nine years for killing a lady in Keene while robbing her in a home invasion."

"Well the bastard stole my knife and worse yet, the book I gave Martha to propose."

"Not the Dickinson?"

"Yeah, the Dickinson."

"Shit."

As they were talking, another couple of staff trucks had pulled in. Bob, Eli. A few others. They didn't interrupt the big boss with George, and quick-stepped to the staff lounge to punch in. Another car arrived as well, a non-descript Bronco that could have been gray or white. That person now walks toward the big boss and George. A parking lot lamp shines a cone of light around the big boss and George; this new man remains in the blackness just beyond. His features are undefined given the snow and shadows.

"Ah, Reeker. Reeker, come on here, come closer. Reeker, this is George, head of engineering. You'll ride with him tonight. He does cold side of the mountain, so he'll show you what working a blizzard is all about. We have to be open by 9:00 a.m., no matter what. We got a record to maintain." From one of ten exterior pockets on his manager's utility coat, the big boss pulls out and shoves a giant, weather-proof walkie in George's hands. He does the same to Reeker. "Take him up."

George hadn't really focused on Reeker as he approached and the boss said all this. He was fuming so hard in his mind his eyes where clouded, which was doubly easy given the blinding snow. But now, now that Reeker is in the spotlight, George shrinks within himself.

A round-head man, with round neck, round torso, round arms, round legs. He can't tell if he's bald, for Reeker wears a thick knit hat.

"Hi there, I'm Reeker," Reeker says to George.

George outstretches his hand, shaking. Reluctant. He's speechless.

The big boss is called to address something in the staff lounge and runs off.

"Right, then," George says to Reeker.

George is not ready to accept that he might be standing in the presence of the Spine Ripper. *Nah. That's nuts.* He's just spun up about Fake-Kyle, he tells himself. *I'm spun up. The news sketch could have been any round, white man. I just want to tell Karen tonight.*

As if on a mind call, George's walkie sizzles.

"Karen to George, Karen to George," Karen calls. She has deep cracks in her voice from frying her vocal cords to an earned brokenness, after spending twenty years of her life as an estate auctioneer and then crying herself voiceless at her husband's grave—a grief so deep she had mental and physical laryngitis a full year, some years ago. George always smiles to hear the strength in how she owns her scars, as if her grief and her vocal strain are braided with her soul. He gets it. He does. Now, widowed at age fifty-two, and having moved here from sunny California to start over, Karen's worked as Safety Captain for the past two years.

"George here, Karen. Good night to you, over," George says. His heart is a pure mixture of excitement to hear her, but outright fright in looking at Reeker who doesn't blink, staring at George in a way that is not seeing George, but seeing thoughts he has about George. The man has black eyes. The man has dead eyes. George, the lumberjack, feels two feet tall and ten pounds total. He fears Reeker could chew him; literally, eat him alive. George eye-measures Reeker as taller and bulkier than even himself. He's a large man to a large man.

"How about we finish those decoys tomorrow. By a fire. I'll make you chili, over," Karen says on the walkie. Because the truth is, Karen and George have played at being best friends for the past year. She doesn't like to duck hunt, that's not her thing. But she does like to paint decoys with George in his heated greenhouse painting room, while they listen to crime podcasts and audiobooks. And she makes him chili. George always tells Karen how he likes her sun-washed blonde hair under her hot pink hat, and how he truly loves her chili. Yes, the feeling is a mutual one, George is sure.

"I never say no to your chili, Karen. I'm heading up with the new guy, Reeker, over," George says, but only half in the conversation, for he's staring back at Reeker. Something is off. The man hasn't blinked.

"Tell him to turn his walkie on, over," Karen Safety Captain says.

Reeker doesn't look down at his walkie as he turns it on. He stares on at George, nimble like a master surgeon with the switch on the walkie.

"It's on, over," George says.

"He number four? Over." Karen asks.

On the back of Reeker's walkie is a round #4 sticker.

"Yes, ma'am, over," George says.

"Good check, I got him. And you're eight-ball as normal? Over?"

"Yes, ma'am, number 8, over."

"Alright then, good check. Take him up. You have cold side, as usual. Don't let your Cat tumble on the steeps. River's a rager in this storm, over."

"Copy. You in your perch? Over."

"Snug as a bug, and my dashboard is lit like a Christmas tree.

All set, over."

"Alrighty then, we're heading up. Out."

"Out."

After driving George's regular Cat out of the barn, past other Cats and several snowmobiles, all with thick, deep treads, George and Reeker sit side by side. Reeker had given a few, rather sparse, answers to George up to now about where he came from and who he was. All George knows is Reeker had come in from another mountain out west and he was living in an apartment in Bloom, Vermont. That is all.

The roar of the Cat engine, the corkscrew-howling wind, and the crush of Cat treads on snow, causes a clatter of vibration through the cab. Reeker sits straight as a pin, silent, and staring out the window, never blinking despite the wild thrust, back and forth, of the scrapers and the thudding of heavy falling snow on the windshield that makes most men blink.

They're halfway up Front Face when Reeker swivels in his seat to face George. He says nothing. Waiting two beats, fearful to acknowledge a man staring at him in such close quarters, for he fears doing so will make it true, George finally braves a slow look at Reeker.

Reeker's black eyes stare back, and in this moment, all doubt leaves George. This is the same man who he'd seen naked and bathing in a stream in the spring. And this is the same killer the news had warned about in a victim's sketch.

Reeker tunnels cold eyes, black eyes, dead eyes, no emotions into George. Says nothing.

Nobody at Malforson's will believe this tale, if George lives to tell it. But *son of a demon from hell, I'm looking into the dead soul of the Spine Ripper.*

Then, as George is about to slam on the brakes and punch him square in the jaw, or do *something*, Reeker spins to his own door, opens it, looks over his shoulder, and yells, "Forgot my thermos," before jumping out of the moving snowcat.

George slams on the brakes, jams the locks on both doors, and searches the rearview mirror through the back glass, which also has wild scrapers scraping, to see nothing. No Reeker. Nobody.

Nothing.

George can't safely turn the snowcat around at this angle on this part of Front Face. He has to continue straight up to Malforson's lift landing and turn around. Malforson being a long-ago village founder, hence the bar name, hence the landing.

George's nerves are on fire, electrified. Prickles, like a million pins, poke up from his core and out his skin, everywhere all over his body. Like when the paramedics gave him blockers to fend off possible tachycardia on the day Martha died in his arms.

He looks to the passenger seat and sees that Reeker has left his walkie, the #4 sticker facing up to the ceiling.

George depresses the talk button on his own #8, "George to Karen, George to Karen."

He gets static in return. He tries several more times in his drive to the top.

At the top, the Malforson lift floodlights allow for visibility, although blurred through driving snow, around the entire landing area, where George starts to turn the Cat. The light bleeds into the snow-drenched evergreens some several dozen feet to the side and backside, which is the cold side of the mountain.

A seam between Front Face and cold side rivers down the side of the mountain, and mid-way down, after and between numerous evergreens, ski glades, and snowmobile trails, sits Karen's Safety Headquarters, a log cabin that the staff calls "The Perch." Down below Karen's Perch, and still within the seam, are three staff cabins. One of which should be emptied by now by fired not-Kyle. And down below and behind those and where nobody goes at night, is the roughest part of a rumbling river that snakes around the backside base of Richard's Mountain and through the village and along the highway, the highway stretch being where George had first seen the naked Reeker. He knows it was Reeker.

As George turns the Cat and marries his headlights with the floodlights of the lift landing, he sees running through the trees, down the seam, and toward Karen's Perch—a man with a robot cardboard box on his head.

George blinks slow. He's still there.

George doesn't wait to consider doubts about all of his

wildest tales colliding tonight. He doesn't care if he is insane and imagining his robot foe. He needs to face all of this lunacy. He stops the Cat, jumps out, and runs headlong for the robot man. It is not Reeker. The man ahead has the frame of a skeleton with skin. This man wears the same jeans and boots as fake-Kyle in the bar. George remembers logging Kyle's mid-calf Timberland's when he removed his snow-cleats in Malforson's mudroom.

"Kyle, it was you! You killed Martha!" George yells. "Stop!"

Robot Man stops, turns, and pauses as George stops short. Facing George, he opens his coat, withdraws the Dickinson, and flings it flat, like a skipping stone, to sink deep in snow between two birches.

Next, he pulls George's hunting knife from his back pocket.

"I guess it's mano a mano now, rude boy," Robot Man says.

In the cold, the smell of George's breakfast sandwich, still hot given the aluminum wrapper, wafts. It blooms around him.

"Take off that fucking box," George yells. His rage will not allow him to assess the danger of a man with an extended knife. He feels his rage and his need to remedy Martha's murder makes him a triple lumberjack and must-be Kyle a toothpick.

Robot Man removes the robot box, throws it to the side.

"Remember me now, rude boy? Ten years ago?"

It is indeed Kyle, but George does not remember him from ten years ago.

"You're a fucking psychopath. I have no idea who you are."

"Of course you wouldn't, rude boy. Of course some big man like you wouldn't see an insignificant ant like me and would stomp on my foot and walk away. No apologies."

"That day in the Strand? I accidentally stepped on you? This is why? That's why you murdered her?" George's voice is hysterical now, he can barely contain himself from launching at Kyle, hell with his own hunting knife in Kyle's hands.

"You know, rude boy, that's the thing with big men like you. You never think you need to care about the people you push out of your way. You never think that maybe, *maybe* us insignificant ants are mightier than you. Never think we're a threat. Well I'm a fucking threat, rude boy. I'll snake away from you, and I'll kill

Karen before you catch up. I'll take all your life away, make you as insignificant as an ant. I was on my way for you, yeah, when I got popped 9 years ago. I've grown madder at you every single fucking day I sat in that cell box. I got your plate number. I knew who you were."

George lunges for Kyle, but Kyle, true to his word, turns swift and snakes away, down the seam of the mountain, towards Karen, weaving between trees. George is having difficulty keeping up with the snake despite his gripping cleats, but as Kyle is leaving the web of light between trees, a galloping beast leaps in the air and onto Kyle. Kyle is stomped by the animal into the deep snow.

George sees his knife at the base of a Douglas fir, a tree owning layers of umbrella limbs that shield the earth beneath from too much snow. He grabs the knife and, looking at the animal that leapt, sees a familiar figure. It's Cope all right. Several coyotes stand around in a circle, yipping at Kyle, and yipping at George's pocket with the breakfast sandwich.

"Cope, off him now, Old Girl. Good Girl. Off."

Cope, barking mad, backs off Kyle, who struggles to get out of the snow and off his back. George quick steps to Kyle, throwing Cope the breakfast sandwich, bends, and grabs Kyle around his scrawny neck with one bear claw of a hand. With his other, he holds the now unsheathed knife to Kyle's temple. "You're coming with me to the river," he says.

George knows the cold side of the mountain like the back of his own ass. He's the only one who can work it. He's got Kyle tied with safety rope, hands and feet, sitting in his passenger seat, right where Reeker was only twenty minutes ago. George is not calling Karen on the walkie now. George has definitely forgotten he wanted to tell Karen he loves her tonight. He has a killer to kill. He has a wrong to right. He has his love's murder to vindicate.

Has George ever been this homicidal?

No, not ever. But love will do that to you sometimes. Ten years of grief and guilt, guilt for not saving her, that will do that to you sometimes. Being stalked for ten years by a psychopath who wears a homemade robot head, that will fucking do that to you sometimes. Knowing your haste and inadvertent rudeness, a simple second of stepping on a stranger's foot, led to death. Such snap insanity, such freak and fatal instances, will do that to you sometimes.

At the bottom of the cold side of the mountain, after barreling through the steeps, blind through the dark, which George did not fear, for he's numb now, they reach the raging river, cold as arctic ice. This violent river never freezes given the constant current.

It's loud here from the roiling water and the howling wind, which funnels through the basin's valley. It sounds like a freight train colliding with a rocket during blast off. Around where George has dragged Kyle, light from the snowcat illuminates a bubble of river bank. George's legs are a foot deep in snow as he removes, with one meatpaw of a hand, the ropes from Kyle's hands and feet. The ropes go in the river. The entire while, George holds Kyle around his neck. He could crush his windpipe with a mere fraction more of pressure.

It must be 2:00 a.m. now, and, having left his gloves in the cab, George's thick fingers are beginning to prickle in tightened circulation.

Ignoring Kyle's throttled cries, which are drowned by the sounds of a train and a rocket, George lifts Kyle as if he's a single log and thrusts him in the freezing cold water. The wild current sucks Kyle in and away, bangs his head against boulders, drowns him, crushes him, kills him of hypothermia in ten seconds flat.

George watches all ten seconds, and when he looks away for a break, there along the bank, in the far-reach edge of his snowcat's light, stands Reeker, naked, his hat off, bald. He wears only snowshoes, which, George guesses, the fucker must have stowed in the woods or stolen from a staff cabin. He's here premeditated. All his round parts, all there, now. Reeker holds a bar of soap in his hands. It dawns on George that this is the Spine Ripper's *modus operandi*: Reeker cleans himself in freezing river water before a kill. At least George hopes it's before, and that nobody from the mountain is already dead. He thinks this because he doesn't see a body dragged here, waiting to be fileted and deboned, as other bodies were left at other watering holes.

"Reeker," George says.

Reeker stares back, that same black-eyed, emotionless expression. Despite this blizzard, despite this cold air, despite it all, George notices the man is aroused. Reeker enjoys the fright he's causing George, the power is a sexual charge. This threat is real. Sure enough, Reeker makes known his weapons by drawing George's eyes to a tree stump, upon which sits a long serrated knife and a small carving knife.

They must have been in his coat pocket.

He looks to Reeker's snowshoes.

Shit.

George is sinking deeper in the heavy snow where he stands, and now it's too late. He might as well be in cement. He's stuck. He can't turn and run. He can't reach any better packed glade, covered in powder, but at least not as keeping as this quicksand. And even if he could run, this larger man, this brutal murderer, would catch him in those snowshoes of his, thrust a knife in George's back to slow him. Then gut him. Filet him.

George is out of moves, and he knows Reeker knows it.

"Saw you kill that man, George," Reeker says, smiling by pushing both lips together in the middle and up. No blinking. His slow tone and cool demeanor changes when he lunges sideways for the tree stump and grabs the long serrated knife. He holds the handle with one hand and keeps the point poking into the palm of the other. He does that weird mouth middle push up thing again, watching George, who's struggling and failing to lift his legs and step away. George keeps sinking.

"You threw him right in the river, George," Reeker says. He slow blinks. Takes a step to George, and George counts the time it takes for Reeker to reach him: three snowshoe steps in three seconds. And in those three seconds, George's body takes over, acting on pure instinct. He falls to his ass, which hard tree fall frees his feet, like a heavy redwood falling and dislodging its root ball: physics. As Reeker lunges down to follow George, leading with his long knife, George sets his spiked cleat feet to Reeker's hip joints and pushes. George pushes the entire weight of his grief, of his guilt, in the thrust, sending Reeker to shimmy backwards— just far enough. Puncture holes from the cleats spray blood on the snow, quickly covered by more falling snow.

In this very second, a roar interrupts, something louder than the water and the wind. A dim light grows brighter through the trees, but blurred, as all is blurred in this blizzard. Out of the trees, a snowmobile bombs out of what was a blackened trail and straight into Reeker, punting him to the river's edge. The snowmobile stops. Backs up. Revs and shoots forward, plowing Reeker into the river.

The river sucks Reeker's circle-stacked body in, greedily dunks him, drowns him, bobbing, screaming and swallowing water, crashing his round skull into boulders, and freezing his balls off in fatal hypothermia in ten seconds flat.

George is on his ass stunned.

The snowmobile driver stands with her legs straddling the snowmobile seat. She takes off her helmet, releasing her sun-drenched California hair.

She looks over to George. "Oh, thank God, George. Thank God. The news kept escalating warnings. They pieced together his name, this guy, he didn't even try to hide his identity. Reeker's the Spine Ripper! I tracked you both by your walkies. They got the upgraded GPS, thank God. Thank Goodness I got here in time, George. I love you!"

"I love you, Karen! I love you!" George yells. He yells it over and over, a gorgeous unending song of *I love you's* as he cries in the snow, on his lumberjack ass, in a blizzard, professing his love for a woman who saved him. He cries, too, with relief that she didn't see him kill the first killer, for that is a tall tale George will never tell, not to Karen, not to those muggers at Malforson's. Nobody's ever going to find either body; this roaring river swallows bodies into deep glacial canyons, pinning them under any of thousands of sunk logging trees, dozens of feet deep. That's why the forest rangers won't let anyone kayak it, no matter their skill. Everyone will hear about Reeker, for Karen and he will tandem tell that tale, but Reeker's gone and no witness no longer to George's crime. As for Kyle, everyone will think he slunk off in the night, disappeared himself into a new identity.

Ayup.

This Kyle tale stays with George, and probably with his

ghost overseer, Martha, who protects him from their heavenly displacement, above these gorge streams, and in her afterlife dog, walks on mountain trails. She's with Cope all right. She is Cope.

Yes, for sure, George doesn't want any mugger to know about Kyle. So he better go find that damn robot head and get rid of it for good. And to punctuate that thought, to underscore that objective, a howl overtakes all noise. George turns to see Cope howling at the blurry moon, right there, within the trail Karen bombed down. When done, Cope bends her head and picks up a leather book in her teeth. She runs off to join her coyote pack.

* * *

ATM

JON LAND

"Don't I know you?" the guy seated across from Venn on the A Train headed uptown toward 207th Street wondered.

Venn tried not to regard him, avoided meeting his eyes. Could be the guy had been a trick in weeks or months past. Somebody he'd picked up in a bar like Tubby's Tavern where he was headed right now, after midnight like always. Venn didn't remember faces like that and didn't want to remember this one either.

"I don't think so, man," he said, not quite regarding the guy and not smiling.

Barely regarding him, in other words, which was normally all it took guys who'd paid him for sex at one time or another to move on in their minds. Sometimes they wouldn't let it go, maybe even wanting more of the same which Venn sometimes provided. He figured he should have been grateful that he remained attractive at the ripe old age of twenty-two.

A glimpse caught in the subway car window across from his seat revealed the tousled hair that swam to his shoulders, mostly brown with some natural blondish streaks. His eyes were the same middle shade, more of a hazel, and a flash of his perfect smile could make any potential trick melt, even the straight ones or ones who at least thought they were straight. Of course, he was also blessed with a great ass which the reflection didn't show, but that Venn regaled in catching guys, and girls, grab stealthy glimpses of that always lingered a bit too long.

Tubby's Tavern wasn't a college bar per se, but its location in a trendy uptown neighborhood was populated by a mix of young professionals, many associated in some respect with nearby Columbia University. A convenient place to gather or stop by alone for a drink.

"Are you sure?" the guy across from him started up again. "Because..."

"You teach at Columbia?" Venn asked, still not fully meeting his gaze. "Maybe you've seen me on campus, something like that."

"Oh, you're a student."

Venn nodded, calculating how many more minutes were left before the train's final stop at 207th and Broadway came up. "Junior."

"You look older."

Ouch, Venn thought. Of course, he couldn't say exactly what he'd looked like when he was younger, since foster homes, group homes, and shelters were not known for keeping photo albums. Venn had grown up in an assortment of those. His was a classic American tragedy, like homeless veterans and that sort of shit. He chose not to dwell on his past—or his future, for that matter. "Live in the moment" was Venn's mantra, out of necessity as much as choice.

There wasn't much glamorous about being a hustler, but Venn had been the subject of a profile in *New York Magazine* and was included, anonymously as well, in the *New York Times Magazine* too. One trick he'd done claimed to be a film producer who wanted to base a movie around him. Venn had pretended to be excited and given the guy a disconnected number, because Venn thought he was full of shit. Months later, the same *New York Magazine* issue containing the article on him included the guy's picture in a story on Hollywood up-and-comers, meaning he'd been legit.

If that didn't beat all.

The train slid into the station and ground to a squealing stop, Venn and the guy across from him rising at the same time.

"You have yourself a nice night," the guy said, a forced smile accompanying his words.

"You, too. Be safe."

The man's face played with a smile, like he knew something he didn't want to share. "I was just going to say the same thing to you."

Now Venn was regarding him closer, the man's features appearing formless, not quite the same as they'd appeared before, but not really different either.

"I hope you find what you're looking for," the guy said, flashing a smile that lingered briefly. "I think this might be the night."

"For what?"

Before he could answer, the doors whooshed open and a swarm of riders swallowed the man up. Venn stepped onto the platform after him, looked one way and then the other, but the man was gone.

* * *

Venn needed cash. Money made for the best disguise. Guys in a bar seeing you paying for your own drinks took the hustler thing off the table until he put it back on. Same thing for clothes and in Venn's case, that meant dressing like a college student. Khakis or jeans to go with the right button-down and jacket courtesy of North Face or something like that.

The problem tonight was that his bank account was closing in on zero, all of fifty bucks left to his name which in his case was "Venn" and nothing more. Using his last name meant acknowledging his past, something Venn avoided at all costs given there was nothing there worth remembering. So why not avoid his surname as much as possible? He never used it when introducing himself, and the people he normally introduced himself to didn't much care.

Still, fifty bucks was fifty bucks and Venn set out in search of an ATM machine to take forty of it out, leaving him ten unless tonight proved to be a profitable one assuming he could find the right trick. Venn could have ventured a bit further uptown to where deeper congestions of bars were clustered. He could have hit the bars frequented more by Columbia students. But he only did that when he needed a place to crash for the night, maybe poach some food for breakfast the next morning, seeing those students as different kinds of marks since any college student worth seducing wouldn't need to pay for what Venn was offering.

ATMs were normally everywhere these days but not so, apparently, here in the area of Broadway and 207th Street. He found two banks but slipping his card into the exterior slot failed in both cases to make the glass door snap open. Since Venn carried the card loose in his pocket, maybe the magnetic strip was fucked up or something.

He walked about in search of an ATM held inside a bodega or all-night coffee shop or convenience store, starting to get anxious when he spotted one on a darkened stretch of Sherman Avenue just off 207th Street squeezed between a shoe repair shop and a cut-rate men's clothing store, both with steel grates bolted down over their facades. The ATM was unique because it was squeezed inside an old-fashioned phone booth of all things which had faded from use around the time Venn was born. The glass was cracked in spider web fashion by what looked like well-placed rocks, reducing previously scrawled graffiti to fractured letters.

Venn unfolded the door after encountering some initial resistance; a single overhead lightbulb flickered to life after he'd folded it back closed. The ATM, too, looked old and beaten down, if such a thing could be said about a machine. In the outdated listing of the various cards it accepted was a selection he'd never seen before: CURRENCY OF with the final word scratched over except for part of the first letter, probably an O or maybe a G. The slot to the right swallowed Venn's card and the ATM's ancient looking screen flashed to life, asking for his password, fresh letters scrolling across the screen after he entered it.

HELLO, VENN.

When did these machines get to be on a first-name basis? Something all wrong about that in Venn's mind, but he was too relieved his card had actually *worked* to ponder that further.

DO YOU NEED CASH THIS EVENING?

There was a Y and N trailing the question, so Venn clicked on the Y.

I'M OUT OF SERVICE RIGHT NOW.

Well, give me back my card, motherfucker, Venn thought.

SORRY, VENN, I CAN'T DO THAT RIGHT NOW.

Had he spoken the words out loud instead of merely formed them?

Venn found the CANCEL button and pressed it a whole bunch of times to no effect.

I NEED YOU TO DO SOMETHING FOR ME. THEN I'LL GIVE YOU YOUR CARD BACK.

What the fuck was this shit?

A TRANSACTION, VENN, THAT'S WHAT THIS IS. DIFFERENT FROM THE ONES YOU'RE USED TO, BUT A TRANSACTION ALL THE SAME.

The light-colored letters scrolled across the screen and froze there, leaving Venn wondering who was messing with him and why. Maybe this was like one of those hidden camera things for some kind of prank show, so he figured he should just go along with it. What choice did he have anyway, since the machine had already swallowed his ATM card?

I'M GOING TO GIVE YOU AN ADDRESS, the scroll resumed. YOU NEED TO GO THERE.

THEN WHAT? Venn used the keyboard to type, the two words appearing beneath the machine's last scroll on the screen.

YOU'LL KNOW WHEN YOU GET THERE. WHEN YOU'RE FINISHED, COME BACK AND I'LL RETURN YOUR CARD.

PROMISE? Venn typed, minus the question mark yet it appeared anyway.

PINKY SWEAR.

That gave Venn a chill because it was his classic follow-up to any lie he formed at the shelters and group homes that would have him. He'd probably said it a thousand times over the years but had never heard another human being utter it even once. Then again, this was a machine.

Venn didn't do drugs, other than weed, because they messed with his head. Had he taken something earlier in the night and forgotten about it? Could he have ingested something without knowing it, maybe been dosed unwittingly? Seemed like that would be something he should remember.

WELL? the ATM machine prompted.

Venn decided to keep going along, typing WHAT'S THE ADDRESS?

9TH AVENUE AND BROADWAY. NOT FAR FROM HERE

A half mile to be covered on foot since the two bucks in his pocket wasn't even enough for another single ride subway ticket.

WHAT AM I SUPPOSED TO DO WHEN I GET THERE? Venn typed.

But the screen went dark at that point, leaving him to recall the machine's previous response that he'd know once he arrived.

WHEN YOU'RE FINISHED, COME BACK AND I'LL RETURN YOUR CARD.

Venn could only hope.

* * *

He was nervously brimming with anticipation when he reached the intersection, recognizing it as one of those listed to be the most dangerous in the whole city from a driving standpoint. There wasn't much still open in the immediate area, save for a Dunkin' Donuts and all-night laundromats. Venn could hear the whirring sound of the driers shuffling clothes about, the scent of drier sheets and fabric softener pouring from the vents and warming him a bit when he passed by. On those occasions when circumstances forced him into the street on a chilly night like this, he'd seek out just such a spot, so the smell didn't carry a lot of happy memories with it.

A steady stream of vehicles flew through the green light even at this late hour, nothing new here in the 'city that never sleeps' which, in Venn's experience, had proven much more than a slogan. It switched to yellow, the oncoming vehicles slowing in reluctant fashion, like bucking horses, eager to get to their destination.

Venn gazed about, no idea what he was looking for exactly since the message scrawled across the ATM's screen hadn't told him anything beyond that cryptic: YOU'LL KNOW WHEN YOU GET THERE.

That's when Venn noticed the woman, early thirties maybe, striding toward the intersection. New York was not lacking for beautiful women and this one certainly qualified, with blonde hair bouncing past her shoulders and leather pants shiny in the streetlights' spill. Venn was free to stare as much as he wanted, since her attention was riveted on her phone screen, her thumbs busy tapping out a text or email.

Not noticing the cross-street traffic light she was approaching switch to red, about to be plowed over by oncoming traffic that would be powerless to stop.

Venn burst into motion, all thoughts of rogue ATM machines

vanished for that moment. He was close enough to a massive SUV that had slammed its brakes in futile fashion to smell the scorched rubber when he grabbed hold of the woman's Angora sweater and yanked her from its path just in time.

"Uh," she gasped, losing hold of the phone that had nearly been the instrument of her death.

Venn retrieved it from the pavement. "Here you go," he said.

The woman, clearly flabbergasted, could say nothing but, "Thank you."

She said a bit more, some muttered explanation, but the words were lost to the hammering of Venn's heart and air pocket that had seemed to form in his head. He backed off. The woman kept her eyes on him until the cross-street light turned green again and she moved back into the street, cocking one last still shaken gaze back his way.

"Whewwwww," Venn said out loud to himself, before a shudder overcame him.

YOU'LL KNOW WHEN YOU GET THERE…

Meaning what he was supposed to do, what the machine had sent him there to do. Had he just done it, saved a woman's life who'd be splattered across the pavement now if not for his intervention?

Only one way to find out.

* * *

The phone booth containing the ATM was dark again when he returned, out of breath more from the rush of what had just happened than keeping a jogger's pace all the way back. He stepped inside and once again folded the door closed behind him, the booth's dome light flickering as the ATM sprang to life.

GOOD WORK, VENN.

HOW DID YOU KNOW? Venn typed on the small keyboard, taking the time necessary to que up the proper letters.

KNOW WHAT?

ABOUT THE GIRL.

In response, Venn heard the familiar thwack of twenty-dollar bills being counted out internally. The cash dispenser opened and a thick wad emerged.

PLEASE TAKE YOUR CASH, the screen reminded.

Venn managed to capture the wad in a trembling hand. "How much is this…"

He'd just been thinking out loud, but the machine answered him anyway.

$1,000. THERE'S SOMETHING YOU NEED TO DO WITH IT. YOU'LL KNOW WHEN YOU GET THERE.

WHAT? Venn typed with quivery fingers.

OR YOU CAN KEEP IT, IF YOU WANT.

WHAT ABOUT MY CARD?

IF YOU KEEP THE MONEY, DON'T BOTHER COMING BACK. IF YOU CHOOSE TO COMPLETE YOUR ASSIGNMENT, GO TO DYCKMAN STREET AND NAGLE AVENUE.

Venn memorized the address, a working-class neighborhood not known for a lot of activity at night. He'd turned more than his share of tricks in the general Inwood area over the years and seemed to recall an apartment building turned rooming house popular among hustlers and prostitutes right in the area of that intersection.

WHAT ABOUT MY CARD?

No response.

WHAT DO I NEED TO DO WITH THE MONEY?

The machine went dark.

* * *

Venn had never had this much cash in his hand before, not even close. He lavished that new bill smell for a time before pocketing the neat stack of fresh twenties, tempted to leave it tucked right there, his ATM card be damned. But something, curiosity as much as anything, made him head down Dyckman Street where it joined with Nagle Avenue, clinging to the shadows to avoid crossing the wrong person's path.

The rooming house he recalled was indeed there, complete with a faded marquee missing all of its bulbs. No one was about, other than the customers inside an all-night diner who were visible through a plate glass window. Except for a few bars that catered to locals, there wasn't much else in view to speak of. Nothing but darkness, still and silent.

Okay, he thought, talking to the ATM in his mind, *I'm here. No one to save this time.*

Then Venn heard a voice.

"Hey, bro, you looking for a date?"

Startled, Venn swung quickly, scaring a kid who looked no more than fifteen.

"'Cause I can give you a good time," the kid resumed, collecting himself. "Guaranteed."

The kid could have been him circa his foster and group home days, the resemblance uncanny, right down to the scent of stale soap and unwashed hair that was mussy and long, casting shadows over the kid's eyes.

"You need a better spiel," Venn said, because he could think of nothing else.

"Huh?"

"For approaching a trick."

"Huh?"

"I should know. I was you, I *am* you."

Something turned in Venn's stomach. The wad of cash burning a hole in his pocket seemed to shift.

"You're new at this, aren't you?" Venn asked the kid.

"What's the difference?"

"Lousy corner to work, that's all. Not enough traffic. And the nearby bars? All locals, guys with families and bills. You might think you could kick ass in these parts but all you're going to do is get your ass kicked. Where do you really live?" Venn added, an afterthought.

The kid tried to look seductive. "Answers'll cost you, too."

"How much?"

THERE'S SOMETHING YOU NEED TO DO WITH IT.

The kid's eyes bulged when Venn slipped the wad of folded twenties from his pocket.

"You're new at this and now you're done, done before you start hating yourself or get something shoved up inside you that won't come out so easy."

He handed the kid the cash, pressed it into his hand but didn't let go.

"Go home. Go anywhere you can that's not here. Hide the money in your shoe and get lost. You hear what I'm saying to you?"

The kid nodded, but his wide blue eyes remained rooted on the cash Venn hadn't quite let go of yet.

"This is your golden ticket off the streets. You hear me?"

Venn let go of the money and the kid ran off into the night without answering him, gone from the world inside the fleabag joint sure to be furnished with ratty, cum-stained mattresses covered by similarly soiled sheets. The kid was already long out of sight when he looked back down the street.

YOU'LL KNOW WHEN YOU GET THERE.

* * *

The telephone booth light flickered to life again when Venn folded it closed behind him, illuminating his ATM card lying on the steel grated floor like it had landed there after the machine spit it out. He had it back, free to bleed its funds from a normal ATM machine or just hightail it back to the homeless shelter away from this fucked-up night.

But something kept him right where he was, staring at the empty black screen. He tapped the glass a few times, as if to roust it back to life. When that produced no result, Venn slid his card back into the slot and watched it be gobbled up.

The screen glowed to life, Venn focusing on a button that he hadn't noticed before, or maybe it hadn't been there, labeled SPEAKER alongside a grid of recessed lines.

"*Good work again, Venn,*" a mechanical voice said, loud enough to echo through the phone booth's cramped confines.

"What's going on? Who are you?"

"*You didn't want your card back?*"

"I want to know what the fuck's going on."

"*You gave it back to me. Another test passed. Congratulations.*"

"Are you going to send me someplace else now?"

"*Many people need help. Few of them know where to find it.*"

"What's that mean?"

"*You found me. You passed the test most fail. You passed twice.*"

320

"I almost kept the money."

"No, you didn't."

"You've got my card."

"You want it back?"

"I want this to stop."

"Then you wouldn't have given it back to me."

"Just tell me where to go. Where am I supposed to go this time?"

"You like helping people."

"What's the difference?"

"It's who you are, who you really are. Look at the screen, your reflection."

Venn did but there wasn't much to be seen, framed by the screen's soft glow. "So?"

"You look different."

"No, I don't."

"I'm talking about on the inside. That's what I see. Just one more test left."

"Where should I go?"

"Your favorite number is thirteen."

Venn suddenly felt hot, almost feverish. "How did you know—?"

"Your mother's name was Carol. You were with her when she died, before they came and took you away."

Venn could feel the sweat soaking through his shirt, gluing his jeans to his legs.

"Thirteen Carol Street."

Five miles from here via Harlem River Drive in what was commonly known as Spanish Harlem. Not the best of neighborhoods but not the worst either.

"Then what?"

"You'll know when you get there. You'll need to take a cab."

And five more fresh twenties popped out of the cash dispenser, followed by his ATM card.

* * *

Cabs normally didn't cruise this part of town much, but he was able to hail one almost immediately.

"Thirteen Carol Street," he told the driver.

The guy behind the wheel, fat unlit cigar hanging from the side of his mouth, cocked a quizzical glance his way. "You sure?"

"Thirteen Carol Street," Venn repeated.

The man shook his head, started the meter and drove off.

* * *

It read $31.50 when they got there, plus a $2.50 surcharge—whatever that was. Venn handed the driver two twenties and climbed out at Thirteen Carol Street on the outskirts of Spanish Harlem.

It was one of those walk-in clinics, open twenty-four hours a day, a security guard manning the entrance behind the thickest glass Venn had ever seen. The man didn't look very formidable and held the door open for Venn's approach.

The waiting area was packed, not a seat to be had. Venn was surprised to see parents with young children plentiful in attendance, including several infants which explained the diaper stench he caught a whiff of on his way to the reception counter. The waiting area was quiet, all voices muffled, and a pair of wall-mounted televisions muted, with the closed-captioning scroll running at the bottom of both screens.

"Can I help you?" the receptionist, a large African-American woman with basketballs for breasts, whose nametag identified her as THELMA, asked him from behind the counter.

"Actually," Venn started, "I think I'm here to help you."

"Come again?"

Venn swept his gaze across the waiting area, hoping whoever the ATM machine had sent him to aid this time would magically appear. "I'm here to help somebody."

"Who?"

Venn shrugged. "I don't know. I will," he added, flashing back to the first two times, "but I don't know now. Any ideas?"

"Of somebody you can help?"

He nodded.

"This is a free clinic, Sweet Cheeks. You see what it looks like now? That's the way it is all day and all night. So you want to know if there's somebody you can help? There's a whole lot of somebodies, starting with yours truly because I haven't had a break in six hours and I've got two aides out with the flu." The woman leaned forward, her breasts bouncing in perfect unison. "So what are you doing for the next few hours?"

* * *

Venn finally left after three, exhausted from the non-stop chores Thelma had assigned him. He shelved supplies, counted inventory, helped patients in and out of wheelchairs, cleaned exam rooms, took down personal information on a clipboard he wore chained to his belt. It kept flapping against his hip, but at least he wouldn't lose it. He even comforted some kids whose parent was being treated inside, got the third wall-mounted television to work, and even found two of the long-missing remotes hidden beneath or between couch cushions. The pace never let up and Venn's head was hammering when he finally ran out of gas.

"I have to go now," he told Thelma, feeling guilty but eager to return to the ATM machine.

"On one condition, Sweet Cheeks," she said to him.

"What's that?"

"You promise to come back tomorrow. Gonna be an especially busy day. You can count on that."

"Why?"

"Because every day here's an especially busy one." She smiled widely. "You get yourself home safe, pretty boy, and make sure to get your ass back here tomorrow."

"Okay," Venn said, actually looking forward to it.

"Promise?"

"Pinky swear."

* * *

He took another cab from East Harlem back to the ATM machine's general address, needing to direct the driver along the final stretch since he didn't have a street number. Another forty bucks blown would leave him twenty plus the few singles in his pocket with which he'd started the night. He had no idea what the machine had in store for him next, but he couldn't wait to find out.

"You sure we got the right place, kid?"

"I...think so."

Everything else looked right, but the ATM was nowhere to be seen. He tightened his focus through the flickering street lights, finally fixing on the relic of a phone booth with its spider webbed glass.

But there was no ATM machine inside.

"Let me off here," he told the driver absently, putting two twenties into the transfer and twisting it toward him. "Keep the change."

The cab drove off and Venn turned his attention back to the phone booth, as if the ATM might reappear now that he was alone. It didn't.

Venn approached the phone booth, folding open the door for some sign the machine had ever been here in the first place, but there was nothing other than street refuse, old fliers and post-its that had collected inside courtesy of the wind. He walked back to the subway stop at 207th and Broadway, dog tired with twenty-two dollars to his name and a promise to return to the free clinic the next day.

The morning's first light was showing when he dropped into the darkness of the station. He bought his ticket and boarded the train that thundered into the station just as he reached the platform. He sat down and squeezed his eyes closed, too tired to even try to make sense of the evening's events. He massaged the lids and manually pried them open.

To find the same guy from earlier in the night seated across from him again. Same seat, same suit, same shoes. Staring right at him.

"Long night?"

Venn nodded. "I'll say."

"Me, too. Lots of work at night."

"How's that?"

"You should know," the man said, leaving it there.

"The ATM machine..."

The man remained silent.

"You?"

The man said nothing, regarding his shoes more than Venn.

The train slid into the next station, aglow in the lights radiating from the platform. The man rose to disembark, stopping before Venn on his way to the door.

"Oh, you must have dropped this earlier," he said, extending something that looked like a credit card toward him. "Glad I got the chance to return it to you in person."

Venn took the card in his grasp. "What happens now?"

The man's expression flirted with a smile. "You'll know when you get there."

Venn glanced down at the Columbia University student ID he was holding with his picture on it. A chill coursed through him. The world seemed to tilt one way and then the other, as the subway train doors whooshed open.

"Hey," he called to the man in the suit. "Hey!"

But the man was already through the door, ambling along the desolate platform and gone from Venn's sight by the time the train started moving again.

* * *

The next day at the Columbia University bursar's office, Venn found he was fully enrolled, his education supported one hundred percent by financial aid. All the paperwork was somehow in order, the application he'd never filed for admission complete and accurate. He even had a room in a dorm and a meal plan. Nobody seemed to know who he was but he didn't know them either. What he did know was that his closet and drawers were full of clothes that were his size and fit perfectly. First time in his life he had more than three sets, so many choices he didn't know what to change into first.

The bursar's office had printed out a class schedule for him. He hadn't registered for a single one, of course, but the classes were exactly what he would have chosen if he had. Venn had plenty of questions, but no one to whom he could pose them. He rode the A train every night for a stretch, hoping to encounter the well-dressed man again, abandoning the effort when it became clear that wasn't going to be the case.

Venn kept his promise to return to the free clinic where he became a volunteer and regularly visited the phone booth in the hopes the ATM machine might someday reappear. Instead, one day when he got there the phone booth had been removed, and he never went back again.

Not a day went by, though, when he didn't think of how a visit to that machine had changed his life forever. He could picture it in his head, right down to the menu of the outdated cards accepted ending with a final entry forming CURRENCY OF *something* that had been scratched off, leaving only a portion of the first letter, an O or maybe a G. For some reason that one stuck in his head, but he didn't realize why until a flier pushed its way beneath his dorm room door, an advertisement for a campus religious group seeking to expand its membership.

The banner at the flier's top, scrawled in bold, brilliant letters, froze Venn in his tracks. He lost a breath and a heartbeat, his eyes holding the banner like they'd never let go.

HOW WILL YOU SPEND THE CURRENCY OF GOD?

Venn could only smile.

* * *

ABOUT THE AUTHORS

JOSEPH BADAL grew up in a family where storytelling had been passed down from generation to generation.

Prior to a long business career, Joe served for six years as a commissioned officer in the U.S. Army in critical, highly classified positions in the U.S. and overseas, including tours of duty in Greece and Vietnam, and earned numerous military decorations.

Joe is an Amazon #1 bestselling author, with 16 published suspense novels. He has been recognized as "One of The 50 Best Writers You Should Be Reading." His books have received two Tony Hillerman Awards for Best Fiction Book of the Year, been top prize winners on multiple occasions in the New Mexico/ Arizona Book Awards competition, received gold medals from the Military Writers Society of America, the Eric Hoffer Award, and Finalist honors in the International Book Awards.

He writes a regular column titled "Inspired by Actual Events" in *Suspense Magazine*.

To learn more, visit his website at www.JosephBadalBooks. com.

LINWOOD BARCLAY, a *New York Times* bestselling author and with nearly twenty novels to his credit, spent three decades in newspapers before turning full time to writing thrillers. His books have been translated into more than two dozen language, sold millions of copies, and he counts Stephen King among his fans. Many of his books have been optioned for film and TV, a series has been made in France, and he wrote the screenplay for the film based on his novel *NEVER SAW IT COMING*. Born in the US, his parents moved to Canada just as he was turning four, and he's lived there ever since. He lives near Toronto with his wife, Neetha. They have two grown children.

RHYS BOWEN is the *New York Times*, *Wall Street Journal* and *USA Today* bestselling author of two historical mystery series, as well as three internationally bestselling standalone novels. Her books have won multiple awards and been translated into over twenty languages. A transplanted Brit, Rhys now divides her time between California and Arizona, where she escapes from those harsh California winters.

JEFFERY DEAVER is an international number-one bestselling author. His novels have appeared on bestseller lists around the world. His books are sold in 150 countries and translated into twenty-five languages. He has served two terms as president of Mystery Writers of America.

The author of forty-three novels, three collections of short stories and a nonfiction law book, and a lyricist of a country-western album, he's received or been shortlisted for dozens of awards. His *THE BODIES LEFT BEHIND* was named Novel of the Year by the International Thriller Writers association, and his *Lincoln Rhyme* thriller *THE BROKEN WINDOW* and a stand-alone, *EDGE*, were also nominated for that prize. *THE GARDEN OF BEASTS* won the Steel Dagger from the Crime Writers Association in England. He's been nominated for eight Edgar Awards.

Deaver has been honored with the Lifetime Achievement Award by the Bouchercon World Mystery Convention, the *Strand Magazine's* Lifetime Achievement Award and the Raymond Chandler Lifetime Achievement Award in Italy.

His book *A MAIDEN'S GRAVE* was made into an HBO movie starring James Garner and Marlee Matlin, and his novel *THE*

BONE COLLECTOR was a feature release from Universal Pictures, starring Denzel Washington and Angelina Jolie. Lifetime aired an adaptation of his *THE DEVIL'S TEARDROP*. NBC television is airing the popular prime time series, *Lincoln Rhyme: Hunt for the Bone Collector*.

His latest novel is *THE GOODBYE MAN*, a *Colter Shaw* thriller.

New York Times and *USA Today* bestselling author, **HEATHER GRAHAM**, majored in theater arts at the University of South Florida. After a stint of several years in dinner theater, back-up vocals, and bartending, she stayed home after the birth of her third child and began to write. Her first book was with Dell, and since then, she has written over two hundred novels and novellas including category, suspense, historical romance, vampire fiction, time travel, occult, and Christmas family fare.

She is pleased to have been published in approximately twenty-five languages. She has written over 200 novels and has 60 million books in print. She has been honored with awards from booksellers and writers' organizations for excellence in her work, and she is also proud to be a recipient of the Silver Bullet from Thriller Writers and was also awarded the prestigious Thriller Master in 2016. She is also a recipient of the Lifetime Achievement Award from RWA. Heather has had books selected for the Doubleday Book Club and the Literary Guild, and has been quoted, interviewed, or featured in such publications as *The Nation*, *Redbook*, *Mystery Book Club*, *People* and *USA Today* and appeared on many newscasts including *Today*, *Entertainment Tonight* and local television.

Heather loves travel and anything that has to do with the water, and is a certified scuba diver. She also loves ballroom dancing. Each year she hosts the Vampire Ball and Dinner theater at the RT convention, raising money for the Pediatric Aids Society, and in 2006 she hosted the first Writers for New Orleans Workshop to benefit the stricken Gulf Region. She is also the founder of "The Slush Pile Players," presenting something that's "almost like entertainment" for various conferences and benefits. Married since high school graduation and the mother of five, her greatest love in life remains her family, but she also believes her career has been an incredible gift, and she is grateful every day to be doing something that she loves so very much for a living.

ALAN JACOBSON is the award-winning, *USA Today* bestselling author of fourteen thrillers, including the FBI profiler *Karen Vail* series and the *OPSIG Team Black* novels. His books have been translated internationally and several have been optioned by Hollywood. Jacobson's debut novel, *FALSE ACCUSATIONS*, was adapted to film by acclaimed Czech screenwriter Jirí Hubac.

Jacobson has spent over twenty-five years working with the FBI's Behavioral Analysis Unit, the DEA, the US Marshals Service, SWAT, the NYPD, Scotland Yard, local law enforcement, and the US military. This research and the breadth of his contacts help bring depth and realism to his characters and stories.

For video interviews and a free personal safety eBook co-authored by Alan Jacobson and FBI Profiler Mark Safarik, please visit www.AlanJacobson.com. You can also connect with Jacobson on Facebook (Facebook.com/AlanJacobsonFans), Instagram (alan.jacobson), Twitter (@JacobsonAlan), and Goodreads (alan-jacobson).

PAUL KEMPRECOS is the author of eight novels in the *Aristotle "Soc" Socarides* private detective series, including *COOL BLUE TOMB*, winner of a Shamus award from the Private Eye Writers of America for Best Paperback, and *SHARK BAIT*, nominated for a Shamus in the same category. Grandmaster of Adventure writer Clive Cussler blurbed: "There can be no better mystery writer in America than Paul Kemprecos." Paul became the first fiction co-author to work with Cussler when they created and wrote the *New York Times* bestselling *NUMA Files* series. After collaborating with Cussler on the first eight books in the *NUMA Files*, Paul wrote two adventure novels including *THE MINOAN CIPHER*, nominated for a Thriller award by the International Thriller Writers. Paul lives on Cape Cod with his wife Christi, a financial advisor.

To learn more about Paul Kemprecos, check out his website at www.paulkemprecos.com.

SHANNON KIRK is the international bestselling and award-winning author of *METHOD 15/33*, *THE EXTRAORDINARY JOURNEY OF VIVIENNE MARSHALL*, *IN THE VINES*, *GRETCHEN*, *VIEBURY GROVE*, and short stories in four anthologies: *THE NIGHT OF THE FLOOD*, *NOTHING GOOD HAPPENS AFTER MIDNIGHT*, and *BORDER NOIR*. Shannon is also a contributor to the International Thriller Writers' Murderers' Row. Growing up in New Hampshire, Shannon and her brothers were encouraged by their parents to pursue the arts, which instilled in her a love for writing at a young age. A graduate of Suffolk Law School in Massachusetts, Shannon is a practicing litigation attorney and former adjunct law professor, specializing in electronic-evidence law. When she isn't writing or practicing law, Shannon spends time with her husband, son, and two cats. To learn more about her, visit www.shannonkirkbooks.com.

JON LAND is the *USA Today* bestselling author of more than 50 books, including the award-winning, critically acclaimed *Caitlin Strong* series, the most recent of which is *STRONG FROM THE HEART*. He has also penned six novels in the *MURDER, SHE WROTE* series and has recently taken over Margaret Truman's *CAPITAL CRIMES* series as well. He's a 1979 graduate of Brown University, lives in Providence, Rhode Island, and can be reached at jonlandbooks.com or on Twitter @jondland.

JOHN LESCROART is the author of twenty-nine novels, nineteen of which have been *New York Times* bestsellers. Libraries Unlimited places him among "The 100 Most Popular Thriller and Suspense Authors." With sales of over twelve million copies, his books have been translated into twenty-two languages in more than seventy-five countries, and his short stories appear in many anthologies.

John's first book, *SUNBURN*, won the Joseph Henry Jackson Award for Best Novel by a California author. *DEAD IRISH*, *THE 13TH JUROR*, and *THE KEEPER* were nominees for the Shamus, Anthony, and Silver Falchion Best Mystery Novel, respectively; additionally *THE 13TH JUROR* is included in the International

Thriller Writers publication "100 Must-Read Thrillers of All Time." *HARD EVIDENCE* made "The Complete Idiot's Guide to the Ultimate Reading List." *THE SUSPECT* was the American Author's Association 2007 Book of the Year. *THE MOTIVE* was an Audie Finalist of the Audio Publishers Association. *THE MERCY RULE, NOTHING BUT THE TRUTH, THE SUSPECT, THE FALL,* and *THE RULE OF LAW* have been major market Book Club selections. John's books have been Main Selections of one or more of the Literary Guild, Mystery Guild, and Book of the Month Club.

> *"John Lescroart's writing skills are a national treasure."*
> —*The Huffington Post*

D. P. LYLE is the Amazon #1 Bestselling; Macavity and Benjamin Franklin Award-winning; and Edgar(2), Agatha, Anthony, Shamus, Scribe, and *USA Today* Best Book(2) Award-nominated author of 22 books, both non-fiction and fiction, including the *Samantha Cody, Dub Walker, Jake Longly* and *Cain/Harper* thriller series and the *Royal Pains* media tie-in novels. His essay on Jules Verne's *THE MYSTERIOUS ISLAND* appears in *THRILLERS: 100 MUST READS,* his short story "Even Steven" in ITW's anthology *THRILLER 3: LOVE IS MURDER,* and his short story "Bottom Line" in *FOR THE SAKE OF THE GAME.* He served as editor for and contributed the short story "Splash" to SCWA's anthology *IT'S ALL IN THE STORY.*

He hosts the Crime Fiction Writer's Blog and the Criminal Mischief: The Art and Science of Crime Fiction podcast series. He has worked with many novelists and with the writers of popular television shows such as *Law & Order, CSI: Miami, Diagnosis Murder, Monk, Judging Amy, Peacemakers, Cold Case, House, Medium, Women's Murder Club, 1-800-Missing, The Glades,* and *Pretty Little Liars.*

Learn more at www.dplylemd.com.

Before his thrillers landed him on the *New York Times* bestseller list, **KEVIN O'BRIEN** was a railroad inspector. The author of 21 internationally-published thrillers, he won the Spotted Owl Award for Best Pacific Northwest Mystery, and is a core member of Seattle 7 Writers. *Press & Guide* said: "If Alfred Hitchcock were alive today and writing novels, his name would be Kevin O'Brien." Kevin's latest nail-biter is *THE BAD SISTER*.

HANK PHILLIPPI RYAN is on-air investigative reporter for Boston's WHDH-TV, winning 37 EMMYs and dozens more journalism honors. A *USA Today* bestselling author of 12 thrillers, Ryan's also an award-winner in her second profession—with five Agathas, three Anthonys, and the coveted Mary Higgins Clark Award. Critics call her "a master of suspense." Her highly-acclaimed *TRUST ME* was an Agatha nominee and chosen for numerous prestigious "Best of 2018" lists. Hank's book *THE MURDER LIST* is an Agatha, Anthony and Mary Higgins Clark Award nominee. Her newest standalone is *THE FIRST TO LIE* (Forge Books August 2020). The *Publishers Weekly starred* review calls it "Stellar."

ACKNOWLEDGMENTS

We'd like to thank our good friend and radio show co-host and author, Jeff Ayers, whose contributions helped to complete the book. We also want to thank Amy Lignor, author and editor-extraordinaire, for being a priceless member of the team and an exceptionally good friend.

What's a book without a title? D. P. Lyle deserves all the credit for the fabulous title—I believe there were drinks and cigars involved and we knew that he'd hit the bull's-eye the moment the words fell from his lips.

We couldn't have done this without the support of the contributors and readers of Suspense Magazine. Your support and love over the years has been motivating and kept us going.

Thank you to our talented friends, who sat down and penned these amazing tales. Shannon and I don't have words for how special you all are to us. It really is a dream come true.

—John and Shannon Raab
Suspense Magazine/Suspense Publishing